NOVELS BY C. P. SNOW

STRANGERS AND BROTHERS

THE LIGHT AND THE DARK

TIME OF HOPE

THE MASTERS

THE NEW MEN

HOMECOMING

THE CONSCIENCE OF THE RICH

These novels, and also

THE AFFAIR

form part of the sequence of novels entitled

STRANGERS AND BROTHERS

THE SEARCH

THE AFFAIR

THE AFFAIR

C. P. SNOW

NEW YORK
CHARLES SCRIBNER'S SONS

E-9.60[H]

THIS BOOK PUBLISHED SIMULTANEOUSLY IN THE UNITED STATES OF AMERICA AND IN CANADA— COPYRIGHT UNDER THE BERNE CONVENTION

PRINTED IN THE UNITED STATES OF AMERICA

LIBRARY OF CONGRESS CATALOG CARD NUMBER 60-6324

CONTENTS

PART I THE FIRST DISSENTIENT

PART II WHY SHOULD ONE ACT?

PART III THE OFFER

THE AFFAIR

I

THE FIRST DISSENTIENT

ONE

AN UNSATISFACTORY EVENING

When Tom Orbell invited me to dinner at his club, I imagined that we should be alone. As soon as I saw him, however—he was waiting by the porter's box, watching me climb up the steps from the street—he said, in a confidential, anxious whisper: "As a matter of fact, I've asked someone to meet you. Is that all right?"

He was a large young man, cushioned with fat, but with heavy bones and muscles underneath. He was already going bald, although he was only in his late twenties. The skin of his face was fine-textured and pink, and his smile was affable, open, malicious, eager to please and smooth with soft soap. As he greeted me, his welcome was genuine, his expression warm: his big light blue eyes stayed watchful and suspicious.

He was telling me about my fellow-guest.

"It's a young woman, as a matter of fact. Lewis, she is really rather sweet."

I had forgotten that this club, like a good many others in London in the Fifties, had taken to letting women in to dine. While he was talking, I had no doubt at all that I was there to serve some useful purpose, though what it was I could not begin to guess.

"You're sure you don't mind?" Tom pressed me, as I was hanging up my coat. "It is all right, isn't it?"

He led the way, heavy shoulders pushing forward, into the reading room. The room was so long, so deserted, that it seemed dank, though outside it was a warmish September night and in the grates coal fires were blazing. By one fire, at the far end of the room, a man and woman were sitting in silence reading glossy magazines. By the other stood a young woman in a red sweater and black skirt, with one hand on the mantelpiece. To her Tom Orbell cried out enthusiastically:

"Here we are!"

He introduced me to her. Her name was Laura Howard. She was, as he had promised, comely. She had a shield-shaped face and clear grey eyes, and she moved with energy and grace. Tom got us sitting in armchairs on opposite sides of the fire, ordered drinks, dumped himself on the sofa between us. "Here we *are*," he said, as though determined to have a cosy drinking evening.

He proceeded to talk, flattering us both, using his wits and high spirits to get the party going.

I glanced across at Laura. One thing was clear, I thought. She had been as astonished as I was to find she was not dining alone with Tom Orbell: quite as astonished, and much more put out.

"When are you going to come and see us again?" Tom was addressing himself to me, tucking into a large whiskey. "We really do miss you, you know."

By "us," he meant the Cambridge college of which I had been a Fellow before the war. I still had many friends there, including my brother Martin, who was himself a Fellow, and went to see them two or three times a year. It was on one of those visits that I had first met Tom, just after he had taken his degree in history. He had made a reputation as a bright young man, and I had heard my old friends saying that they would have to elect him. That had duly happened—so far as I remembered, in 1949, four years before this dinner in his club.

"We really do miss him," Tom was explaining confidentially to Laura. "It's like everywhere in this country, the right people are never where you want them. Everything's got into the hands of those awful old men, and when anyone like Lewis comes along he goes and does something frightfully important and leaves the old men to sit on the heads of the rest of us. He's a very powerful and slightly sinister figure, is Lewis. Oh, yes, he is. But he's on the right side. I assure you he is. We miss him very much, do you believe me?"

"I'm sure you do," she said, in a tone which could scarcely have been less interested.

Tom continued to talk—was he trying to distract her?—as though we were all in a sociological conspiracy. Generalisations poured out: the good young middle-aged, said Tom, flattering me, for I was forty-seven, had got caught up trying to keep the country afloat. The generation coming up, he said, flattering her, for she was about thirty, had got to fight some other battles, had got to smash the "awful old men."

"We are all in it together," he said. He had had three stiff drinks, he sounded both hearty and angry. "We're going to show them. I mean it very sincerely, both of you."

Upstairs in the dining-room, with Laura sitting between us at a dark corner table, Tom went on with his patter. There were a couple of decanters waiting for us, shining comfortably under the three candles, and soon Tom had put down the best part of a bottle of wine. But, though he showed the effects of drink very quickly, he did not get any more drunk. He was spontaneous, as he usually seemed to be, but whatever his policy was for this evening he had not lost hold of it. He was spontaneous, at the same time he was wily: somehow he managed to use the spontaneity as part of his stock-in-trade.

Meanwhile he was enjoying his dinner with a mixture of appetite and discrimination, with a gusto so intense that he appeared to be blushing. After he had ordered our meal with analytical care, he suddenly had a second thought about his own. Beckoning the waitress, he whispered to her almost as confidentially as though they were having a love-affair. She reappeared with some gulls' eggs while Laura and I forked away at the smoked salmon.

"Delicious, delicious," said Tom Orbell, in a gourmet's transport.

It was when he repeated this performance over the savoury that Laura lost her patience. As he talked at large, she had been half-polite, half-sulking. Not that she was irritated because he was not paying attention to her as a woman. Actually, he was. He was a susceptible young man, he wanted to make a hit with her. To which she was totally indifferent; something was on her mind, but not that.

Tom had just had a new and delectable afterthought about the savoury. When our mushrooms on toast arrived, he had another piece of happy whispering with the waitress. "Do you think I could possibly have . . .?" Soon he was munching away at chicken livers and bacon, murmuring with content.

Then Laura said to him:

"I do want to get down to business, if you don't mind."

Tom looked at her, his glance at the same time defensive and bold:

"Is there really anything we can do to-night?"

"When are any of you going to move?"

"It isn't any use me moving by myself, is it?"

"That's not the point."

"But isn't it the point, my dear? Do you think that the blasted Court of Seniors is going to listen to a solitary junior Fellow? Remember this is the last shot you've got, if you don't mind me speaking frankly. And I'm speaking with great affection for you, even more than for Donald, and that isn't a monstrous thing to say, is it?"

She was looking angry and determined, which made her seem more handsome, and he gazed at her admiringly. "Forgive me," he said, "I'm afraid I'm slightly drunk." He was not: he was trying to put up a smoke-screen.

"If you don't mind me speaking very frankly, you've got

to be very, very careful about your tactics," he went on. "And so have I, because there might come a time when I could be a bit of use to you, in a minor way, and it would be a mistake to have shot my bolt before the right time came, wouldn't it?"

"Not so much a mistake as doing nothing at all."

"Is there any reason why I shouldn't let Lewis into this?" he said, beating another retreat.

"Haven't you heard about it already?" Almost for the first time, she spoke to me directly.

In fact, as I had been listening to them, I knew something of the story. My brother was the most discreet of men: but he and Francis Getliffe had thought that, as an ex-Fellow, I had a right to know. Even so, they had told me the bare minimum. The scandal had been kept so tightly within the college that I had not caught a whisper from anyone else. All I had picked up was that one of the younger Fellows had been caught out in a piece of scientific fraud. Without any noise at all, he had been got rid of. It was a kind of dismissal that had only happened in the college once within living memory. It had been done, of course, after something like a judicial investigation. I assumed that it had been done with more obsessive care even than in a process at law. The final dismissal had happened six months before: and, as I had realised as soon as Laura set to work on Tom Orbell, the man concerned was her husband, Donald Howard.

I said that I knew what they were talking about.

"Have you heard that it's a piece of unforgivable injustice?" she demanded.

I shook my head.

"You've got to remember, just for the sake of getting your own tactics right," said Tom, "that no one in the college takes that view, haven't you got to remember that?"

"Have you heard that it's the result of sheer blind prejudice?"

I shook my head again, and Tom put in:

"With great respect, my dear Laura, that's just misleading you. Of course there's some strong feeling about it, it wouldn't be natural if there wasn't. Of course most of them don't agree with his opinions. I don't myself, as you know perfectly well. But then, I don't agree with Lewis's opinions either, and I think Lewis would feel pretty safe in his job if I suddenly came into power. Speaking with great affection, you're really on the wrong track there."

"I don't believe it for an instant."

"Truly you're wrong—"

"I will believe it when you've done something to prove it."

I watched them as she went on bullying him. Tom Orbell was as clever as they came; psychologically he was full of resource and beneath the anxiety to please there was a tough, wilful core. But his forehead was sweating, his voice was not so mellifluous or easy. He was frightened of her. While she sat there, pretty, set-faced, strong-necked, she had only one thought in her head. She had come to talk to him and make him act. Talking to Tom, who was so much cleverer, she had the complete moral initiative.

She said: "I'm not asking you anything difficult. All I want is to get this business re-opened."

"How can you expect me to do that? I'm just one out of twenty, I'm a very junior person, I'm not a majority of the college. And I've tried to explain to you, but you won't realise it, that you're dealing with a society and a constitution, that you need a majority of the college before the thing can be so much as raised again."

"You can't get a majority of the college unless you make a beginning now," she said.

Tom Orbell looked at her with something like appeal. I thought she had got him down. Then I realised that I had underrated him, when he said:

"Now look, my dear. I've got a serious suggestion to make,

and I want you to consider it very carefully. I don't believe that anyone as junior as I am is going to make any impact on this situation at all. What I suggest, and I mean it very deeply, is that you should try to persuade Lewis here to talk to some of his friends. I'm not saying that you could possibly want him to commit himself to an opinion one way or another, any more than I could commit myself, as far as that goes. But if you could get him so much as to raise the question with the people he knows—after all, he's become the nearest approach we have to an elder statesman, has Lewis. He can talk to them as I can't possibly and shan't be able to for twenty years. I do mean that, I assure you."

So now I understood why he had enticed me there.

She looked at me with steady, bright, obstinate eyes.

"You don't see much of them there nowadays, do you?" she asked.

"Not very much," I said.

"You can't possibly be really in touch, I should think, can you?"

I said no.

"I don't see what you could expect to do."

She said it dismissively and with contempt. Contempt not for Tom Orbell, but for me. I felt a perceptible pique. It was not agreeable to be written off quite so far. But this young woman had decided that I was no good at all. She did not seem even to be considering whether I was well-disposed or not. She just had no faith in me. It was Tom in whom she still had her faith.

When we returned to the reading-room, even she, however, was deterred from forcing him any more. Tom sat there, his face cherubic, sketching out visions of the future like roseate balloons, high-spirited visions that seemed to consist of unworthy persons being ejected from positions of eminence and in their places worthy persons, notably the present company and in particular Tom himself, installed. I thought Laura would start on him again as soon as she got him alone. But for that night, at any rate, he was secure. For he had revealed to us that he was staying in the club, and at last it became my duty to take Laura out into Pall Mall and find her a taxi.

She said a cold good-night. Well, I thought, as I went along the street, looking for a taxi for myself, it would not be easy to invent a more unsatisfactory evening. None of the three of us had got away with what he wanted. Laura had not cornered Tom Orbell. He had not managed to slide her off on to me. And I had not done any better. I was not much interested in the story of her husband: it did not even begin to strike me as plausible that there had been an injustice of that kind. No, I was not thinking of that at all, but I was faintly irked. No one likes to be treated as a vacuum inhabited solely by himself.

TWO

NO SENSE OF THE PAST

A few weeks after the evening in Tom Orbell's club, I was sitting in my brother's room in college. It was a routine visit: I had gone down, as I did most years, for the Michaelmas audit feast. It gave me a curious mixture of comfort and unfamiliarity to be sitting there as a guest; for I had once used that great Tudor room as my own dining-room, and had sat talking in it as I now sat talking to Francis Getliffe, on October nights like this one, with draughts running under the wainscot, the fire in the basket grate not quite hot enough to reach out to the window seats.

In the study next door, my brother was interviewing a pupil, and Francis Getliffe and I were alone. He was a couple of years older than I was, and we had known each other since we were young men. I could remember him thin-skinned, conquering his diffidence by acts of will. He still looked quixotic and finefeatured; his sunburned flesh was dark over his collar and white tie. But success had pouched his cheeks a little and taken away the strain. In the past few years the success which he had wanted honorably but fiercely as he started his career and which had not come quickly, had suddenly piled upon him. He was in the Royal Society and all over the world his reputation was as high as he had once longed for it to be. In addition, he had been one of the most effective scientists in the war. It was for that work, not his pure research, that he had been given the C.B.E. whose cross he wore on his shirt-front. For a combination of the two he had, two years before, been knighted.

He was chatting about some of our contemporaries who also had done well. He would always have been fair about them, because he had a strict code of fairness: but now, it occurred to me, he was just a shade more fair. He was showing that special affection which one who has in his own eyes come off feels towards others who have done the same.

Martin came in through the inside door. He had changed before his tutorial hour, and was already dressed for the feast. Straight away he began to ask Francis's advice about the pupil he had just been seeing: was he, or was he not, right to change from physics to metallurgy? Martin worried away at the problem. He had recently become junior tutor, and he was doing the job with obsessive conscientiousness. He enjoyed doing it like that.

Unlike Francis, whose prestige had been rising for years past, Martin's had been standing still. A few years before, he had had the chance of becoming one of the atomic energy bosses. He had got the chance, not through being a scientist in Francis's class, which he never could be, but because people thought he was hard, responsible and shrewd. They were not far wrong: and yet, to everyone's surprise, he had thrown up the power and come back to the college.

He did not seem to mind having a future behind him. With the obsessive satisfaction with which he was now speaking of his pupil's course, he applied himself to his teaching, to the bread-and-butter work that came his way. He looked very well on it. He was getting on for forty, but he might have passed for younger. As he spoke to Francis, his eyes were acute, brilliant with a kind of sarcastic fun, although everything he said was serious and business-like.

Then he mentioned another pupil called Howarth, and the name by chance plucked at something at the back of my mind to which, since it happened, I had not given a thought.

"Howarth, not Howard?" I said.

"Howarth, not Howard," said Martin.

"As a matter of fact," I said, "I heard something about your ex-colleague Howard. In September young Orbell introduced me to his wife."

"Did he now?" said Martin, with a tight smile. "She's a pretty girl, isn't she?"

"She was crying out loud that there had been a miscarriage of justice. I suppose that's all nonsense, isn't it?"

"Quite nonsense," said Martin.

Francis said:

"There's nothing in that."

"She seemed to think that he'd been turned out because of some sort of prejudice, which I never got quite clear—"

"That's simple," said Francis. "He was, and I suppose he still is, a moderately well-known fellow-traveller."

"He wouldn't be the favourite character of some of our friends, then, would he?"

"If I'd thought that was deciding anything, I should have made a noise," said Francis. "I needn't tell you that, need I?"

He said it stiffly, but without being touchy. He took it for granted that no one who knew him, I least of all, would doubt his integrity. In fact, no one in his senses could have done so. In the Thirties, Francis himself, like so many of his fellow scientists, had been far to the left. Now he was respectable, honoured, he had moved a little nearer to the centre, but not all that much. In politics both he and Martin remained liberal and speculative men, and so did I. It was a topic on which the three of us in that room were close together.

"I don't want to give you a false impression," Francis said. "This man was disliked inside the college, of course he was, and there's no getting away from it, with most of them his politics made them dislike him more. But that wasn't the reason why we had to throw him out. It was a reason, if you like, why we found it difficult to get him elected in the first place. We had to be pretty rough with them, and tell them that politics or no politics, they mustn't shut their eyes to an Alpha man."

"In which," said Martin, "we don't seem to have done superlatively well."

Francis gave a grim smile, unamused.

"No," he said, "it's a bad business. He just went in for a piece of simple unadulterated fraud. That's all there is to it."

So far as he could make it intelligible to a layman, Francis told me about the fraud. A paper of Howard's, published in collaboration with his professor, an eminent old scientist now dead, had been attacked by American workers in the same field—and the attack had said that the experimental results could not be repeated. Francis and some of his Cavendish colleagues had had private warning that there was something "fishy" about Howard's published photographs. Two of the scientists in the college, Nightingale and Skeffington, had had a look at them. There was no doubt about it: at least one photograph had been, as it were, forged. That is, a photograph had been enlarged, what Francis called "blown up," to look like the result of a totally different experiment: and this photograph became the decisive experimental evidence in the paper.

The fraud could not be accidental, said Francis. Neither he nor Martin had worked on Howard's subject, but they had looked at the photograph. It was only too straightforward. The technical opinion that Nightingale and Skeffington had given was the one that any other scientist would have had to give, and it was on this technical opinion that the Court of Seniors had acted. The Court of Seniors, so Francis and Martin told me, had been the Master, the Senior Tutor, Arthur Brown, old Winslow, and Nightingale, this time in his capacity as Bursar. "Of course," said Francis, "they had to go on what the scientists told them. Nightingale's the only one of them who'd have any idea what a diffraction photograph was."

"Still," he added, "they went into it very thoroughly. If it hadn't been a clear case, they would still have been at it."

Somehow a question of mine set him reflecting on other cases of scientific fraud. There hadn't been many, he said, less even than one might expect. Considering the chances and the temptation, the number was astonishingly low. In the last fifty years, he could tick off the notorious ones on the fingers of two hands. He produced names at which Martin nodded, but which, of course, meant nothing to me. Rupp, the J-phenomenon ("but that, presumably, was an honest mistake"): Francis spoke of them with the incredulous relish which professional scandals often evoke in a hyper-scrupulous man. He was wondering about the motives of those who perpetrated them, when the college bell started clanging for the feast.

As we picked up our gowns and went downstairs into the court, Francis was saying:

"But there's no mystery why Howard did it. He just wanted to make his marble good."

Sitting in hall in the candlelight, I let the story drift comfortably out of mind. It was over and tied up now, and the college was going on. I was enough of a stranger to draw an extra pleasure out of being there. I was also enough of a stranger to be put up on the dais among the old men. This was not such a privilege as it looked: for my next-door neighbour was so old that the places beside him were not competed for.

"Ah," he said, gazing at me affably. "Excuse me. Do you mind telling me your name?"

The colour in his irises had faded, and they were ringed with white. Otherwise he did not show the signs of extreme age: his cheeks were ruddy pink, his hair and beard silky but strong.

I said that I was Lewis Eliot. It was the second time since dinner began that he had asked the question.

"Indeed. Tell me, have you any connection with the college?"

It was too embarrassing to tell him that we had been

Fellows together for ten years. This was M.H.L. Gay, the Icelandic scholar. In his presence one felt as though confronted by one of those genealogical freaks, as I once felt when I met an old lady whose father, not as a boy but as a young man, had been in Paris during the French Revolution. For Gay had been elected a Fellow over seventy years before. He had actually retired from his professorship before Tom Orbell and half a dozen of the present society were born. He was now ninety-four: and in a voice shaky, it is true, but still resonant, was loudly demanding a second glass of champagne.

"Capital. Ah. That's a drink and a half, if ever there was one. Let me persuade you, sir"—he was addressing me—"to have a glass of this excellent wine."

He began to speak, cordially and indiscriminately, to all around him:

"I don't know whether you realise it, but this is positively my last appearance before my annual hibernation. Indeed. Yes, that is a prudent measure of mine. Indeed it is. I adopted that prudent measure about ten years ago, when I had to realise that I was no longer as young as I used to be. So after this splendid audit feast of ours, I retire into hibernation and don't make the journey into college until we have the spring with us again. That means that I have to miss our fine feast for the Commemoration of Benefactors. I have suggested more than once to some of our colleagues that perhaps the summer might be a more opportune time for that fine feast. But so far they haven't taken the hint, I regret to say."

For an instant his face looked childish. Then he cheered up:

"So I retire to my own ingle-nook for the winter, indeed I do. And I listen to the great gales roaring over the Fens, and I thank God for a good stout roof over my head. Not one of those flat roofs these modern architects try to foist off on us. A good stout pitched roof, that's what a man wants over his head. Why, one of those flat roofs, our Fenland gales would have it off before you could say Jack Robinson."

A few places along the table, a distinguished Central European architect was listening. "I do not quite understand, Professor Gay," he said, with a serious, puzzled and humourless expression. "Are you thinking of the turbulent flow round a rectangle? Or are you thinking of the sucking effect? I assure you—"

"I am thinking of the force of our Fenland gales, sir," cried Gay triumphantly. "Our ancestors in their wisdom and experience knew about those gales, and so they built us good, stout, pitched roofs. Ah, I often sit by my fire and listen, and I think, 'That's a gale and a half. I'd rather be where I am than out at sea.' "

Old Gay kept it up throughout the feast. Sitting by him, I found it impossible to feel any true sense of the past at all. The candles blew about, in the middle of the table the showpieces of gold and silver gleamed, all, like Gay's conversation, as they would have been at a feast twenty years earlier. The food was perhaps a little, though only a little, less elaborate, the wines were just as good. No, I got pleasure out of being there, but no sense of the past. True, I now knew half the Fellows only slightly. True, some of those I had known, and the one I had known best, were dead. But, as I sat by Gay, none of that plucked a nerve, as a visitant from the true past did. I could even think of the Baron de Charlus's roll-call of his friends and say to myself, "Despard-Smith, *dead,* Eustace Pilbrow, *dead,* Chrystal, *dead*: Roy Calvert, *dead.*" Not even that last name touched me; it was all a rhetorical flourish, as though one were making a nostalgic speech after a good dinner. Now I came to think of it, wasn't Charlus's roll-call just a flourish too?

In the shadows on the linenfold, I noticed a picture which was new since my last visit. Above the candle-light it was too dark to make out much of the face, although it did not look any better done than most of the college portraits. On the frame I could, however, read the gold letters:

Doctor R.T.A. Crawford, F.R.S., Nobel Laureate, Forty-First Master.

Master 1937—

My eyes went from the picture to the original, solid, Buddha-faced, in the middle of the table. His reign, so they all said, had been pretty equable. There did not seem to have been much to scar it. Now it was nearly over. They had prolonged him for three years above the statutory age of seventy, but he was to go in a year's time: he would preside at the next Michaelmas audit feast, and that would be his last.

"Ah. Master," Gay was calling out. "I congratulate you on this splendid evening. I congratulate you. Indeed I do."

From his previous conversation, I thought he was not clear which, of all the Masters he had known, this was. Masters came and Masters went, and Gay, who was telling us that port did not agree with him, applied himself to the nuts.

In the jostle of the Combination Room afterwards, I felt my arm being squeezed. "Nice to see you," came a round, breathy, enthusiastic whisper. "Slip out as soon as you decently can. We still finish up in my rooms, you know."

It was Arthur Brown, the Senior Tutor. Some time passed before I could get free and when I entered Brown's sitting-room it was already full. Brown gripped my hand.

"This is more like it," he said. "I've been telling them, people got into the habit of dropping in here after feasts more years ago than I care to remember. I take it amiss that you haven't been here since this time last year. You mustn't forget us altogether, you know. Now I hope I can tempt you to a drop of brandy? I always think it's rather soothing after a long dinner."

He was a man of sixty-three, padded with flesh, broad-jowled, high-coloured. The residual wings of hair were white over his ears. He looked kind, he looked like someone who enjoyed seeing others happy: and that was true. He looked a bit of a buffer—to those who did not notice the eyes behind his spectacles, sparkling with inquisitiveness, or how, under the paunchy flesh, he carried his stomach high. In fact, when I had been a colleague of his in the college, I thought that he was one of the shrewdest managers of people that I had met. I still thought so, after meeting a good many more. He contrived to be at the same time upright, obstinate and very cunning.

The room was cosier, the temperature higher, than in most college sets. On the walls hung a collection of English water-colours, of which Brown had come to be a connoisseur. There were so many men in the room that they had split up into groups: that would not have happened in the first after-feast parties which I had attended there. The college was larger now, the average age of the Fellows lower, the behaviour just perceptibly less formal. Glass in hand, Francis Getliffe was talking to a knot of three young scientists; Martin and a handsome man whom I recognised as Skeffington, were away in a corner with two arts Fellows, Clark and Lester Ince, both elected since I left.

By the fire, Brown and I were sitting drinking our brandy when Tom Orbell came and joined us. His face was pink, flushed and cheerful, but in Brown's presence he was comporting himself with decorum, with a mixture of expansiveness and caution. What could be done about the Chaplain? he was asking. Apparently there was a danger that he would be enticed away. He was intelligent, so Tom was saying, and it wasn't all that easy nowadays to find an intelligent man in orders.

"Of course," he turned to me with a flush of defiance, "that wouldn't matter to you, Lewis. You wouldn't mind if every clergyman in the country was mentally deficient. I expect you'd think it would make things easier if they were. But Arthur and I can't take that view, can we?"

"I should have thought it was slightly extreme," said Brown.

But he was not prepared to let Tom flaunt his piety at my expense. Brown was a "pillar of society," conservative and Anglican, but he went to church out of propriety more than belief, and he was not entirely easy when young men like Orbell began displaying their religion. So Brown told a story in my favour, designed to show how careful I was about others' faith.

"I'm sorry, Lewis," said Tom, at his jolliest and most repentant, instantaneously quick to catch the feeling of someone like Brown, "it was absolutely monstrous of me to accuse you of that. You're frightfully good, I know you are. And by the way, it was absolutely monstrous of me to inflict that evening on you with Laura Howard."

"What's that?" said Brown, his eyes alert and peering, "how did you come to be meeting Mrs. Howard, Lewis?"

"I saddled him with it, I'm afraid," Tom replied. "You see, she was wanting me to raise Cain in the college about her husband—which I couldn't very well do as I believe all those protests of hers are just sheer nonsense, could I? Just sheer nonsense which she's managed to make herself believe because she loves him, God knows why. So I didn't want to make it easy for her to get to work on me, did I? Mind you, Arthur," he said, "if I thought there was the slightest bit of sense in her case or even the chance that there could be a bit of sense in it, I'd have come and told you straight out that I was going to bring it up. I do mean that. I think it's very important that people of my age should be ready to throw their weight about. I know you agree, Arthur, don't you?"

Soon afterwards, Tom attached himself to Martin's group. I was thinking that, as he explained himself to Brown, he had shown a delicate blend of the deferential and the man-to-man, beautiful to listen to. In private, out of hearing of persons in authority, few people rebelled as eloquently as Tom Orbell. In the hearing of persons in authority, the eloquence remained, but the rebellion not. In the company of Arthur Brown, Tom seemed above all desirous of growing into someone just like Arthur Brown—solid, rooted, statesman-like, a man on top.

"So our young friend has been involving you with the Howards, has he?" asked Arthur Brown.

"You've been having more trouble than I thought, haven't you?" I said.

"I need hardly say," said Brown, "that none of this ought to be so much as mentioned outside the college. I needn't tell you that, I know. Put it another way: I should have thought it was safer, if you only talked about it, even in this place, with Martin or the people you know well."

"What's this man Howard like, Arthur?" I asked.

The colour, heavy puce, deepened in Brown's cheeks. He was frowning as though angry with me even for asking the question.

"He's an unmitigated swine," he said.

For an instant I was both astonished and thrown off my stride. I did not know many people more tolerant of others than Brown was. Also, he had spent so many years guarding his speech that it often seemed he couldn't speak in any other way.

Even Brown himself seemed startled at hearing his own outburst. He said, once more judicious, weighing his words: "No, I don't think I feel inclined to withdraw what I've just said. I never have been able to find anything to set down in his favour. He's a twister, but there are plenty of twisters that have some redeeming qualities, and I can't recall this chap showing a single one. He's graceless, he's never been able to get on with anyone, and I shouldn't be surprised if that's why he wants to pull the world down round our ears. But I might have been able even to put up with that, if he hadn't behaved so vilely to the people he owed everything to. When he started biting the hand that fed him, I decided

I wasn't going to look for any more excuses or listen to anyone else making them. He's no good, Lewis. I don't mind telling you that I considered at the time, and I still do, that we ought to have gone the whole hog and struck his name off the books."

Brown had been speaking in a reasonable, moderate tone, but heavily, almost as though he had been giving his judgment to the other seniors. He added:

"There's only one good thing to be said about this wretched business. The whole college was absolutely solid about it. I don't need to tell you that that's not exactly common form. But if the college hadn't been solid for once, it would have made things difficult. The place wouldn't have been any too comfortable to live in. And I don't want to exaggerate, but we might have walked straight into trouble outside. This is just the kind of thing that could have got us into the papers, and if that had happened, it would have done us more harm than I like to think about."

Francis Getliffe had already gone, and the party was breaking up. Just as Martin said good-night to Brown, and waited to take me across the staircase to his rooms, I was remarking on the new picture of the Master in the hall. "There's exactly room for one more beside it," I said as I stood up to go, "and then you'll have to think again."

I noticed Brown glancing sharply at me. Still sitting in his armchair, he tugged at my sleeve.

"Stay here a few minutes," he said. He smiled at Martin: "He can find his own way to your bedroom, can't he? After all, he's done it plenty of times, more than you have, I suppose. And I don't get many chances to talk to him these days."

Martin said that it was time he went home to his wife. Like me, he suspected that Arthur Brown was not just idly keeping me back for the sake of company. When we were left alone, Brown made sure that I was settled in the chair opposite to him. He became more than ever hospitable and deliberate. "More brandy?"

No, I wouldn't drink any more that night.

"Old chap," he said, "it's very nice to see you sitting there again."

He had always been fond of me. At times he had defended and looked after me. Now he had the warm, sharp-edged, minatory affection that one feels for a protégé who has done pretty well. Was everything going all right? How was my wife? My son?

"So everything's reasonably smooth just now, is it? That's perfectly splendid. Do you know, Lewis, there was a time when I was afraid things weren't going to turn out smooth for you."

He gave me a kind, satisfied smile. Then he said, quite casually: "By the way, when you were talking about the Master's picture, it just crossed my mind that you might have heard something. I suppose you haven't, by any chance, have you?"

"No," I said, surprised.

Brown said: "No, of course, I thought you couldn't have."

His expression was steady and unperturbed.

"Just for a moment, though on second thought I can see you couldn't have been, I fancied you might be casting a fly."

I shook my head, but now I thought I was following him.

"Well, what's happening?" I said.

"The trouble is," said Brown with satisfied gravity, "I'm not quite sure how much I'm at liberty to tell you. The whole matter is very much at the stage where no one has wanted to come out in the open. In my judgment the longer they put it off the more chance we have of avoiding ructions and coming to a decent conclusion."

"What's the point?"I asked again.

Brown pursed his lips. "Well, within these four walls, I

think I'm not breaking any obligations if I tell you this. When the present Master retires, which is at the end of next year, not the academic but the calendar year, some of the society have asked me whether I would consider offering myself as a candidate."

Yes, I had got there five minutes before. But, until he began to talk, I had not been expecting it. I had taken it for granted that Francis Getliffe had the next Mastership in the bag. On and off over the last two years, I had heard it discussed. The only name that anyone mentioned seriously was that of Francis.

"Who are your backers, Arthur?" I asked.

"No," he said, "without their permission I don't think that I ought to specify them at this stage, but I believe they'd let me say that there are enough of them to make the suggestion not entirely frivolous. And I think I might indicate that there were one or two of them recently present in this room."

He was smiling blandly. He did not seem anxious, elated or depressed.

"If I were to ask for your advice whether to let my candidature go forward or not, Lewis, I wonder what you'd say?"

I hesitated. They were both friends of mine, and I was glad that I should be out of it. But I was hesitating for a different reason. I was afraid, despite what Brown had just said, that he would get few votes—perhaps so few as to be humiliating. I did not like the thought of that. I could not see any college not preferring Francis Getliffe when it came to the point.

"I think I know what's in your mind," Brown was saying. "You're thinking that our friend Francis is out of comparison a more distinguished man than I am, and of course you're right. I've never made any secret of it, I should be satisfied to see Francis Getliffe as Master of this college. Between ourselves, there are only three distinguished men here, and he's one of them, the other two being the present

Master and I suppose we've still got to say old Gay. I've never had delusions about myself, I think you'll grant me that, old chap. I've never been really first rate at anything. It used to depress me slightly when I was a young man."

He meant, I knew, precisely what he said. He was genuinely humble: he did not credit himself with any gifts at all

I said: "I was thinking something quite different."

Brown went on: "No, it's perfectly right that the college should consider whether they could put up with an undistinguished person like me, in comparison with a very distinguished one like Francis. But one or two members of the society have put an interesting point of view which has made me think twice before saying no once and for all. Their view is that we've just had a Master of great external distinction, even more so than Francis's. So one or two people have represented to me that the college can afford someone who wasn't much known outside but who could keep things going reasonably well among ourselves. And they paid me the compliment of suggesting that I might have my uses in that respect."

"They are dead right," I said.

"No," he said, "you've always thought too much of me. Anyway, sometime within the next twelve months I shall have to decide whether to let my name go forward. Of course, it's my last chance and it isn't Francis's. Perhaps I should be justified in taking that into account. Well, I've got plenty of time to make up my mind. I don't know which way I shall come down."

He had, of course, already "come down." He was thinking, I was sure—although he had no vanity, he was a master-politician—about how his supporters ought to be handling his campaign and about how much more capably he would do it in their place. He was thinking too, I guessed, that it had been useful to talk to me, apart from warmth, affection and reciprocal support. I believed that he was hoping I should mention this conversation to Martin.

THREE

A SEALING-DAY

About half past twelve the next morning, which was a Sunday, Martin and I were sitting in one of his window-seats gazing out over the court. On the far wall, most of the leaves of creeper had fallen by now, but in the milky sunlight one or two gleamed, nearer scarlet than orange. Martin was just saying to me—did I notice one difference from before the war? There were no kitchen servants carrying trays round the paths, green baize over the trays. Martin was saying that for him green baize was what he first remembered about the college, when the telephone rang.

As he answered it, I heard him reply: "Yes, I can come. Glad to." Then he was listening to another question, and answered: "I've got my brother Lewis here. He'll do for one, won't he?" Martin put the receiver down and said, "The Bursar's polishing off some conveyances, and he wants us to go and sign our names."

"Is he working on Sunday?"

"He enjoys himself so much," said Martin with a sharp but not unfriendly grin.

As we climbed up the Bursary staircase, which was in the same court, Nightingale had thrown open the door and was waiting for us.

"I must say, it's good of you to come." He shook hands with me. He greeted me with a kind of cagey official courtesy, as though anxious to seem polite. He was much better at it than he used to be, I thought. When we had both lived in the college, we had never got on. So far as I had had an enemy, it had been he. Now he was shaking hands, as though we had been, not friends exactly, but at any rate friendly acquaintances.

He was getting on for sixty, but he had kept his fair wavy hair, and he was well-preserved. He did not look anything like so strained as he used to. Several times I had heard Martin and others saying that he was a man whose life had been saved by the war. When I knew him, he had been a scientist who had not come off, and at the same time an embittered bachelor. But he happened, so it seemed, to be one of those people who were made for the military life. He had had a hard war, spectacularly hard for a man of his age: he had been decorated, as he had been in 1917, and he finished up as a brigadier. On top of that, while in hospital, he had managed to get married to a nurse. When he returned, people in the college thought he was transformed. They were so impressed that they wanted to do something for him. As it happened, the Bursar died suddenly: and almost unanimously, or so I gathered, they had given Nightingale the job. They all said that he loved it. No incumbent had ever spent so much time in the bursarial office. As he showed us in, his whole manner was active and proud.

"I'm sorry to drag you up here, Martin," he said, "but there's no point in letting things pile up."

"That would be very serious, wouldn't it?" Martin was teasing him. I was surprised to see that the two of them were on such easy terms. Yet I ought to have known that when, as with Nightingale and me, two people dislike each other without reason, or more strongly than reason justifies, either of them often tends to make it up with some close attachment of the other.

The Bursary was like a lawyer's office, the walls piled with metal boxes painted black, letters standing out in white. From the window one could see the hall and lodge, newly washed, light gold Ketton stone in the autumn sun. The room was full of the smell of melted wax.

"I don't know whether you've ever taken part in a sealing, Martin," Nightingale said with bustling officious pride. "I'm afraid we shall have to leave you out of this one, Eliot," he turned to me, with the same pleasure in performing the ceremonies, in getting the ritual right. "Only present Fellows are allowed to sign after the college seal. When I put the seal on, I am afraid that for our purpose ex-Fellows don't exist." He gave a triumphant smile.

In the mould, the wax shone crimson and he tested it with the tip of a finger. Steadily, with a scientist's precision, he laid the wafer-covered seal on top, closed the mould, and took it to an antiquated iron vice. He spun the arm of the vice round and back, putting pressure on the mould: then he brought it out, replaced it on the table, and undid it. "If it hasn't taken," he said, "I shall just have to do it again, of course."

Meticulously he studied the wax.

"No, it's all right," he cried.

As a matter of fact, the result was not startling: for on each side of the impress was a wafer of paper, so that all one could see were indentations something like a faint brass rubbing.

"Now, Martin, if you don't mind," said Nightingale, "will you sign on this line here? I shall want another Fellow's signature, of course. I've asked Skeffington to come along. To make it absolutely watertight he ought to have witnessed the sealing too, but I think I'm prepared to stretch a point."

Within a few minutes, Skeffington had entered the office, while Nightingale was cleaning the great seal. As Skeffington wrote his name on the line beneath Martin's, Nightingale with delicate, patient fingers extracted fragments of wax. Then reverently he laid the seal on the table in front of us.

"It is a beautiful thing, isn't it?" he said.

It was not really beautiful. It was a piece of fifteenth-century silver-work, heavy and over-elaborate. Nightingale looked at it as though there could not be a more delectable sight. To him it was lovely. He looked at it with piety for all it meant to him. He had had so many grudges, he had never trusted anyone; he had longed for the college to trust him, and had not expected them to. Now here he was in the Bursary. What to most men would already have become a habit, was to him a delight, a security, a joy.

"Well," he said, "now this is where Eliot comes in. If you don't mind filling in your present address and occupation, we want those too. You're not allowed to put 'sometime Fellow of the College,' I'm afraid."

His voice was gleeful. He liked reminding himself that others—particularly me, that morning—were outside the charmed circle, that they did not possess the *mana* of the college, the *mana,* that he shared in and loved.

After we had signed, Nightingale brought out a bottle of sherry and three glasses. It was a surprise to me, for he had always been a teetotaller, the only one in the college in my time. He still was, so it appeared: but somehow, he was explaining, he always liked to let people celebrate a sealing.

As we were drinking the sherry and getting ready to go, Martin pointed to one of the black boxes on which was painted, in white letters, PROFESSOR C.J.B. PALAIRET, F.R.S.

"Howard's professor," he remarked.

"What?" I said.

"The old man Howard worked with. Francis G. was telling you about him last night."

Even now, I was slow to pick up the reference. In the Howard affair I was an outsider; it still meant nothing to me. Whereas they had been living within the situation. They had kept it to themselves, and so all three in that room and Brown, Getliffe, Orbell and the others, had lived within the situation more completely even than a society as closed as theirs was used to doing. They all knew every move that had been made.

"The old man's left a nice bequest to the college, I'm glad to say," said Nightingale. "Which makes it all the worse."

"It was a bad enough show anyway, God knows," said Skeffington. "But I agree, that last gambit—that's more than anyone can take."

Just for a second, they were showing their anger. Then Nightingale said:

"Wait a minute. I suppose we oughtn't to discuss it while Eliot is with us, ought we?"

I was irritated. I said:

"I'm not quite a stranger here, you know."

"I'm sorry," said Nightingale. "But I believe that no one outside the college ought to have heard a word."

"Arthur Brown and Getliffe didn't take that view. They were talking to me about it last night."

"I'm sorry. But I think they're wrong."

"I also heard some of it from Howard's wife," I said, "and I can't for the life of me see how you're going to keep her quiet."

"We shall keep it all quiet enough for our purposes," said Nightingale.

When we had left Nightingale alone in the Bursary, and the three of us were walking through the court, Skeffington said: "Bad mark from the Bursar. Loose talk."

He was a very tall man, and he threw back his head. Just as I had been irritated, so was he. He was a man of means, he had been a regular officer in the Navy: he did not like being what he called "ticked off." He seemed arrogant and also vain: vain of his striking looks, among other things, I thought. He had strong features, a fleshy chin and handsome eyes; they were the kind of looks that seem to chime with riches, an influential family, an easy life. Nevertheless, he had not chosen such an easy life as he could have had. He was about

Martin's age, just under forty: his career in the Navy had been going according to plan, when he decided that he wanted to make himself into a scientist. That had happened just after the war, and at thirty-two he had started as an undergraduate, taken his degree, and then gone on to research. It was only two years before that the college had elected him a research fellow. Academically he was junior not only to Martin and his other contemporaries, but to young men like Tom Orbell. His Fellowship was not yet a permanent one, and within the college he was on probation.

"The Bursar would have been right, if it had been anyone but you, don't you think?" Martin said to me. He was himself tight-mouthed as a clam.

"The trouble is," I said, "keeping it a secret as you have done—if ever the story breaks, you're in a worse mess than ever, aren't you?"

"There's something in that," said Skeffington.

"There's something in it. But it's not the whole story," said Martin. We had stopped at the foot of his staircase. "We took the risk into account. You don't think we were all that careless, do you?"

"If I'd been you," I replied, "I'm sure I should have wanted the college to come right out with it as soon as you'd made up your minds."

"And I'm moderately sure that you'd have been wrong. The point is," said Martin, "we've got enough against this man so that it's a fair bet he'll have to go on holding his tongue. Then if he doesn't hold his tongue, we shall have to bring it all in the open and explain in so many words why we've been keeping it dark."

"Softlee softlee catchee monkey," said Skeffington.

Quietly, his eyes sharp, Martin explained what they had done. I began to think I had been airy-fairy in my criticism. The more I heard of the story, the more I thought that they had been decent, cautious, hard-headed. When the two men who were asked to enquire into Howard's work—that is, Nightingale and Skeffington himself—reported to the Master and Seniors that at least one of Howard's photographs could not be explained in any way other than as a fraud, he had been asked for any defence he wanted to put up. He had been interviewed twice by the Court of Seniors, and each time he had said nothing to the point. Both the Master and Brown had written to him formally, telling him to put his case on paper. He had still produced nothing as a defence: until, quite suddenly, he asked to appear again before the court. Then he announced that he had now decided there had been a fraud, but that the fraud was not his but old Palairet's.

"Which must have taken some cooking up," said Skeffington.

At last I could understand some of the eddies of anger. Palairet had just died; as long as most of us could remember, he had been a college worthy. Not that he had visited the place much, even when he was younger. I recalled seeing him at a feast once or twice, twenty years before, when he must have been in his fifties. He had gone off to be a professor at a Scottish university when he was a young man and had stayed there till he died. He had had a long and eminent career, not quite as distinguished as the Master's, but about on the level of Francis Getliffe's.

Just then a couple of undergraduates passed by us on the path and Skeffington, his face flushed and authoritative, had to hold himself in. When he could speak, he had got more savage, not less so.

"It's a bad show," he said. "Only the worst sort of Red would have done anything like that."

"Does that come in?" I asked. But my detachment, which usually had an effect on Skeffington, only vexed him more.

"If the man had had anything to keep him straight," he said furiously, "if he'd had a faith or even had the sort of code you two have, he might have done lots of bad things, but he would never have done that."

I said that the younger generation in the college were moving to the Right so fast that survivals like myself would soon be left standing outside the gates. Skeffington was not amused. He was a devout Anglo-Catholic, more pious, so I thought, than Tom Orbell, though not so given to protesting his faith. He was also a Tory, as Tom Orbell claimed to be. In fact, my gibe was somewhere near the truth. Most of the young Fellows were conservative, if they were political at all. At High Table one heard a good deal of the reactionary apologists Tom and his friends had resurrected, such as De Maistre and Bonald. I did not mind that so much: but I did mind the tone in which Skeffington had just introduced Howard's politics.

Nevertheless, I thought, as Martin went on explaining, no body of men could have been much more thorough, when it came to investigating the fraud. When Howard made his accusation-cum-defence, the seniors had insisted that, though it was the most improbable anyone could have invented, they must act as though it might be true. The old man's executors were asked to turn over his working note-books to the college, which, since he had bequeathed them his entire estate, was within the rules. He had, incidentally, left thirty-five thousand, and Nightingale wanted to put the money into a building fund and call it after him.

"It was a slap in the eye for the family," said Skeffington. Then I discovered, what was news to me, that his wife was Palairet's niece.

The note-books, scientific papers, fragments of researches, had arrived in batches at the Bursary, and after Nightingale and Skeffington had inspected them, were filed in the college archives. If Howard's story had had any foundation, there would have been signs of faked evidence in some of the old man's recent notebooks: all the scientists were certain of that. There was no such sign. Not only Skeffington and Nightingale, but also Francis Getliffe and Martin, and those who worked in related subjects, had gone through the notebooks. Each one of the old man's diffraction photographs, taken either by himself or his collaborators, had been studied millimetre by millimetre.

"It was about as likely we should find anything wrong," said Skeffington, "as that any of us would be nabbed in the buttery lifting a case of whiskey."

To him there was no doubt. All that search had seemed disrespectful to the dead. It was to his credit, I thought, that he had worked as scrupulously as anyone. I also thought, once again, that no body of men I knew of would have been more punctilious and fair.

FOUR

TWO UNITED FRONTS

One night in December, not long before Christmas, the telephone rang in the drawing-room of our flat. My wife answered it. As she listened, she looked puzzled and obscurely amused.

"Won't I do?" she asked. She went on: "Yes, I can get him if it's really necessary. But he's very tired. Are you certain it can't wait?"

For some time the cross-talk went on. Then Margaret raised an eyebrow and held the receiver away from her. "It's Mrs. Howard," she said. "I'm afraid you'd better."

Down the telephone came a strong, pleasant-toned, determined voice.

"This is Laura Howard. Do you remember that we met one night in Tom Orbell's club?"

I said yes.

"I'm really asking if you can spare me half an hour one day this week?"

I said that I was abnormally busy. It was true, but I should have said it anyway. Somewhere in her tone there was an insistent note.

"I shan't keep you more than half an hour, I promise you."

I began reciting some of my engagements for the week, inventing others.

"I can manage any time that suits you," her voice came back, agreeable, not at all put off.

I said that I might be freer after Christmas, but she replied that "we" were only in London for a short time. She went on: "You were in Cambridge a few weeks ago, weren't you? Yes, I heard about that. I do wish I'd had a chance to see you there."

She must, I thought, have revised her first impression of me. Presumably she had made enquiries and people had told her that I might be useful. I had a feeling that she didn't in the least mind her judgment being wrong. She just wiped the slate clean, and resolved to chase me down.

Margaret was smiling. She found it funny to see me overborne, cut off from all escape routes.

Aside, I said to her:

"What in God's name ought I to do?"

"You're under no obligation to spend five minutes on her, of course you're not," said Margaret. Then her face looked for a second less decorous. "But I don't know how you're going to avoid it, I'm damned if I do."

"It's intolerable," I said, cross with her for not keeping her sense of humour down.

"Look here," said Margaret, "you'd better ask her round here and get it over. Then you've done everything that she can possibly want you to."

That was not quite so. Laura was also set on having me meet her husband. Since his dismissal, she told me over the telephone, he had been teaching in a school in Cambridge: that was the reason he could not often get to London. In the end, I had to invite them both to dinner later that same week.

When they arrived, and I looked at Howard for the first time—for now I realised that I had not once, visiting the college while he was still a Fellow, so much as caught sight of him—I thought how curiously unprepossessing he was. The skin of his face was coarse and pale; he had a long nose and not much chin. His eyes were a washed-out blue. He had a long neck and champagne-bottle shoulders; it was a kind of physique that often went with unusual muscular strength, and also with virility. Somehow at first sight he would have struck most people as bleak, independent, masculine, even though his voice was high-pitched and uninflected. As he spoke to me, he seemed awkward, but not shy.

"I believe you know that chap Luke don't you?" he said.

He meant Walter Luke, the head of the Barford atomic energy establishment, knighted that January at the age of forty, one of the most gifted scientists of the day. Yes, I said, Luke was an old friend of mine.

"He must be an extraordinary sort of chap," said Howard.

"Just why?"

"Well, he's got a finger in this bomb nonsense, hasn't he? And I don't know how a scientist can bring himself to do it."

I was annoyed, more annoyed than I was used to showing. I was fond of Walter Luke: and also I had seen how he and his colleagues had tried to settle it with their consciences about the bomb, Luke choosing one way, my brother Martin the other.

"He happens to think it's his duty," I said.

"It's a curious sort of duty, it seems to me," replied Howard.

Meanwhile Margaret and Laura had been talking. Glancing at them, vexed at having this man inflicted on me, I noticed how young and slight Margaret looked beside the other woman. Against Laura's, Margaret's skin, still youthful over her fine bones, seemed as though it would be delicate to the touch. Actually it was Margaret who was ten years the elder, who had children; but she seemed like a student beside the other, dark, handsome, earnest.

I could not hear what they were saying. As we sat round the table in the dining-room, Howard mentioned one or two more acquaintances he and Margaret and I had in common. Listening to him, I had already picked up something that no one had told me. He was farouche and a roughneck, and some of his manners might—to anyone without an English ear—have seemed working-class. Actually he was no more working-class than Margaret, who had been born among the academic aristocracy. His parents and hers could easily have gone to the same schools, though his probably came from Service families, not from those of clerics or dons. It was his wife who had gone up in the world, Howard not at all.

Margaret, who was watching Laura's face, did not let the chit-chat dribble on.

"You've come to tell Lewis something, haven't you?" she said before we had finished the soup. She was kind: and she did not like being oblique. "Wouldn't you rather do it straight away?"

Laura smiled with relief. She looked across at her husband: "Who's going to begin?"

"I don't mind," he said, without any grace.

"We're not going to ask you very much," said Laura to me, her brows furrowed. "There's still shilly-shallying about opening the case again, and we want you to use your influence on them, that's all."

Suddenly she said, in a formal, dinner-party manner, addressing Margaret in full style: "I'm afraid this is boring for you. How much have you heard about this difficulty of ours?"

"I think about as much as Lewis has, by now," said Margaret.

"Well, then, you can understand why we're absolutely sickened by the whole crowd of them," cried Laura. Her total force—and she was a passionate woman, one could not help but know—was concentrated on Margaret. But Margaret was the last person to be overwhelmed. She looked fine-nerved, but she was passionate herself, she was tough, and her will was at least as strong as Laura's.

She was not going to be bulldozed into a conviction she did not feel, or even into more sympathy than she had started with.

"I think I can understand the kind of time you've had," she said, gently but without yielding.

"Perhaps I ought to say," I broke in, "that I know a good deal more about this business now—"

"How do you know?" she cried.

"I heard a certain amount in college."

"I hope you were pleased with everything you heard," she said.

There had been a time when I should have found this kind of emotion harder to resist than my wife found it. Though it was difficult for people to realise it, though Laura exerted her first effort on Margaret because she seemed the softer option, I was more suggestible than she was. I had had to train and discipline myself out of it. But actually I had no temptation to acquiesce too much that night. Laura had not got me on her side; I felt antipathy for Howard; I was ready to speak plainly.

"That's neither here nor there," I said. I waited until the next course was in front of us, and then spoke to Laura again: "You talked about people in the college shilly-shallying about opening your case again. That's nothing like the situation."

"What do you mean?"

"I mean that, so far as I heard, and I think I should have heard if it was being talked about, no one there has the slightest intention of opening the case again."

"Do you believe that?" said Laura to her husband.

"I shouldn't be surprised," he said.

She stared at me steadily, with angry eyes. She came straight out: "If you were there, would you be content with that?"

For an instant I caught Margaret's eye, and then looked at Howard on her right. His head was lowered, as it were sullenly, and he did not show any sign of recognition at all. I turned back to his wife and said:

"I am afraid I haven't yet heard anything which would make me take any steps."

I felt, rather than heard, that Howard had given something like a grin or snigger. Laura flushed to the temples and cried:

"What right have you got to say that?"

"Do you really want me to go on?"

"What else can you do?"

"Well, then," I said, trying to sound impersonal, "I couldn't take any other view, in the light of what the scientists report about the evidence. Remember, I'm totally unqualified to analyse the evidence myself, and so are most of the people in the college. That's one of the difficulties of the whole proceedings. If I were there, I should just have to believe what Francis Getliffe and the other scientists told me."

"Oh, we know all about them—"

I stopped her. "No, I can't listen to that," I said. "Francis Getliffe has been a friend of mine for twenty-five years."

"Well—"

"I trust him completely. So would anyone who knew him."

"Getliffe," Howard put in, in a tone both sneering and knowing, "is a good example of a man who used to be a progressive and has thought better of it."

"I shouldn't have thought that was true," I replied, "If it were true, it wouldn't make the faintest difference to his judgment."

"Then I should like to know what would," Howard went on in the same sneering tone.

"You must know what would." I had nearly lost my temper. "And that is what he thought, as a scientist, of the evidence under his eyes."

"I suppose they weren't prejudiced when I gave them the explanation?"

"I've heard exactly what they did about it—"

"Who from?"

"Skeffington."

Laura laughed harshly.

"Did you think *he* wasn't prejudiced?"

"I don't know him as I know Getliffe, but he strikes me as an honest man."

"He's a religious maniac, he's the worst snob in the college."

"I also heard from my brother."

"Do you really think he worried?" Laura burst out. "All he wants is to step into old Brown's shoes—"

I saw Margaret flinch, then look at me with something like apprehension, as if she felt responsible for her guest.

"I suppose you think," said Howard, "that the precious Court of Seniors weren't prejudiced either? I suppose they weren't anxious to believe what Skeffington and that crowd told them?"

I had got tired of this. I went on eating and as I did so, organised a scheme of questions in my mind, just as I used to when, as a young man, I had practised at the bar.

Everyone was quiet.

"I'd like to clear up two or three points, simply for my own satisfaction," I said to Howard. "May I?"

"I don't mind," he said.

"Thank you. According to my information, you actually appeared before the Court of Seniors several times? Is that true?"

He nodded his head.

"How many times?"

"I suppose it must have been three."

"That agrees with what I've been told. The first time you appeared there you were told that the scientists had decided that one of the photographs in your paper was a fraud. Were you told that?"

"I suppose that is what it amounted to."

"It must have been clear one way or the other, mustn't it? It's important. Were you told in so many words that the photograph was a fraud?"

"Yes, I suppose I was."

His eyes had not dropped but risen. They were fixed on the picture-rail in the top left-hand corner of the room. It was a long time since I had examined a witness, but I caught the feel of it again. I knew that he had gone on the defensive right away: he was hostile, slightly paranoiac, beating about to evade the questions. I asked:

"Was it, in fact, a fraud?"

He hesitated: "I don't quite get you."

"I mean just what I say. Was that photograph a fraud? That is, was it faked to prove something in your paper?"

He hesitated again: "Yes, I suppose you could say that."

"Is there any shade of doubt whatsoever?"

Just for a second, his upturned, averted eyes looked at me sidelong with enmity. He shook his head.

"Did you agree with the Court of Seniors, then, when they told you it was a fraud?"

"Yes, I told them so."

"My information is that you denied it totally the first couple of times you appeared before them. Is that true?"

"I told them."

"On your third appearance?"

"Yes."

"Why did you deny it?"

"Because I didn't believe it was true."

"Yet every other competent scientist who saw the evidence didn't take long to be certain it was true?"

He broke out: "They were glad of the chance to find something against me—"

"That won't get us anywhere. Why did you take so long to be certain? Here was this photograph, you must have known it very well? But even when you'd been told about it, you still didn't admit that it was a fraud? Why not?"

He just shook his head. He would not answer: or rather,

it seemed that he could not. He sat there as though in a state of hebephrenia. I pressed him, but he said nothing at all.

I took it up again:

"In the long run, you decided it really was a fraud?"

"I've told you so."

"Then when you decided it was a fraud, you were able to produce an explanation?"

"Yes, I was."

"What was it?"

"You must have picked up that," he said offensively, "among the other information they've given you."

"In fact, you blamed the fraud on to your collaborator?"

He inclined his head.

"Who'd just died, at the age of, what was it, seventy-five? Your explanation was that he had faked one of your own photographs?"

"Yes, it was."

"Did that seem to you likely?"

"Of course it didn't," Laura broke in, her expression fierce and protective. She spoke to her husband: 'You had a great respect for him, of course you had."

"Did you have a great respect for him?" I asked.

"Not specially," he answered.

"What reason did you think he could have, at that age and position, for this kind of fraud?"

"Oh, he must have gone gaga," he answered.

"Were there any signs of that?"

"I never noticed."

"One last question. When you decided that he had faked this photograph of yours, you also said that you'd seen similar photographs before—did you say that?"

"Yes."

"Who had taken those photographs?"

"The old man, of course," he said.

"How many had you seen?"

He looked confused. His reactions seemed very slow.

"I can't tell you," he said at last.

"Many?"

"I shouldn't think so."

"Only one?"

"I don't know."

"You're sure you saw one? At least one more, besides yours?"

"I've told you I did."

"Did you know there are no signs of any such photographs in the whole of his scientific notebooks?"

His face went vague and heavy. "I suppose they told me that," he said. Then he asked: "What I want to know is, who looked?"

Then I stopped. "I don't think it's any use going further," I said.

Margaret tried to make some conversation, I joined in. Howard fell into silence, with an expression that looked both injured and apathetic. Even Laura had lost her nerve. She did not refer to the case again. The evening creaked slowly on, with gaps of strained silence as Margaret or I invented something to say. I offered them whiskey within half an hour of the end of dinner: Laura took a stiff one, he would not drink at all. At last, it was only a few minutes after ten, she said that they must go. Margaret, usually gentle-mannered and polite, was out of her chair with alacrity.

As we stood by the door, waiting for Howard to come out of the lavatory, Laura suddenly looked up at me.

"Well? Will you talk to Getliffe or your brother?"

I was startled. Even now, she did not know when she was beaten.

"What do you think I could say?"

"Can't you just tell them that they've got to open this business all over again?"

Her eyes were wide open. She looked like a woman making

love. She was so fervent that it was uncomfortable to be near her.

"I shall have to think whether there's anything I can do," I said.

By then Howard was on the way towards us, and she did not speak any more.

As the door closed behind them, Margaret remarked, "*Of course* there isn't anything you can do."

"Of course there isn't," I said.

"He hasn't got a leg to stand on, has he?"

"Less than that, I should have thought."

We sat down, neither of us in good spirits, and held hands.

"No one," I said, "could call that a particularly agreeable party."

"Anyway," said Margaret, "you're not required to see them again."

I said no.

Margaret was smiling.

"I must say, I thought you got pretty rough with them."

"I couldn't think of anything else to do."

"That's not quite all, is it?"

I smiled. We knew each other's intuitive likes and dislikes too well.

"I can't pretend," I said, "that he's exactly my cup of tea."

"Whereas, if he hadn't done what he unfortunately has done, you wouldn't be surprised if I thought he'd got a sort of integrity, would you?"

We were laughing at each other. The fret of the evening was passing away. We were reminding each other in the shorthand of marriage that, when we made mistakes about people, they were liable to be a specific kind of mistake. As a young man, I had been fascinated by, and so had overvalued, the ambivalent, the tricky, the excessively fluid, and even now, though they no longer suggested to me the mystery of life as they once did, I had a weakness for them. I saw value in

Tom Orbell, for instance, that others didn't. Certainly not Margaret, whose own weakness was the exact opposite. The moral roughneck, the *mauvais coucheur,* often seemed to her to have a dignity and elevation not granted to the rest of us. She was not taken in by the fluid, but on the other hand, just because a character was not fluid, was craggy in its egotism, she was likely to think it specially deserving of respect. If, as she said, grinning at her own expense, Howard had come to us with different credentials, I could easily have imagined her regarding him as a man of fine quality.

"I grant you that he's not two-faced," I said. "But what's the use of that, when the one face he has got is so peculiarly unpleasant?"

FIVE

A PARTY FOR A PURPOSE

During our parting with Laura Howard, when she was demanding that I talk to my brother, we had not told her that we were spending Christmas in his house. In fact, we arrived there on Christmas Eve, and after dinner Martin's wife and I were for a few minutes alone in the drawing-room. Or alone, to be more exact, in a room of which the drawing-room was only half: for Irene had invited some of the Fellows and their wives for wine and cheese at nine o'clock, and she had already furled back the bronze doors between drawing-room and dining-room. Yes, bronze doors: the house, before the college acquired it, had been a piece of luxurious modernist building of a generation before. Now it was divided into two sections, and let out to college officers. By the standards of the Fifties, Martin's section, which was the larger one, was sizeable for a professional man's house.

The children were all in bed, their boy and girls, Margaret's son by her first marriage, and ours. Margaret was upstairs: Martin was uncorking bottles in the kitchen: Irene and I sat alone on opposite sides of the fire. She had been asking me about my work, and presumably I gave a heavy reply, for she broke out with a yelp of glee: "The trouble is, Margaret doesn't make fun of you enough!"

If one had just heard her voice without seeing her, one would have guessed that she was a very young woman, mischievous, light, high-spirited. Actually, as I glanced across the fireplace, I saw a woman in the early forties, looking much more worn than her husband. She had always been tall and big-framed, but recently her shoulders had rounded and she had put on weight; not only had her bosom got full and shapeless, but she had thickened through the middle. By contrast to this body, comfortably slumped into middle-age, her face seemed thinner and fined-down; the skin of her cheeks had lost its bloom, and underneath the make-up there was a faint, purplish undertint. And yet, it was still a reckless face. Some men would still find her attractive. Underneath full lids, her eyes were narrow, treacle-brown, disrespectful and amused.

Nevertheless, when Martin came in with a complaint, she was not amused, but dead serious. Where was the specimen he had picked up yesterday on Wicken Fen? Who could have moved it? Martin was for once off-balance. There was a distraught, hare-like look in his eye. As a small boy he had been more of a collector than any of us. Now the addiction was coming back. Was it because he was reconciling himself to not making a go of academic physics? Was that why he concentrated so much on his pupils, and then in his spare time went off in search of botanical species? Anyway, he was methodically ticking off the English flora. That night he thought he had lost one: he was showing the signs of a phobia of loss.

Worried, active, Irene started from her chair and went out with him. Within three minutes she was back.

"That's all right," she said, her expression relieved and earnest.

"The trouble is," I said maliciously, "you don't make fun of him enough."

Irene giggled, but she did not really think that it was funny. She broke out: "But how do you think he is?"

"Don't you know?"

"I think so," she said honestly, "but I'm never sure."

I nodded. He was a secretive man: people, even those nearest to him, thought him cautious, calculating, and capable of being ruthless.

"I don't believe you need worry," I said. "I fancy he's pretty happy."

"Do you?" She shone with pleasure.

"I should be surprised if he wasn't."

"I must say," she cried. "I should like to bring off something for him."

"What do you mean?"

"Wouldn't it be good if he could get something?"

For a second, I was surprised at her. She was no fool. She knew that, after throwing away the chance of power, even if he had thrown it away for a qualm or set of qualms that she did not share or understand, he must have times when he would like the chance back again. So, with the energy she had once scattered on her own adventures, she was now not only longing, but working, for him to get another kind of job. It was mildly ironic, when one thought how, as a young woman, she had shocked the bourgeois, to find her set on seeing him a cosy, bourgeois success. She had closed her mind to what she used to think of as "the big world": she wanted him to climb in the college's little one.

"That's what this is in aid of," she said, pointing to the glasses in the dining-room.

She was doing it without hypocrisy. She did not possess in the slightest degree the gift, so desirable in the life of affairs, of being able to keep the right hand from knowing what the left is doing. Her right hand knew, all right. Shamelessly, innocently, she wanted to help push him up the college ladder and install them both in the Lodge before the end.

When I realised what she was up to, I thought she was pitching her hopes far too high. The Mastership, the Vice-Chancellorship—her fancy was making pictures of them, just as it used to make pictures of the dashing ideal lover when she was a girl. But Martin had no chance at all of ever becoming

Master. She was not cut out for politics, she did not know when to hope and when not to hope. The most she could expect for Martin was that, if Arthur Brown were elected next year (which I still could not believe was on the cards), Martin might get the senior tutorship. That was his ceiling, so far as the college was concerned. Then I remembered Laura Howard's sneer, that Martin was planning to step into Brown's shoes. Was that true, I wondered? I had seen my brother's command of tactics when he was spending his time in the corridors of power. Why should I think he was committed to Francis Getliffe? Why should not Martin be preparing to come in on Brown's side, incidentally freeing an agreeable niche for himself?

At any rate, I was prepared to bet that this was in Irene's mind. Soon the first guests were coming into the room, and I could not get more out of her. But I began to watch those whom she had invited. Was it just a coincidence that the Getliffes were not coming? Were the people here going to form the hard core of Brown's party?

Standing up, plate and glass in hand, overhearing a conversation about the English faculty, I found myself talking to G. S. Clark. Like the other Fellows at that party, he had been elected since the war; but unlike Tom Orbell and Ince, and two or three of the others, he was not a young man. I did not know for certain, but I guessed that he was over forty. He had been paralysed by poliomyelitis as a child, and his face had the gentle, petulant, youthful and hopeful expression that one sometimes sees in cripples; his skin was pink and fresh. Although his left leg was in a metal brace, he would not sit down. He stood there obstinately and argued with me.

"No," he said, "with great respect, I don't agree."

I teased him. I said I had only made the modest suggestion that the examination system as it existed in Cambridge that night, December 24th, 1953, might just not possibly be perfect for all time. Was that so shocking? He smiled, a gentle, patient, invalid's smile.

"But I'm making the modest suggestion," he said, "that it's easy to tamper with things just now and make them worse."

Whenever I met him, which was fairly often, since he occupied the other section of Martin's house, I liked his sweet and hopeful smile and then ran up against this kind of brick wall. But this was not the night for an argument: I asked him about his work. He was a don in Modern Languages, and he was writing a book about the German novelist Fontane. His accent became broader and flatter as he warmed up to the Nineteenth Century romantic-realists: he came from Lancashire, his origins were true working-class. It was very rare, I had thought before, for anyone genuinely working-class to struggle through to the High Table, though a sprinkling had come, as I did myself, from the class just above. In the whole history of the college, there could not have been more than three or four who started where he did.

Just then his wife's voice, just a shade off-English, the consonants a little too sharp for English, broke in.

"I'm going to take Lewis from you, G.S. Remember, I have known him longer than I have you."

That was true. When she first knew me, she had been a refugee and the wife of another. Then she had been called Hanna Puchwein; she had been a pretty, elegant young woman with a neat, glossy, hamitic head, snapping black eyes, disconcerting in her integrity and bitter temper. She had got rid of Puchwein in what seemed a fit of pique; there were plenty of men round her, and she nearly married the most unsuitable. We had thought her then the worst of pickers: even so, I was astonished when I heard that she had suddenly married Clark. It was not only astonishing to hear, it was obscurely disagreeable.

That night, her face was still pretty, her forehead bland and intelligent in her pointed, cat-like face: but the black hair was going grey, and she was not bothering to do anything with it, even to keep it tidy. She used to be beautifully groomed, but she seemed to have given up.

She said that she had been talking to Margaret, she asked after our child, but with the touch of impatience of people who haven't any. In turn, I asked her how she liked Cambridge now.

"It is all right," she said, with sharpness and pride.

Did she see much of the college, I asked her.

"As much as a woman can."

"What are they thinking about just now?"

"Are they ever thinking about anything?" She said it just as contemptuously as she would have in the past. I was glad, it showed the old Adam was not dead. She corrected herself: "No, that is not fair. Some of them are clever men, some of them do good work. But a lot of them are not precisely what I was brought up to think of as intellectuals. Even those who do good work are often not intellectuals. Perhaps that is one of the secrets of this country that a foreigner is not expected to understand."

I asked her, were there any major rifts in the college at present?

"What is there for them to have rifts about?" she said.

I grinned to myself. She had always had a lucid grasp of theoretical politics: I imagined that unlike her husband she was passionately radical still. But, intelligent as she was, she had not much insight, less perhaps than anyone of her intelligence I had known.

"Lewis!" came an enthusiastic, modulated voice over my shoulder. "Hanna, my dear Hanna!" Tom Orbell came between us, carrying not only a glass but a bottle, his cheeks gleaming pink almost as though they were a skin short, sweat on his forehead, his blue eyes cordial and bold. Punctiliously he gave me the bottle to hold, murmuring happily, "I'm afraid I'm rather drunk," seized Hanna's hand and bent over it to kiss.

"My dear and most admired Hanna!" he said.

"Have you finished that article?" Her tone was cross, but there was a dash of affection in it.

"Of course I have," said Tom, with the indignation of one who, for once, is in the right. As a matter of fact, I knew, and she ought to have known, that he was an industrious man.

"I'm very glad to hear it," said Hanna.

"Will you let me tell you about it? When will you let me give another little dinner-party for you?"

"Oh, in the New Year," she said. "Now look, Tom, I don't often see Lewis—"

"Why have I got to leave you with him? He's a bit of a menace, is Lewis—"

Hanna frowned, and Tom, who had regripped the bottle, gave it to me again. Once more with great elaboration, and a bow that became something like a genuflexion, he kissed her hand.

When he had merged into the party, Hanna said,

"Why does that young man behave in the way he imagines Continentals to behave? I suppose he imagines that Continentals are polite to women. Why does he think so? Why does he think I should like it? Why do young Englishmen like that go in for hand-kissing? Is it only those like that young man who are sexually insecure?"

She still sounded ratty. Nevertheless, I thought she had a soft spot for him.

"Yes," she was saying with asperity, "I think it is because he is sexually insecure that he kisses hands. You can not imagine Martin performing like that, can you?" I could not. "Or that *lourdon* Lester Ince?"

Irene split us up, and for a few moments I stood on the fringe of the party, watching Martin, as usual deliberate, easy-mannered, planted among his guests, while his wife moved avidly about.

As a young woman she would have been on the look-out for a man. She still moved about just as frenetically, just as darting-eyed. Yet that had gone, all gone. Not that she regretted it much, I thought. She was happy here, and across the room I could hear her squeals of glee.

I heard another sound of glee at my shoulder, and Tom, in a state of airborne hilarity, was whispering to me a story about Mrs. Skeffington. She had not long arrived, and within two minutes, Tom was telling me, had dropped "her biggest clanger" yet. I did not know her, and across the room he pointed her out. She was very tall, almost as tall as her husband, but as plain as he was handsome. According to Tom she was something of a *grande dame* and, what made it worse, spoke like one. Apparently she had improved the occasion, soon after she got to the party, by announcing to Irene: "I think it's so sensible of people to think out how to entertain, and strike out for themselves. If they *can't* give dinner-parties, why *shouldn't* they give bits and pieces afterwards?"

Tom rejoiced. Observant, labile, malicious, he was a very good mimic. Somehow he managed, not only to sound, but to look like Mrs. Skeffington, county to the bone, raw-faced.

"It still goes on, my dear Lewis," said Tom. *"It still goes on."*

"At some levels," I said, "I think it's getting worse."

"Give me your hand." Tom, half-way between inflation and rage, insisted on gripping my hand in his, which was unexpectedly large and muscular for so fat a man. He wanted to go on denouncing exponents of English snobbery, radicals, complacent politicians, unbelievers, all the irreconcilable crowd of enemies that he managed to fuse into one at this time of night. He had not said a word about the Howards. They had not been so much as mentioned since I arrived at Martin's house.

"But what do you *want,* Tom?" I enquired, getting impatient.

"I want something for this college."

"Do other people here—" I waved my hand at the party—"want anything definite?"

He gazed at me with eyes wider-open, but guarded. He was deciding not to let me in.

"I want something for this college, Lewis. I mean that very sincerely."

Before long I was confronted by Skeffington, who called his wife and introduced me to her. I thought that, though his manner was as lofty as ever, he looked jaded and ill at ease. He did not say much, while his wife and I conscientiously made some Cambridge exchanges—new buildings, traffic, comparison of college gardens. Suddenly Skeffington interrupted us: "What are your plans for tomorrow?" he said.

It seemed a curious question.

"Well," I said, "we've got four children in this house—"

"Yes, but when the fun and games are packed up and you've got them to bed?"

It still seemed an odd cross-examination. However, I said that, since we should have the big meal at mid-day ("quite right," said Mrs. Skeffington) Martin and I had thought of giving our wives a rest and dining in hall at night.

"I've never done it before on Christmas Day."

Skeffington was not interested in my experiences.

"That's cut and dried, is it? You're going to show up there?"

"Well, we've put our names down," I said.

Skeffington nodded, as though for the time being placated.

He did not appear to resent it, when Lester Ince, who had broken away from his own group, put in:

"Well, I call that a nice Christmassy programme for old Lew."

No one, either living or dead, had been known to call me Lew before. I was senior enough, however, to find it agreeable. It was not often that I met anyone as off-handed as this young man. He had a heavy, pasty, cheerful face. Although his stance was slack, he was thick-set and strong. He was not really a *"lourdon"* as Hanna thought. He had a sharp, precise mind which he was devoting—incongruously, so it seemed to most people—to a word-by-word examination of *Nostromo.* But though he was not really a *"lourdon,"* he liked making himself a bit of a lout.

"Come to that," he said to Skeffington, "how do you propose to celebrate the Nativity?"

"Much as usual."

"Early morning service with all the highest possible accompaniments?"

"Certainly," Skeffington replied.

"Stone the crows," said Lester Ince.

"It happens to be a religious festival. That's the way to do it, you know." Skeffington looked down at Ince, who was not a short man, from the top of his height, not exact snubbingly, but with condescension and a gleam of priggishness.

"I tell you what I'm going to do," said Ince. "I shall have to do my stuff with wife and kiddies, confound their demanding and insatiable little hearts. I shall then retire with said wife—who's doing herself remarkably well over there in the corner, by the way—I shall retire with her and three bottles of the cheapest red wine I've been able to buy, and the old gramophone. We shall then get gently sozzled and compare the later styles of the blessed Duke with such new developments as the trumpet of Miles Davis. You wouldn't know what that means, any of you. You two wouldn't know, it's since your time," he said to Skeffington and his wife. "As for old Lew, he's certainly non-hep. I sometimes have a suspicion that he's positively anti-hep."

Soon after, just as the Skeffingtons were leaving, Tom Orbell wafted himself towards me again. "I wish I could get Hanna to myself," he confided, "but she's holding a court and they won't leave her alone, not that I'm in a position to blame them." He was the only person in the room who had been drinking heavily, and he had now got to the stage when from second to second, he was switched from exhilaration to fury, and neither he nor I knew which way he was going to answer next. "It is a great party, I hope you agree that it's a great party, Lewis?" I said yes, but he wanted more than acquiescence. "I hope you agree that the people here ought to throw their weight about in the college. These are the people who ought to do it, if we're not going to let the place go dead under our feet." He looked at me accusingly.

I said, "You know the position, and I don't."

"That's not good enough," said Tom Orbell.

He seemed just then—did this happen often?—to have changed out of recognition from the smooth operator, the young man anxious to please, and on the make. He nodded his head sullenly: "If that's what you think, then that's all right." He said it as though it were at the furthest extreme from being all right.

"What do you want me to say?"

"I've told you, I want something for this college. There are some people I'll choose for my government, and some people I'll see in hell first."

He spoke of "my government" as though he were a Prime Minister who had just returned from the Palace with the job. His own studies of history seemed to be taking possession of him. "Some of these chaps I'll have in my government straight away. There are some in the college we've got to keep out, Lewis, or else the place won't be fit to live in. I know he used to be a friend of yours, but do you think I'm going to have *Sir Francis Getliffe* in my government?"

"What do you mean? Now then, what is all this about?" I spoke brusquely, to make him talk on the plane of reason.

Without paying attention he went on.

"There are one or two others who think as I do, *I* can tell you. I wish we knew what your brother Martin thought."

He was still enough in command of himself to be trying to sound me. When he got no response, he gave his sullen nod.

"Martin's a dark horse. I should like to know what he wants for the college. I can tell you, Lewis, I want something for it."

"So you should," I said, trying to soothe him.

"Give me your hand," he said. But he was still obscurely angry, with me, with Martin, with the party, with—I suddenly felt, though it seemed altogether overdone—his own fate.

Just then I noticed that Skeffington, though he was wearing his overcoat, had still not left the house. For once he looked dithering, as though he was not sure why he was hanging about. All he did was check with Martin, in the peremptory tone he had used to me, that we were likely to be dining in college the following night.

SIX

COLLEGE DINNER ON CHRISTMAS DAY

The Cambridge clocks were striking seven when, on Christmas Day, Martin and I walked through the Backs towards the college. It was a dark night, not cold, with low cloud cover. After the noisy children's day, we, who were both paternal men, breathed comfortably at being out in the free air.

As we made our way along the path to Garret Hostel Bridge, Martin said, out of the dark, in his soft, deep voice:

"Stinking ditches."

We smiled. We had not been talking intimately: we had not done so for a long time: but we still remembered what we used to talk about. That was a phrase of a colleague of Martin's when he first started his researches, an Antipodean who had come to Cambridge determined not to be bowled over by the place.

"Wouldn't some of these boys like Master Ince think that was a reasonable description?"

"I must walk along the Backs with him and see," said Martin. He sounded amused. I asked him more about the people I had been speaking to the night before. Yes, he found Ince's knockabout turn a bit of a bore: yes, he wished Ince had settled down rather less and Tom Orbell considerably more.

Of course, said Martin, G. S. Clark was the strongest character among them.

If so, I had quite misjudged him. It set me thinking, and I asked:

"What are they like inside the college?"

"Well, it's never been altogether an easy place, has it?"

Whether he had his mind on politics at all, I still did not know. If he had, he was not going to show it. Nevertheless we were both relaxed, as we went through the lane, all windows dark, to the back of the Old Schools and out into the market place. There it was empty: no one was walking about on Christmas night, and the shop-windows were unlighted. It was the same down Petty Cury: and in the college itself, entering the first court in the mild blowy evening we could see just one window shining. Everything else was dark under the heavy sky. The Lodge looked deserted, nothing but blank windows in the court: but between the masses of the Lodge and the Hall, there was a window glowing, dull red through the curtains, golden through a crack between them.

"Cosy," said Martin.

It was the Combination Room. Unlike most colleges of its size, ours kept up the tradition of serving dinner every night of the year; but in the depth of vacation, the Fellows dined in the Combination Room, not in Hall. When we entered, the table, which at this time on a normal night would be set out for the after-dinner wine, was laid for the meal. The napery gleamed under the lights; the side of the table-cloth nearest the fire had a rosy sheen. In the iron grate, the fire was high and radiant, altogether too much for so mild a night. Old Winslow, the only man to arrive before us, had pulled his chair back towards the curtains, out of the direct heat. He gave us a sarcastic smile, the lids hooded over his eyes.

"Escaping the cold supper at home, as a colleague of mine used to say?" he greeted us.

"Not entirely," I said.

"We don't expect the singular pleasure of the company of married men on these occasions, my dear Eliot."

"I'm afraid you're going to get it," I said.

When I had lived in the college, I had got on better than most with Winslow. Many people were frightened of him.

He was a savage, disappointed man who had never done more than serve his time in college administrative jobs. When he was Bursar, people had been more frightened of him than ever. After he retired, it seemed for a time that the old sting had left him. But now at eighty, with the curious second wind that I had seen before in very old men, he could produce it again, far more vigorously than ten years before. Why, no one could explain. His son, to whom he had been devoted, was living abroad and had not visited him for years: his wife had died, and in his late seventies he had come back to live in college. By all the rules he should have been left with nothing, for the bitter, rude old malcontent had had a marriage happier than most men's. But in fact, whenever I met him, he appeared to be in some subfusc fashion enjoying himself. He looked very old; his cheeks had sunk in; his long nose and jaw grew closer together. To anyone unused to old men, he might have seemed in the same stage of senescence as M.H.L. Gay. Yet, as one talked to him, one soon forgot to take any special care or make any allowances at all.

"My dear Tutor," he was saying to Martin, "I suppose we ought to consider ourselves indebted to you—for producing your brother to give us what I believe is known as 'stimulus' from the great world outside."

"Yes, I thought it was a good idea," said Martin, in a polite but unyielding tone. Like me, he did not believe in letting Winslow get away with it. "Perhaps I might present a bottle afterwards to drink his health?"

"Thank you, Tutor. Thank you."

Tom Orbell came in, deferential and sober, and after him the new chaplain, a middle-aged man who was not a Fellow. Then two young scientists, Padgett and Blanchflower, whom I knew only by sight, and another of the young Fellows whom I did not know at all. "*Doctor* Taylor," Winslow introduced him, inflecting the 'doctor' just to make it clear that he, in the old Cambridge manner, disapproved of this invention of the

Ph.D. "Doctor Taylor is our Calvert Fellow. On the remarkable foundation of Sir Horace Timberlake."

It did not strike strange, it sounded quite matter-of-fact, to hear of a Fellowship named after a dead friend. Taylor was stocky, small and fair: like all the rest of us except one of the scientists, he was wearing a dinner-jacket, since that was the custom when the college dined in the Combination Room on Christmas Day. I was thinking that, since the college, which in my time had been thirteen, had expanded to twenty, some of the young men seemed much more like transients than they used to. Blanchflower, for example, stood about like a distant acquaintance among a group of people who knew each other well.

I was thinking also that, if Martin and I had not dropped in by chance, no one present would have had a wife. One old man who had lost his: one bachelor clergyman: and the rest men who were still unmarried, one or two of whom would never marry. About them all there was that air, characteristic of bachelor societies, of colleges on days like this, of the permanent residents of clubs—an air at the same time timid, unburdened, sad and youthful. Somehow the air was youthful even when the men were old.

We took our places at table, Winslow at the head, me at his right hand. We were given turtle soup, and Tom Orbell at my side was muttering, "Delicious, delicious." But he was on his best behaviour. Champagne was free that night, as the result of a bequest by a nineteenth Century tutor: Tom, shining at the thought of his own lack of self-indulgence, took only a single glass.

Smoothly he asked Winslow if he had been to any Christmas parties.

"Certainly not, my dear Orbell."

"Have you really neglected everyone?"

"I gave up going to my colleagues' wives' parties before you were born, my dear young man," Winslow said.

He added: "I have no small talk."

He made the remark with complacency, as though he had an abnormal amount of great talk.

Just then I heard Taylor talking in a quiet voice to his neighbor. Taylor was off to Berlin, so he was saying, to see some of the Orientalists there: he produced a couple of names, then one that, nearly twenty years before, I had heard from Roy Calvert, Kohlhammer. The name meant nothing to me. I had never met the man. I did not know what his specialty was. Yet hearing that one word mumbled, in a pinched Midland accent, by Taylor, I was suddenly made to wince by the past. No, it was not the past, it was the sadness of the friend dead over ten years before, present as it used to be. That single name gave me a stab of grief, sickening as a present grief—whereas the name of Roy Calvert himself I had heard without emotion. Often enough in the college, I had looked up at the window of his old sitting-room, or as at the feast made up my own Charlusian roll-call of the dead—all with as little homesickness as though I were being shown round a new library. But at the sound of that meaningless German name, I felt the present grief.

When the table, the glasses, the fire, which had retreated to the far distance came back and focussed themselves, I could still hear Tom Orbell deferentially baiting Winslow.

"Have you been to any services to-day, Winslow?"

"My dear young man, you should know by now that I don't support these primitive survivals."

"Not even for the sake of *gravitas?*"

"For the sake of what you're pleased to call *gravitas*—which incidentally historians of your persuasion usually misunderstand completely—I am prepared to make certain concessions. But I'm not in the least prepared to give tacit support to degrading superstitions."

The chaplain made a protesting noise.

"Let me bring it to a point, my dear chaplain. I'm not in

the least prepared to lend my presence to your remarkable rituals in the chapel."

"But I've seen you set foot in the place, haven't I?" I said.

Winslow replied: "I've now been a Fellow of this college for slightly more than fifty-eight years. I was elected fifty-eight years last June, to be precise, which is no doubt not a date which many of my colleagues would feel inclined to celebrate. During that period I have attended exactly seven obsequies, or whatever you prefer to call them, in the chapel. Each of those seven times I went against my better judgment, and if I had my time again I should not put in an appearance at any one of them. I believe you have never gone in for these curious superstitions, Eliot?"

"I'm not a believer," I said.

"Nor you, Tutor?"

Winslow turned to Martin with a savage, cheerful grin.

"No."

"Well, then, I hope you will keep my executors up to the mark. In my will, I have given strict instructions that when I die, which in the nature of things will be quite shortly, there is to be not the faintest manifestation of this mumbo-jumbo. I have endeavoured to make testamentary dispositions which penalise any of my misguided relatives who attempt to break away from these instructions. I should nevertheless be grateful to men of good sense if they keep an eye open for any infringement. Your co-believers, my dear chaplain, are remarkably unscrupulous and remarkably insensitive about those of us who have come perfectly respectably, and with at least as much conviction as any of you, to the opposite conclusion."

Winslow was enjoying himself, so were some of the others. I thought the chaplain was not fair game, though Tom Orbell would have been, and so I said:

"You've been in chapel more than seven times, you know."

"My dear boy?"

"Electing Masters and so on."

"I take the point," said Winslow. "Though I'm not sure that those occasions can fairly be counted against me. But yes, I grant you, I've been inside the building four times for magisterial elections. Three of which, it became fairly clear soon after the event, showed the college in its collective wisdom choosing the wrong candidate." He added: "Now I come to think of it, I suppose that by this time next year I shall have to go inside the building again for the same purpose. My dear Tutor, have you worked out when the election falls due?"

"December 20th," said Martin without hesitation.

"Unless I die first," said Winslow, "I shall have to assist in the French sense at that ceremony. But I'm happy to say that this time I can't see even this college being so imbecile as to make a wrong choice. Just for once, the possibility does not appear to be open."

"You mean—?"

"It's not necessary to ask, is it? Francis Getliffe will do it very well."

No one contradicted the old man. I could not resist making things slightly more awkward for Tom Orbell.

"I seem to remember," I said, "having heard Brown's name mentioned."

"My dear Eliot," said Winslow, "Brown's name was mentioned last time. I then said it would mean twenty years of stodge. I should now say, if anyone were crass enough to repeat the suggestion, that it would mean seven years of stodge. It is true, seven would be preferable to twenty, but fortunately it is impossible for my colleagues, even with their singular gift for choosing the lowest when they see it, to select stodge at all this term."

"Getliffe is generally agreed on, is he?"

"I've scarcely thought the matter worth conversation," said Winslow. "The worthy Brown is not a serious starter by the side of Francis Getliffe. And that is the view of all the seniors in the college, who are showing surprising unanimity for once in a way. I had a word with the Bursar recently. We agreed that there would have to be a pre-election meeting, but we saw no reason why there should be more than one. Which, I may tell you young men—" Winslow looked round the table—"is entirely unprecedented in the last sixty years in this college. I even find that our late Senior Tutor, the unfortunate Jago, is completely at one with the Bursar and myself. As I say, we all think Getliffe will do it very well."

As my eyes met Tom Orbell's, his were bold, light, wide-open. For whatever reason, he was not going to argue. Was it deference, or was he just not ready to show his hand? While Martin, listening politely to Winslow, gave no sign whether he agreed or disagreed. In a moment he got the old man talking of past college follies: of how a "predecessor of mine in the office of Bursar showed himself even more egregiously unfitted for it" by selling the great Lincolnshire estate. "If it hadn't been for that remarkable decision, which shouldn't have been made by anyone with the intelligence of a college servant, this institution would be approximately half as rich again."

Further inanities occurred to Winslow. As we stood up while the waiters cleared the table and arranged chairs in a crescent round the fire, he was reflecting on the number of Fellows in his time who had been men of a "total absence of distinction."

"A total absence of distinction, my dear Tutor," he said to Martin, with even greater cheerfulness.

"Wasn't there something to be said for old—?" said Martin, his own eyes bright.

"Nothing at all, my dear boy, nothing at all. He would have made a very fair small shopkeeper of mildly bookish tastes."

He settled into the President's chair, which was the second as one proceeded anti-clockwise from the far side of the fire-place. In the middle of the room, the rosewood table shone polished and empty: when the college dined in the Combination Room, it was the habit to drink wine round the fire.

"It can't be too often said," Winslow addressed himself to Taylor and the youngest of the others, both in their twenties, well over fifty years his juniors, "that, with a modicum of exceptions, Cambridge dons are not distinguished men. They are just men who confer distinctions upon one another. I have often wondered who first uttered that simple but profound truth."

The port glasses were filled as Winslow announced:

"I believe this bottle is being presented by Mr. Eliot, for the purpose—correct me if I am wrong, my dear Tutor—of marking the appearance here of his brother. This is a remarkable display of fraternal good wishes."

With sardonic gusto, Winslow proposed my health and then Martin's. We sipped the port. The fire was warm on our faces. Martin and I, not to be outfaced by Winslow, spoke of previous times when we had dined together in that room. The old man, satisfied with his performance, was becoming a little sleepy. The room was hot and comfortable. Some of the young men began to talk. Then the door clicked open: for a second I thought it was the waiter with the coffee, coming early because it was Christmas Night: but it was Skeffington.

Winslow roused himself, his eyes red round the rims.

"My dear boy," he said, "this is a most unexpected pleasure. Pray take a glass of port."

"I apologise, Mr. President," said Skeffington. I noticed that his first glance had been in the direction of Martin.

"Don't apologise, but sit down and fill your glass."

It was unusual, but not startlingly so, for Fellows who had missed dinner to drop in afterwards for wine. As a rule, one would have taken it without curiosity, as most of them were taking it that night. But I couldn't: nor, I felt sure, could Martin. Skeffington had sat down, and in silence watched his glass being filled. He was not dressed: for him, so formal and stiff with protocol, that was odd in itself. In a blue suit, his head thrown back, his cheeks high-coloured, he looked out of place in that circle.

The conversation went on, but Skeffington did not take part in it and Winslow was nearly asleep again. It was not long before Martin got to his feet. When we had said our good-nights, and were outside in the court, I was not surprised to see Skeffington come up behind us.

"As a matter of fact," he said to Martin, "I should like a word with you."

"Do you want me alone?" said Martin.

"I'd just as soon Lewis heard," said Skeffington.

Martin said that we had better go up to his rooms. They struck dank and cold, even on that muggy night. He switched on the electric fire, standing incongruously in the big sixteenth century grate.

"Well, Julian?" said Martin.

"I didn't think I ought to keep it to myself any longer."

"What is it?"

"The last few days I've been going more into the business of this chap Howard."

"Yes?" Martin was still impassive, but bright-eyed.

"I can't see any way out of it. I believe that he's been telling the truth."

SEVEN

THE COMPONENT OF CONTEMPT

For an instant, none of us moved. It would have been hard to tell whether Martin had heard what Skeffington had just said. He was not looking at Skeffington. He gazed steadily at the chimneypiece in which the electric fire had one small incandescent star, much brighter than the glowing bars, where a contact had worked loose.

"What made you go into the business again?" he said at last, as though merely curious, as though that were the only question on his mind.

"I tell you," said Skeffington, temper near the surface, "that he's been telling the truth."

"Can you prove it?" said Martin sharply.

"I can prove it enough to satisfy myself. Damn it, do you think I *want* to blackguard the old man?"

"That's fair comment," said Martin. "But have you got a hundred per cent proof that'll satisfy everybody else?"

"Have you?" I asked.

"What do you mean?"

"I don't know what you intend to do," I said, "but can you do anything without what a lawyer would think of as a proof? Have you got one?"

He looked flushed and haughty.

"In that sense," he said, "I'm not sure that I have. But it will be good enough for reasonable people."

"Then what *do* you intend to do?" Martin took up my question.

"The first thing is to get this chap Howard a square deal. That goes without question."

He said it simply, honorably, and with his habitual trace of admonition and priggishness.

"When did you decide that?"

"The moment I realised that there was only one answer to the whole business. That was yesterday afternoon, though for forty-eight hours I hadn't been able to see any other option."

"I'm sorry," said Martin, turning to him, "but it's not so easy to accept that there can't be one."

"Don't you think I've made sure that I've closed all the holes?"

"Don't you think you might be wrong? After all, you're saying you've been wrong once before, aren't you?"

"You'll see that I'm not wrong," said Skeffington. "And there's one point where I'd like your advice, both of you."

He began answering the question Martin had asked first—what had made him "go into the business again?" It happened that, though Skeffington's wife had not often seen her uncle Palairet while he was alive, she was on good terms with his solicitors. A partner in the firm had mentioned to the Skeffingtons that the last box of the old man's papers was being sent to the college. Skeffington had, of course, thought it his duty to go through them.

As he explained, I thought, as I had done before, that his voice did not live up to his looks. It was both monotonous and brittle. But his mind was more competent than I had given him credit for. It was precise, tough, not specially imaginative, but very lucid. People had given me the impression that he was an amateur, and lucky ever to have been elected. I began to doubt it.

I was interested in his attitude towards old Palairet. Obviously he had not known him well. Skeffington seemed to have had an impersonal respect for him as a scientist of reputation, such as Skeffington himself longed to be. For Skeffington felt a vocation for science. He might be rich, he might be smart: he was not at ease with the academics, he could not talk to them as he had been able to talk to his brother-officers: the reason why he could get on with Martin and me was that he had met us in the official world, and knew some of the people we knew. Yet for all that, though he could not in his heart accept most of "those chaps" as social equals, he longed to win their recognition. He longed to do good work, as Palairet and Getliffe had done; he might have said this was setting his sights too high, but he was seeking exactly that kind of esteem.

"How did your wife get on with her uncle?" I asked, just as he was leading off into the scientific exposition.

"Oh," said Skeffington, "he never saw her jokes."

For a second I caught a sparkle in Martin's eye. As I had heard him give both Skeffingtons maximum marks for humourlessness, I wondered what astonishing picture that reply conveyed.

As Skeffington went on, I found both him and Martin agreeing that whatever the old man was like, most of his scientific work was sound and safely established on the permanent record. His major set of researches were "textbook stuff," Skeffington insisted.

"That's what I don't understand," said Skeffington, simple, high-minded, incredulous. "Because, assuming that he cooked this other business, it couldn't have done him tuppence-ha'penny worth of good. It just doesn't count beside the real good, solid stuff he'd got behind him. Was he *crackers,* do you think?"

The old man had done first class scientific research, they told me: his major work, on the diffraction of atomic particles, was "quite water-tight": some of the photographs were reproduced in the standard books. Martin fetched down a couple of volumes, and showed me the photographs, rather like rifle targets with alternate rings of light and dark. Those results were beyond dispute: they had been repeated, time and time again, in laboratories all over the world.

It was also beyond dispute that Palairet had become interested in an extension of his technique—not an important extension, something which only counted "marginally," by the side of his established work. He had expected to be able to apply his technique to a slightly different kind of particle-diffraction. "For a rather highbrow reason, that no one could possibly have thought up a year ago, we now know it couldn't work," said Skeffington. But the old man had expected it to work. So had Howard, doing his research under the old man's eye. The photograph in Howard's paper demonstrated that it *did* work, said Martin, with a grim chuckle: demonstrated it by the unorthodox device of taking a genuine diffraction film and "blowing it up," just like enlarging an ordinary photograph, so as to increase the distances between the light-rings and the dark. It was from these distances that Howard in his paper had calculated the wave-lengths of the particles. "After blowing it up, someone got the results he expected," said Skeffington.

For the first time I heard how the fraud had been detected. When the film had been "blown up," the hole left by a drawing-pin which had held it up to dry in the dark room had been expanded too. As soon as the result had been proved to be theoretically impossible, the Americans had enquired why the white blob in the top centre of the picture seemed so singularly large. It was just as simple as that.

According to Howard, when at last he gave the Court of Seniors his explanation, that photograph had not been the first the old man had shown him. He had told me the same.

To credit his story, one had to assume that he was absolutely trusting. If it were feasible at all, it meant that he had been indoctrinated beforehand. However uncritical he was, he must have been ready to believe in the evidence, he must have taken for granted that the technique was "on," before he put that final photograph into his paper.

"Even so," said Martin, "he would have to be pretty wooden."

"That's as may be," said Skeffington, who had until a few days before thought the whole account so preposterous as to be an insult. It was only out of mechanical duty, automatic conscientiousness, that when he heard that more of the old man's manuscripts had reached the college, he went into the Bursary, borrowed the key of the Palairet box, and took them away.

"Had the Bursar told you they'd arrived?" asked Martin.

"The usual piece of formal bumf," said Skeffington. As soon as any scientific document arrived from Palairet's executors, Nightingale sent a reference number to Skeffington, so I gathered.

Without interest Skeffington had sat in his rooms, reading through the last note-books.

"Have we got them all now?" asked Martin.

"So far as they know, we've got them all."

Without interest, Skeffington had read on. "Old man's stuff, most of it," he said. Jottings about researches which Palairet would never do: occasional sets of data, corrections of earlier papers. But at last, on the Saturday afternoon before Christmas, something had turned up. "I don't mind telling you, I didn't take in what it meant. I was sitting in my rooms in the Fellows' building, and I went out and walked in the garden, and I couldn't see anything that made sense. I don't mind telling you, I wasn't very bright about it."

He looked at Martin. "As a matter of fact, I've brought it along with me."

"May I see it?" Even Martin's politeness was wearing sharp.

Skeffington opened a briefcase which he had brought with him into the room, and produced a thick exercise book, such as I remembered using in the Oxford Senior class at school. Sticking out of it was a bookmarker. "Yes," said Skeffington, "I've kept the place." It sounded so matter-of-fact as to be absurd. Just as it did when he assured us that he had signed a receipt for the exercise book with the Bursar's clerk.

"All right, Julian," said Martin. Then Skeffington put his fingers, delicate, square-tipped, on the marker and said: "Here we are."

I had gone across to glance at the book over Martin's shoulder. My first impression was of an almost empty page. Then I read at the top, in a spiky, old-fashioned holograph, the date, July 20th, 1950. Underneath the date were several lines of handwriting, which began: *Tried diffraction experiments using neutron source A and crystal grating B, encouraging results.* Then a blank space in the middle of the page, with a rim of sticky paper, as though something had been removed. Underneath, at the bottom of the page, the handwriting went on: *Above print gives strong support for view that diffraction of neutrons at higher speeds, corresponding to wave-lengths shown above, follows precisely the same pattern as at low speeds (see J.B.P., Proc. Roy. Soc. A. . . . 1942, 1947) Have always predicted this. Follow up.*

"The photograph's missing, is it?" said Martin.

"The point is," Skeffington said loudly to me, "that what he says at the bottom can't be true. This is where the Howard paper starts off." He tapped the page. "It can't be true."

"If there ever was a print there," Martin was reflecting, "either it couldn't have shown anything at all—"

"Or else that had been blown up too."

"Where is it?" said Martin.

Skeffington shrugged his shoulders.

"Something was there once, wasn't it?"

"The point is," he went on loudly again, "if Howard saw that print and that entry, then his story stands up as near as makes no matter. However you read that entry, the old man was fooling himself, if he wasn't fooling anybody else. I don't know what he was up to—he must have been crackers. But I do know that it gees with the Howard story, and I don't believe that there's any way out of it. *Can you see one?*"

"If the print was there," said Martin in a soft, deliberate tone, "then I don't think I could."

"But still."

Martin sat frowning. He asked me for a cigarette. After a time he said:

"I can't believe there isn't a way out of it."

"Do you think *I* want to believe it?" Skeffington's tone, just as when he started to explain, was haughty and annoyed. "It isn't exactly pleasant for me to stir up mud about the old man —and, if I had to stir up mud about anyone connected with my family, I shouldn't choose to do it on behalf of anyone like Howard. We never ought to have let in a chap like that. But the point is, we did let him in, and I believe he's an innocent man—"

"Oh, yes, Julian," Martin roused himself, and for once was speaking restlessly, sarcastically, and without civility. "We know that you believe that. It's like G.H. Hardy's old crack—If the Archbishop of Canterbury says he believes in God, that's all in the way of business, but if he says he doesn't, one can take it he means what he says. We don't need persuading that you mean what you say. We know you believe it. But I don't see that recognising your conviction gets us very far."

At Martin's tone, so untypically sharp, Skeffington showed no resentment. He just threw his head back and said:

"It might get us a bit further when I've settled what to do next."

Martin was composed and cautious again. He said:

"I hope you won't do anything until we've all thought it over."

"I can't wait long."

"I'm not asking you to wait long."

"I should like to see Nightingale tomorrow."

"I hope you won't do anything," said Martin, "until we've thought it over."

"I can't put it off. That isn't good enough—"

"No one's asking you to put it off. Look, it's Boxing Day

tomorrow. I'd be grateful for another twenty-four hours after that. Then I'll be ready to talk."

Reluctantly, Skeffington acquiesced. He went on:

"But there's something I want your advice on now. Lewis, you've heard the state of the game. I want to know, shall I write to this chap Howard tonight? I mean, I don't feel specially inclined to talk to him. But he hasn't had a square deal, and I think he's entitled to know that someone like me is going to make it his business to see that he gets one."

"It would be a good thing to write to him, I should have thought," I said. "So long as you make it clear you're only speaking for yourself."

I was thinking, Skeffington was a brave and honorable man. He had not had an instant's hesitation, once he believed that Howard was innocent. He was set on rushing in. Personal relations did not matter, his own convenience did not matter, nor how people thought of him. Both by nature and by training, he was single-minded: the man had his rights, one had to make sure that justice was done. Yet, inside that feeling, there was no kindness towards Howard. There was no trace of a brotherly emotion at all. The only residue of feeling he had for Howard was *contempt*. Contempt not because he and Skeffington had not an idea in common, but just because he was an object of justice. I had seen the same in other upright men: one was grateful for their passion to be just, but its warmth was all inside themselves. They were not feeling as equals: it was *de haut en bas:* and, not only towards those who had perpetrated the injustice, but also, and often more coldly, towards the victim, there was directed this component of contempt.

"The chief thing is, isn't it," I said, "that you mustn't raise false hopes?"

"I think it would be much better," said Martin, "if you didn't write at all until we've talked it over. Won't that give you a clearer idea of just what you can and cannot say?"

II

WHY SHOULD ONE ACT?

EIGHT

AMBIGUOUSNESS AND TEMPER

Through the wet and windy Boxing Day, Martin played in the big drawing-room with the children—played just as I remembered him in our own childhood, concentrated and anxious to win. Irene and Margaret were laughing at us when he and I had a game together. He had invented a kind of ping-pong, played sitting down with rulers at a low table, and complicated by a set of bisques.

Though our wives knew what was on Martin's mind, for we had told them last thing the night before, no one would have guessed it. He was out to win, within the rules, but just within the rules. His son, Lewis, watched with the same bright eyes, the same concentration, as his father's: so did my son. When we had finished, Martin coached them both, patiently showing them how to cut the ball, repeating the stroke while the minutes passed, as though going through his head there was no thought of Skeffington's conversion, no thought of anything except the cut-stroke at ping-pong. Outside, through the long windows, one could see the trees lashing and the grass dazzling in the rain.

Just before tea, the children went off to put records on their gramophone. Martin said to me:

"I don't know. I don't know. Do you?"

For years we had talked like acquaintances. But we could still get on without explanation: we caught the tone of each other's voice.

I replied: "I wish I understood the scientific evidence

better. I suppose understanding that does make it a bit easier, doesn't it?"

"I suppose it might," said Martin, with a tucked-in smile.

He did not say any more that day. At the same time the following afternoon, when again we were having a respite from the children, we were sitting with Irene and Margaret. The rain was slashing the windows and the room had turned dark except for a diffused gleam, reflected from the garden, of green and subaqueous light.

"This is a wretched business," said Martin at large, not with worry so much as annoyance. Again I knew he had not been thinking of much else.

"Tomorrow morning I shall have to have this talk with Skeffington," he said to me.

"Can't you put him off?" said Irene.

"What are you going to tell him?" I said.

He shook his head.

Margaret said: "I can't help hoping you'll be able to agree with him."

"Why do you hope that?" Irene broke out.

"If Skeffington's right, it must have been pretty shattering for Howard, mustn't it? And I should have thought it was even worse for her," said Margaret.

"What are you going to say tomorrow?" I came back at Martin.

Margaret asked: "Is Skeffington right?"

Martin looked straight at her. He had a respect for her. He knew that, of all of us, she would be the hardest to refuse an answer to.

He said: "It makes some sort of sense."

She said: "Do you really think he could be right?" Her tone was even, almost casual: she did not seem to be pressing him. Yet she was.

"It seems to make more sense," said Martin, "than any other explanation. But still, it's very hard to take."

"Do you believe he's right?"

Martin replied: "Possibly."

Unexpectedly, Margaret burst into laughter, laughter spontaneous and happy. "Have you thought," she cried, "what awful fools we should all look?"

Martin said:

"Yes, I've thought of that."

"All of us thinking how much we know about people!"

For once Irene did not see any sort of joke. Frowning, she said to Martin:

"Look here, have you got to get yourself involved too much with all this?"

"What do you mean?"

"Suppose Skeffington goes ahead. There's going to be a row, isn't there?"

Martin glanced at me. "That's putting it mildly."

"Well, have you got to get into it? I mean, have you got to start it? It isn't your business, is it?"

"Not specially, no."

"Whose is it?" Margaret asked.

He told her that constitutionally it would be for the subcommittee—Nightingale and Skeffington—to take the first steps.

"Well then," said Irene, "do you need to do much yourself?"

"No, I don't need to," said Martin. He added: "In fact, if I don't want to quarrel with half the society, I can keep out of it more or less."

"*Can* you?" said Margaret. She had flushed. She said passionately to Irene, "Do you really want him to sit by?"

Almost as though by reflection, Irene had flushed also. Surprisingly, she and Margaret got on well. Neither then nor at any time could Irene bear to have her sister-in-law disapprove of her, much less to think her crude and selfish. For Irene, despite, or to some extent because of her worldliness, had both a humble and generous heart.

"Oh," she said, "someone will put it right if there's anything to put right. If old Martin were the only chap who could, I suppose he'd have to. But let Julian S. do the dirty work, that's what he's made for. Those two won't mind getting in bad with everyone here. All I meant was, we're settling down nicely now, we haven't got any enemies for the first time in our lives."

"Isn't there a danger—you're frightened that if Martin makes a fuss over this—it might stand in his way?"

Irene replied, shamefaced with defiance: "If you want the honest truth, yes, I'm frightened of that too."

Margaret shook her head. Even now, after marrying me, and meeting my colleagues, and getting a spectator's view of the snakes and ladders of power, she could not quite credit it. Her grandfather and great-uncles had resigned Fellowships over the Thirty-Nine Articles. I sometimes teased her, did she realise how much difference it had meant to them and even to her, that they had all been men of independent means? Yet she stayed as pure as they had been. She did not think that Martin or I were bad men: because she loved me, she thought that in some ways I was a good one: but she could not sympathise with the shifts, the calculations, the self-seekingness of men making their way.

"Do you think," she said, apparently at random, "that Laura ever had any doubts about him?"

"No," I said.

"She's totally wrapped up in him," said Martin. "I don't imagine she ever had a second's doubt."

"In that case, she must be the only person in the world who didn't. I wonder what it's been like for her?"

Margaret, I knew, was deliberately playing on our human interest. She, too, was subtle. She knew precisely what she wanted Martin—and, if I could take part, me also—to do.

But Irene sidetracked her by saying casually: "Well, she'd never tell *me*. She just can't bear the sight of me."

"Why ever not?" I asked.

"I just can't think."

"I expect she fancies," said Martin, "that you've cast an eye at Donald."

"Oh, she can't think that! She *can't!*" cried Irene, as usual hilarious (though she detested Howard and had been for years a faithful wife) at the bare prospect of adultery.

Then she said to Margaret: "It isn't going to be fun, doing anything for them, don't you see that?"

"I tell you, that's putting it mildly," said Martin.

"You won't stick your neck out if you don't need to? That's all I'm asking you. Will you?"

"Do you think I ever have done?" said Martin.

None of us was certain how he proposed to act, or whether he proposed to act at all. Even when he sounded for opinion that night at the Master's dinner table, he did it in the same ambiguous tone.

Until Martin began that sounding, the dinner had been a standard and stately specimen of the Crawford régime. It would not have happened if I had not been in Cambridge, for the Crawfords had only returned to the Lodge late on Boxing Day. But Crawford, who had never been a special friend of mine, had a kind of impersonal code that ex-Fellows who had achieved some sort of external recognition should not stay in Cambridge uninvited: so that night, in the great drawing-room at the Lodge, ten of us were drinking our sherry before dinner, the Nightingales, the Clarks, Martin and Irene, me and Margaret, and the Crawfords themselves, the men in white ties and tails, for Crawford, an old-fashioned Cambridge radical, had refused in matters of etiquette to budge an inch.

He stood, hands in pockets, coat-tails over arms, warming his back at his own fireplace, invincibly contented, so it seemed. He was a heavy, shortish, thickly-made man who still, at the age of seventy-two, had a soft-footed, muscular walk. He looked nothing like seventy-two. His Buddha-like face, small-featured and round, had something of the unlined youthfulness, or rather agelessness, that one sees often in Asians, but very rarely in Europeans: his hair, glossy black, was smoothed down and did not show any grey at all.

He talked to each of us with impersonal cordiality. He said to me that he had "heard talk" of me in the "club" (the Athenaeum) just before Christmas, to Nightingale that the college had done well to get into that last list of American equities, to Martin that a new American research student seemed to be highly thought-of. When he had gone into dinner and settled down to the meal, with the same cordiality he addressed us all. The subject that occurred to him, as we ate an excellent dinner, was privilege. He went on: "Speaking as the oldest round this table by a good few years, I have seen the disappearance of a remarkable amount of privilege."

Crawford continued to deliver himself. The one thing on which all serious people were agreed, all over the world, was that privilege must be done away with; the amount of it had been whittled away steadily ever since he was a young man. All the attempts to stop this process had failed, just as reaction in its full sense had always failed. All over the world people were no longer prepared to see others enjoying privilege because they had a different coloured skin, or spoke in a different tone, or were born into families that had done pretty well for themselves. "The disappearance of privilege—if you want something that gives you the direction of time's arrow," said Crawford, "that's as good as anything I know."

Hanna could not restrain herself. With a sharp smile, she said:

"It's still got some way to go, shouldn't you say?"

She looked round the table at the white ties, the evening dresses, the panelled walls beyond, the amplitude of the Lodge dining-room, the lighted pictures on the walls.

"Fair comment, Mrs. Clark," said Crawford, imperturbable, gallant. "But we mustn't be misled by appearances.

Speaking as the present incumbent, I assure you that I can't imagine how my successors in the next generation are going to manage to run this Lodge. Unless indeed a society which is doing away with privilege decides to reward a few citizens for achievement by housing them in picturesque surroundings that no one else is able to afford. It would be interesting if a certain number of men of science in the next generation were still enabled to live in Lodges like this or the Carlsberg mansion at Copenhagen."

As the talk became chit-chat, I was paying attention to Mrs. Nightingale, whom I had not met before. She was a plump woman in the late thirties, a good twenty years younger than he was. Her shoulders and upper arms were beginning to ham out with fat; her eyes were full, sleepy, exophthalmic. But that sleepy plumpness was deceptive. Underneath she seemed energetic and quick-moving. When I said to her, pompously, as we were considering whether to pour sauce on to the pudding: "Now if we're wise—," she replied, deadpanned but instantaneous: "*Don't* let's be wise." Between her and Nightingale there passed glances sparkling with both humour and trust. She referred to him as the Lord Mayor, a simple private joke which continued to delight him. They were happy, just as Martin and the others had told me. I was astonished that he had found such a nice woman.

I had been half-expecting Martin to lead in Howard's name. All through dinner he did not mention him; he was still playing his part in the chit-chat when the women left us. But in fact it would have been surprising if he had not waited until the men were alone. College manners were changing in some of the young men, but not in Martin. He would no more have thought of discussing college business in the Lodge in front of wives than Crawford would, or Brown, or even Winslow. Though Martin was used to the company of women like Margaret or Hanna, though he knew how they detested the

Islamic separation, Martin would not have considered raising his question that night until they had gone.

When the door had closed behind him, Crawford called for us to sit nearer to him. "Come up here, Nightingale! Come beside me, Eliot! Will you look after yourself, Martin?" It occurred to me, still thinking of Martin's manners, that while he kept some of old-style Cambridge, Crawford had, in just one respect, dropped his. Crawford called his contemporaries by their surnames, and that had been common form until the Twenties. Even in my time, there were not many Fellows who were generally called by their Christian names. But, since the young used nothing else, since Martin and Walter Luke and Julian Skeffington had never been known by anything but their Christian names to their own contemporaries, the old men also began to call them so. With the result that Crawford and Winslow, who after fifty years of friendship still used each other's surnames, seemed oddly familiar when they spoke to the younger Fellows. As it happened, I came just at the turning-point, and to both Crawford and Winslow, though my brother was "Martin," I remained "Eliot."

The five of us had been alone for some time, the decanter had gone round, before Martin spoke. He asked, in a casual, indifferent, almost bored manner:

"Master, I suppose you haven't thought any more about the Howard business?"

"Why should I? I don't see any reason why I should, do you?" said Crawford.

Martin replied:

"Why should you indeed?"

He said it dismissively, as though his original question had been silly. He was sitting back in his chair, solid and relaxed, with Clark between himself and Crawford. Though he looked relaxed, his eyes were on guard, watching not only Crawford, but Nightingale and Clark. He said:

"As a matter of fact, I thought I heard that it was just possible that some fresh evidence might still turn up."

"I don't remember hearing the suggestion," said Crawford. He spoke without worry. "I must say, Martin, it sounds remarkably hypothetical."

"I suppose," said Martin, "that if more evidence really did turn up, we might conceivably have to consider re-opening the case, mightn't we?"

"Ah well," said Crawford, "we don't have to cross that bridge till we come to it. Speaking as a member of our small society, I've never been fond of hypothetical situations involving ourselves."

It was a reproof, good-humoured, but still a reproof. Martin paused. Before he had replied, Nightingale gave him a friendly smile and said:

"There's a bit more to it than that, Master."

"I'm getting slightly muddled," said Crawford, not sounding so in the least. "If there is any more to it, why haven't I been informed?"

"Because, though there is a bit more to it on paper," Nightingale went on, "it doesn't amount to anything. It certainly doesn't amount to enough to disturb you with at Christmas. I mean, Martin is perfectly right to say that a certain amount of fresh evidence has come in. It's not fair to accuse him of inventing hypothetical situations."

Crawford laughed. "Never mind about that. If he's not used to being misjudged at his age, he never will be."

"No," Nightingale persisted. "I for one am grateful that he mentioned the matter."

"Yes, Bursar?" said Crawford.

"It gives us the chance to settle it without any more commotion."

Martin leaned forward and spoke to Nightingale:

"When did you hear about this?"

"Last night."

"Who from?"

"Skeffington."

Just for an instant, Martin's eyes flashed.

"It's all perfectly in order, Master," Nightingale said to Crawford. "You'll remember, Skeffington and I were the committee deputed to make a technical report to the Seniors in the first instance. Naturally we've assumed it was our duty to keep our eyes open for any development since. It happens that the last instalments of Professor Palairet's scientific papers have arrived at the Bursary since the Seniors made their decision. Both Skeffington and I have gone through them. I think it's only fair for me to say that he's made a more thorough job of it than I've been able to do. The only excuse I've got is that the Bursary manages to keep me pretty busy."

"We all know that," said Crawford.

"So these very last notebooks I hadn't been able to do more than skim through. It was those that Skeffington brought to my attention last night."

"When did *you* hear?" Suddenly Clark spoke in a quiet voice to Martin, but Nightingale had gone on:

"I'm glad to say that I saw nothing which makes the faintest difference to my original opinion. If I were writing my report to the Seniors again to-day, I should do it in the same terms."

"That's exactly what I should have expected." Crawford said it with dignity and authority.

"I don't think I ought to conceal from you, in fact I'm sure I oughtn't," said Nightingale, "that in the heat of the moment Skeffington didn't take entirely the same view. He gave to one piece of evidence an importance that I couldn't begin to, and I think, if I have to take the words out of his mouth, that he would have felt obliged to include it, if he were rewriting his own report. Well, that's as may be. But even if that happened, I am quite sure that in the final result it wouldn't have had the remotest effect on the Seniors' findings."

"Which means," said Crawford, "that we should have been bound to take the same action."

"Inevitably it does," said Nightingale.

"Of course," said Clark.

Crawford had settled himself, his hands folded on his paunch, his eyes focussed on the wainscot.

"Well, this is a complication we could reasonably have been spared," he said. "I am inclined to think the Bursar is right, Martin has done us a service by bringing up the subject. Speaking as Master for a moment, there is one thing I should like to impress upon you all. I should also like to impress it on Skeffington and our other colleagues. In my judgment, this college was remarkably lucky to avoid a serious scandal over this business. I never took the violent personal objection to Howard that some of you did, but a piece of scientific fraud is of course unforgivable. And any unnecessary publicity about it, even now, is as near unforgivable as makes no matter. We've come out of it internally with no friction that I know of. And externally, better than any of us could have hoped. I do impress on you, this is a time to count our blessings and not disturb the situation. In my view, anyone who resurrects the trouble is taking a grave responsibility upon himself. We did justice so far as we could, and as the Bursar says, we have every reason within the human limits to believe that our findings were the right ones. Anyone who tries to open it all over again is going to achieve nothing except a certain amount of harm for the college, and a risk of a good deal more."

"I'd just like to ask again, as I've asked you all in private often enough," said Nightingale, "if this man felt he had been hard done by, why in Heaven's name didn't he bring an action for wrongful dismissal?"

"I agree with every word you've both said," Clark broke in. He was hunched round to ease the weight on his leg. His smile was sweet, a little helpless, a little petulant. All of a sudden I realised that, just as Martin had said, he was a man of formidable moral force. "Except, if I may say so, personally I think worse of the man responsible for it all. I always thought it was a mistake to elect him, and I was sorry that our scientific friends got their way. I know we all kept off the question of his politics. Politics is becoming a taboo word. I'm going to be quite frank. I should have to be convinced that, in present conditions, a man of Howard's politics can be a man of good character, as I understand the term. And I am not prepared to welcome such men in the name of tolerance, the tolerance that they themselves despise."

"I wish I'd had the courage to say that earlier," Nightingale broke out.

Martin had not spoken for a long time. In the same tone, neither edgy nor over-concerned, in which he had made his first approach, he said: "But that isn't really the point, is it? The real point is what the Bursar said about the evidence."

Clark replied:

"What the Bursar said settled that, didn't it?"

The curious thing was, I thought, that Nightingale, Clark, and Martin liked one another. When we went into the drawingroom there was no sign of argument on any of them. In fact, there had not been a word of disagreement spoken.

As the college clock struck the half hour, it must have been half-past eleven, Martin and Irene, Margaret and I, were walking up Petty Cury on the way home. In the empty street, Martin said softly:

"I got even less change than I reckoned on."

He had spoken in a matter-of-fact tone, but when Margaret said:

"The Nightingales know all about it, don't they?" he turned on her:

"How did you hear that?"

"I wanted to see what she and Hanna were thinking—"

"You talked about the Howard business, did you?"

"Of course—"

"You told them that Skeffington was worried?"

"Naturally."

"Can none of you be trusted?" Martin broke out.

"No, I won't take that—"

"Can none of you be trusted?" He had quite lost his temper, something so rare for him that Irene and I glanced at each other with discomfort, a discomfort different from just looking on at her husband and my wife snacking. As his voice sharpened, his face lost its colour: while Margaret, whose hot temper had risen to meet his cold one, was flushing, her eyes snapping, looking handsome and less delicate.

"Has everyone got to talk the minute you get hold of a piece of gossip? Has that fool Skeffington got to blurt out the whole story before any of us have had a chance to have a look at it? Has none of you any idea when it's useful to keep your mouths shut?"

"Don't you realise Connie Nightingale is a good sort? She and Hanna will have some influence—"

"They'll have that, without your talking to them before the proper time."

"Why should you think no one else can judge the proper time?"

"Just from watching the mess you're all getting into."

"I must say," said Margaret violently, "you seem to assume this is a private game of yours. I'm damned if that is good enough for me. You'd better face it, this isn't just your own private game."

Speaking more quietly than she had done, but also more angrily, Martin said:

"It might be more convenient if it were."

NINE

TREAT FOR A WORLDLY MAN

The next morning, the 28th, Martin was as controlled as usual. Without fuss, without making an explicit apology to Margaret, he did apologise to her, by asking if she could bear to sit round and join the "conference" with Julian Skeffington. "I remember that you've shown an interest in the matter," Martin permitted himself to say, unsmiling but bright-eyed.

Skeffington was due at ten o'clock: Margaret and I had to go back to London that afternoon. It was a bright morning, the sunny interval in the warm cyclonic weather, and the children were playing in the garden. The air was so mild that we left the french windows open, and from the end of the long lawn we could hear them shouting, as they chased each other through the bushes. On the grass there shone a film of dew, gossamer-white in the sunshine, with firm black trails of footsteps across it, like a diagram in a detective story.

When Skeffington came in, punctual to the first stroke of ten, he gazed round the room with what looked like distaste or pity for our sloppiness. Where we had had breakfast, in the garden end of the big double room, Irene had not yet cleared away; I was wearing a sweater instead of a jacket. Himself, he stood there beautifully groomed, blue tie pinned down, hair smooth, skin ruddy. Before we had moved from the table he was into his problem.

"I've got to admit it," he told Martin, "I can't come to terms with some of those chaps of ours."

"Who in particular?"

"I was dining in the Combination Room last night, there

were only one or two chaps there, I told them that Howard's case would have to be re-opened."

"You did, did you?" said Martin.

"I didn't see any point in beating about the bush," said Skeffington. "Well, one of those chaps—they were both very junior—said that meant getting a majority of the college. Do you know what he said then?"

Martin shook his head.

"He had the brass to tell me that he didn't feel very much like helping to form that majority."

"Who was this?"

"That man Orbell."

Irene yelped with surprise, Margaret caught my eye. Martin was saying, at his most disciplined, without any sign of irritation: "I can't help wishing you hadn't jumped the gun. You know, it might have been better to tackle Orbell later—"

"It couldn't have been worse," said Skeffington. "I'm sorry. False move."

"By the way," Martin went on, "you spoke to Nightingale the night before, so I heard. I thought we were going to leave that until we'd thought it over?"

"Yes, I spoke to him. I'm not sorry about that. He's the other man on the committee. After I saw you, I decided I was under an obligation to tell him. It was the straightforward thing to do."

"I suppose it was the straightforward thing to do." Martin's voice was neutral. Just for an instant I saw in his face the temper of the night before. But he knew when to cut his losses. He had realised that it was profitless to scold Skeffington. It was done now. Martin contented himself by saying: "You're not making it any easier for yourself, you know."

"That can't be helped."

"You understand that it isn't going to be easy, don't you?"

"I hadn't thought much about it. But it's not going to be a pushover, I see that."

"Doesn't Orbell's reaction show you something?"

"It was a bit of a facer, yes." Skeffington threw back his head, and his expression was puzzled, irritated, sulky.

"It's a good deal more than that." Martin leaned forward into the fireplace, picked up a spill from the holder, twisted it into a knot. Then he looked across at Skeffington and began to speak easily, naturally, and in earnest. "Look, that is what I wanted to talk to you about. I want you to be absolutely clear what the position is. I wouldn't like you to do any more, I really didn't want you to do anything at all, before you realise what you're running yourself in for."

"I think I know the form," said Skeffington.

"Do you?" Martin was watching him. "I intend to make sure you do. That's the whole object of this exercise."

Skeffington had begun to ask me a question but Martin interrupted:

"No, I really want to say this. There are just two courses you can take, it seems to me. Now this evidence has come along, and taking the view of it you do—"

"And you do too," Margaret broke in.

"Taking that view of it, you're bound to do something. If you wrote a statement and sent it to the Master saying, for the sake of argument, that some new technical data made it seem to you extremely unlikely that Howard had been responsible for any fraud—that's all that reasonable men could expect you to do. I think you're obliged to do that. I'm the last man to run into unnecessary trouble, but if I were you I'm afraid I should have to do that."

"I should think you damned well would," said Skeffington.

"And I shouldn't expect it to have any effect," said Martin with a grin that was calculating, caustic, and uncharacteristically kind. "You see, the evidence isn't quite clinching enough to convince anyone who desperately doesn't want to be convinced. There are quite a number of our friends who desperately don't want to be convinced. I suppose you have realised that?"

"They've got to be, that's all," said Skeffington.

"Well, that is the second course. Which means you set yourself first to get the case re-opened and then, which I might remind you isn't the same thing, make the Seniors go back on their decision about Howard. I don't say that's impossible—"

"That's something," Skeffington said.

"—but it's going to be very difficult. Some of the steps you've taken already have made it slightly more difficult. It's going to need a certain number of qualities I am not sure you possess."

Martin said it simply. Skeffington blushed. His haughtiness had left him for an instant: he wasn't used, as Martin and I and our friends were, to direct personal examination.

"Come clean. What does it need?"

"Obstinacy," said Martin. "We're all prepared to credit you with that."

Irene laughed as though glad of the excuse, just to break the tension.

"Patience," said Martin. "How do you fancy yourself in that respect?"

Skeffington gave a sheepish smile.

"Persuasive power," said Martin. "There you might be better than you think. And, I'm afraid that is going to be necessary, considerable command of tactics. I mean, political tactics. I don't think you'll like it, I don't think Margaret will, but it's going to need a good deal of politics to put Howard in the clear."

"Perhaps you know more about that than I do—"

"I do, Julian."

Martin was still explaining carefully. "This business is going to split the college from top to bottom. Anyone who's seen anything of this kind of society would know that. Lewis knows that as well as I do. It will make the place unliveable in and do some of us a certain amount of harm into the bargain. And that's the last thing I want to say to you. I wouldn't feel quite easy until I'd said it in so many words, before you plunge in. If you do plunge in, you've got to be ready for certain consequences to yourself. You're bound to make yourself conspicuous. You're bound to say things which people don't want to hear. The odds are that it will damage your chances. Look, let me be brutal. I know you want your Fellowship renewed when it runs out. I know you'd like to be a fixture. I'd like you to be, too. But if you make too much of a nuisance of yourself, there's going to be a cloud round the name of Skeffington. I don't mean that they'd do anything flagrantly unjust, or that they thought was unjust. If you were Rutherford or Blackett or Rabi or G.I. Taylor, they would keep you as a Fellow even if you insulted the Master every night of your life. But most of us aren't all that good. With most of us there is a perfectly genuine area of doubt about whether we're really any better than the next man. And *then,* if there's a cloud round your name, they're liable to think, and it's very hard to blame them, that perhaps they might let your Fellowship run out, and give someone else a go. Just as they might think, perfectly reasonably, that half a dozen people would do the Senior Tutorship as well or better than I should. So, if they have anything against us, the net result is liable to be that Skeffington is out, and M.F. Eliot doesn't get promotion."

"What does all that add up to?" said Skeffington.

"I just wanted you to know. If I'm going to take a risk myself, I like to reckon out the chances beforehand."

"Do you seriously think any of that is going to keep me quiet?" Skeffington had flushed again, and he looked at Martin as though he despised him.

"No, I didn't think so."

"So you are going in up to the neck, are you?" Irene asked Skeffington.

"What else do you expect me to do?"

Suddenly she turned to her husband, and said:

"What about you?"

Martin answered straight away:

"Oh, there's nothing for it. I shall have to help him as much as I can."

"I knew you would! I knew you would!" Irene cried out, half in reproach, half in pleasure, still youthful, that he should do something dashing.

Of us all, Skeffington was the only one totally surprised. He sat with his mouth slightly open; I wondered if Martin remembered that our mother used a word for just that expression—"flabbergasted." Just for an instant, Skeffington did not seem pleased to have a comrade; he had an expression of resentment, as if Martin had made a fool of him. He liked Martin, and he expected people he liked to behave like himself, simply and honorably. He had been led astray by Martin's deviousness, his habit, growing on him as he became older, of giving nothing away.

Myself, I believed that Martin had two motives. The nearer one was to him, the more often he seemed hard, selfish, cautious, calculating. With his wife, for instance, he was so inconsiderate that it could be harassing to be in their house. And he could not stop himself planning the next move ahead on the chessboard of power. I was pretty sure that the rumours about him were right, that he had not been able to resist working out the combinations for the next magisterial election. I was pretty sure that he had decided it was worth trying for Brown as Master, so that if it came off, he could walk into the Senior Tutorship himself.

That was all true. But it was not all. There was something else within him which made him a more interesting man. At its roots it might not be more amiable than those other roots which made him a hard self-seeker; but it certainly made him more surprising and more capable of good. It was something like a curious kind of self-regard. He knew as well as anyone else that he was hard, selfish, obsessively careful: but he knew, what no one else did, that he had sometimes wanted to be different from that. This self-regard, "romantic" if you like, had twice in his life made him step right out of his ordinary casing. He had, as it were deliberately, made an imprudent marriage, not only by his own standards but by anyone else's. He had been more than imprudent when humanity got the better of him and, with real power waiting on his table, he had quit the atomic establishment and come back to hide himself within the college.

Now he was doing it again. Not out of patrician high principle edged with contempt, as in Skeffington. Martin, who was not such a lofty character, had no contempt for his brother men. No, out of that special kind of self-regard, tinged with and disentangleable from his feeling that he had to be responsible. He did not like being pushed so—out of the predictable, calculating life, with its pickings, small-scale but predictable for years ahead. That would be disturbed now. He did not like it: that was why he had been so bad-tempered the night before. But he was pushed, and he could not stop himself.

That was one motive. The other, it seemed to me, was much simpler. Martin was a natural politician. Inside the college, there was no one in his class, except Arthur Brown. Like anyone with a set of unusual skills, Martin enjoyed using them. This was a perfect opportunity. He felt like an opening bowler on a moist morning, his first two fingers itching for the ball. It looked to Martin a situation adapted to his talents. Skeffington would certainly mishandle it. If anyone could take it through to success, Martin could.

There was one other thing, I thought. Martin enjoyed using his political skills. As a rule, he had used them for his own purposes, sometimes petty, often selfish. It was a treat for him—and I believed that unless one understood that, one didn't understand him or other worldly men—to think of using them for a purpose which he felt, without any subtlety or complexity at all, to be nothing but good.

TEN

PREOCCUPATION OF A DISTINGUISHED SCIENTIST

As we sat in the sunny room after Irene had cried, "I knew you would," Martin got down to tactics. He reiterated what he had already told Skeffington, that getting a majority to re-open the case was only the start. This wasn't the sort of argument that would be settled by "counting heads." The essential thing was to bring in men who would "carry weight." Could Skeffington, or Martin himself, persuade Nightingale to stay neutral? Even after the night before, Martin thought it worth trying. Above all, Francis Getliffe was a key man. Get him active, and all the scientists, the Master included, would have to listen.

Within half an hour, Martin had telephoned the Cavendish, and he and Skeffington and I were on our way there. At first I was surprised that Martin had not only asked if I would care to come with them, but pressed me to. Then I realised that he had a reason. He wanted Francis at his easiest. He knew that with me Francis still sometimes talked like a young man, like the young man I still—with the illusion that invests a friend one has known since twenty—half-thought him to be. But his juniors in the college, even Martin, did not think of him in the least like that. To them—it struck me with one of the shocks of middle-age—he had become stiff and inaccessible.

Yet, when we had climbed up the steps of the old Cavendish, and walked down the dingy corridors to his room, we found him lit up with happiness. The room, which was not his laboratory but his office, was dark and shabby, a room that minor Civil Servants would have refused to live in. On the walls were graphs, scientific photographs, pictures of scientists, one of Rutherford. At one side stood two packing-cases covered with dust. On the desk, under two anglepoise lamps, were pinned down what looked like long stretches of photographic print, with up and down curves in white clear upon them.

"Have a look at this," called Francis. No man could have been less stiff. "Isn't this lovely?"

He explained to them, he explained to me as though I knew as much as they did, what he had found out. "It's a new *kind* of source," he was saying. "I've been keeping my fingers crossed, but this is it."

They were all three talking quickly, Martin and Skeffington asking questions which were incomprehensible to me. Out of it all I gathered that he was "on to something," not as big as his major work, but scientifically both unexpected and sharp-edged. He had made his name by research into the ionosphere, but since the war he had moved into radio astronomy; he was over fifty, he was keeping on at creative work when most of his contemporaries had stopped. As I watched him, his long face warm with delight, I thought this discovery was giving him as much joy as those of twenty years before—perhaps a purer joy, because then he had not satisfied his ambitions. Now he was free to be enraptured with the thing itself.

"Really it is beautiful," he said. He smiled at us all, shamefaced because he was so happy.

Then reluctantly, in a sharp brisk tone, he broke off: "But I mustn't go on talking all morning. I think you had something to see me about, Martin?"

"I'd rather go on with this," said Martin.

"Oh, this can wait—that is, if your job is important. Is it?"

"In a way, it might be. But we want your advice on that."

"You'd better go ahead."

With dexterous care, Francis was fitting a plastic cover over the print; he was still studying the trace, and as he spoke his eyes did not leave it.

"As a matter of fact, it's Julian's show more than mine."

"Well then?"

Skeffington began to explain, much as he had done on the night of Christmas Day. The story was better organised than it had been then; he had had time to get it into proportion. The instant he said that they had been blaming the wrong man, Francis looked up from the print. He gazed at Skeffington without any interruption or gesture, except to draw at his pipe. As he gazed, his expression, which had been happy, receptive and welcoming when we first saw him, changed so much that one did not know what to expect.

When Skeffington paused, Francis said in a harsh voice:

"That all?"

"Yes, I think it puts you in the picture," Skeffington replied.

"Is that what you call it?" Francis broke out. "It's just about the most incredible picture I've ever heard of." He was flushed with resentment. His courtesy, which was usually just a shade more formal than most of ours, had quite left him, and he was speaking to Skeffington with the special hostility kept for those who bring bad news. In fact, he spoke to Skeffington as though he, and only he, were the culprit and that it was his duty to obliterate the bad news and restore the peace of the morning.

"What do you mean, incredible?" said Martin, in a conversational tone. "Do you mean it's incredible that we've all been such fools?"

"I should like to be told when we stop being fools," Francis snapped. Then he tried to collect himself. In a level, reasonable voice, but his face still stern, he said to Skeffington:

"Don't you see that your explanation is very hard to take?"

Skeffington had become angry too. He answered back: "Then are you prepared to make a better one?"

"From what you've told me, I shouldn't have thought it was beyond the wit of man."

"If we'd believed that," said Skeffington, "we shouldn't have come to waste your time."

I said something, and Francis was sharp with me: "Lewis, you're not a scientist, after all."

"If you studied the evidence, what else do you think you could make of it?" said Skeffington. He had begun his exposition with much deference towards Francis, and now, though he looked angry and baited, the deference had not all gone.

Francis ignored the question and spoke coldly and sensibly: "Don't you want to realise how this is bound to strike anyone who isn't committed one way or the other?"

"We not only want to realise that, we've got to," said Martin.

Was he as puzzled as I was by Francis's response? He did not know him so well: perhaps that made it less mystifying to Martin than to me. But he was certainly at a loss to know how to get on terms with Francis, and was feeling his way.

"Remind me," Francis said to Skeffington, "who acted as referees on Howard's work when we elected him?"

"There was one external—old Palairet, naturally. One internal—Nightingale. I was asked to write a note along with Nightingale's. Of course, I was still a new boy myself."

"And you and Nightingale reported on his work when we dismissed him. That's fair enough. But you admit that it isn't precisely convincing when you suddenly tell us that you and Nightingale have ceased to agree?"

"He's not got a leg to stand on—"

"That won't do," said Francis. "He knew as much as you did about the whole background, didn't he?"

"Yes."

"And you showed him the new data and told him your explanation, and he didn't think there was much in it?"

"He didn't think there was anything in it," said Skeffington.

"Well, there it is," said Francis. "If you're going to attack the memory of a distinguished old man, you'll want something firmer than that."

"The facts are firm," Skeffington broke out.

Martin spoke quietly and fairly, still trying to persuade Francis to match his tone:

"At any rate, they're as firm as one could expect. If only that photograph weren't missing."

"Presuming that there was ever a faked photograph there," said Francis.

"Presuming that. Given that photograph, I should have thought there was enough evidence to satisfy a court of law. What do you think, Lewis?"

I also set out to be fair.

"It would be a terribly difficult case for an ordinary court, of course. Too much would depend on the technical witnesses. But I think I agree with Martin. I believe that if that photograph weren't missing, a court would probably see that Howard was cleared. Without it—without it he wouldn't stand more than an even chance."

Francis looked from Martin to me, but without any sign that he was willing to talk our language. He said to Skeffington:

"I take it Nightingale knows all the facts you know, by now?"

"He's seen everything."

"And he still doesn't admit the facts are firm?"

"I told you right at the beginning. I didn't want to give you any false impression. Nightingale wouldn't admit to me—

and I hear he said the same a good deal more strongly when these two were at the Lodge—he wouldn't admit that the facts add up to anything."

For some instants Francis sat silent. Somewhere in the room a clock gave a lurching, clonking tick: I thought I had noticed it as we came in, tapping out the half-minutes, but I did not look round. I was watching Francis's expression. Despite his strong will, he hadn't any of the opacity that I was used to in men of affairs. By their side his nerves were too near the surface. When in the war he was successful among men of affairs, it had been through will and spirit, not through the weight of nature most of them had. As he sat at his desk, faced with a situation that colleagues of mine like Hector Rose would have taken in their stride without a blink, the shadows of his thoughts chased themselves over his face as theirs never would. His expression was upset and strained, out of proportion, much more than Skeffington's or Martin's had been at any time in the last few days. As he sat there, his eyes clouded, his lips pulled themselves in as though he had had a new thought more vexing than the rest.

At last he said, putting his hands on the table, making his voice hearty and valedictory:

"Well, that seems as far as we can go just now." He continued, in the same dismissive tone, but deliberately, as though he had been working out the words:

"My advice to you—" he was speaking to Skeffington—"is to keep on at Nightingale and see if you can't convince each other of the points that are still left in the air. By far the best thing would be for the two of you to produce a combined report. The essential thing is that the two of you ought to agree. Then I'm sure nearly all the rest of us would accept your recommendation, whether you wanted us to stay put or take some action. In fact, I'm sure that's the only satisfactory way out, either for you or the rest of us."

"Do you think it's likely?" Martin asked sharply, pressing him for the first time.

"That I don't know."

Francis's thoughts had turned into themselves again. Martin rose to go. He knew they were getting nowhere: it would be a mistake to test Francis any more that day. But Skeffington, although he got up too, was not acquiescing. In an impatient, aggrieved tone, he said to Francis:

"When you mentioned me changing my mind about the explanation, you don't seriously think that's on the cards, do you? You don't seriously think that now I've had this evidence through my hands, I could possibly change my mind, do you? If you still think I could, why don't you have a look at the evidence for yourself?"

"No," said Francis. "I've got enough to do without that."

He had replied bleakly. When he was opening the door for us he said to Skeffington, as though intending to take the edge off the refusal: "You see, these new results of mine are taking up all my time. But if you and Nightingale do a report, either alone or together, then I'll be glad to have a look at that."

ELEVEN

LOOKING OUT INTO THE DARK

That night, when we were back in our flat in London and the children had gone to bed, Margaret told me that she would like to write to Laura Howard. Just as Skeffington felt on Christmas Day, she wanted them to be sure she was on their side.

"Do you mind?" she asked, her eyes steady and clear. She would take care not to harm me; but she was irking to act, springy on her feet with restlessness. She was more headstrong than the rest of us.

"I'm thinking of writing to her fairly soon," said Margaret speculatively, as though it might be within the next month, while she was moving with the certainty of a sleepwalker towards her typewriter.

During the weeks which followed, she heard several times from Laura, and it was in that way that I kept an insight into the tactics. Nothing had come of Francis Getliffe's idea of a combined report. It became common knowledge that both Skeffington and Nightingale were writing to the Master on their own. Before either report was in, the sides were forming. They were still three or four votes short of a majority for reopening the case. By the end of January Skeffington's report was known to be complete and in the Master's hands. It was said to go into minute detail and to run to a hundred pages of typescript. (I wondered how Martin had let that pass). Nightingale's, which was delivered a little later, was much shorter. Within the college, these reports were not secret and any Fellow could read them who chose. But it had been agreed, for security reasons, that there should only be three copies of each in existence.

Laura's letters were a curious mixture of business-like information and paranoia. Margaret said:

"Has it ever struck you that when people get persecution mania, they usually have a good deal to feel persecuted about?"

It all seemed to be going slowly, but on the lines one could have forecast. It was clear that Martin could not risk putting forward a formal motion for re-opening until he had his majority secure.

One Friday evening in February, I arrived home later than usual, tired and jaded. It was raining hard, and I had had to walk from Marble Arch the quarter of a mile or so along the Bayswater Road. The warmth of the flat was comforting. From the nursery I could hear Margaret playing with the little boy. I went into the drawing-room looking forward to the quiet, and there, sitting under the standard lamp by the window, the light full on her face, was Laura Howard.

I saw her with surprise, and with something stronger than surprise, involuntary recoil. I had a phobia of entering a room expecting to be by myself, and finding someone there. For an instant I was inclined to gibber. Was Margaret looking after her? I asked, my tongue feeling too large for my mouth, resentfully wishing to push her out, knowing—what usually I did not know at all—exactly what it is to be pathologically shy. Of course Margaret was looking after her, said Laura, firm, composed, utterly unflirtatious. She added:

"We've been putting our heads together."

"Have you?"

"I'm not satisfied with the way things are going. I don't want them to get stuck, and they will get stuck unless we're careful."

I was recovering myself. She did not think of explaining

what "things" were. She was as single-minded as ever. I had never seen a woman of her age so inseparably fused into her husband's life. She sat there, pretty, healthy, and most men would have felt that beneath her skin there was the inner glow of a sensual, active, joyous woman. Most men would have also known that none of that inner glow was for them.

When Margaret came in, she heard Laura repeating that "things were getting stuck."

"Yes," said Margaret, glancing at me guiltily, her colour high, "Laura rang me up and so I thought it might be useful if she came along."

"I see," I said.

"Would you like to hear what she's been telling me?"

I could not refuse.

Succinctly, competently, Laura brought out something new. According to "information from the other side," there had been a suggestion that, if the feeling became strong enough, the Seniors ought to offer to re-open the case before a majority asked for it. I nodded my head. That sounded reasonable, precisely the sort of step that experienced men would consider. Apparently the suggestion had been made by Crawford first, and "the other side," or rather, the more influential members, Arthur Brown, Nightingale and Winslow, had spent some time discussing it. Now they had decided that it wasn't necessary: the feeling was not more than "a storm in a teacup," it would soon blow over. All they had to do was "stick in their heels."

Even the phrases sounded right.

"Your intelligence service is pretty good, isn't it?" I said to Laura.

"I think it is."

"Where does it come from?"

"I'm not at liberty to say," she replied without a blench.

She was not worried. The situation was less promising than three weeks before—"We've gone backwards," she said. But, like so many active people, like Margaret herself, she was freed from worry just by taking action. Why had things deteriorated, I was trying to get her to explain. So far as I could gather, it must have been the effect of the reports. Nightingale's seemed to have been fair in tone, but uncompromising in its conclusion, and that had gone home.

What were Martin and Skeffington doing? I asked her. Martin was "plugging on." She did not complain of the way he was handling the tactics. To her, men were good or bad. Skeffington and Martin, who had been bad men the first time she came to our house, had now been transformed into good. When she trusted, she trusted absolutely. But she wanted "to put on some more pressure." One waverer had decided not to vote for re-opening: they were now four short of a majority. Who was against, of the people I knew, I asked? The old men and the reactionaries, she said with passion (whether she started with any politics I could not tell, but she had taken over her husband's), Arthur Brown, Winslow, Nightingale of course. One or two—such as Gay, because he was "too old to understand," and Crawford from magisterial neutrality—would not vote either way, but that was equivalent to voting against. The "young reactionaries," like G.S. Clark and Lester Ince, were flat against. So was Tom Orbell. As she mentioned his name, Laura swore and Margaret joined in. Abusing him, they made a united front—"Blast the fat snake," said Margaret.

Francis Getliffe? I asked. Laura cursed again. "He's still sitting on the fence." She gave an account, second-hand from her husband, with the pained, knowing smile of the innocent being cynical, of how one can never trust people who pretend to be liberal. They were always the worst. It seemed hardly tactful of her, since she was disposing of Margaret, Martin, and, Skeffington apart, their entire side.

Meanwhile Margaret was frowning, not because Laura was being heavy-footed, but because Francis was a favorite of hers. Of my old friends, he was the one she respected most.

While Laura was with us, Margaret did not ask me anything direct. I could see that she was anxious for Laura to go. Once or twice Laura missed her cue. Then Margaret promised to ring her up during the week, and at last we were alone.

I had gone to the window, and was looking down on the road, over the centre of which the vapour lamps were swinging in the wind. A bare and lurid glimmer reached the trees opposite, but it was too dark to make out the fringes of the park. As I stood there, Margaret had put her arm round me.

"This isn't going too well, is it?" she said.

"Well, it looks as though it might take some time."

"Is that fair?"

"I should have thought so." I was being evasive, and we both knew it. She wanted us to be loving, but she was too much committed to stop.

"No," she said. "Doesn't it look as though it might go wrong?"

"Everything that can be done is being done, you needn't worry about that. Martin knows that place like the palm of his hand."

"But it can go wrong, can't it?"

"However do I know?"

Just for an instant, she smiled at me, the smile of marriage, the smile of knowledge. Then, with all her ardour, she broke out:

"Do you feel like taking a hand yourself?"

She knew, just as well as I did, that I should be cross, should feel trapped. She had known that, when she let Laura stay there, so that I was plunged into the middle of it. She knew, better than I did because she had struggled with it, how I disliked a choice forced upon me, not approached by myself "in my freedom." Now she had done precisely that.

The choice was there. Left to myself I could have blurred it. I wasn't unused to living with situations which were morally ambiguous, or aspects of myself that I didn't especially like. I didn't have so much self-regard as Martin, and thus I hadn't so much compulsion to make a gesture. I had lived for a long time in the corridors of power. It was a condition of living there that the gestures were not made. Most of my colleagues, the men who had the power, would not have considered interfering about Howard. They would have said it wasn't the business of anyone outside the college. They were not cynical, but they kept their eyes on the sheet of paper in front of them. They were not in the least cynical: they believed, quite humbly though comfortingly for themselves, that "the world was usually right."

I was too much of an odd man out to believe that. In fact, doing so seemed to me one of the less dramatic but most dangerous of all the temptations of power. Yet I had lived that disciplined life for nearly twenty years. Perhaps I was the last person to see the changes it made, just as one doesn't see the changes in one's own face, and then, in a photograph, notices an ageing man—can that be me?

I could fairly think to myself that I had no responsibility about Howard. It just was not my business. If I did as Margaret was pressing me, some of my old friends would resent it, because I was being a busybody. They would resent it more, incidentally, because I was being a busybody on the opposition side. I was not likely to be in Arthur Brown's confidence again. That would be a sacrifice, nothing like so heavy a one as Skeffington risked in the line of duty, but still a sacrifice. Why should I make it, when I had lost any taste for exhibition that I ever had, when I plain disliked even the prospect of being thought officious?

If I had added up the arguments, there would scarcely have seemed any in favour. True, I was inquisitive, acutely so, and my inquisitiveness was not weakening: the only way I could satisfy it in this business was to get right inside. Also I knew, and I knew it with the wreckage and guilt of part of my life behind me, that there were always good, sound, human, sensitive reasons for contracting out. There is great dignity in being a spectator: and if you do it for long enough, you are dead inside. I knew that too well, because it was only by luck that I had escaped.

As I stood there, though, gazing down on the road, Margaret's arm round me, I was not searching down into my experience. I was merely aware of a kind of heavy vexation. I was thinking, I had met few people who, made aware beyond all self-deception of an inconvenient fact, were not at its mercy. Hypocrites who saw the naked truth and acted quite contrary—they were a romantic conception. Those whom we call hypocrites simply had a gift for denying to themselves what the truth was. On this occasion, that was a gift which I did not possess.

I said to Margaret, ungraciously, that I would think it over. She had heard me say, often enough, that choices never took as long to make as we pretend: the time was taken in finding the reasons to justify them. She was watching me, face averted, looking out into the dark. She knew precisely what was going on. She knew that I was fretted and sullen because she had not let me evade, or put off, the choice—and that I was not willing to admit to her that it was already made.

TWELVE

THE STARE OF DELUSION

There was another result of the disciplined life, I thought when I was in a better mood, as well as the temptations. It was a week before I could manoeuvre even a day or two free in Cambridge. So far as leisure went, I was living my life backwards: while Martin and the others in the college were no more tied than I had been as a young man.

On the Thursday afternoon following Laura's visit, Martin, to whom I had telephoned, had arranged for us both to meet Howard at his school. My train was late: the taxi slithered through the wet streets, the shop windows already spilling pools of light on to the pavement; through the streets of Romsey town, in which I could not recall, in my time at Cambridge, having been before, which seemed as remote from the collegiate Cambridge as the town where I was born. The school was right at the edge of the suburb: as the taxi drove up, there outside the gates, in the February murk, stood Martin.

He wanted a word about some questions we should ask Howard. While the rain drizzled on us, we agreed how to try it. Then we started to push our way through crowds of children, rushing and squealing into the corridor, just set free from the last lesson of the afternoon.

A boy took us into the physics classroom where Howard was sitting on the lecture table. As we went in, he muttered some sort of greeting, but, if he looked at us, it was only out of the corner of his eye. To make conversation I said, glancing round the room, that it was an improvement on those I had been taught in as a boy.

"If they had some apparatus," said Howard, "you might begin to talk."

"Still, it's better than nothing—"

"Not much," he said.

That seemed the end of that. It was, in fact—I was gazing round for want of anything to say—a model of a room, new, bright, shining, with seats with a good rake and windows taking up the two side walls. On the blackboard behind the table Howard had been writing: the smell of chalk hung in the air. His writing was high, spiky, broken-backed. There were calculations I couldn't follow: this must have been a sixth-form lesson. One word stuck out—"inductence." Could that be right? It didn't seem possible, even in scientific English. Was he one of those people, without visual memory, who just couldn't spell?

"Can we talk here?" said Martin.

"I don't see why not."

Martin settled himself against one of the desks in the front row.

"I don't think I've got any news for you yet awhile—" he began.

"Why did you want to see me, then?"

"There are one or two things we'd like to ask—"

"I'm sick and tired of going over stuff you know as well as I do," said Howard, not meeting Martin's eye, staring unfocussed beyond the darkening windows.

"It's mainly for my benefit," I said.

"I'm not clear where you come in."

"Perhaps Lewis had better tell you," said Martin, glancing at me.

"Yes," I said. "It's very simple. I should like to say that I believe you are in the right in this business. I'm sorry that

I doubted you before. If I can be of any use at this stage, I should like to do what I can."

For an instant, Howard's eyes flickered in my direction and then away again. He said:

"You don't expect me to be exactly overcome with gratitude, do you?"

As a rule I was not touchy, but Howard had a knack of getting under my skin. Martin intervened.

"Come off it, Donald." His tone was hard but comradely. "We've got enough to cope with without you."

Howard, whose head had been turned away, brought it round to face us: but it sank down on to his chest and he was gazing, not at the window, but at his feet.

"Anyway," he said, without a mollifying word, "I don't see what you can do."

He was speaking to me, and I replied: "I've known some of these people a long time. I've arranged to see Francis Getliffe tomorrow morning. I thought it might be worth while."

"A fat lot of good that will do."

"I'm glad you're doing that—" Martin was saying, but Howard interrupted:

"I don't believe in seeing these people. The facts are on paper. They can read, can't they? Well, let them get on with it."

The curious thing was that, though he spoke with such surliness, he was full of hope. It wasn't simply one of those flashes of random hope that come to anyone in trouble. This was a steady hope that he had kept from the beginning. At the same time he managed to be both suspicious and childishly hopeful.

Martin started to question him about the missing photograph. It seemed to be old ground for both of them, but new to me. Had Howard still no idea when old Palairet could have taken such a photograph? Had he never seen one which fitted the caption at the bottom? Couldn't he make his memory work and find anything that would help?

"I'm not a lawyer," he said, gibing at me, "it's no use asking me to cook up a nicer story."

"That isn't specially valuable, even in the law," I replied. Martin, who knew him better, was rougher with him.

"We're not asking you that. We're asking you to use what you're pleased to call your mind."

For the first time that evening Howard grinned.

I went on to say that anything he could tell us about Palairet might be a point in argument. Even people whose minds were not closed couldn't be swung over until they had some idea what had happened. None of us seemed to have a completely clear idea: I certainly hadn't myself.

"Why should you think I have?" asked Howard. "I didn't have anything to do with him apart from the work. He was always decent to me. I don't pay any attention to what other people say about a man. I take him as I find him, and by how he is to me."

"And you're satisfied with the result?" I could not resist saying, but he did not see the point. He described how Palairet had given him the photograph which he had used in his thesis—the photograph with the dilated pin-mark. According to Howard, Palairet had said that it would "help out" the experimental evidence. Howard had not wondered for an instant whether it was genuine or not. He had just taken it with gratitude. Even now, he could not imagine when Palairet had faked the photograph. He said, with a curiously flat obstinacy, that he was not certain it was a conscious fake at all.

"What else could it be?" said Martin sharply.

"Oh, just an old man being silly."

"No," said Martin.

I was thinking that Howard was one of the two or three worst witnesses I had listened to. So bad that it seemed he could not be so bad. Once or twice I found myself doubting my own judgment.

Howard said that he had seen another photograph of the same kind: he had repeated that often enough. But that photograph could not have been the one missing from the notebook. Whatever the photograph in the notebook had been, he had never seen it.

"You're positive about that?" I said.

"Of course I am."

"It's a pity," said Martin.

"Then it's got to be a pity," said Howard.

Martin said, "If that photograph was still in the notebook, there might have been a bit of resistance but there's no doubt we should have got you home in the end."

As Martin spoke, not with any special edge, saying something which we all knew, Howard's expression had undergone a change. His eyes had widened so that one could see rims of white round the pupils; the sullen, dead-pan, sniping obstinacy had all gone; instead his face seemed stretched open, tightly strained, so exposed that he had lost control over his eyes and voice. In a high, grating tone he said:

"Perhaps that's why it isn't there."

"What do you mean?" Martin asked him.

"Perhaps the people who wanted to get at me found it convenient to get rid of that photograph. Perhaps it isn't an accident that it isn't there."

I had heard someone, in a state of delusion, speak just like that. Martin and I glanced at each other. Martin nodded. We both knew what had to be said, and Martin began:

"You must never say anything like that again. That is, if you want to have a fighting chance. We can't do anything for you, we couldn't even take the responsibility of going on, if there's the slightest risk of your saying that again."

"I don't see why not."

"It's time you did," said Martin. I broke in:

"Don't you see that it's a very serious accusation? Don't you see that, if it once got round the college, you'd have to answer for it—"

"So would the people who were standing up for you," said Martin. "Either you cut it out, or we should have to wash our hands of the whole business."

Without speaking, without any sign of acquiescence, Howard had lost the wild open look. He had slumped back again, his eyes looking at his feet, his head on his chest.

"All right?" said Martin.

Howard raised his eyes and Martin was satisfied. The classroom clock showed five to six, and he said that it was time to go out for a drink. As he led us out of the room, Martin said: "All aboard," like a cricket captain calling his men out to field, or like an old leader of mine before we went into court. He could put on that kind of heartiness very easily. That evening, it worked better with Howard than anything I could have done. In the pub, he was less suspicious than I had seen him. It was a new and shining pub, as bright, as freshly-built as the school. Among the chromium plate and the pin-tables, Howard sank into a corner as though he were for the time being safe, and put down a pint of bitter. The second tankard was soon in front of him, and he was replying almost good-naturedly to Martin, who had abandoned his normal carefulness and was questioning him head on. Did he like teaching? Yes, said Howard surprisingly, he wouldn't have minded making his career at it. Why had he settled in a Cambridge school? Was it just to embarrass the college? Howard, who had previously shown no sense of humour, thought that was a good joke.

Martin, who had drunk a couple of pints himself, asked if he were deliberately following the good old college pattern. There had only been one other Fellow in living memory who had ever been dismissed. Did Howard know the story? Howard, prepared to think Martin a remarkably good comedian, said no. Martin said that he was disappointed. He had hoped Howard was following suit. The story was that during the Nineties, the college had elected someone from outside, actually from as far away as Oxford, as a Fellow. He had turned out to be an alcoholic of a somewhat dramatic kind, and his pupils, attending for supervision at five o'clock, had found him not yet out of bed and with empty bottles on the floor. So the college had sacked him. He had promptly married a publican's daughter and set up in a fish-and-chip shop two hundred yards from the college's side gate. I remembered hearing the story used, forty years later, by one of the old men as an argument against electing a Fellow from outside.

"Don't you admit the precedent is rather close?" Martin said to Howard. "You must have decided that by staying in Cambridge you could make more of a nuisance of yourself. Now didn't you?"

"Oh, well," said Howard, "if I'd cleared out it would have made things easier for them. I was damned if I could see why I should."

That reminded me of another question, which Nightingale had brought up at the Lodge.

"In that case," I said, "I wonder you didn't think of appealing to the Visitor, and then bringing an action for wrongful dismissal."

"I did think of it."

"Why didn't you bring it, then?"

"Should I have won it?"

"I don't think so. But it wouldn't have made things easier for them, would it?"

He hedged. He did not want to answer straight. I was nothing like so good with him as Martin was. He prevaricated, became embarrassed, and wrapped up in his own thoughts. He said that he had preferred other methods. I did not begin to understand why he was suddenly so shy. I asked again:

"I should have thought, when nothing happened, you might have brought an action?"

"I wasn't keen on washing that kind of dirty linen in public."

That was all I could get out of him. After we had all three taken a bus into the town, he left us in the Market Place. He offered to drop my bag in the college, where I was sleeping, since I wanted to go off with Martin to have supper at his house.

"Do you mind?" I said.

"Do I mind putting my head in the porter's lodge," said Howard, prickly but not at his most offensive, "is that what you mean? The answer is, I don't."

As Martin and I were walking towards the Backs, Martin said:

"Not as useful as it might have been, was it?" He meant the last few hours.

"Have you ever got anything more out of him?"

"Nothing to speak of." Martin went on: "I suppose we might have got someone more difficult to work for, but offhand I can't think of one."

Then he asked, how was I going to handle Francis Getliffe next day? He thought I ought to come right out in the open, and say that we should probably never be able to prove our case "down to the last drawing-pin." Without the second photograph we could not do it. With a man like Francis, it would be a mistake to minimise the difficulties or try to cover up where we were weak.

As we planned, each of us felt kinship and a curious kind of support. It was comforting—it was more than comforting, it was an active pleasure—to be at one, to be using our wits on the same side.

THIRTEEN

TURNS ACROSS THE LAWN

The next morning after breakfast, I was looking out of the guest room window into the Fellows' Garden when Francis Getliffe arrived. The trees were bare, the branches were not stirring. It seemed to be a windless day with the cloud-cap very low. Francis said that it was warm outside, we might as well walk in the garden, I should not need a coat.

The turf was soft with rain, still springy under our feet, brilliant as moss. In the flower-bed to our right I could not see a single flower, not even the last of the snowdrops. We were walking slowly, but Francis nevertheless moved with lunging strides, a foot longer than mine, although he was two or three inches the shorter man.

We had not gone far, we had not gone out of the formal garden into the "wilderness," when Francis said:

"I think I know what you've come for."

"Do you?"

"It doesn't really need an inspired guess, does it?" Then he said, stiffly and proudly, "I'm going to save you a certain amount of trouble. I'd better say straight away that I regard myself as very much to blame. I'm sorry that I've delayed so long. There's no doubt about it, Martin and Skeffington have produced a case that no one has got a serious answer to yet. I'm sorry that I didn't tell them so, when they first came to see me. The sooner this business is cleared up, the better."

I felt a sense of anti-climax, a sense of absurd let-down, as though I had put my shoulder against a door which was on the latch. I also felt embarrassed, because Francis was so ashamed of himself, stiff with me because he was ashamed.

"What are you going to do?" I asked.

"It's done."

"What have you done?"

"I've just sent this out. It went off before I came to see you."

"This" was a mimeographed note with *"Confidential: to All Fellows"* in the top left-hand corner. It read: "I have now studied the new evidence relating to the thesis and publications of D.J. Howard and the notebooks of the late C.J.B. Palairet, F.R.S. In my view, Dr. Skeffington is right in representing that there is a case to answer. I think it is urgent that the college should request the Court of Seniors to consider this case without delay. F.E.G. 19.2.54."

This note, as I knew, would be taken round by the college messenger. It would reach most of the Fellows by the lunchtime delivery, and all of them that day.

"I should have thought," I said, "that ought to collect the majority for re-opening the case, anyway."

"I should hope so," Francis said.

"I notice you don't say that you're a hundred per cent convinced yourself?"

"That was as far as I felt inclined to go."

In silence we walked through to the inner lawn, right at the bottom of the garden, close to the college wall. In the greenhouse in the corner great carnations shone into the aqueous morning, into the green and grey. Francis suddenly broke out, his voice tight with anger:

"This man Howard must be as stupid as they come."

I asked what had gone wrong now. Francis paid no attention and went on:

"I want you to realise one thing. It's his fault we've got into this absurd position. I mean, by that, if he had had the scientific judgment of a newt, he'd never have taken the old man's experiments on trust. It's almost unbelievable that anyone working in that field allowed it without having another look. If Howard's innocent, which I'm inclined to think he is, then he must break all records for stupidity. I must say, there are times when stupidity seems to me the greater crime."

We did another turn across the lawn. Francis broke out again:

"Of course, we never ought to have elected him in the first place."

I told him, because I wanted to make him easier, that that reminded me of his father-in-law on an occasion we both knew, looking for a first cause. Francis gave a reluctant grin, but his voice did not soften.

"Now we've got to clear up this mess," he said. "All I hope is that it doesn't take too long."

"Why is the time it takes worrying you so much?"

I asked him straight out, not knowing whether he wanted to reply. We had been friendly for nearly thirty years, and I had not seen him at such a disadvantage before. I was bewildered to know why. True, he didn't like being wrong, even less than most of us. Like most men of his granite-like integrity, he had a streak of vanity inextricably fused within it. He did not like falling below the standard he set himself, either in his own eyes or anyone else's. He did not like my having to make this visit, to remind him of his duty. It was the first time it had happened, though several times in our friendship he had reminded me of mine. None of that seemed to explain a malaise as strong as his, as we walked backwards and forwards across the lawn. We had walked like that before. The inner lawn was not overlooked by any window, and as young men we used to go there at night and talk out our plans or troubles undisturbed.

After a time, he said in a voice no longer angry but quiet and surprised:

"You're quite right. I didn't want any friction in this place just now."

I did not say anything. On the next turn he went on: "I'm afraid it's only too simple. When those two came to see me, I wasn't as completely impressed by their case as they were. That was genuine, and to a limited extent it still is. But if I'd been reasonably responsible, I should have got down to what they had to say. The fact was, Lewis, I didn't want to."

He was speaking with the candour, the freshness, that sometimes comes to men not given to introspection when they talk about themselves.

"No, I didn't want to. I didn't want the risk of making myself unpleasant to everyone who counts for anything here. I just didn't want to blot my copybook. I needn't tell you why, need I?"

I did not say anything.

"You know, Winslow and Nightingale and those others, they're my backers. The election's coming on this autumn, and the fact of the matter is"—he hesitated—"I should like it."

As we turned, he went on:

"The curious thing is, I can't really tell why I should like it so much. I should make a pretty fair job of it, as good as anyone else they're likely to put in the Lodge, by and large. But that doesn't come into it. It's not really the sort of thing that matters to me, I should have said. All I seriously wanted was to do some adequate research and leave some sort of record behind me. Well, I haven't done as much as I should have liked, but I've done something. I believe I've got ten more years work in me, and I shall do some more. The work's come off pretty well, all things considered. Looking back to the time we both started, I should have been moderately content with what I've been able to do. That's all that ought to matter. As for the rest, I've had more than my share of the honours going round. I didn't think I was specially greedy: and so why should I want the Mastership into the bargain? But I do, you know. Enough to make me put up a disgraceful exhibition about this wretched case."

As we went on walking, in a silence more relaxed than before, I was thinking, I could have given him one reason why he wanted it. Francis, who had gone through so many struggles, in college, in government, even in public, was not a rebel by nature. His politics had come through duty and intellect, not through a passion of nonconformity, not even through that residue of identification with those outside, pushing their noses against the shop-window, that I, on the surface a more compromising man than Francis, and one who had lived closer to the Establishment, still preserved. In the long run Francis, who out of principle would stick out as one dissenting voice in the council of the Royal or any group of respectable bosses, wished to end his days with them. His intellect, his duty, would not let him alter his opinions, but in a curious sense he wanted to be "respectable," and to be received by the respectable. He would be soothed, a final uneasiness assuaged, if the men he had argued with so long, the Winslows and Nightingales and Arthur Browns, made him Master. He still would not qualify anything he said: but he would have come home.

Suddenly I was reminded of another person who, comically different in temperament, also wished for what Francis did. It was Irene, who in her youth had been a reckless manchaser and who now wanted nothing better than for her and her husband to end up staidly in the Lodge. The resemblance pleased me, but, as I walked with Francis in the quiet damp garden—his face lighter but surprised because he had made a confession, the first I had heard from him, his voice comradely and quite free from resentment, as though glad to have me there—I did not tell him so.

FOURTEEN

TWO VIEWS OF RETIREMENT

After Francis, there was no one else I had arranged to see that Friday until I dined in Hall. So in the afternoon, with nothing to do, I went on a round of bookshops. It was in the third of these, not Heffer's, not Bowes and Bowes, that, as I was glancing at the latest little magazine, I heard a voice I used to know well.

"I'm sure you're right. I'm sure you've laid your finger on it."

The voice was plummy, thick and muffled, but it spoke warmly, with teasing affection. I was standing by the rack of periodicals near the door: as I looked up I saw in the inner room, just visible behind the main display shelf, Paul Jago talking to his wife.

As I looked up, so did he. I was certain that he had seen me. But he darted his eyes back to his wife, talked to her rapidly and intimately as though pretending that they were quite alone, as though hoping that I should not notice or disturb them.

Should I slip out, I thought? It would be easy to get into the street, so that he would not be embarrassed. Then I revolted. I had known him well once, and had been fond of him. He had been Senior Tutor during my time at the college and had just missed the Mastership, when Crawford was elected. That had been a traumatic blow to him. He had gone on with his routine duties, but he had given up dining and—so I had heard—no one, not even his closest friends, had seen much of him.

I went into the inner room and said:

"Well. It's a long time since we met."

Not for ten years, not since Roy Calvert's memorial service. Jago's appearance had altered since then, but in a way I could not define. He had always looked older than his age, and now his age was catching up with him; he was bald, the fringe of hair had gone quite white, but he was sixty-eight and looked no more. His cheeks and neck were fleshy, but the moods seemed close beneath the skin, so that his expressions were liquid, and even now one could not say that it was a sad face. Behind thick lenses his eyes were still brilliant.

"Why, it's you!" he cried. Even though he was prevaricating, even though he wanted to evade me, he could not help the warmth flowing out.

Then I thought I saw what had changed. He had become much fatter, but fatter in a way that did not suggest self-indulgence. As a younger man he had had a paunch, but moved lightly; now he showed that special kind of discouraged heaviness which sometimes seems linked with a life of dissatisfaction or strain.

"Darling," he turned to his wife with an elaborate mixture of protectiveness, courtesy and love, "I think you remember —" Formally he introduced me. "I think you know him, don't you?"

Of course she knew me. I must have been inside her house twenty or thirty times. But she dropped her eyes, gave me a limp hand and what appeared to be her idea of a *grande dame* being gracious to someone who might, in the multitude of her acquaintances, conceivably be one.

"Do you spend much time in Cambridge—?" and she addressed me in full style as though it were a condescension on her part.

"I think he's kept pretty busy in Whitehall," said Jago. She knew it perfectly well.

"I wish we could offer you better weather," said Alice

Jago. "Cambridge can look very attractive at this time of year."

Now she was speaking as if I did not know the town. She too had grown fatter, but she was stronger-boned and muscled than her husband and could carry it better. She was a big woman with a plain, white, anxious face. She had a sensibility so tight-drawn that she could detect a snub if one said good-morning in the wrong tone; but it was the kind of sensibility which took it for granted that though her own psychological skin was so thin, everyone else walked about in armour. She was so insecure that the world seemed full of enemies. In fact, she had made many. She had done her husband much harm all through his career. But for her, he might have got the Mastership. They both knew it.

His manner to her, which had always been tender, had become more so. When he spoke, he was trying to make her happy, and even while he listened to her he seemed to be taking care of her.

"How are you?" I asked him.

"I've quite retired now, I'm thankful to say."

"He has to spend all his time with me," said Mrs. Jago.

"We're reading all the books that we've always wanted to read," said Jago. "I've been looking forward to this for a long time."

I asked: "Do you see any of our old friends?"

"Oh, I run into them now and then," said Jago. He said it as though he wished to drop the subject.

"Don't you think they miss him?" I let slip the remark to Alice Jago.

"If you think I try to prevent my husband going to the college, then you're very much mistaken."

"No," said Jago, "I was glad when I'd shaken hands with my last pupil. The chains had been chafing for a long time, can you understand that? When I used to go into my study in the morning, for my first tutorial hour, I used to think, I shall only have to do this another thousand times. Then another hundred. Then another ten."

I had seen many people get through years of routine, and come to their last day. Nearly all of them were sad. I asked, didn't he feel just a tinge of regret at the end?

"Not for a single instant," said Jago with a flash of pride. "No, I felt that for a good many years I had been wasting too much of my life. Now I was ceasing to. And I was also ceasing to be reminded of some associations that I should willingly forget."

He looked at me. He was a man of quick human sympathy and recognised it in others. He knew that I had followed him.

"Mind you," he went on, "I'd taken care not to be reminded of them more than I could help. It was one thing to go on with my pupils and do my best for them. It was quite another to inflict myself on some of our colleagues. I haven't seen some of them for years, apart from college meetings, which I couldn't cut until I gave up office—"

"And now you needn't go to any more of them," cried Alice Jago triumphantly.

"I think I can bear that deprivation, don't you?" he said to me.

"I suppose, while you were still attending, you heard of this Howard business, didn't you?"

I hesitated about trying it. Mrs. Jago looked blank and resentful, as though the name meant nothing and I was shutting her out.

"I couldn't very well help hearing, could I? I might have had to waste some time over it, because I was third Senior and was due to serve on the Court. But I thought that that was another deprivation I could bear, and so I begged leave to be excused."

"I should think you did," she said.

He seemed quite uninterested in the case. I wanted to find

out if Francis Getliffe's circular had reached him: but apparently he did not open his college documents until days after they arrived.

He asked after my doings. He still couldn't keep back his interest and looked friendly when I spoke about my wife and son. But he brought out no kind of invitation. He did not suggest that I should see him again.

"Well," he said, a little over-busily, "we mustn't take up your time. We must be going ourselves."

"I hope," said Alice Jago graciously, "that you enjoy the rest of your visit." She added, "And good luck in your career," as though I were one of her husband's pupils and she was safely projecting me into the future.

Getting back to my rooms after tea, I found a letter on the table. It was addressed in an old man's hand that I had either forgotten or did not know. When I opened it and looked at the signature, I saw to my astonishment that it was M.H.L. Gay. The handwriting was bold in outline, only a little shaky, and the letter read:

"My dear Eliot,

I learn upon good authority that you are residing temporarily in the college. I must ask you most urgently to visit me to-night after my evening meal, which I take at six-thirty upon medical advice, and before eight, which is the time when I nowadays have to suspend my labours for the day. Pray regard this visit as having first priority. *The question we have to discuss will brook no delay. You are essential to me because of your legal studies.*

I shall await you at seven-fifteen or thereabouts.

Yours ever sincerely,

M.H.L. GAY."

I was irritated even more than astonished. Perhaps it wasn't so odd that he should, out of the blue, remember who I was: even when he was less senile, his memory had come and gone. Why should he want me? I was irritated, because

I had planned to see Arthur Brown in Hall and on the side pick up such gossip as was going. I didn't fancy missing my dinner for the sake of conversation with someone who might not recognise me. Still, there seemed nothing for it. One could not refuse the very old. I had to telephone Brown, saying that instead of that night in Hall it would have to be Sunday. I explained why, and Brown, who had guessed the reason for my visit and was at his most impenetrable, nevertheless gave a fat man's chuckle over the wire. "You'll find him pretty exigent, old chap. He'll never let you get away at eight o'clock. If I were you, I should make sure that there are some sandwiches waiting for you in your rooms when you get back."

The joke seemed even more against me as I walked up the Madingley Road. I had made a mistake in walking at all, because it had begun to rain, a steady seeping rain; the road was dark, Gay's house was close to the Observatory, and the lights of the Observatory seemed a long way off. The rain was percolating inside the collar of my mackintosh: I could feel the damp against my neck, and wet sleeves against my wrists.

In the hall of Gay's house, the pretty young housekeeper gazed at my clothes. In a foreign accent she asked if I wanted a towel.

From an open door, Gay's voice resounded:

"No, indeed, he doesn't want a towel! He wants to get down to business! You be sure he does."

Her brow puzzled, she led me through the door into his study, where Gay, a scarf round his neck was sitting in an armchair by an enormous fire. Fitting on the armchair was an invalid's tray, and he still had spoon in hand, working away at his meal.

"That's the man," said Gay. He seemed to know my face. "You're not wet, are you? You're not wet, I'll be bound." He felt the shoulder and arm of my jacket. "Ah, that's nothing," said Gay, "that's not what I call wet. You don't understand about our English climate yet, my dear," he said to his housekeeper. "A fine climate ours is, it's a climate and a half. It makes us the men we are, I've not a shadow of a doubt about that." He gazed at me with faded eyes. "Pray sit down, Eliot. Pray sit down and enjoy yourself."

I was too much occupied with discomfort, crude physical discomfort, to be amused. As for his housekeeper, pretty as she was, she did not seem to be amused in any circumstances. She kept her puzzled frown.

"Please to offer our guest some cocoa," Gay said to her.

No, I put in rapidly, I didn't drink cocoa.

"Now that's an error on your part, my dear boy. A splendid drink, cocoa is. Why, I sometimes drink a dozen cups a day. Indeed I do."

Did he mind if I smoked? I asked.

"Ah, now *that's* not good for you. It's not good for me either. I have to be careful with my bronchials at this time of year. I don't want bronchial trouble at my time of life. It could turn to pneumonia, the doctors say. Old man's friend, they used to call pneumonia, when I was born. Old man's friend—no, I don't like the sound of that. I'm not prepared to give up all that easily, I assure you I'm not."

I sat in my armchair, not smoking, steam rising from my trouser-legs, while Gay finished his supper. He finished it in an unusual fashion. On one plate he had what appeared to be some sort of trifle, on another a piece of Cheshire cheese and two slices of bread. Methodically Gay cut the cheese into thin sections and put them in the trifle. Then he took a slice of bread and crumbled it over the mixture, which he stirred vigorously with his spoon and then swallowed in six hearty mouthfuls.

"It all goes the same way home," he explained himself to me.

I had known some old men, but not anyone as old as this.

Sitting there, watching him, I thought he was pretty far gone. Then all of a sudden he seemed at least as lucid as he would have been at eighty. He had rung a handbell to fetch his housekeeper back. She removed the tray and went out again, followed by cries of: "Splendid! That was a splendid supper you gave me!"

I was studying the drawings on the walls, drawings of the Saga heroes that he had made himself, some of which I remembered from my visits before the war, when he said:

"Ah, I thought to-day—it's very fortunate we have Eliot here. Eliot is a lawyer by training, he's the man to go to for legal guidance. Indeed he is."

"How did you know I was here at all?"

"Ah ha! I have my spies. I have my spies." (How in the world, I wondered, did the old man pick up jargon of the Forties and Fifties, like that phrase, or "first priority"?)

He stroked his beard with self-satisfaction and asked:

"Do you know, Eliot, why I thought of you to-day? He's the man, I thought. No, you can't be expected to see the connection. Why, I've just received a remarkable communication from one of our Fellows. If you go to that desk, my dear chap, you'll find this communication under the paper-weight. Certainly you will. I don't mislay important communications, whatever certain people think."

The "communication" was Francis Getliffe's note. I handed it to Gay who, from the interstices of his chair, brought out a reading glass.

"There it is. *To all Fellows.* No, I don't like that. I think a special copy should have been sent to me, what? Initialled at the bottom by 'F.E.G.' I have looked up our college list, and I find that must be young Getliffe. *To all Fellows.* These young men aren't careful enough. Indeed. But still, this isn't a time to think of our *amour propre.* These are important issues, Eliot, important issues."

"Do you mean," I said, "that you're concerned about what Getliffe says?"

With cunning, with a certain grandeur, Gay replied:

"I'm concerned in a very special way about what Getliffe says."

"You mean, you're interested in forming a majority—?"

"Oh, no, my dear chap. I've seen too many fly-sheets in my time. What do you think of that? I must leave these *minutiae* to the younger men. They must make up their own majorities. I trust them to get on with their own little squabbles, and I expect they'll do very well. Fine young men we've got. Getliffe's a fine young man. Brown's a fine young man. Oh no, I'm not the one to take part in little differences within the college. They all come right in a few years. But no, my dear chap, *that isn't the point at all.*"

"What is the point?"

"I want to draw your attention to a very remarkable feature in this communication."

"What is it?"

"Come and look here. Over my shoulder. You see those words—'The Court of Seniors?' You're sure you see them?"

I said yes.

After I had gone on saying yes, he let me go back to my chair.

"Well, now. What do those words suggest to you?"

I was at a loss, and shook my head.

"Come now. This isn't being on the spot. This isn't what I expect from a lawyer. Tell me, who is the Senior Fellow of this college?"

"You are, of course."

"Indeed I am. Now that *is* the point, my dear chap. Does it surprise you to hear that when the Court of Seniors was meeting—over this little trouble of Getliffe's, I presume, but that's neither here nor there—when that Court was meeting I was not invited to take my rightful place?"

Gay threw back his noble head.

"I'd never thought—" I began.

"But you should have thought. Does it surprise you that I was not only not invited to take my rightful place, but absolutely discouraged? I had letters from the Master implying that it might be too much for me, if you please. Letters full of flattering sentiments, but fine words butter no parsnips, my dear chap. They even implied that I could not make the journey into college. Stuff and nonsense! Why, the Court could meet in the summer, couldn't it? Or if they were in a special hurry, what was to prevent them meeting here? If Mahomet can't go to the mountain! Yes, indeed. No, they are treating me as though I were not *compos mentis*. That's the long and short of it. And I think it's time they were taught a lesson."

I tried to soothe him, but Gay, his scarf slipping from his shoulder, had taken a second wind.

"This is where you come in, Eliot," he said in triumph. "Tell me, am I or am I not entitled to sit on the Court of Seniors, unless I withdraw of my own free will?"

I said that I must re-read the Statutes.

"Tell me, have they or have they not deprived me of my place without my consent?"

"So it seems."

"Tell me, will or will not the fact that I have been deprived of my place be known to all the Fellows of the college?"

"Certainly to some of them."

"Tell me, will or will not that fact be taken to mean that in the opinion of the Master and his advisers I am no longer *compos mentis?*"

"Not necessarily—"

"That's what it will be taken to mean. I have been libelled, Eliot. That is why I am contemplating seeking legal redress from the college."

I had been expecting various things, but not this. Trying

to humour him, I said that it could not, in technical terms, be a libel. Gay was not to be humoured.

"I believe there must still be justice in England. You remember Frederick the Great—there are still judges in Berlin. A fine city, they gave me an honorary degree in that city. I am positive that damaging a man's reputation cannot be done with impunity. And that ought to be true of people who have achieved some little distinction, quite as much as of anyone else. Indeed it ought. Not letting a man take a place which is his of right—that is a comment on his fitness, my dear chap, and I am absolutely convinced people cannot make such comments with impunity."

He was becoming more obstinate. Incredulously, I began to think that he might not forget this. How far, I was calculating, with a faint suppressed *Schadenfreude* at Arthur Brown's expense, could he go before he was stopped?

"If I proceed against them," said Gay, "that will be an action and a half."

I said his situation was more complicated.

"You're too genteel, you young men."

Gay was chuckling with gusto and malice. Oddly enough, it did not sound like senile malice. I was astonished at how much vigour he had summoned up. The prospect of litigation had made him younger by twenty years. "You're too genteel. I'm absolutely positive that this action of mine would lie. Indeed it would. That would teach them a lesson. I don't believe in being too genteel, my dear chap. That's why I've attained a certain position in the world. It's a great mistake, when one has attained a certain position in the world, to be too genteel about teaching people a lesson."

FIFTEEN

'NEVER BE TOO PROUD TO BE PRESENT'

The following afternoon, Saturday, Martin rang me up in college. Some progress, he said. No special thanks to us: after Francis's circular, we couldn't avoid it. Anyway, two people had come over—Taylor (the Calvert Fellow) and another man I did not know. On paper the score was now ten to nine against. That is, nine men were pledged to sign the request for re-opening the case. "I think we're pretty well bound to pick up another. Then the real fun begins," came Martin's voice with a politician's mixture of optimism and warning.

For reasons of tactics—"just to show we mean business"—Martin was anxious to get the majority decided soon. Would I have a go at Tom Orbell? Would I also dine in Hall and see if there was anyone I could talk to? It would be better if he and I were acting separately. We could meet later that night at his house.

I obeyed, but I drew blank. In the mizzling afternoon, so dark that the lights were on all over the college, I walked through to the third court. For an instant I looked up at Tom Orbell's windows: I could have sworn that they were lighted too. But when I climbed the stairs his outer door was sported. I rattled the lock and called out that I was there. No response. I had a strong suspicion that Tom had seen me coming.

Frustrated, irritated, I gazed at the name above the door, "Dr. T. Orbell." The letters gleamed fresh on the unlit landing. I remembered faded letters there, and the name of Despard-Smith, who had been a Fellow for fifty years. He had been a sanctimonious old clergyman. At that moment I felt a mixture of rancour and disgust; it seemed that the rancour, long suppressed, was directed at that old man, dead years before, not at Tom Orbell who kept me waiting there.

However, I met Tom before the end of the afternoon. I had been invited to tea by Mrs. Skeffington, to what, I discovered when I arrived, was something very much like an old-fashioned Cambridge tea-party. That was not the only odd thing about it. To begin with, the Skeffingtons were living in one of a row of two-storied houses just outside the college walls, which used to be let to college servants. Why they were doing it, I could not imagine. They were both well-off: was this Skeffington's notion of how a research Fellow ought to comport himself? If so, they were not making all that good a shot at it: for in the tiny parlour they had brought in furniture which looked like family heirlooms, and which some of the guests were cooing over. Sheraton? someone was asking, and Mrs. Skeffington was modestly admitting: "Oh, one must have something to sit on."

Round the wall there were pictures that did not look at all like heirlooms, and I recalled that I heard Skeffington had taste in visual things. There was a Sickert, a recent Passmore, a Kokoschka, a Nolan.

So, in the parlour, smaller than those I remembered in the back streets of my childhood, we sat on Sheraton chairs and drank China tea and ate wafers of brown bread-and-butter. Another odd thing was Mrs. Skeffington's choice of guests. I had imagined that Skeffington wanted to talk over the case with me and that everyone there would be on his side. Far from it—there was Tom Orbell, hot, and paying liquid compliments, and also, though without their husbands, Mrs. Nightingale and Mrs. Ince. To balance them, Irene was there without Martin. Did Mrs. Skeffington think it was her duty to pull the college together? Quite possibly, I thought. Not through policy. Certainly not through doubts of her husband's case: she was as firm as he was. But quite possibly through sheer flat-footed duty, as though to the tenantry.

The case was not referred to. What was referred to, was a string of names, as though everyone were playing a specifically English kind of Happy Families. Someone mentioned an acquaintance in the Brigade: Mrs. Skeffington trumped that by having known the last Colonel. County names, titled names, token names, they all chanted them as though the charmed circle were tiny and as though one kept within it by chanting in unison. And yet those who were chanting the loudest needn't have done so. There was nothing bogus about the Skeffington's social roots: Tom was the son of an Archdeacon, Irene the daughter of a soldier. I discovered that Mrs. Ince, whom I rather liked, had been to a smart school. That I shouldn't have guessed. She wore spectacles, like her husband she had adopted a mid-Atlantic accent, she was cheerful, ugly, frog-faced, and looked as if she enjoyed a good time in bed.

The only person not chanting was Mrs. Nightingale. With unfailing accuracy Mrs. Skeffington asked if she knew—.

"Oh, no," said Mrs. Nightingale, impassive, exophthalmic.

Had she known—or—?

"Of course not," said Mrs. Nightingale with complete good-temper. "We were living in Clapham Junction at the time."

"Were you, now?" Mrs. Skeffington could not help speaking as though a junction were a place that one passed through. She brightened. "Then you may have known the —s when they had one of those nice Georgian places over in the Old Town?"

"Oh, no, my father could never have lived there. That was before the big money started to come in."

Tom guffawed. Soon afterwards he slipped out. When he found that I had followed him and caught him up on the cobbles outside, he said, in a defiant tone:

"Hullo, Lewis, I didn't know you were coming."

I had just been quick enough to prevent him letting himself into the college by a side gate, to which I did not have a key. Instead we walked round by the wall. Under a lamp, I caught sight of his eyes, blue, flat and mutinous. I said: "What were you doing this afternoon?"

"What do you mean, what was I doing?"

"I came up to your rooms. I wanted to talk to you."

"Oh, I was working very hard. I did some really good work. I was extremely pleased with it for once."

"I'm glad of that—"

"Hanna's always bullying me to produce more, you know she is. But you know, Lewis, I'm really producing quite as much as anyone of my age—"

He was steering the conversation into a comparison of the academic output of young historians. I interrupted:

"You know what I wanted to talk about, don't you?"

"Don't you think I've had enough of that?"

"Who from?"

"Hanna, of course. She says that I'm behaving like a beast."

I had not realised till then that she was taking such an open part. That remark was right in her style. I wondered, did she think he was weaker than he really was? He seemed—it might have crystallised by now—in love with her. It would be like Hanna to assume that he was easy to persuade. But in fact, though he was so labile, he was also intensely obstinate. When one dug deeper into him, he became both less amiable and less weak.

"I don't think you're behaving up to your usual standard."

"I'm sorry to hear that."

"I've always thought you tried to be detached, when it came to a personal issue," I said.

"I'm sorry we don't agree on this. I mean that very sincerely." He was speaking with hostility.

"Look here, won't you talk this over on the plane of reason? Preferably with Martin—?"

"I haven't the slightest desire to talk to Martin. I shall only hear what you've just said and what Hanna says, ten times worse."

We had come round to the front of the college. Tom caught sight of a bus slowing down before the stop. "As a matter of fact," he said, moving towards it, "I've got to go off to see a pupil. He's not well and I said I'd supervise him in his rooms. Perhaps I shall see you in Hall. Is that all right?"

I did not expect to see Tom return from his putative visit, and I did not expect to see him in Hall. In fact, there were only six names on the list when I arrived in the Combination Room, and one was that of an old member of the college up for the week-end. Of the four Fellows dining, three were young men whom Martin had already made sure of. The other was old Winslow. He had a bout of sciatica and was in a temper that made ordinary civil conversation hard enough. The six of us sat chastened at the end of the High Table; Winslow was scarcely speaking, the young men were over-awed. As for the old member making a pious return to the college, it seemed to be a sad Saturday night.

Down in the body of the hall the undergraduates were making a hubbub. Winslow roused himself.

"To what do we owe this curious display?" he asked.

Someone thought the college Fifteen had won a cup tie.

"I've never been able to see why we should encourage dolts. They would be far happier at some decent manual work." Winslow regarded the old member. "I apologise if you've ever been concerned with this pastime. Have you?"

The old member had to say yes. Winslow made no further comment.

Back in the Combination Room after dinner, Winslow announced that his complaint made wine seem like poison. "Poison," he said. "But don't let that deter the rest of you."

It did. Lugubriously we sat, Winslow's chin sunk down as though he were studying the reflection of his coffee-cup in the rosewood, two of the young Fellows talking in low voices.

Leaving the room in that devastated hush, I reached Martin's house so early that he thought I must have news. I said that I had never spent such a useless day. As I described it, Martin grinned with brotherly malice.

"Well," he said, "I've got one last treat for you. We're going next door to see G.S."

I cursed, and asked to be let off.

"He says we can have some music."

"That doesn't add to the attractions."

Martin smiled. He knew that I was tone-deaf.

"No," he said, "we must go."

He was too realistic to think there was a chance of winning Clark over. But he was acting on rule-of-thumb experience. In this kind of struggle—neither of us needed to tell the other—the first maxim was: forget you're proud, forget you're tired. *Never be too proud to be present.*

Between their half of the house and the Clarks', they had kept a communicating door and Irene unlocked it and came with us. As soon as we crossed into the Clarks', it was like going from Italy into Switzerland. The Clarks' passage, even, was immaculate and bright: the drawing-room shone and glistened, with the spotlessness of a house without children. Clark struggled to his feet to greet us, but there was pain tucking up his mouth as he stood in his brace, and soon Hanna helped him back into his chair.

Coffee and Austrian cakes were waiting for us. When we all three refused drinks, it was a relief to them both. Clark was a hospitable man, he liked displaying the bottles on the sideboard, but he had never forsaken his Band of Hope piety. While as for Hanna, she could not, after twenty years in England, eradicate her belief in both Anglo-Saxon phlegm and Anglo-Saxon alcoholism.

"Delicious," said Irene, munching a cake, glancing at Hanna. She sounded mischievous: was she deliberately mimicking Tom Orbell?

"Before we start to enjoy ourselves," said Clark gently, "I think we'd better put one thing behind us, hadn't we?"

He was looking at Martin, then at me, with his beautiful afflicted eyes.

"If you like," said Martin.

"Well, I've thought over this *démarche* of Getliffe's. I don't think I ought to make any bones about it to you two. I'm very much afraid that my answer has to be no."

"I'm sorry about that," Martin replied, but easily and without indignation.

"I think I can understand the position you're all in. I mean, you two and Getliffe. I exclude Skeffington, because I don't pretend to know how his mind works. And I'm not convinced that he's a man of any judgment. But you others were in a genuinely difficult position, I can see that. You had to balance the possibility that there's been a certain amount of individual injustice—you've had to balance that against the certainty that if you raise the point, you're going to do a much larger amount of damage to us all. I can see that you were in a difficult position. Granted all your preconceptions and back histories, I can understand what you chose to do. But, with great respect, I'd like to suggest that it was the wrong choice."

"We're tied up with the word 'possibility'," Martin said.

"You're not prepared to say 'certainty'," said Clark.

"Can't I explain to you the nature of scientific evidence?" said Martin. But he was more respectful to Clark than to most men. There was no doubt that, in some fashion, Clark had the moral advantage over him.

"I must say," I put in, "your view seems to me almost unbelievably perverse."

"We've got different values, haven't we?" he said, with sweetness and composure.

"I told him that I disagreed," Hanna said to me.

"Of course you disagree, my dear. Of course these two do. As I say, with your preconceptions and back histories, it would be astonishing if you did anything else."

"What do you mean?"

"I mean, that you and the Eliot brothers and Getliffe have

been what you'd call liberals all your lives. I haven't, and I don't pretend to be. That's why I can understand some of your attitudes, which you all think are detached and based on the personal conscience, but which really aren't quite as detached as you'd all like to think. In the long run, anyone who has been as tinged with liberal faiths as you have is bound to think that by and large the left is right, and the right is wrong. You're bound to think that. It's the whole cast of your minds. And it shows itself in quite small issues like this present one, which *sub specie aeternitatis* isn't quite as earth-shaking as we're making out. *Of course* you want to think that this man has been a victim. *Of course* all your prejudices, your life-histories, your *Weltanschauung* are thrown in on his side. You must forgive some of us if we're not so easily convinced."

"Do you really think a scientist of international reputation, like Francis Getliffe, is quite as capable of deceiving himself on a point like this?" I said.

"I've got to be persuaded that he isn't."

"You would seriously take Nightingale's opinion rather than Getliffe's—that's what it amounts to, doesn't it, G.S.?"

Martin was talking to him better-temperedly than I could. It struck me that there was a protective tone in Martin's voice. I wondered—it was the kind of thing near the physical level, that one did not easily recognise in a brother—whether if, like many robust men, he wanted to turn his eyes from a cripple and so had to go out of his way to compensate.

"Yes, I think that's fair. It amounts to that."

"Forgetting Skeffington," said Hanna. "Whom even you could not regard as a man of advanced opinions, I should think."

"Forgetting Skeffington." He brushed her aside more contentedly than anyone I had seen. "You see, I can respect Getliffe's opinions and the Eliots', even when I disagree with them. But I'm not going to give equivalent weight to playboys."

"That's special pleading," I said.

"Take it as you like," said Clark. "In my view, and you're naturally at liberty to think it's wrong, the question is very much as Martin put it. If I've got to take a side, I've got to decide between Nightingale's opinion and Getliffe's. Now I'd be the last person to say that Getliffe wasn't by far the more distinguished scientist. People competent to judge have decided that for me, and of course there's no room for reasonable doubt. But, with respect, it seems to me that their scientific merits aren't under discussion. So far as I'm concerned, there is room for reasonable doubt about whose guidance I accept on a piece of scientific chicanery."

"How well do you know Nightingale?" I was provoked enough to say it. As soon as I did, I knew it was a false step.

"I know them both well enough to form my own judgment. And that's something one must do for oneself, isn't it?" He looked around with his fresh smile, the smile edged with physical strain. "Well, we shan't convince each other, shall we? I think this is the time to agree to differ, don't you?"

After Clark had said that he was going to play us some Berlioz, I was left out of the party. All of the others were musical, Clark passionately so: while as soon as he had put on the record, I drifted into the kind of wool-gathering that music induced in me. On the bright wall opposite I caught sight of a couple of Piranesi prints. They set me speculating on what sort of inner life Clark had, Berlioz and Piranesi, the march to the scaffold, the prisons deep under the earth.

Why in the world had Hanna married him? Throwing over a husband, a healthy man with, I recalled, a sly eye for women, to do so. There Hanna sat, curled up on the sofa, in her mid-forties, her body lean, tense, still young, her face still young apart from the grey in her hair which, before she married Clark, when she was one of the most elegant of women, she would never have left there. Why had she married him? She was not happy here. It did not need her ambiguous relation to Tom Orbell to say she was unhappy. She had not taken Clark into her confidence, even at the start, so far as I could see. There had been a time when she was far more politically committed than he thought. When he spoke of her as in the same political grade as Francis Getliffe, he did not know what Martin and I knew.

Did he know that once she had been fond of Martin?

Yes, Martin had been fond of her in return. A good many men were roused by her sharp, shrewish charm and wanted to tame her. But though she liked such men, they were not the ones she disrupted her life for. Instead she seemed to be searching for someone to look after. It must have been that, it could only have been that, which led her to break one marriage and take on Clark.

As the music went on, I felt both indulgent to her and impatient. For, of course, the irony was that she could scarcely have picked worse. She was so brave, much more than most of us, she was intelligent, she had her farouche attractions. But she had no insight. She was a good judge of men's intellects, but compared with a hundred stupid women she despised, she had no idea what men were like. It did not take a clairvoyant to see that, though Clark might be crippled, he had a character like a rock. Not an amiable character; one fused out of bad luck and pain, not giving pity to others, and not wanting it himself. One might help him across a room, but he would not like one the better for that. As for offering him tenderness—one ought to know that gently, inexorably, he would throw it back in one's teeth.

Sitting there, daydreaming in the sound, I believed Hanna knew that now. She had no insight, but she learned. I was not specially sad for her. She was younger than most women of her age, she still had force and nerve and the hope of the fibres. She was capable of sacrificing herself and enduring more than others could take. In the past she had gone on with a sacrifice for years, and then come to a snapping-point. Then she had saved herself. Could she do so again?

SIXTEEN

THE GOVERNMENT

When the butler came into the Combination Room on the Sunday night and ritually announced, "Master, dinner is served," Crawford told me that, since there were no visitors dining, I was to follow him in and sit at his right hand. As we stood in our places waiting for the Grace to finish, I saw the heavy back of Arthur Brown, dead opposite to me, as he faced down the Hall.

It was a full Sunday night, and we had scarcely spoken in the Combination Room. Once we had sat down to our soup, he gave me a smile of recognition, and told me that he had already asked the Master's permission to present a bottle after dinner to drink my health. He knew why I was in the college, but he was at the same time too warm-hearted and too cunning to let that effect his welcome. Crawford nodded, with impersonal cordiality. He liked a glass of port, he didn't mind me, he wasn't what Gay would have called "on the spot" as to what had been going on that week-end.

Brown gazed down the table. He noticed, just as I did, that neither Francis Getliffe nor Nightingale were dining. Martin was there, so were Tom Orbell and most of the younger Fellows: there were also several members of the college present who were not Fellows but had university jobs. Brown must have been calculating that, until and unless they dispersed, there was no chance of a show-down that night. Whether he found the thought satisfactory, I could not guess. As though it were the only trouble on his mind, he was informing the Master that Winslow's sciatica was worse.

"Ah, well," said Crawford, who was inclined to take a biological, or alternatively a cosmic, view of human miseries, "a man of eighty ought to expect that bits of the machine are beginning to run down."

"I don't think he'd find that much consolation just at present," said Brown.

"Speaking as one trained in medicine, I should have thought he'd been remarkable lucky with his physical constitution. And with his medical history, if it comes to that, I can't think of many men who've lived as long and had so little wrong with them."

"The old chap seemed rather sorry for himself when I dropped in on him before Hall," Brown said.

"That was very considerate of you, Senior Tutor," said Crawford. Without irony at his own expense, or anyone else's, he said: "Do you think I ought to visit him?"

Brown considered: "There's certainly no need to put yourself out. No, I'm inclined to think that he's had enough visitors for twenty-four hours. But if you could send round a note? And perhaps a book? He complained of being short of reading matter."

"That shall be done," said Crawford. He kept his Buddha-like, contented smile. He was either oblivious that he was being told how to do his job, or else he accepted it. He was capable of thinking 'Brown is better at these *personalia* than I am,' and it would not disturb him in the least.

That was the way things worked, I thought. Since Chrystal's death, those two had been the government of the college. No doubt other people had been let in, sometimes and for some things—Nightingale now and then, after he became Bursar, and occasionally Francis Getliffe. But if I knew Brown, they would never have been let right in. Nor should I, though he liked me better, if I had stayed in the college.

The curious thing was, as men, Crawford and Brown had not much use for each other. Crawford was not one to whom friends mattered: he probably thought of Brown as a dullish colleague, a run-of-the-mill administrator, one of those humble persons who kept the wheels going round. While Brown had once had a positive dislike for Crawford. Deep down, I believed—Arthur Brown was loyal and tenacious in all things, including his antipathies—that it remained. He had opposed Crawford's election with every resource that he could pull out. When he lost, people thought that his days of influence in the college were over. They could not have been more wrong. Crawford was arrogant, not over-active, not interested in men's motives, but quite a fair judge of what they could do. He was also human enough to like the support of a man who had previously been all against him. It was not a friend to whom a normal man wanted to give the spoils of office, but an enemy who had just come over. So when Crawford saw Brown settling himself to help, the supreme college manager, he took him with open arms.

As for Brown, he loved managing so much, that, whoever had been Master, he could not have avoided waiting there at his side. For people like him, who lived in affairs, it was part of the rub of life to put loves and hates, particularly hates, out of sight, and almost out of mind. Brown's happened to be unusually strong, stronger than a politician's ought to be: even so, he could behave, not for days but for years, as though he had forgotten. For the practical purpose, like running the college, in front of him, he seemed able to conceal from himself an inconvenient personal dislike. I thought that if I reminded him what he really felt for Crawford, he would be shocked, he would take it as a blemish on good taste.

Through dinner, Crawford, in good world-historical form, was enquiring of me, of Brown, of anyone at large, how China could avoid becoming the dominant power on earth? Not in the vague future, but in finite time: perhaps not in our time, but in our sons'. It was not until we were sitting round the table in the Combination Room that Brown got in much of a word.

The company had dwindled. I watched Brown peer inquisitively as several of the younger Fellows, not waiting for wine, said good-night and went out in a bunch. There was a party at Lester Ince's house, Martin told Brown. "In my young days," said Brown, "our seniors would have looked down their noses if we hadn't stayed in the room on Sunday night. Still, it leaves a nice little party to drink Lewis's health." In fact, it left him and the Master, Martin, Tom Orbell and me, and a couple of non-Fellows. "Which means one glass apiece," said Brown. "That's rather meagre for a beastly winter night and an old friend. I think I should like to ask permission, Master, to order another bottle."

"Very generous of you, Senior Tutor, very generous indeed."

I was now certain that Brown wanted to keep the non-Fellows at the table and so avoid an argument. He did not manage it. They each of them drank their port but, quite early before half-past eight, they had got up and gone. The rest of us were alone, one of the bottles still half-full. I glanced at Martin, who gave the slightest of nods. I was just going to lead in, when Crawford himself addressed us round the table:

"I suppose you've all had the opportunity to read Getliffe's fly-sheet by now, haven't you? I seem to remember, Eliot—" he said, imperturbably gazing at me—"that you're familiar with this unfortunate business."

"I think we can take it," said Arthur Brown, "that Lewis is quite familiar with it. I fancy he was able to study Francis Getliffe's production at least as soon as any of us."

He spoke with his usual lack of hurry, but he was irritated that the Master had opened the subject. Himself, he would have let others make the running.

"I know the situation pretty well," I said to Crawford. "I think I ought to say straight away that I am *parti pris*."

"What exactly do you mean, Eliot?"

"I mean, that if I were a Fellow now, I should be in favour of re-opening this case, without any qualification at all."

"I'm surprised to hear you say that," Crawford said. "You must forgive me, Eliot, but it does sound like a premature judgment."

"I'm surprised to find that you feel in a position to make any judgment whatever," said Brown sternly. "Do you think that the people who decided this issue were altogether irresponsible? I think you might remember that we spent several months devoting as much care to our decision as I for one have ever devoted to anything."

"It's not a decision which anyone in a position of trust could have taken lightly," said Crawford.

"Do you seriously think," said Brown, "that we were as irresponsible as what you've just said seems to indicate? I should like you to consider that question too, Martin."

Martin met my eye. This was going to be rough. Tom Orbell, who had been quiet all the evening, was effacing himself and listening. I thought the only thing was to take the offensive.

"All you say is fair," I replied. "Of course you're not irresponsible men. I've never known people less so. But on your side, do you think that Francis Getliffe is a man to go in for premature judgments? Do you think he would have written as he did, unless he were convinced of it?"

"To an extent, I think you have a point there," said Crawford. "Getliffe is a distinguished man of science—"

"I'm sorry, but I can't accept that as a reason for giving up our own responsibility." Brown's voice was steady and full. "I've known Francis a long time. Of course we all recognise how distinguished he is. But I have known him make mistakes in judgment. If you were a scientist, Lewis, and were giving your opinion on this case, I should be disposed to give more weight to it than I feel able to give to Francis's. Put it another way. There are two of you who are trying to make us take what to my mind would be a false step. Francis is a scientist and a master of technicalities, but gives me some reason to have reserves about his judgment. While I have respect for your judgment, Lewis, but I know you can't master the technicalities any more than I can."

Conciliating, flattering, dividing and ruling, even when he was angry—he was very angry, but he had not lost his touch.

"Of course, I'm in general agreement with you, Senior Tutor," said Crawford, "but for the sake of fairness we ought perhaps to remember that this isn't simply a matter of one individual's judgment. I still consider we were right to resist them, but several men of science in the college, not only Getliffe, have suggested there was a case for enquiry. That's still your feeling, for instance, Martin, isn't it?"

"It is, Master."

"I'm obliged to say," Brown put in, "that I'm not specially happy about the way all this is being done. I exempt you from that remark, Martin. I can't pretend I think you've been well advised—" He gave his jolly laugh, but his eyes were sharp—"but I'm prepared to admit that any step you've taken has been correct. But I'm afraid I can't say as much for most of your associates. I'm very disappointed in Skeffington. I should have thought he'd have known the way to do things. When we elected him, I didn't imagine for a second that he'd turn out to be a trouble-maker. As for Francis Getliffe, he's done nothing more nor less than put a pistol to our heads."

"The danger about pistols," said Crawford, "is that sometimes they go off."

That was as near to a joke as I had heard him make. Tom Orbell gave a suppressed snort, and for an instant Crawford beamed, like a humorist who is appreciated at last. Brown was not beaming, and said:

"In a small society, I've always felt that it's a mistake to rush your colleagues as he's tried to do. Some of us are not all that fond of being threatened."

"Agreed," said Crawford.

"If he'd come to see you about his difficulty, Master," Brown was now turning his full weight on to Crawford, "I might feel differently about it. That would have been the proper thing to do. He ought to have spoken to you before he put a word on paper. Then perhaps we could have smoothed things down in a reasonable fashion. But the way he's gone about it, it's making the college into a beargarden."

"Again, I agree," said Crawford. "One would have thought that Getliffe wouldn't have wished to create unnecessary commotion. I'll try to have a word with him next Thursday at the Royal Society."

"Meanwhile," Brown was continuing to talk, not to the rest of us but to the Master, "I've thought about the proper position to adopt, and I think I can say I've come down to this. If the college chooses to let itself be rushed, and there's a majority for asking the Seniors to re-open the case, then by the Statutes the Seniors naturally have to do so. That's all cut and dried. But I don't see the college losing its head like that. I believe we're interpreting the wishes of the college if we go on resisting attempts to sweep us off our feet against our better judgment."

"Are you sure you're interpreting the wishes of the college?" asked Martin.

"Yes."

"I don't want to do too much counting heads," Martin went on, speaking Brown's own language, "but there are nine out of nineteen feeling the other way."

"Is that a firm figure, Martin?" Crawford asked.

"There are nine Fellows willing to vote for re-opening."

"I confess I should be happier," said Crawford, "if there were a clearer weight of opinion one way or the other."

"I accept Martin's figures," said Brown. Well he might, I thought: those two knew each other's measure and also the score, ball by ball. "But I'm sure he'd agree with me when I say that the nine he's referred to don't include, apart from Getliffe and himself, any of our more influential and senior members."

"That's quite true," said Martin. He was not going to overstate his case.

"Still," said Crawford, "it would be more satisfactory to all concerned if the numbers were wider spaced."

Once again Martin and I glanced at each other and saw that we agreed. It was time to stop. Quickly I got in before Brown and said that they might be in for another kind of trouble. I explained that old Gay was asking advice about how to sue the college.

Crawford did not think that that was funny. He went to a cupboard and fetched a copy of the Statutes. He showed us that, in order to disqualify Gay from the Court of Seniors, the college would have to pass a formal motion. That had never been done, so far as the college history had been traced. So they—not only the Master, but Brown and Winslow—had visited him, written him letters, assuming that he was withdrawing of his own free will. He had not made much protest, once or twice he had verbally acquiesced: but, with a kind of old man's cunning, more animal than senile, he had not acquiesced on paper.

I had a feeling that Brown felt the Master had not been resourceful or punctilious enough. When Crawford asked me what the legal position was, I said that they didn't have much to worry about. I could help them string the old man along for a time. If he went to his solicitors, they wouldn't let him bring such an action. It was just possible that, if he had enough stamina, he could get into touch with an unscrupulous firm—but I couldn't imagine a man of ninety-four keeping up a grudge long enough, not even Gay.

"I shan't believe we're out of that particular wood until we've attended his Memorial service in the chapel," said Arthur Brown. His previous annoyance made him less emollient than he would normally have been. Conscientiously he added, "Not that he hasn't been a grand old boy in his way."

SEVENTEEN

CONTRACTING OUT

A few minutes later, Martin and I were in a taxi on our way to Lester Ince's house in Bateman Street. Martin was asking: didn't I think that, when the argument over the case got sharp, Brown had spent all his effort keeping the Master up to scratch? Yes, I said. It wouldn't take much, probably one conversation with Getliffe, for the Master to decide that the case ought to be re-heard.

That meant the majority was in the bag, said Martin. He went on: "But we don't want it to come like that, do we? They've made a mistake, not offering a re-hearing the minute three or four people wanted it. Just for once, Arthur hasn't played his hand right. It's a point to us if we can force this majority on them, so that they're up against it as soon as they start the case again. We don't want them to let us have it as a favour."

On the pavement in Bateman Street we could hear the noise of the party three storeys above. After I rang the bell we could still hear the noise, but no footsteps coming downstairs. It took minutes of ringing before Ince came down to let us in. Out of the hall, lights streamed into the dark and dripping street. "Hallo, Lew," said Lester Ince. There were two prams in the hall, and the smell, milky and faecal, of small children. As we climbed up the stairs of the old, high, narrow-fronted Victorian house, Martin and I were whispering. "You needn't bother," said Ince in his usual voice, "it would take the crack of doom to wake them up."

Bits of the wall were peeling, a banister leg was loose. The four children were sleeping "dotted about", said Ince, on the first two floors. He owned the whole of the shabby house, and let off the basement. When we got into the party, it seemed to me—I thought it must have seemed to Martin—like going back to parties we used to know when we were poor young men in the provincial town. Beer bottles on the table: the room, which in earlier days would have been a main bedroom, cleared for dancing: a gramophone in the corner: the floor full of couples. There were just two differences. Ince's gramophone was a handsome new record-player, and the couples were jiving.

Ince picked up a glass of beer from the table, drank it, grinned all over his robust, pasty face, and said: "I'm not going to miss this." He crooked his finger at a pretty young woman, and began swinging her round with vigour. His wife winked at him. About the whole party, certainly about Ince, there was a cheerful, connubial, sexy air.

Like his wife, I was thinking, even more than his wife, Ince was a bit of a social fraud. But a fraud in reverse, so to speak. Instead of wanting to be taken for something grander than he was in fact, he seemed to be aiming at the opposite. He was actually a doctor's son, born in the heart of the middle classes, educated like the quintessence of the professional bourgeoisie, middling prep-school, middling public school. He insisted on behaving, talking, and often feeling, as though he had come up from the ranks. Just as with the other kind of social mimic, one listened to his speech. Beneath the curious mixture of what he thought, often not quite accurately, to be lower-class English or happy-go-lucky American, one could hear the background of an accent as impeccably professional as Arthur Brown's.

One odd thing was, that while the Inces imitated those lower down the social ladder, they were not in the least political. I had been used, years before, to upper-class left-wingers, conscientiously calling each other Des, and Pat, and

Bert, on envelopes punctiliously leaving off the "Esquire." But this was nothing like the same thing. It was not a "going to the people." The Inces did not even trouble to vote. They weren't making an intellectual protest. They just felt freer if they cut the ties of class.

It seemed to suit them. If they weren't happy that night, they gave a remarkable impersonation of being so. Between each dance Lester Ince drank a bottle of beer; he had the sort of heavy, games-playing physique, not unlike Martin's, that could mop it up. He danced with his wife as though he were uxorious and glad of it. Ugly, frog-like, cosy, she had such appeal for him that she took on charm for us watching. The temperature of the room, thermometric and psychological, was rising. The young dons were getting off with the women. Married couples, research students with an eye for girls, intellectual-looking girls with an eye for the research students—I was speculating about the curious *idée reçue* dear to men of action, business men and people in the great world, that intellectual persons were less interested in sex than they were. So far as one could generalise at all, in my experience the opposite was true.

In the taxi, Martin had said that we should have to talk to Ince. It wasn't a good time, but in view of Crawford's "wobbling", we mightn't have another. And so, after we had been there an hour, Martin caught him on the landing outside the room and beckoned to me.

"Christ," Ince was saying, "I'd a hell of a sight sooner go back to my wife."

"Two minutes," said Martin. Then he said straight out that Getliffe's note had "put the cat among the pigeons", and he wanted just one more vote.

"You've got a one-track mind, Marty. Strike me pink you have."

"I shouldn't have thought so," said Martin, "but still—"

Ince had drunk a lot of beer but he was not drunk, just

cheerful with drink. Standing with heavy legs firmly planted, he considered and then said:

"It's no go. I'm not playing."

"You can't dismiss it like that, you know."

"Can't I hell?"

I did not know him well, but I felt that at heart he was decent, sound and healthy. It came as a shock to find his tone not only flippant, but callous. I said that I was surprised.

"It's good for you to be surprised, Lew. If it comes to that, why in Christ's name are you messing about here?"

I replied, just as rudely:

"Because people like you are behaving like fools or worse."

"I won't take that from you or anyone else."

"You've damned well got to take it," said Martin.

Ince stared at us, legs immovable, with a matey smile. He was neither abashed nor at a loss.

"I'm just not playing, Marty," he said.

"Why not?"

"I don't feel obliged to give a reason. I didn't know they'd made you a sort of confessor for anti-God men—"

For an instant I saw Martin's face go pale. He was more provoked than I was by the insolence of younger men. But though his temper had risen he did not let it go. He would not do that, except as a tactical weapon or at home.

"I think you are obliged to give a reason," he said.

"Why?"

"If you want to be taken seriously. Which I hope you do."

For the first time, Ince's expression was clouded. He was a strong character, but he gave me the impression that he had not often crossed wills with other strong characters: while for Martin, this was nothing new.

"I'm not interested," he said.

"That's a meaningless thing to say," Martin replied.

"So far as I'm concerned, this is a squabble among scientists. All I want is for you to go and sort it out among yourselves, and good luck to you and a nice long good-bye kiss."

"It's not a squabble among scientists," I said. "That's just letting yourself out. We're telling you, you can't—"

"I'm telling you, can't I hell?"

"Look," I said, "you must admit, there's a chance, we think it's a near certainty, that an innocent man has been victimised. Do you think that's so good?"

"Oh, if that sort of thing happens, it always comes out all right in the wash."

"Good God above," I said, "that's about the most optimistic statement on human affairs that I've ever heard."

"Oh, it's not true of your sort of affairs. Not the big stuff. Not on your life," said Ince. "How many people have you seen done down in your time?"

"Quite a lot," I said, "but not quite—"

"Then why the sweet hell don't you go and put that right?"

"I was going to say," I replied, "not quite in this way. And just because a lot of people are done down inevitably, that's no reason to add another."

"If you really want to know, that's why I wash my hands of this schemozzle," said Ince. "There's too much Pecksniffery about it for me. Christ knows what you've seen, Lew, but then you come here and do a Pecksniff on me. And you're not the worst of them. There's too much Pecksniffery about you scientists, Marty. You think you can do anything you like with the rest of us, and switch on the moral uplift whenever you feel good. That's why I'm bleeding well not playing. You go and do good, I shan't get in your way. But I don't want to hear about it. I'm nice and happy as I am, thank you very much."

EIGHTEEN

CONVERSION

Next day, when Martin came to my rooms to take me to lunch, neither of us had any more news. In Hall, where half a dozen Fellows were already sitting, no one spoke a word about the case, though there were some there, such as Nightingale and Tom Orbell, who must have known each move that had been made. Apart from an old man, a deaf clergyman from a village outside the town, who had come in to lunch each day since before my time, the rest of them had been lecturing or working in the laboratories. Lester Ince announced that he had been talking to a class about Beowulf.

"What have you been telling them?" asked Tom Orbell.

"That he was a God-awful bore," said Ince.

Below the High Table, relays of undergraduates came in and out. The doors flapped, the servants slapped down plates. It was a brisk, perfunctory meal, the noise level in the Hall very high: afterwards only four of us, Martin and I, Nightingale and Orbell, went into the Combination Room for coffee.

After the cosiness of the room at night, it looked bleak, with no fire to draw the eye, no glasses on the table to reflect the light. Through the windows one could see the head and shoulders of a young man running round the court; but the room seemed darker than at night, the beams of the ceiling nearer to one's head.

The four of us sat round the gaping fireplace, with the coffee jug on a low table close by.

"Shall I be mother?" said Nightingale, as though he were in the mess, putting on a cockney accent. As he poured out, he seemed in high spirits, quite unresentful of my presence, less worried by the situation than either Crawford or Brown had been the night before. He was not exactly indifferent to it, but full of a suppressed, almost mischievous satisfaction. He behaved like a man with inside knowledge, concealed from us, which if it were disclosed, would make us recognise that we did not stand a chance.

He was talking about his plans for a new building. He had an ambition, perhaps the last ambition he had left, to leave his mark upon the college. He wanted to put up a building with another eighty sets of rooms.

"If we're going to do it, we've got to do it properly," said Nightingale, "I intend to do the young gentlemen well."

Of course, he said, in the minatory tone of someone talking about past waste of money, if the college had built in the 'thirties it would have cost only seventy thousand. "That's what we ought to have done in your time, Eliot." As it was, the building he was determined on would "run us in" for a quarter of a million. "But the college has got to pay for its mistakes," said Nightingale. "I won't have bed-sitters. I mean to put up a building that we shall be proud of when we're all dead and gone."

He explained his scheme for choosing an architect. He intended to select two "orthodox" men and two "modernists", and ask them to submit plans. "Then it will be up to the college!" said Nightingale triumphantly.

"Do you know, Bursar," I said, "I'm prepared to have a modest bet in bottles that I've just the faintest sneaking suspicion which the college in its taste and wisdom will prefer?"

"Oh, I don't know about that, Eliot. I don't know about that."

Brisk and busy, Nightingale stood up, said that he had a Bursars' meeting at two-thirty, and must spend half an hour in his rooms briefing himself beforehand. He glanced at Tom Orbell. Confident as he was, Nightingale was a little chary of leaving him with Martin and me.

"Coming, Orbell?" he said affably.

"Not just yet, Bursar. Will you excuse me?" said Tom in his most honeyed tone. "As a matter of fact, I've got a letter I ought to send off. Is that all right?"

I was puzzled that he was willing to face us. I was even more puzzled when, after we had heard Nightingale's steps down the passage, Tom said:

"Well, now, how is the Affair going?"

"From whose point of view?" Martin was on his guard.

"It came over me, when we were here last night, that it is pure Dreyfus, you know. At least, there really is something similar between Dreyfus and poor old Howard. And Julian Skeffington would make a reasonably good Picquart, at a pinch. I can't cast you, Martin, you don't seem to fit in. And one's got to stretch a point to cast the others, I suppose. But still, hasn't it ever struck you, either of you, that it is a bit like *'l'Affaire'?*"

Tom Orbell was flushed, excited, apparently with the sheer beauty of the historical analogy. Martin shook his head.

No, it hadn't, he said. "Actually, things are going none too badly—"

"I'm very glad. I mean that, very sincerely."

"How do you cast yourself?" I said.

"No, that isn't so easy either."

"I shouldn't think so," I was saying, when Tom gave me what seemed a defiant stare, and said:

"You haven't got your majority yet, have you?"

"Not yet," said Martin, "but we shall."

"How are you going to do it?"

Tom knew too much of the detail for Martin to bluff.

"If the worst comes to the worst, the Master will have to make it up. Just to give us a hearing—"

"That's exactly the kind of thing he would do," Tom burst out.

"Yes, that's what he was chewing over last night, God rot those awful old men and their beastly, puritanical, unbelieving, Godless, so-called liberal souls. Well, I can save him the trouble, or alternatively we can stop him having the satisfaction. I'll come in with you, by God I will!"

"You're sure?"

"I mean it."

"Do you need some time to change your mind?" said Martin deliberately.

"By God, I've got to come in with you. I can't stand awful old men. When I heard Crawford talking about 'trouble-makers', that was the last straw. Trouble-makers! What else in the name of heaven and earth do they expect honorable men to be? Have they forgotten what it was like to think about one's honour? God knows I don't like Howard; but was one word said last night, was one word even thought, about the man himself? It was so de-humanised it made my blood boil. Have they forgotten what it's like to be human?"

"This business apart," I said, "Arthur Brown is a very human man."

"I'm very glad to hear you say that," said Tom, "because it's only on this business that I've changed sides, remember. Mind you, I don't agree with either of you on many things. We think differently. Nothing's going to persuade me that Getliffe ought to be the next Master of this college. What I'm saying now isn't going to affect what I do this autumn. I'm not joining you about him—that is, presuming you want him?"

Martin did not reply, and Tom stormed on:

"I'd sooner have Arthur Brown a hundred times. Even though some of your friends say he's a stick-in-the-mud. But as for the rest of the old guard, I just can't sit down under them. Trouble-makers. Judgment. Keeping us in our places till we're fifty! I can't abide it, and I won't. It's about time someone spoke up for honour. By God, this is the time to do it!"

With a smile both forced and curiously sweet he said:

"Anyway, it'll be nice being on the same side as you two again. We're all in the same lobby this time, aren't we?"

We had known, for minutes past, almost from his first question, that he was changing sides. But his tone was not what one might have expected. He kept some of his desire to please; he was trying to sound warm, to feel what most of us feel when we are giving our support. He did not manage it. He had thrown away his prudence, his addiction to keeping in with the top; but he had not done it out of affection for us. Nor out of devotion to Hanna. Nor out of the honour that he was protesting about. Instead he seemed to be acting partly from direct feeling for a victim, partly from frustrated anger. One felt, under the good-living, self-indulgent, amiable surface, how violent he was to himself. He was a man who couldn't take authority just as it was; he surrounded it with an aura, he longed for it and loathed it. He couldn't listen to the Master as though he were just a brother human being speaking. In fact, he listened wrong. The phrase which had inflamed him—'trouble-makers!'—he attributed to the Master, but it had actually been spoken by Arthur Brown.

"Good," said Martin. But he was less at home with natures like Tom's than I was. Now that Tom had committed himself, my instinct would have been to trust him. Martin's wasn't. He was not as easy as usual, as he said:

"Look here, I'd like to get this cut and dried. It would be a good idea to tell Crawford to-night that we've got a majority signed, sealed and delivered. I wonder if you'd mind writing me a note?"

Tom flushed. "You'd like it on paper, would you?"

Martin said, "Well, it would be a final piece of ammunition—"

"Very well," said Tom. He went, shoulders pushing forward, eyes hot, to the writing-desk by the window. He wrote a few lines, signed his name, put the sheet of paper in an envelope. Then, with his back to us, he started laughing. It was a loud laugh, both harsh and hearty.

"I told Nightingale I was going to stay to write a letter, didn't I?"

III

THE OFFER

NINETEEN

REMARK FROM AN OFFICIAL GUEST

The Court of Seniors was taking its time, so Margaret and I heard in London. Weekly meetings, a summons to Howard to give written evidence, a summons to Francis Getliffe—it all looked, both inside the college and to us, as though they were being stately to save their faces. Laura told Margaret that, when Howard was reinstated, they proposed to stay a couple of years at Cambridge and then move. There seemed surprisingly little gossip about the affair within the college: certainly none reached us. Some of them were beginning to get busy about the autumn election, however, and there were reports that both Brown's "caucus" and Getliffe's had already met.

For myself, I received one direct communication from the college. It came from old Gay. He reminded me that I had promised to "take legal soundings" and finished up by a reference to "certain infractions of privilege, of privilege won by a lifetime's devotion to scholarship, which, for the sake of others, are not lightly to be borne nor tamely to be brooked."

In April I had to go to Cambridge on official business. On business which was, as it happened, at that time top secret: for Walter Luke, the head of the Atomic Energy Establishment at Barford, wanted to talk to the Cavendish about the controlled thermo-nuclear reaction. There was a slice of the work he planned to divert to Cambridge. It had to be done with what Luke called our "masks and false noses" on, and when he went to negotiate I, as his boss in the hierarchy, went too.

Outside the conference room windows it was a piercing blue April afternoon, a sunny afternoon with a wind so cold and pure that it made one catch one's breath. As we sat there in the Old Schools, I looked out at the bright light, resentful at being kept in, resentful without understanding why, as though the springs of memory were being plucked, as though once I had been out in the cold free air and known great happiness. And yet, my real memories of days like that in Cambridge were sad ones.

Shaking myself, I got back to the argument. Round the table were the Vice-Chancellor, Crawford as an ex-Vice-Chancellor, three scientists, one of them Francis Getliffe, Walter Luke, and me. Negotiations were going slowly, and not well. They were not going well partly because Luke, as well as being a good deal the youngest man present, was also a good deal the most impatient. Incidentally he was—and that didn't make it easier either—probably the most gifted. There was a fair amount of ability in the room, two Nobel Prize winners, five Fellows of the Royal Society. For imagination and sheer mental drive, I would have put Luke before any of them. But for persuasive power in a genuinely difficult situation, he wouldn't have been the first partner I should have chosen.

It was a genuinely difficult situation. In principle, they were all ready for the Cavendish to take on some of the thermo-nuclear work. Luke told them, though one or two knew beforehand, the minimal facts about it. It was peaceful, he said, no one need have any moral qualms. In fact, the reverse. The only people who need have moral qualms were those who in any way obstructed it. For this, if it came off, would meet the human race's need for energy for ever. If this country got it first, it would stay as a major power for a couple of generations. "I'm not going to sell you something we haven't got," said Luke. "It's not in the bag yet. But if I were going to stick my neck out, I should say the chances weren't worse than evens."

So far, so good. Everyone liked the sound of that. The first trouble was that, if any of the research came to Cambridge laboratory, it would mean a special kind of security. "You won't like it," said Luke, "I don't like it. No one in his senses likes it. It's mostly bloody nonsense, anyway. But we've got to have it. If you want to know why, you'd better ask Lewis Eliot."

Some of them were uneasy. It wasn't that they were unused to security. But, as I had to explain what this special kind would mean, they thought it would be not only a nuisance inside the university, but something worse. The Vice-Chancellor and Crawford questioned me. I thought it was bad policy to gloss over the difficulties; I was ready to be as patient as they were, but Luke was getting restive.

"I can't credit that we're going to hold it up just because of a couple of flatfoots and a bit of vetting and the other thing—"

Towards six o'clock, negotiations adjourned until the next day, Crawford, Getliffe, Luke and I walked back to the college. Not willing, not able, to let the controversy fade out, Luke was saying that all these doubts and hesitations were anachronisms, they'd forgotten the time they were living in, the first thing we'd got to make sure was that "this country can earn its living." If this reaction came off, then the country could earn a living till our grandchildren's time or longer. Anything which got in its way was suicidal. Unless, Luke said, someone else was brighter than he was and could see another way to keep us "a jump ahead." Luke's voice, which still kept the rumble of the Devonport dockyard in which he had started, rolled out unsubdued as we entered the First Court.

In the bright and dramatic twilight, I looked at him. It was the kind of light which, after a brilliant day, suddenly gives shadows and moulding to faces—so that one has something like an optical illusion that the day, instead of darkening, is getting brighter. Luke's cheekbones stood out through flesh that was no longer full: his skin was matte, and the colour was washed out: his bristly, strong hair had gone quite grey. Although his backbone was ramrod stiff as he walked, he had a limp that had not left him since a radiation accident. He had aged more quickly than anyone I knew. When the college had first elected him—and it was only eighteen years before—he had been younger-looking than most men of twenty-four. His cheeks had been fresh and high-tinted; he had been quiet, discreet, determined to get on, certain that he would leave a great corpus of scientific work behind him.

It hadn't gone like that. War and the scientific revolution had played tricks on him. As a young man, he would never, not even in a fantasy, have imagined himself as he was that night, walking into his old college, possessed in his early forties of power, a title, a place in the Establishment. Not that he disliked these things: people did not get what they didn't want. But he had expected quite different successes, and still valued them more. Compared with these two older men, Crawford and Getliffe, he knew that in natural talent he was their equal or superior; he had got into the Royal Society younger than either of them; he had a touch of genius which they hadn't. And yet, his creative work was slender by the side of theirs. In fifty years' time, when students read through the scientific textbooks, there would be pages about Crawford's discoveries; there would be descriptions of the Getliffe layer and the Getliffe effect; there would be a little, but only a very little, to keep alive Luke's name.

I did not know how much he regretted it. He was not an introspective man and, argumentative and articulate as he was, he did not often confide. All his imagination, vitality, crude and crackling force, seemed to have become canalized into the job he had set himself, what he called "seeing that the country can earn a living." Somehow his ambition, his scientific insight, his narrow and intense patriotism, had all fused into one.

When Francis had gone up to his rooms, Crawford asked Luke and me into the Lodge. There, in the study, after he had given us a drink, Crawford said; fingers together, gazing across the fireplace:

"I *think* I hope you get your way about this matter, Luke, I'm not certain, but I *think* I hope you get your way."

"I should damned well hope you do," said Luke.

"No, speaking as an old-fashioned man of science, I don't see it's as straight-forward as that," said Crawford imperturbably. With his usual respect both for ability and position, he approved of Luke: but he wasn't to be bulldozed when an idea was being talked about. Crawford didn't like disagreement on 'personalia', but when it came to an idea, he remembered that he was a son of the manse and became, at about half the speed, as disputatious as Luke himself.

As they argued (Crawford kept saying "you *aver* that . ." which I could not recall having heard anyone say before) they were enjoying themselves. I wasn't, for I had less taste for amateur metaphysics.

Just as we were getting ready to go, Crawford remarked:

"By the by, I'm afraid that I shan't be able to be with you tomorrow."

I said that we shouldn't reach a decision anyway.

"As a matter of fact," said Crawford, "I've got to attend to a rather troublesome piece of college business."

"What's that?" Luke asked, "The Howard flap, I suppose?"

For once, Crawford was taken aback, Buddha-smile dissolved into an astonished fretting stare.

"I really don't understand how you've heard that, Luke," he cried.

"God love me," Luke gave his harsh guffaw, "it's all round

the scientific world. Someone told me about it at the Ath. God knows how long ago."

"Then I'm very distressed to hear it."

"Never you mind." Luke was still grinning. "You couldn't have stopped it. Nothing's ever going to stop scientists talking, as you ought to know. Hell, that's what we've been chewing the rag about this afternoon! As soon as the boys in the Cavendish heard there was something fishy about Howard's paper, nothing could have stopped it going round. If you ask me, you've been bloody lucky that it's been kept as quiet as it has."

"I should be very sorry to think," said Crawford, "that anyone in the college has spoken a word outside."

"That's as may be," Luke replied.

"I've never had the slightest indication," Crawford went on, "that anyone in the university outside this college knows anything of the unpleasantness we've been through."

"Like a bet?" said Luke.

Crawford had recovered his equilibrium. He gave a smile, melon-lipped, contented with himself. "Well," he said, "I don't want to say any more, but tomorrow I think there's every chance we shall have finished with this unfortunate business once for all."

TWENTY

A PIECE OF PAPER

After another day of meetings, which had again been adjourned, without giving Luke and me what we were asking for, I went in the evening to Martin's rooms. Earlier in the day I had telephoned him, telling him what Crawford had said. The lights in the high eighteenth century windows, late additions to the court, did not dominate it as they would when it was full dark: they just stood welcoming. I expected Martin to be waiting for me with the result.

What I did not expect was to enter the room and find not Martin, but Howard and his wife waiting there. Howard, who was reading an evening paper, looked up and said hullo. Laura said good-evening, addressing me in full, politely, formally, brightly.

"Martin let us know that the verdict was coming through to-night," she explained.

"Nothing yet?"

"Not yet." She remarked that Martin had gone out to see if he could "pick up anything." Both she and Howard seemed quite undisturbed.

Their nerves were steadier than mine, I thought. If I had been in their place, I couldn't have endured to plant myself in the college waiting. However certain I had been of what I was going to hear. In fact, the more certain I had been, the more I should have been impelled, by a streak of superstitious touching-wood, which they would both have despised, to make it a bit hard for the good news to catch up with me. In their place, I should have gone for a walk, away from telephones or messengers, and then returned home, hoping the news was there, still wishing that the envelope could stay unopened.

Not so these two. They were so brave that they seemed impervious. Howard had found in the paper something about an English soldier being killed on what he called "one of *your* colonial adventures." He would have liked to make me argue about politics. The curious thing was that, as he talked, protruding the Marxist labels, making them sound aggressive, he was also cross because the platoon had walked into an ambush. A cousin of his was serving with that brigade, and Howard suddenly slipped into a concern that I might have heard at Pratt's, irritated, paternal, patrician. One felt that, change his temperament by an inch, he would have made a good regimental officer.

There was a sound of footsteps on the staircase outside. I knew them for Martin's, though they might have sounded like a heavier man's. I stopped talking. Howard was looking towards the door.

Martin came in. He had a piece of paper in his hand. His eyes were so bright that, just for an instant, I thought that all was well. We were sitting round the chimney-piece, and he did not speak until he had reached the rug in front of us.

"I am sorry to be the one to tell you this," he said to them in a hard voice. "It's bad."

Without another word he gave the note to Howard, who read it with an expression open and washed clean. He did not speak, passed the note to his wife, and once more picked up the evening paper. In a moment Laura, her colour dark, a single furrow running across her forehead, gave me the note. It carried the address of the college Lodge, and read:

The Court of Seniors, at the request of the College, have re-considered the case of Dr. D. J. Howard, formerly a Fellow. They have concluded that there is no sufficient reason for them to amend their previous decision.

R. T. A. Crawford.
Master of the College.

In a tone so quiet that it became a whisper, as though we were in a sick-room or a church, Martin told me that the notice had not yet gone round: it was just being duplicated in the college office, and he had collected a copy there. As he sat down, without saying any more, he looked at me, as if for once he did not know the etiquette, as if he was lost about what to say to these two or do for them. I hadn't any help to give. He and I sat there in silence, watching Laura gaze with protective love at Howard. He was holding the newspaper low, so as to catch the light from the reading-lamp. The only movement he made, the only movement in the whole room, was that of his eyes as they went down the page.

He did not turn over. I could not tell whether he had stopped reading, or whether he was reading at all.

All of a sudden he let the paper drop. As it fell, the front page drifted loose and we could see the headlines, bold and meaningless, upon the rug.

"I hope they're satisfied now," he shouted. He began to swear, and the curses came out high and grating. "Oh, yes," he cried, "I hope they're satisfied!" He went on shouting and cursing, as though Martin and I were not there. At last he sat up straight, looked at Martin, and said with a curious sneering politeness; "If it comes to that, I hope you're satisfied too."

"Don't speak like that to me!" Martin broke out. Then, getting back his usual tone, he said: "Look, this isn't going to get us anywhere—"

"What I want to know is, why wasn't I asked to talk to that Court again, after they said they'd probably want me? I want to know, who stopped that? I suppose you're all pleased by the masterly way you've handled things. It's not important to be fair, all that matters is that everything should look fair."

Howard did not seem to have noticed the flash of Martin's temper. For him, everyone was an enemy, everyone was a part of "them," most of all those who had pretended to be working on his side. His voice changed. "I'm positive, if I could explain how I wrote that paper, if I could explain quietly and sensibly and not get panicked, then the Court would see the point." He was looking ingenuous and hopeful, as though the issue were still in the future and the Court could still be influenced. He was caught up by one of those moments of hope that come in the middle of disasters, when time gets jangled in the mind and it seems that one still has a chance and that with good management one is going to emerge scot-free and happy.

Another splinter of mood: he began to shout again. "By God, they wanted to get me! I should like to have heard what they've been saying this last fortnight. I should like to know whether it's just a coincidence that *you* happened to be here," he said to me, with the same jeering courtesy that he had used to Martin. "But I don't suppose they wanted any extra help. They were determined to get me, and one's got to hand it to them, they've made a nice job of it."

"It isn't finished yet," said Laura. She had gone near to him; she was speaking with impatience and passion.

"They've made a very pretty job of it. I think they deserve to be congratulated," cried Howard.

"For God's sake," said Laura, "you're not giving up like that!"

"I should like to know—"

"You're not giving up," she said. "We've got to start again, that's all."

"You know nothing about it."

He spoke to her roughly—but there was none of the suspiciousness with which he would have spoken to anyone else that night. Between them there flared up—so ardent as to make it out of place to watch—a bond of sensual warmth, of consolatory warmth.

"It's not finished yet, is it?" she appealed to Martin.

"No," he said. He spoke to Howard. "Laura's right. I suggest we cut the inquests and see about the next step."

Martin's manner was business-like but neither enthusiastic nor friendly. He was no saint: He had none of the self-effacingness of those who, in the presence of another's disaster, don't mind some of the sufferings being taken out on themselves. He didn't like being accused of treachery. He would gladly have got Howard out of sight and never seen him again. Martin had himself taken a rebuff, more than a rebuff, in the Seniors' verdict that night.

"You've got a formal method of appeal," said Martin. "You can appeal to the Visitor, of course."

"Oh, that's pretty helpful," said Howard. "That's your best idea yet. Do you really think a bishop is going out of his way to do any good to me? And when I think of that particular bishop—Well, that ought to be the quickest way of finishing me off for good and all." He said it with his paranoid sneer.

A bite in his voice, Martin replied:

"I said that it was the formal method. I mentioned it for one reason and one reason only. You're probably obliged to go through the whole formal machine before you bring an action for wrongful dismissal. I still hope we can get this straight for you without your bringing an action."

"Do you?"

Martin's tone kept its edge, although he went on without being provoked: "But after what's happened, I couldn't blame you if you went straight ahead. I don't think any of us could."

Howard looked startled. He was startled enough to go in for a practical discussion: did Martin really advise him to see a solicitor straight away? No, Martin replied patiently, but it was only fair to say that most men would think it justified. How did one start going about an appeal to the Visitor? Howard went on, beginning to look tired, confused, and absent-minded, his eyes straying to his wife, as though it was she only that he wanted.

Martin continued to reply, ready to bat on about procedure. It was Howard who said that he wasn't going "to do anything in a hurry," that he had "had enough for one night." He left the room with his arm round Laura, and once more the two of us, watching them, felt like *voyeurs*.

After the door had closed behind them, Martin sat gazing into the grate. At last I said: "Were you prepared for this —?" I pointed to the slip of paper with the Seniors' verdict.

"I wish I could say yes."

He answered honestly, but also in a rage. Despite his caution and his warnings—or perhaps because of them—he had been totally surprised, as surprised as any of us. He was furious with himself for being so, and with the men who caused it.

"There'll have to be a spot of trouble now," he said, able, since the Howards went, to let the anger show. People often thought that those who "handled" others, "managers" of Martin's kind, were passionless. They would have been no good at their job if they were. No, what made them effective was that they were capable of being infuriated on the one hand, and managerial on the other.

Vexed as he was, Martin did not lose his competence. There were two tasks in front of him straight away; first to prevent any of his party doing anything silly, second to keep them together. Without wasting time, he said that we had better walk round and see Skeffington; he had heard him say that he was going to dine at home.

When we got to the bottom of the staircase, Martin looked across the Court. The chapel door was open wide, a band of light poured on to the lawn; a few young men, gowns pulled round them, were hurrying away from evensong.

"It isn't anything special in the way of festivals, is it?" said Martin, nodding towards the chapel.

We paused for an instant. There was no sign of Skeffington coming round the path; there was only the chaplain, shutting the door behind him.

Not there, said Martin. We went through the screens, bustling and jostling with young men, some pushing early into hall, some swinging off with beer-bottles. In the second court there were lights in old Winslow's rooms.

"I wonder what *he* thinks he's doing," I said.

"He's never had any judgment," said Martin. "He took you all in, but he never had much sense."

I was thinking, as Martin unlocked the side door, how I had seen Winslow in his full power, a formidable man: and how the stock exchange of college reputations went up and down, so that Martin, nine years younger, saw him only as a failure. On that stock exchange, Brown's reputation had kept steady since my time, Crawford's had climbed a bit, Nightingale's had rocketed—while men whose personalities filled the college when I was there, Winslow, Jago, had already been written off long before their deaths.

We crossed to the row of cottages and Martin pulled at the handbell on Skeffington's. There was no answer, although from the living-room, faintly lit, came a sound of voices. Martin pulled again. Suddenly lights sprang up behind the curtains, and substantial steps came to the door. It was Mrs. Skeffington. As she opened the door, her face was reddened, her manner flustered. She said: "Oh, it's you two, is it? I'm afraid you've caught me on the wrong foot."

Martin asked if Julian was there.

No, she was alone, he had gone off for a meal at a pub.

Could we come in, since Martin wanted to leave a message for him?

"You've caught me on the wrong foot," Mrs. Skeffington repeated, as we sat there in the living-room. I thought I knew why she was so embarrassed. It wasn't, or at least not immediately, because Julian had gone off alone. She had lived a long time with a marriage which had worn dry, so that she had forgotten how to conceal it, if indeed she had ever tried. No, it was something much sillier. She had been sitting by herself in that little parlour, with a tray in front of her, scrambled eggs on toast and a good stiff whisky: and the sound of voices which we had heard from the lane outside came from the television set. It was now safely turned off, but Mrs. Skeffington looked like a great, chapped-cheeked schoolgirl caught in the act: her hearty, brick-dropping, county assurance had dropped from her quite. She couldn't believe that men like Martin and me would have spent such an evening. She had an impression, which filled her with both ridicule and awe, that her husband's colleagues spent their entire existence at their books. She was certain that if we saw what she had been enjoying, we should despise her. With dazzled relief, she realised that we were not going to question her or comment. She poured out whiskies for us both, drank her own and helped herself to another. She drank, it seemed to me, exactly as her brothers would have done after a day's hunting.

Martin was set on getting her to understand his news. "Look, Dora, this is important." Next morning, by the first delivery, Julian would get the Court's decision. Martin told her the form of words.

"That's a slap in the eye for some of you, isn't it?" she said. "They're as good as saying that old Uncle Cecil (Palairet) wasn't up to any monkey-business, aren't they?"

"Yes, they're certainly saying that."

"Well," said Dora Skeffington, "I must say I'm rather glad. None of my family ever thought much of Cecil. My mother used to say that he was a bit common, though I never understood how she made that out. But still, he did more than some of them and he was always decent to me when I was a little girl."

She sat back, basking in the comfort of family piety and several drinks. But she was neither stupid nor, except when she felt it was due to herself, obtuse. She felt the absence of response. She said:

"What's the matter? Don't you believe the old man's all right?"

"Not for a minute. Nor will Julian. That's why I don't want him to fly off the handle—"

Martin told her that this meant that the affair had only got worse. None of the revisionists could accept this verdict, neither Julian, nor he, nor Francis, nor any of their followers. All it meant was that they were back where they started, with passions higher. The danger was, Julian might make things worse, if he insisted on behaving like a "wild man." Martin's plan was to call a meeting of the majority by the end of the week. Would she tell Julian to keep out of action until then?

"I'll tell him," said Dora. "Mind you, I don't know what good it'll do."

She sounded both sad and jocular. Sad because it was a disappointment that old Palairet wasn't going to be left in peace, and sad too because she couldn't answer for her husband and spoke of him as one might speak of a not-very-close friend. And at the same time amused, because somehow she thought of her husband, not only as someone worth a certain kind of admiration, but also as a bit of an ass. Superb, handsome, high-minded, priggish, high-principled, extravagantly brave—that was how others saw him, but not she. Yet she was utterly loyal. Loyal partly because it was both her nature and training to be so: but also, oddly, just because their marriage had worn so thin and dry. Somehow that strengthened their knockabout, not-very-close friendship, instead of weakening it. They had become allies, neither of them humorous, each of them priding themselves on "seeing the joke" in the other. It meant that, when she had to choose between Palairet's good name and her husband's principles, or even her husband's whims, there was no choice for her. She would make higher sacrifices than that for him. With her own kind of clumsy devotion, she was with him whatever he wanted to do. Others might admire him more, other women might long for the chance of admiring him, but she happened to be married to him.

TWENTY-ONE

TWO APPROACHES TO A STATESMAN

The next evening, Walter Luke and I came back from a day of negotiations late but pleased with ourselves. It was too late to talk in our rooms: we went straight into the Combination Room, affable because, as Luke was saying, most of what we had come for was "in the bag." As soon as we entered the room, however, no one could have stayed affable. We had walked right into the hiss and ice of a quarrel. G. S. Clark was standing there, his useless leg braced against the table, Nightingale behind him. Two or three of the young scientists were talking angrily and did not lower their tone as we came in. Francis Getliffe was listening, with an expression fine-drawn, distressed, furious. One of the young men was saying that it was "an outrage."

"Aren't you going in for propaganda?" replied Clark.

"I've got to say," Getliffe interrupted, "that I've never seen anything worse handled."

"What do you mean, worse handled?" said Nightingale, smiling, more in control than the others.

"Do you really think you can fob us off without an explanation?" said a scientist.

"Do you really think the Court didn't consider that?" G. S. Clark was asking.

"Do you know better than we do what they considered?"

"I'm prepared to trust them," said Clark.

"I should like to know why."

"I'm sorry," said Clark, "but that seems a little adolescent

I should have thought it reasonable to trust a Court of Seniors of this college to behave at least as responsibly as you would yourself."

For some instants, Luke had been standing, for once looking stupefied and incapable of action, on the edge of the fracas. He asked: "What is all this?"

"I don't know how much you ought to hear, Luke, not being a Fellow—" Nightingale began.

Luke broke in:

"Oh, come off it, Alec. Is the business I was talking to Crawford about two nights ago?—"

"I think you're bound to be told this some time," said Nightingale. "The Seniors have been sitting on an appeal on behalf of a man called D. J. Howard. We've just informed the college that we've had to decide against him."

Luke stared round at the angry faces.

"Well," he said, "I hope to God you've got it right."

He was oddly at a loss. He had forgotten, if indeed he had ever paid much attention to it, how intense and open the emotions could show in a closed society like this. For fifteen years he had been used to high scientific affairs. He had seen great decisions taken, and had at least twice forced a great decision himself. He had been in the middle of a good deal of politics, but it had been controlled, official politics, with the feelings, the antagonisms, the hates and ambitions, kept some distance beneath the skin. It hadn't been different in kind from the college's politics, but there was a difference—Luke had forgotten how much—in nakedness and edge. The curious thing was, in terms of person-to-person conflict, when one moved from high affairs to the college one moved from a more sheltered life to a less.

It was the precise opposite of what most of us would have imagined. Just as, I thought, most of us would never have imagined another move, from a more sheltered life to a less. Observe the lives of tycoons, like my acquaintance Lord

Lufkin, or boss administrators, like Hector Rose; they had much power, they carried responsibility, they were hard-working to an extent that the artists I knew could not begin to conceive. And yet in a special sense, they were also sheltered. Neither Lufkin or Rose had met a direct word of hostility for ten years: they did not have to listen to a breath of criticism of themselves as persons. While people whom they, the bosses, thought passed happy-go-lucky lives, the artists living right out of 'the world,' had to take criticism, face to face, as straightforward as a school report, each week of their lives as part of the air they breathed.

As the butler announced dinner, Brown had walked into the Combination Room. President for the night, he took Luke and me into hall behind him. After grace, his eyes peered down the high table. Francis Getliffe and Martin were several places down from the President—and beyond them, having arrived late, was Skeffington, his head inches above any man's there. Brown's face was composed, high-coloured and full; his eyes were sharp behind their spectacles, not missing a trick. For all his heavy composure, he responded to atmosphere as one of the most sensitive of men. He had only had to get inside the combination room to sniff the trouble in the air.

From the head of the table, he watched the faces—and then, in his unfussed way, he talked to Luke and me as though it were a perfectly ordinary evening, as though, after his ten thousand dinners at the high table, this was just his ten thousand and first. The immemorial topics: new buildings: the flowers in the garden: which head of a house was retiring next. Walter Luke wasn't specially designed to meet that unflurried pattern. Once Brown broke it, and asked us a question, wrapped up but shrewd, about the "military side" of Luke's work. Brown did not approve of pacifism; if horrific bombs could be made, of course his country ought to make them. Then he returned to harmless talk, deliberately small beer, produced—since Brown was not afraid to seem boring—to damp down controversy, and to prevent anyone raising "awkward subjects."

It went on like that at our end of the table. It might have been a college evening at its most placid. To Luke, who went away immediately after dinner, it must have seemed that the excitement had died. When Brown took his seat in the combination room, he asked the junior Fellow to see whether the company wanted wine, and himself called out to Francis and Martin—"Won't you stay for a few minutes?" They were standing up: they glanced at each other, and Francis said that they had some business to attend to. Still speaking as though all were smooth, Brown said, "Well, Julian, what about you?" Skeffington also had been standing up: but when he heard Brown's question, he dropped into a chair not far from Brown at the Combination Room table.

"That's right," said Brown.

"No, Mr. President," Skeffington threw his head back, "it's not right at all."

"Can't you stay?"

"All I want to do is to tell you this is a bad show, and I for one am not prepared to sit down under it."

"I'm sorry to hear you say that," Brown said, playing for time. "I suppose you must be talking about this decision, which the Seniors couldn't see any alternative to making—"

"There was a very simple alternative, Mr. President."

"What was that?"

"To admit that there'd been a crashing mistake. Then to make it up to the poor chap."

"I'm sorry," said Brown. "We're all human and liable to error, but on this particular issue, speaking for myself, I've seldom been more certain that I was right."

"Then it's time we had someone unprejudiced on this wretched Court—"

"Are you seriously suggesting that we should give up our

places on the Court of Seniors simply because we don't find ourselves able to accept your judgment?"

"No. Simply because you don't want to admit the facts when you see them."

Brown said, dignified and still equable in tone: "I think we'd better leave this for to-night. I don't think you will persuade us to abdicate our responsibility, you know. I fancy we'd better leave it for to-night and talk it over later, if you feel disposed."

"No. I feel disposed for something which will bring results."

At that, Martin, who had been standing behind us, said to Skeffington that it was time to go.

"I intend to have results and have them quickly," cried Skeffington. "I am not going to have this innocent chap left with a black mark against him while you put us off with one sidestep after another. If you can't give us a decent constitutional method of getting a bit of simple justice, then we shall have to try something else."

"I'm not clear what else you can try," Brown replied.

"I am ready to make the whole case public," said Skeffington. "I don't like it, it won't do any good to any of us or to this college. But it will do some good to the one chap who most needs it. The minute we've let a breath of fresh air into this wretched business, you haven't got a leg to stand on."

"I hope I don't understand you, as I am afraid I do," said Brown. "Are you intending to say that you're prepared to get the college *into the papers?*"

"Certainly I am."

"I'm obliged to tell you," said Brown, "that I'm astonished to hear the bare suggestion. All I can hope is that when you've slept on it you will realise how unforgiveable all of us here would judge any such action to be."

Skeffington replied, "Don't you realise some of us here

won't sleep at all? It's better than letting this chap be done down for ever."

"I repeat," said Brown, "I hope you'll sleep on it."

"Unless someone else can think up a nice way, I'm ready to blow the whole thing wide open."

"I should be surprised if you didn't think better of it."

"I shan't."

Skeffington's wild irritability seemed to have left him. He glanced over his shoulder at Francis and Martin, still waiting for him. He stood up, proud, vain, sure of himself. With the return of a naval officer's politeness—towering over the table, he appeared so theatrically handsome that he looked more like an actor playing a naval officer—he said, "Good-night, Mr. President," and the three of them went out.

Brown returned the good-night, but for a few moments he sat thinking, the decanter static before him in its silver runner. Two or three of the scientists had followed the others, and there were only half a dozen of us scattered around the long table. Of these Nightingale stayed until the decanter had gone round, and then, apologising to Brown, said that he had an hour's work to do before he went home. He spoke good-temperedly, not making any reference to the scene we had all witnessed. Neither did Clark, who departed soon after; he did mention, however, that he would be ringing Brown up that night or next morning, and it sounded like business. I hadn't much doubt that there would be other telephone calls about Skeffington's threat before the end of the night.

Soon Tom Orbell and I were left alone with Brown. He summoned Tom from the far end of the table, telling him to sit at his left hand. "It's rather a small party for an April evening," said Arthur Brown, and proceeded impassively to tell us how, as a junior Fellow, he had found himself the only man dining at High Table, one night in full term. But Brown's front was not impregnable. At the end of the story he became silent; just for an instant, he was too much preoccupied to be master of ceremonies; he turned to me and said, "I know you are inclined to believe that the Seniors' judgment isn't the right one, Lewis."

"I'm afraid I do," I said.

"But you wouldn't deny that our friend Skeffington made an exhibition of himself, would you?"

For once Brown, the most solid of men, was asking for support. He was speaking to me not as an opponent, but as an old friend.

I could not help replying:

"I should have preferred him to do it in a different way. Of course I should."

"I thought you would," said Brown, with a smile relieved, comradely, but still brooding. "I thought we should agree on that."

Just then Tom put in, deliberately innocent, his eyes wide open, as though he were exaggerating his youth: "I wonder if you'd let me say something, Arthur?"

"My dear chap?"

"I think you know that, like Lewis, I don't see quite eye to eye with you over this. On this one single occasion, I do very sincerely think you're wrong."

"I appreciate that," said Brown.

"It's the only time since I've been here that, when it's come to a decision, I haven't felt you were incomparably righter than anyone else."

"You're much too kind to me."

Brown was watching Tom with care. He knew—it didn't take a wary man to know—that Tom was up to something. For what purpose Tom was trying to get round him, he couldn't foresee. I was thinking, Tom, quite apart from his hidden violence, was a subtle character. He was fluid, quick-moving, full of manoeuvre, happy to play on other men. But, like other subtle characters, he was under the illusion that his manoeuvres were invisible. In fact, they were seen through, not only by people like Brown and me, but by the simplest. And that was true of most subtle men. As they went round, flattering, cajoling, misleading and promising, the only persons who found their disguise totally convincing were themselves.

"So I was wondering if you'd let me ask one question. Don't you think it might be a mistake to be too intransigeant over this? I respect your attitude, I respect your opinion on the justness of the affair, though quite sincerely I can't agree with it. But don't you think it might be a mistake—well, one might call it a mistake in tactics, if you don't misunderstand me, to be too intransigeant? Because there are several people like me who would follow your lead over anything else, who simply can't do it over this. And I do suggest it might be a mistake to put them off too much."

Brown replied, "I think I can speak for the other Seniors. Naturally we realised that the decision couldn't be a popular one."

"I really wasn't thinking of the other Seniors. If I may say so, Arthur, I was thinking of you."

"No," said Brown. "Again I'm not betraying a confidence, I think, when I say there is no difference between us or the Court."

"There is one very important difference, if you'll allow me to say so."

"What do you mean?"

"I mean, that none of the other Seniors is a candidate for the Mastership this autumn, and you most certainly are."

Brown's face was heavy: "I don't see where this is leading us."

"There's something I've wanted to say for a long time. Perhaps I oughtn't to. I don't think you'll like it. It isn't my place to say it anyway."

"I'd rather you did."

Tom was put off by Brown's tone, formal and stern. Would Tom realise, even at the last second, I was praying, that he had misjudged his man? He hesitated; then, once more acting the innocent, making his spontaneity into a technique, he cried:

"Yes, damn it, I will say it! Arthur, you know I want to see you get the Mastership. I want it more than anything in the college, I mean that most sincerely. And you know that some of us are working for you as hard as we can. Well, we've been a little worried, or at least I have, about the effect your part in this affair is going to have. You see, it can't be helped, but everyone takes it for granted that you're the toughest obstacle to doing anything for Howard. If you hadn't been there, everyone assumes that something might have been patched up. That may or may not be fair, but it's what a lot of people are thinking. And, don't you see, it's bound to have a bad effect on some of those who ought to be your supporters. There's Taylor and one or two others. I've been counting on their votes, and now I can see us losing them unless we're careful. There's Martin Eliot. He's not committed to anyone. But I can't see that it would even be possible for him to vote for you if this affair goes much further. Arthur, I'm not asking you to change your mind. Of course, I know you can't. You believe what you believe, just as much as we do. But I am asking you to slip into the background and let people think you're being as fair-minded as they always expected you to be. I'm asking you to slip into the background, and let the others do the fighting."

Brown had heard him out, but his own reply was prompt and hard. "I should like to believe that you don't intend it."

"I do, very sincerely."

"You're asking me to alter my behaviour in a position of trust. I oughtn't to have to tell you that I can't consider it."

Brown was plucking his gown round him, ready to get up from his chair. "And it oughtn't to be necessary for me to tell you, which I will do now, since I don't wish the subject to be raised again, that during the whole course of this unfortunate business, I have not given a second's thought to any possible reactions on the mastership election or on my chances in it."

Brown stood up.

"I'm sorry to leave you a little earlier than I expected, Lewis," he said. With steady steps he walked out of the room.

The interesting thing was, all Brown said was true. He had been manipulating the college for a generation. He was cunning, he knew all ropes, he did not invent dilemmas of conscience for himself. He wanted the mastership, and he would do anything within the rules to get it. But it had to be within the rules: and that was why men trusted him. Those rules were set, not by conscience, but by a code of behaviour—a code of behaviour tempered by robustness and sense, but also surprisingly rigid, surprising, that is, to those who did not know men who were at the same time unidealistic, political, and upright. 'Decent behaviour,' for Brown, meant, among other things, not letting anyone interfere with one's integrity in a judicial process. On the Court of Seniors, he felt in the position of a judge, and so, automatically, without any examination of conscience, he fell into behaving as he thought a judge should behave. At the same time he was following, move by move, the campaign of G. S. Clark to get him votes for the autumn: but when he said that he had not so much as considered how many he would lose or gain by his judge-like stand, it sounded unrealistic for such a realistic man, but it was true.

That was a temptation which did not exist for him. It existed much less for him than for a more high-principled man like Francis Getliffe, who had wavered about Howard when he knew his duty was clear. Brown was under no such temptation; he believed that he had to condemn Howard, and guided by his code, he was not tempted to examine either his own motives or any price he might have to pay.

That was why men trusted him. His cunning, his personal skills, his behaviour, his mixture of good-nature and unbendingness, were all of a piece. As a young man, I believed, he had known unhappiness. He had known what it was like not to be loved; he always had sympathy, which came from a root deeper than good-nature, for those who had got lost in their sexual lives. But all that was long over. As an ageing man, he was utterly, sometimes maddeningly, unshakeably, at one.

Tom watched as the door closed behind Brown, utterly astonished. He could not conceive what he had done. What he had said, seemed to him quite innocent. He was just giving legitimate political advice. It was unimaginable to him that it hit Brown as something like blackmail.

I was thinking—uncomfortably, for I had an affection for Tom and was getting concerned about him—that a subtle man like him would be wiser not to play at politics.

TWENTY-TWO

'UNDER WHICH KING, BEZONIAN?'

Sitting in my room the following afternoon, I found myself with nothing to do. The bargain with the university was made, except for a formality which I could knock off next day: Luke had returned to London: I could stretch myself out on the sofa like an undergraduate, and read a book. I had the luxurious feeling that all time was spread out ahead. Did one feel that as a young man, and if so, did one chafe against it? Was it luxurious now just because it was the contradiction of the official life?

Before I lay down, the head porter had rung up to know if I was in my rooms. It seemed a little odd: I thought it might have to do with Arthur Brown's dinner party that night. At what he called "shamefully short notice", Brown was organising a dinner in his rooms. For whom, and for what, I wasn't told, only that he needed me. It sounded as though he were acting fast, as though he were not glossing over the previous night.

I had not been reading for half an hour when I heard steps, a muttering of steps, outside. A tap on the door, and then the head porter, bowler hat in hand, unctuously calling out my name, and announcing:

"Professor Gay!"

The old man was wrapped in a fur coat, with a silk muffler under his beard and round his neck. On his head he wore a wide-brimmed homburg, such as I had not seen for a generation. The head porter was supporting one arm, an assistant porter the other. Another college servant had been conscripted to follow behind, and so a phalanx of four entered the room.

"Ha, ha, my dear fellow! I've run you to earth, indeed I have!"

There was nothing for it but to get him into an armchair. He progressed in movements a few inches at a time, but neither embarrassed nor, so far as I could see, physically discomforted. His lungs did not seem to be troubling him, his breathing was easy. He dismissed the porters with a jaunty wave. "Stay at your posts, men. We shall require you later. When we have conducted our business. We shall summon you by telephone. That's what we shall do."

When they had gone, he informed me that he was going to continue to wear his hat—"the draughts in these old rooms, one has to be careful of them nowadays."

He looked at me, cheeks blooming, pupils white-rimmed but glance eager.

"Well, this is a surprise and a half for you, I'll be bound!"

It was.

"You can guess what's brought me here, I'll guarantee you can guess that."

I could.

"But you couldn't guess that I should be able to find you, indeed you couldn't. Ha, ha. I have good spies. They keep me *au fait,* my spies do. I know more of what is going on than some people in this college realise. Why, you hadn't been in Cambridge half a day before I had you taped, my dear chap. Had you taped, indeed I had. That was the day before the special meeting of our so-called Court of Seniors. I knew you were here. I said to myself; 'Young Eliot is here. A very promising lawyer, that young man is. He's well spoken of. He's got his name to make. Why, he might be the man for me!' "

He chuckled.

"You don't think I've come here just to make conversation, do you? Oh, no. If you think that, you're vastly mistaken. No, my dear chap, I've come here for a purpose. I've come here for a purpose and a half. I wonder if you have any intimation what the purpose is?"

I had.

"Certain persons thought that I should forget," said Gay. "Not a bit of it. The psychological moment has arrived. I've given them every chance. If they had made amends in their last notification, even if they had mentioned my name, I should have been disposed to let them off. But no, it's no use looking back. Forward! Forward, that's the place to look. So now is the time that I bring my suit against the college."

I was asking about his solicitors, but he interrupted me, his face shining with triumph, guile, and joy.

"Ah, my dear chap, this is where we help each other. This is a case of mutual help, if ever there was one. That's why I sought you out this afternoon. I don't mind telling you, I can do with a good, cool legal head like yours, just to see that we bring all our guns to bear. Fine, cool heads you lawyers have. But I don't intend to take advantage of you, my dear Eliot. Indeed I don't. I've come here with a proposition. If this case goes into court, I shall insist that you act for me. That will be a fine step in your career. Why, it will make your name! This is going to be a case and a half. It's a fine thing for a young man like you, to have his chance in a *cause célèbre*. After all, it isn't every day that a man of some little note in the learned world brings an action against his own college. I said to myself: 'This will be a god-send to young Eliot. It will put his foot right on the ladder. There's no one who deserves to have his foot on the ladder more than young Eliot.' "

Whether he was genuinely under delusions about me, I could not tell. Did he really think that I was still in my twenties? On the envelopes, when he wrote to me, he punctiliously put down style and decoration: had he forgotten what

I was doing now, or was he just pretending? Of one thing I was certain. He was completely set in his monomania, and I did not see how we were going to distract him. He wasn't the first old man I had seen whose monomania kept him very happy. And also—what one had always forgotten in the presence of his preposterous and euphoric vanity—he had throughout his life been more tenacious than most of us. It wasn't for nothing, it wasn't simply because he was enthusiastic and vain, that he had made himself into a great scholar. There had been within him the kind of tenacity that could hold him at the same job for sixty years. It was that tenacity that I had walked into the teeth of now.

I repeated, because I could think of nothing better, what did his solicitors advise?

"Ha ha, ha ha!" said Gay. "It's what you advise that I want to hear."

No, I told him, he couldn't take the first step without his solicitors. He gave me a look sly and meaningful, what my mother would have called "an old-fashioned" look.

"I'll be candid with you, my dear chap, indeed I will. My solicitors are not encouraging me to bring this action, that they're not. They're absolutely discouraging me from any such thing."

"Well," I said, "that makes it very awkward."

"Not a bit of it!" cried Gay. "Why, you young men lose heart at the first fence. Who are these solicitors of mine after all? Just a firm of respectable professional men, in Cambridge. What is Cambridge, after all? Just a small market town in the Fens. I strongly advise you young men to keep a sense of proportion. My dear Eliot, there is a world elsewhere."

That did seem a bit cool, after he had lived in the place for over seventy years.

"If you're not satisfied with them," I said, "I'll gladly give you the names of some firms in London—"

"And who might these be?"

"Oh, they're as good as any in the country."

"I suppose they'll take their time, my dear chap? I suppose they're good old stick-in-the-muds? *I suppose you might tip them the wink that there wasn't any special hurry about old Professor Gay?*"

Gay waved a finger at me, not in the slightest disturbed, but triumphant, full of genial malice and *bonhomie*. "Ah, you see, my dear chap, I know your little game. You're trying to play out time, indeed you are."

I felt the joke was against me. I said:

"Oh, no, I just need to be sure that the case is in good hands. After all, anything that concerns you is rather special. If it were anybody else, we shouldn't take such care—"

"Now I think you're *humouring* me," said Gay, still triumphant. "Don't humour me. That's not the point at all. I want to get down to business. To business, that's where I want to get."

I tried another tack. Professionally, there was no business I could do, I explained. If I were a barrister taking his case, I could only receive instructions through a solicitor—

"Opportunity only knocks once! Remember that!" cried Gay. "I shall soon be absolutely obliged to ask you a question, my dear Eliot. Yes, it's a question and a half. Which side of the fence are you coming down on, young man? I've told you, it's all very well to humour me. That's all very fine and large. But it's not enough, indeed it's not. We've got to make progress. I'm not the one to be content with marking time. So that's why I'm asking you the vital question. 'Under which king, Bezonian?' "

Baffled, I said that he knew he had my sympathy—

"Not good enough, my dear chap. Not good enough for the needs of the moment. Time is not on our side. Indeed it isn't. You see, I've got a little surprise for you. You could absolutely never guess what my little surprise is, could you?"

I had an awkward feeling that I could.

"I'll put you out of suspense. Yes, indeed. It's no use talking to me about solicitors. I've already provided myself with one. A fine solicitor he is. Not the man to let the grass grow under his feet. If I tell him you're our man, you'll get a letter from him before you can say Jack Robinson. So I can't give you long to make up your mind. That's as plain as a pikestaff, isn't it?"

Triumphant, he seemed ready to go.

"This is the time for action," he cried. "Action, that's what I want to see!"

TWENTY-THREE

BARGAINS AT A SMALL DINNER PARTY

Under the chandeliers in Brown's room, eight of us sat at the dinner-table. The names themselves would have had a simple eloquence for anyone inside the affair: Nightingale, Winslow, Clark, and Brown himself, on one side; Getliffe, Martin, me, and yes, though I hadn't expected it, Skeffington, on the other. It meant, and everyone present knew that it meant, some attempt at peace-making, it was a kind of response, almost instinctive and yet at the same time calculated, which any of us had seen before in the college when feeling ran high. Perhaps Brown had a point to score or a bargain to make: that was more likely than not. But also he wanted, unsentimentally but also unquestioningly, out of a desire for comfort as well as piety, to prevent "the place getting unliveable-in," to ensure that it "didn't come apart at the seams."

On the other side, men like Francis Getliffe and Martin wanted the same thing. In bodies like the college, I was thinking, there was usually a core with a strong sense of group self-preservation. That had been true in the struggles I had seen there. Passions had gone from violence to violence, the group emotions were spinning wildly, and yet, from both sides of the quarrel, there had come into existence a kind of gyroscopic fly-wheel which brought the place into stability once more. This was the fiercest quarrel I had seen in the college. It was not accidental that Brown and the others, the bitterest of partisans, were behaving at dinner as though they were not partisans at all.

It was such a dinner as Brown liked to give his friends. Not lavish, but carefully chosen: only Brown could have got the kitchens to produce that meal at twelve hours' notice. There was not, by business men's standards, or writers', much to drink; but what there was was splendid. Brown was a self-indulgent man in a curious sense; he liked drinking often, but only a little, and he liked that little good. That night he brought out a couple of bottles of a '26 claret. Very rare, he said, but drinkable. Winslow made a civil remark as he drank. With most of them, I thought, it was going down uncomprehending crops. No one in the college nowadays, except Brown himself and Tom Orbell, cultivated a taste in wine.

As I ate my devils on horseback and drank the last of the claret, I was wondering whether, if he had not made his démarche to Brown the night before, Tom Orbell might have been at this dinner. True, he was junior to everyone there. But still, he was committed in the Affair, and yet in all other respects was a Brown man. I couldn't help feeling that Brown would have seen good reasons for having him along. Nightingale, Winslow and Skeffington had, so I had heard, attended the first Getliffe caucus; Clark was the only man present pledged to vote for Brown. Seeing them together, seeing how differently, while they were fighting out the Affair, the alignment ran, I couldn't begin to prophesy how many of these allegiances were going to survive intact until the autumn.

While dinner went on, no one mentioned the Howard case. The nearest anyone came to it was myself, for, sitting next to Brown, I gave him a précis of my talk with Gay and said that in my view they had no choice but to placate the old man, and the sooner the safer. Brown asked Winslow if he had heard.

"No, my dear Senior Tutor, I have been sunk in inattention."

Did he realise how often that happened to him now? Was he brazening it out?

"I think we may have to ask you to form a deputation of one and discuss terms with the Senior Fellow."

Winslow roused himself.

"I have done a certain amount of service for this college, most of it quite undistinguished, in a misspent lifetime. But the one service I will not do for this college is expose myself to the conversation of M. H. L. Gay. It was jejune at the best of times. And now that what he was pleased to call his mind appears to have given up the very unequal struggle, I find it bizarre but not rewarding."

There were grins round the table, though not from Skeffington, who throughout the meal had sat stiffly, participating so little that he surrounded himself with an air of condescension. Winslow, encouraged because his tongue had not lost its bite, went on to speculate whether Gay was or was not the most egregious man who had ever been awarded fifteen honorary degrees. "When I was first elected a Fellow, and had quite a disproportionate respect for the merits of my seniors, he was in his early thirties, and I simply thought that he was vain and silly. It was only later, as the verities of life were borne in upon me, that I realised that he was also ignorant and dull."

In an aside, Brown told me that Gay would have to be "handled." "I blame myself," he whispered, while the others laughed at another crack by Winslow, "for having let it slide. After the first time you gave us the hint."

Quietly, his voice conversational, he began talking to the party, when for an instant everyone was quiet. There did seem a need, said Brown, for a little discussion. He was glad to see them all round his table, and he had taken the liberty of asking Lewis Eliot for a reason that he might mention later in the evening. All sensible men were distressed, as he was, by the extent to which this "unfortunate business" had "split the college."

Then Brown, with dignity and without apology, made an appeal. He said that the Court of Seniors had spent months of their time and had now reached the same decision twice. "I needn't point out, and I know I am speaking for my two colleagues among the seniors present to-night, that if we had felt able to modify our decision on Tuesday, we were well aware that we should make personal relations within the college considerably pleasanter for ourselves." But they had felt obliged to reach the same decision, without seeing any way to soften it. They knew that others in the college—including some of their own closest friends—believed that they were wrong: "it's even worse than voting on plans for a new building," said Brown, with the one gibe that he permitted himself, "for dividing brother from brother." But still the decision was made. He didn't expect their critics to change their minds. Nevertheless, wasn't it time, in the interests of the college, for them to accept the decision at least in form? It had been a deplorable incident. No doubt some of the trouble could have been minimized if the Seniors had been more careful of their friends' sensibilities. He felt culpable himself on that score. Nevertheless, it wouldn't have affected the decision; that was made now. In the interests of the college, couldn't they agree to regard the chapter as closed?

Martin and Getliffe, who were sitting side by side, glanced at each other. Before either had spoken, Skeffington broke in. "So far as I'm concerned, Senior Tutor, that's just not on."

Brown pursed his lips and gazed at Skeffington with sharp eyes.

"I hoped," he said, "that you would consider what I've just said."

"It doesn't touch the issue," said Skeffington.

"I'm afraid," said Getliffe, "that several of us can't let it go at this stage."

"No, that's not acceptable, Arthur," Martin put in. "We didn't want to, but we've got to take it further."

That meant, since he and Brown understood each other and spoke the same language, an appeal to the Visitor. Brown was considering, but again Skeffington was quick off the mark.

"You know, Martin, that's no good for me." He turned to Brown with arrogant awkwardness. "I spoke out of turn last night. I'm sorry. I oughtn't to have hit the ceiling with a senior. That was a bad show. But I stick to every word I said. If there's only one way to get this poor chap a square deal, then I've got no option."

Brown did not hesitate any more. In a round, deliberate tone, as though he were dealing with a commonplace situation, he said, addressing himself to Martin and Getliffe: "Well, I can see that you haven't lost your misgivings. In that case, I have a proposition to make which might ease your minds. Put it another way: it might show you that we on the Court of Seniors realise that you still have grave doubts on your consciences."

There was no question that Arthur Brown had come equipped. If the first offer failed, as he expected it to, then he had the second ready. There was no doubt also why he was doing it, and why in the last few hours he had worked so fast. It wasn't because Francis and Martin stayed inflexible. Brown addressed his offer to them, but really all the time it was to Skeffington that he was speaking. Skeffington's threat had forced him, even while he thought it was an outrage.

To bring the college into the public light, to "get it into the papers," was to Brown inadmissible and inexcusable. For Skeffington to threaten him, took him out of the area of responsible men. From now on, Skeffington could not be trusted in college affairs, nor could his opinion carry any weight. And yet, it was he who had broken through.

The curious thing was, Brown and Martin and all good performers in closed politics often exaggerated the importance of the shrewd, the astute, the men who knew the correct moves. At least as often as not, in a group like the college, the shrewd moves cancelled each other out and the only way to win was through the inadmissible and the inexcusable.

Brown's offer was conciliatory and well-prepared. He said that he made it after consulting the other seniors. Nightingale nodded his head, but Winslow was sleepy after dinner in the warm room. The proposal in essence was that the Seniors volunteered of their own free will and without pressure from the college to have a third and final enquiry. But, Brown said, it was pointless their doing this without some difference in procedure. Therefore the Seniors proposed, again of their own free will, one minor and one major change. The minor change was that, under the Statutes, they had the power to co-opt other members: their suggestion was that they should ask Paul Jago to serve. If he had been willing in the first instance, he would have been one of the Court all through. "Some of us know him well, though he's rather dropped out of things in late years," said Brown, who used to be his closest friend. "We feel that he would bring a fresh mind to our problems. And I don't think that his worst enemies would ever have said that he was lacking in human sympathy and kindness."

"I'm sorry to say," G. S. Clark remarked, "that I've hardly spoken to him."

"Oh, in the old days, G. S., he'd have done a lot for you," said Brown, quick to meet the unspoken opposition.

"Could you give us a little information about him?"

"What do you want me to tell you? I think Lewis will agree, he was always very good about anyone in trouble—"

That was why I wanted him on the Court. He had more human resources than most men. But it did not satisfy Clark, who looked so sensible, so reasonable, so sweet-eyed, the knuckles of his bad hand purple-raw on the table, that I felt half-hypnotised and at a loss.

"Has he any strong attachments?" Clark persisted.

"I should have said, he had strong personal attachments, if that's what you mean—"

It wasn't.

"I meant rather, is he attached to causes?"

"I shouldn't have thought so," Brown replied.

"Well, then, is he a religious man?"

"No, I couldn't say that. His father was in Orders, he was a Fellow of Trinity, Dublin, but I always imagined Paul reacted against Papa pretty early on."

Clark was looking troubled. Brown added, with the cheerful laugh of one man of sane opinions talking of another, "Of course, Paul has always been a sound Conservative. In fact, he sometimes went a bit further in the right direction than I was able to follow him. You know what these old Protestant Irish families are like."

Clark had broken into a beautiful, acceptant smile. Now at last I had it. He had been suspicious in case Jago happened to be a man of progressive views. Paranoia didn't only exist on one side, I was thinking. Clark was ready to detect the sinister whenever he heard a radical word. And that air had blown round the college, more than Francis or Martin thought, living in it, right through the course of the Affair. Even at this table, most of them felt a kind of group-content and group-safety, as they heard of a sound Conservative. Certainly Skeffington, the "trouble-maker."

Paranoia wasn't all on one side: and then by free association, the thought of Howard, staring blank-eyed, deluded with persecution mania, asking who could have removed the photograph, flickered through my mind.

It was agreed to ask Jago.

The second change—"and this," said Brown, "is why I took it upon myself to bring Lewis Eliot into our exchange of views," came as a surprise. It was that the Court should have two lawyers in attendance, "one, to look after the interests of Howard, and the other, if I may say so, to give some help to the Seniors themselves."

For the first, Brown said, at his most cordial and benign, he hoped that they might obtain "the good offices of our old friend here"—he beamed at me. He knew that Lewis hadn't practised law for a long time, but this wasn't a formal trial. He felt sure that Francis Getliffe and Martin and the others would rest quieter if they knew that Lewis was there to give Howard guidance. As for the other lawyer, it meant letting someone else into the secret, but they had in mind "a distinguished member of the college, known to the older people here, and someone who wouldn't be overweighted by Lewis, which I think we should all feel that the circumstances required."

Brown finished by saying to Francis and Martin that he made the offer with the full authority of the Master. Just for an instant, he sounded like a shogun speaking formally of the Kyoto Emperor. The Seniors realised they couldn't make much claim on the lawyers' time; they believed that the entire re-hearing could be compressed into a few days.

Francis Getliffe was asking me if I could manage it. Running through my pocket-book, I said that I hadn't three consecutive week days free until the end of June.

"That's all right," said Martin. "So you'll do it, will you?"

"If you can wait that long—"

"Good." Martin spoke suddenly, freshly, and with enthusiasm. For a second, across the dinner-table, we had gone back over the years. He was no longer the hard and independent man more capable in so many ways than I was myself. He was a younger brother speaking to an older, investing in me, as when he was a child, greater faith than I deserved.

This would mean another two months' wasting time, Skeffington burst out.

"I'm sure we all regret that," said Brown, steady but not cordial. "But I hope we should all agree that it would be a mistake to spoil the ship for a ha'p'orth of tar."

"I don't know that I can take it."

"You've got to take it," Francis Getliffe said. "Brown has gone a long way to meet us. It's a fair offer, and we've got to make it work." Francis said it with authority. Skeffington acquiesced with meekness because, as well as having an overweening sense of his duty, he had also a capacity for respect. He had a simple respect for eminence: to him, Francis was near the peak of eminence, and he both listened to him and was a little afraid of him.

Suddenly, however, Skeffington drew support from someone who had little respect for eminence and was afraid of no one. G. S. Clark, with his gentle, petulant smile, broke in: "I must say, with due respect, I've got a lot of sympathy for Julian's view. I couldn't disagree with him more over the merits of this case, but heaven's above, I think he's right to push on with it."

"No," said Nightingale, "we've got to get the right answer."

"You're preaching to the converted," Clark replied. "I'm sure we've already got the right answer, and we're going to get it again."

"We'll see what happens," Nightingale answered, with a smile open and confident.

"I'm sorry, I still support Julian on the time-table," said Clark. "I don't feel like accepting delay."

"Then you'd better feel like it. Because that's the way it's going to be."

Nightingale said it amiably enough, and, like Francis, with authority—though Francis's came from himself and Nightingale's from his office.

"The general opinion does appear to be against you, G.S.," said Brown. Winslow roused himself and muttered, "Hear, hear."

Clark smiled across Winslow at Skeffington.

"We seem to be in a minority of two. If it were a meeting, we could have our names written in the minutes."

There was a curious accord between them. They stood at the two extremes, both utterly recalcitrant. As often with extremists, they felt linked. They had a kinship, much more than with their own sides, the safe and sensible people in the middle.

Well then, said Brown, we were agreed. He was just putting a last question, when I slipped in one of my own. I had been thinking over to myself the chance of having Jago on the Court. Would Brown mind if I took a hand in persuading him to act? Brown, anxious to concede us any inessential point, agreed at once and went on with his question.

"I should like to ask everyone round the table, presuming that the Seniors reach a decision according to the methods we've agreed on to-night, whether they could see their way to pledge themselves to regard that as the finish. I'm not asking anyone to answer here and now. I expect you'll want to sleep on it. But I suggest to you that it wouldn't be unreasonable, if we're to get this place back on an even keel."

"Content," said Winslow, suddenly revivified.

"I am very happy," said Nightingale.

"I'm not fond of hypothetical pledges," said Francis, "but, yes, I think it's reasonable."

"I agree, this must be all or nothing," said Martin.

Brown looked at Clark.

"What is your present feeling, G.S.?"

"Oh, it's bound to turn out right," said Clark.

"And you?" Brown said to Skeffington.

"I shall try to accept what the Seniors decide," Skeffington replied, after a long pause, his head high, staring at the wall. "But I'm not making any promises to-night. And I don't see how I shall ever be able to."

TWENTY-FOUR

HERMITAGE

Next morning, the clock on the Catholic church was striking eleven as I walked along by Fenner's to the Jagos' house. The trees were dense with blossom; the smell of blossom weighed down the air, the sky was heavy. I was coming unannounced, and I had no idea what reception I should get. All I knew was that Brown, wishing to clinch the bargain of the night before, had seen to it that the Master sent a letter to Jago by messenger.

In the dark morning, the petals shone luminescent, the red brick houses glowed. Jago's was at the corner of a side street. I had not been there before, as, when I knew him, they had been living in the Tutor's residence: but he had owned this house for forty years, since the time when, as a young don, he had married one of his pupils. They had lived there in the first years of the marriage, and when he retired they had gone back. It was ugly and cosy from the outside, late nineteenth century decorated, with attic gables, and, through a patch of garden, a crazy pavement leading to the front door.

After I rang, the door was opened by Mrs. Jago. She stood there massive, pallid, and anxious. She looked at me as though she did not know whether to recognise me or not.

"Good-morning, Alice," I said.

At her stateliest, she replied in form.

I said that I was sorry to appear without warning, but could I have a quarter of an hour with Paul?

"I'm afraid my husband is much too busy to see visitors," she said.

I said: "It is fairly important—"

"On matters of business, I'm afraid my husband has nothing to say to anyone."

"I should like you to tell him that I'm here."

Once she had disliked me less than she had disliked most of Paul's colleagues. She stared at me. I did not know whether I should get the door slammed in my face.

"Please be good enough to come in," she said.

Preceding me down a passage, she was apologising for the state of the house—"not fit for *visitors,*" she cried. In fact, it was burnished and spotless, and had a delicious smell. That, too, she had worked at, for it came from bowls of pot-pourri chosen to complement the smell of wood-fires. For anyone with a sharp nose, it was the most welcoming of houses. Not in other respects, however. When Alice Jago opened the study door and cried out that I had come to see him, Jago's voice did not express pleasure.

"This is unexpected," he said to me.

"I shan't take much of your time."

As he stood up to shake hands, he was watching me with eyes shrewd and restless, in the fleshy face.

"Perhaps I have an idea what brings you here," he said.

"Perhaps you have," I replied.

"Ah well, sit you down," said Jago. His natural kindness was fighting against irritability. He might have been a man essentially careless and good-natured, intolerably pressed by his job, not knowing what it was to have five minutes free, driven mad by the latest distraction.

The study could not have been more peaceful. Out of the french windows one saw the garden, with blossoming trees spreadeagled against the wall. The room was as light, as bright, as washed free from anxiety, as though it looked out to sea. They used it together. There was one chair and table and rack of books for him, the same for her, and another rack between them. Jago saw me examining the third rack. Realising that I was puzzled, quick to catch a feeling, he said:

"Ah, those are the books we're reading to each other just

now. That was a good custom your generation didn't keep up, wasn't it?"

He was saying that one of them read to the other for an hour each evening, taking it in turns. That winter they had been "going through" Mrs. Gaskell. It all seemed serene. Perhaps, in spite of her neurosis, his pride, the damage she had done him and the sacrifice he had made for her, they truly were at peace together, more than most couples in retirement, provided that they were left alone.

I was not leaving them alone. Mrs. Jago gazed at me, uncertain how to guard him, protect herself. With her most lofty impersonation of a *grande dame,* she said:

"May I offer you a cup of coffee?"

I said that I would love one.

"It will be cold, needless to say."

It was not cold. It was excellent. As I praised it, Alice Jago said with rancour:

"When I was obliged to entertain because of Paul's position, no one ever wanted to come to see *me*. So naturally I had to give them decent food."

"Darling," said Jago, "that's all past history."

"I expect," said Alice Jago to me, "that now you've had your coffee you'd like to talk to Paul alone."

"I hope he doesn't expect so," said Jago. He had not sat down again, and now he moved, on soft slippers, towards her.

"I think he'll appreciate that I don't see anyone alone nowadays. Anything he wants to say, I'm sure he'll be ready to say to us together."

"Of course," I said. To myself, I was wishing it wasn't so. While I was thinking about it again, I noticed the books on their two reading-racks. As with others who had waited a lifetime "to catch up with their reading," Jago's didn't appear very serious. There were half a dozen detective stories, a few of the minor late nineteenth century novels, and a biography. On Mrs. Jago's rack stood the Archer translations of Ibsen, together with a Norwegian edition and dictionary: it looked as though she were trying to slog through the originals. She used to be known in the college as "that impossible woman." She could still put one's teeth on edge. But it was she who had the intellectual interest and the tougher taste.

"I suppose," I said, "you did receive a letter from Crawford this morning?"

"Yes," Jago replied, "I received a letter from the Master."

"Have you answered it?"

"Not yet."

"I hope you won't," I said, "until you've listened to me."

"Of course I'll listen to you, Lewis," said Jago. "You were always a very interesting talker, especially when the old Adam got the better of you and you didn't feel obliged to prove that there wasn't any malice in you at all, at all!" His eyes were sparkling with empathy, with his own kind of malice. He had scored a point, and I grinned. He went on:

"But I oughtn't to conceal from you that I don't feel inclined to accept the Master's kind invitation."

"Don't make up your mind yet."

"I'm very much afraid it is made up," said Jago.

Mrs. Jago was sitting in the chair next to mine, both of us looking out to the garden as to the sea. He was sitting on her chair arm, with his hand on hers.

"I don't feel inclined," he said, "to get involved in college affairs again. I can't believe it's good for them, and it certainly isn't good for us."

"I'm asking you to make one exception."

"When I was looking forward to retiring," he replied, "I thought to myself that I would make just one exception. That is, I should have to drag myself away from here and set foot in the college once more. But not for this sort of reason, my dear Lewis."

"What was it, then?"

"Oh, I think I shall have to cast my vote when they elect the next Master. This autumn. It would be misunderstood if I didn't do that."

"Yes," said Alice Jago. "It's a pity, but you must do that."

At first hearing it seemed strange. The last time those votes had been cast—that was the wound, which, except perhaps in this room, the two of them had not been able to get healed. And yet, it was the sort of strangeness one could, at least viscerally, understand. I had heard more than once that he was committed to vote, not for his old friend Arthur Brown, but for Getliffe—as though choosing the kind of distinction which he didn't possess and which had been thrown up against him. I thought of asking, and then let that pass.

"Look," I said, "this is a human situation." I told him, flat out, why I wanted him on the Court of Seniors. He was much too shrewd and perceptive a man to dissimulate with. I said that I believed Howard was innocent. Jago might not agree when he heard the complete story and studied the evidence—all his prejudices, I said, for I too knew how to dig in the knife of intimacy, would be against Howard. Nevertheless, Jago had more insight than any of them. I wanted to take the chance. If he happened to decide for Howard, that would make it easier for the others to change their minds than anything I could say.

"I don't see what claim you have on me," said Jago. "It would be different if I knew anything about this man already."

"Don't you feel some responsibility?"

"Why should I feel responsibility for a man I don't know and a college I've had no control over for seventeen years?"

"Because you have more sympathy than most people."

"I might have thought so once," he replied simply and gravely, "but now I doubt it."

"You like people."

"I used to think so," said Jago, in the same unaffected tone, "but now I believe that I was wrong." He added, as though he were speaking out of new self-knowledge and as though I deserved the explanation:

"I was very much affected by people. That is true. I suppose I responded to them more than most men do. And of course that cuts both ways. It means that they responded to one. But, looking back, I seriously doubt whether I genuinely liked many. I believe that, in any sense which means a human bond, the people I've liked you could count on the fingers of one hand. I've missed no one, no one now living in this world, since we thought we hadn't enough time left to waste, and so spent it all with each other." He was speaking to his wife. It sounded like flattery, like the kind of extravagant compliment he used to give her to bring a touch of confidence back. I believed that it was sincere.

"Haven't you found," he turned to me again, in a tone lighter but still reflective, "that it's those who are very much affected by people who really want to make hermits of themselves? I don't think they need people. I certainly didn't, except for my own family and my wife. I've got an idea that those who respond as I responded finally get tired of all human relations but the deepest. So at the end of their lives, the only people they really want to see are those they have known their whole lives long."

He glanced at me, his eyes candid, amused and searching.

"If your man has had the atrocious bad luck you think he has, I'm sure you'll persuade them, Lewis. But, as far as I'm concerned, I think you can see, can't you?—it would have to be something different to make me stir."

It was no use arguing. I said good-bye almost without another word. I thanked Alice Jago for putting up with me.

"Not at all," she said, with overwhelming grandeur.

I went out into the street, the blossom dazzling under the leaden cloud-cap. I felt frustrated, no, I felt more than that: I felt sheer loneliness. I wasn't thinking of the Affair: it would mean working out another technique, but there was time for that. Under the trees, the sweet smell all round me, I couldn't stay detached, and reflect with interest on the Jagos. I just felt the loneliness.

IV

SUSPICION IN THE OPEN

TWENTY-FIVE

ADDRESS FROM THE MODERATOR

In the Fellows' Garden, the tea-roses, the white roses, the great pink cabbage-roses glowed like illuminations in the heavy light. The garden, when I entered it that afternoon, had looked like a steel-engraving in a Victorian magazine, the sky so boding, the roses bulbous. A week earlier, there would have been young men lying on the grass, staying in college to receive their degrees: but this was the last Friday in June, and as I strolled by the rose bushes, scuffing petals over the turf, the garden was dead quiet, except for the humming by the bee-hives.

It was a cold day for midsummer, so cold that I could have done with a coat. I had seen no one since I arrived in Cambridge that lunch-time. In fact, I had taken care to see no one. This was my last chance to get my thoughts in order before tomorrow, the first day of the Seniors' hearing.

The college clock struck four. The time had gone faster than I wanted, the garden had a chilly, treacherous, roseladen peace. It was irksome to be obliged to leave: but there had been an invitation waiting for me in the guest-room, asking me to tea with the Master to meet my "opposite number," Dawson-Hill.

As I walked through the college, it seemed deserted, and I could hear my own footsteps, metallic on the flag-stones. The only signs of life in the second court were a couple of lights (Winslow's for one) in the palladian building. Once past the screens, though, and the first court was as welcoming as on a February afternoon, with windows lighted in the Bursary, in Brown's set, Martin's, the drawing-room and study in the Lodge. As I let myself into the Lodge and went upstairs, I could hear Crawford's laugh, cheerful, pawky, and quite relaxed.

In the study, Dawson-Hill was in the middle of an anecdote. Crawford was contentedly chuckling as I came in: At once Dawson-Hill, slender and active as a young man, though he was a year my senior, was on his feet shaking my hand.

"My dear Lewis! How extremely nice to see you!"

He spoke as though he knew me very well. It was not precisely true, though we had been acquaintances on and off since we were pupils in the same Inn over twenty-five years before.

Looking at him, one found it hard to believe that he was fifty. He stood upright in his elegant blue suit, and with his Brigade tie discreetly shining he might have been an ensign paying a good-humoured, patronising visit to his old tutor. His face was smooth, as though it had been carved out of soapstone; his hair, sleekly immaculate, had neither thinned nor greyed. His eyes were watchful and amused. In repose, the corners of his mouth were drawn down in an expression—similar to that of someone who, out of curiosity, has volunteered to go on to the stage to assist in a conjuring trick—surprised, superior, and acquiescently amiable.

He said:

"I was just telling the Master about last week-end at—." He mentioned the name of a ducal house. Crawford chuckled. He might be an old-fashioned Edwardian liberal, but he wasn't above being soothed by a breath from the high life. The ostensible point of the story was the familiar English one, dear to the established upper-middle classes—the extreme physical discomfort of the grand. The real point was that Dawson-Hill had been there. Crawford chuckled again; he approved of Dawson-Hill for being there.

"*She* is rather sweet, though, isn't she, Lewis?" Dawson-Hill went on, appealing to me as though I knew them as well as he did. He wasn't greedy or exclusive about his social triumphs. He was ready to believe that nowadays I had them too. His own were genuine enough; he had been having them since he was a boy. He never boasted, he just knew the smart world, more so than any professional man I had met: and the smart world had taken him unto themselves. Why, I had sometimes wondered? He had been born reasonably luckily, but not excessively so. His father was a modest country gentleman who had spent a little time in the army, but not in the kind of regiment Dawson-Hill found appropriate for himself in the war. Dawson-Hill had been to Eton; he had become a modestly successful barrister. He had agreeable manners, but they were not at first sight the manners one would expect to make for social triumphs. He was no man-pleaser, and he wasn't over-given to respect. His humour was tart, sarcastic, and as his hosts must have known by now, not what they would describe as "loyal." And yet—to an extent different in order from that of any of the tycoons I knew, or the bureaucrats, or the grey eminences, the real bosses of the establishment, or even of the genuine aristocrats—he was acceptable everywhere and had become smart in his own right.

That must have been the reason, I thought, why, when Crawford and Brown were, out of the college's three or four Q. C's., choosing one to advise them at the Court of Seniors, they had picked on him. At one time Herbert Getliffe, Francis's half-brother, would have been the automatic choice: but Brown was too shrewd not to have smelled the air of failure, not to have suspected, as I had heard Brown say, that "the unfortunate chap does seem to be going down the hill." Nevertheless, the college, usually pretty good judges of professional success, had overestimated Dawson-Hill's—not very much, but still perceptibly. He was a competent silk, but not better. He was earning, so my old legal friends told me, about

£9000 a year at the Common Law bar, and they thought he'd gone as far as he was likely to. He was clever enough to have done more, but he seemed to have lacked the final reserve of energy, or ambition, or perhaps weight. Or conceivably, just as the college was dazzled by his social life, so too was he.

"Well," said Crawford, loath to say good-bye to high life, "I suppose we ought to have a few words about this wretched business." He began asking whether we had been supplied with all the "data."

"I must say," said Dawson-Hill, suddenly alert, "it isn't like being briefed by a solicitor, Master. But I think I've got enough to go on with, thank you."

"I fancy our friend Eliot, who has been in on the ground floor, so to speak, has the advantage of you there."

"That's the luck of the draw." Dawson-Hill gave a polite, arrogant smile.

"About procedure, now," said Crawford, "you'll appreciate that this isn't a court of law. You'll have to be patient with us. As for your own procedure," he went on massively, "we were hoping that you'd be able to agree at least in principle between yourselves."

"We've had some talk on the telephone," said Dawson-Hill.

I said that we proposed to spend the evening after Hall working out a *modus operandi.*

Crawford nodded, Buddha-like. "Good business," he said. He went on to ask if he was correctly informed that Wednesday night, June 30th, five days hence, was the latest Dawson-Hill could spend in Cambridge. If that was so, we had already been told, had we not, that the Court was willing to sit on all the days between, including Sunday? We had already received the names of the Fellows who wished to appear before the Court? We both said yes.

"Well, then," said Crawford, "my last word is for your ear particularly, Eliot. My colleagues and I have given much thought to the position." He was speaking carefully, as though he had been coached time and time again by Arthur Brown. "We feel that, in the circumstances of this hearing, the onus is on you, representing those not satisfied with the Seniors' previous and reiterated decision, to convince the Court. That is, we feel it is necessary for you to persuade a majority of the Court to reverse or modify that decision. There are, as you know, four members, and if we can't reach unanimity I shall be compelled to take a vote. I have to tell you that, according to precedents in the Court of Seniors, which as far as we can trace has only met three times this century, the Master does not possess a casting-vote. Speaking not as Master but as an outside person, I'm not prepared to consider that that precedent is a wise one. But those are the conditions which we have to ask you to accept."

All this I knew. The college had been seething for weeks. Minute-books, diaries of a nineteenth century Master, had been taken out of the archives. I contented myself by saying: "Of course I have to accept them. But it doesn't make it easy."

"The only comfort is," said Crawford, "that, whatever rules one has, sensible men usually reach a sensible conclusion."

Dawson-Hill caught my eye. He was deeply conservative, snobbish, perfectly content to accept the world he lived in: but I thought his expression was just a shade more like a conjuror's assistant, just a shade more surprised.

"And now," Crawford shrugged off the business and Arthur Brown's coaching, and became his impersonal, courteous self, "I should like to say, speaking as Master, that the entire college is indebted to you two for giving us your time and energy. We know that we're asking a good deal of you without any return at all. I should like to thank you very much."

"My dear Master," said Dawson-Hill.

"I wish," said Crawford, still with imperturbable dignity, "that the next stage in the proceedings were not an extra tax on your good nature. But, as I expect you know, we have to reckon with a certain amount of *personalia* in these institutions. In any case, I think you have had due notice?"

Yes, we had had due notice. I felt irritably—for I was anxious enough about next day to have lost my taste for farce—that it was something we could have been spared. The college had had to buy old Gay off. The way they had found, the only way to placate him and prevent him from insisting upon his place on the Court, was to resurrect the eighteenth century office of Moderator. This was an office I had never heard of, but the antiquaries had got busy. Apparently, in days when the Fellows had been chronically litigious, one of the Seniors had been appointed to keep the ring. So solemnly, in full college meeting, M. H. L. Gay, Senior Fellow, had been elected "Moderator in the present proceedings before the Court of Seniors"—and that evening after tea, Crawford, Winslow and Nightingale in one taxi, Brown, Dawson-Hill and I in another, were travelling up the Madingley Road to Gay's to be instructed in our duties.

I said that this must be one of the more remarkable jaunts on record. Brown gave a pursed smile. He was not amused. Not that he was anxious: in times of trouble he slowed himself down, so that he became under the surface tougher and more difficult to shift. No, he was not anxious. But he was also not viewing the proceedings with irony. For Brown, when one was going on a formal occasion, even on a formal occasion he had himself invented, the ceremonies had to be properly performed.

We filed, Crawford leading us, into the old man's study. Gay was sitting in his armchair, beard trimmed, shawl over his shoulders. He greeted us in a ringing voice.

"Good-afternoon, gentleman! Pray forgive me if I don't rise for the present. I need to husband my energies a little nowadays, indeed I do." Then he said disconcertingly to Crawford; "Tell me, my dear chap, what is your name?"

Just for a moment Crawford was at a loss. His mouth

opened, the impassive moon of his face was clouded. He replied:

"I am Thomas Crawford, Master of the College."

"I absolutely remember. I congratulate you, my dear chap," said Gay, with panache. "And what is more, I absolutely remember why you have attended on me here this very evening."

He had not asked us to sit down. The room was dark. Out of the window, one saw, under the platinum sky, more roses. That day the town seemed to be full of them.

"I trust you had a comfortable journey out here, gentlemen?"

"Where from?" Crawford replied; he was still off his stroke.

"Why, from the college, to be sure." Gay gave a loud triumphant laugh. Someone said that it was a cold afternoon and an awful summer.

"Nonsense, my dear chap. Bad summer? You young men don't know what a bad summer is. Indeed you don't. Now, '88, that was a bad summer if ever there was one. Why, I was in Iceland that summer. I was just getting into the swim of what some critics have been kind enough to call my great work on the Sagas. Great work—ah, indeed. Mind you, I've always disclaimed the word 'great.' I've always said, Call the work distinguished if you like, but it's not for me to approve of the higher appellation. Certainly not. I was telling you, gentlemen, that I was in Iceland, that bitter summer of 1888. And do you know what I found when I got there? None of you will guess, I'll be bound. Why, they were having the best summer for a generation. It was fifteen degrees warmer than in our unfortunate Cambridge. Iceland—that country was very poor in those days. They were living hard lives, those poor people, like my Saga-men. Do you know, that year they managed to grow some fresh vegetables? And for those poor people that was a luxury and a half. I remember sitting down to a meal with a dish of cabbage, I can taste it now, and I told myself, 'Gay, my boy, this country is welcoming you. This country is giving you all it can.' I'm not ashamed to say it seemed like an omen for my future work. And we should all agree that that was an omen which pointed true."

We were still standing up. Crawford coughed and said:

"Perhaps I ought to introduce my colleagues to you—?"

"Quite unnecessary, my dear chap. Just because one has a slip of memory with your face, it doesn't mean that one forgets others. Indeed it doesn't. Welcome to you all."

He waved magnanimously to Brown, Winslow and Nightingale, who were standing together on Crawford's left. None of us was certain whether he really knew who they were. "In any case," Crawford started again, "I expect you don't remember our legal advisers here. May I present—?"

"Quite unnecessary once more. This is Eliot, who was a Fellow of the College from 1934 until 1945, although he went out of residence during the war and then and subsequently did service to the State which has been publicly recognised. He has also written distinguished books. Distinguished, yes; I never protested about people calling my own work that. It was when they insisted on saying 'great' that I felt obliged to draw in my horns. And this must be Dawson-Hill, whom I don't recall having had the pleasure of meeting, but who was a scholar of the college from 1925 to 1928, took silk in 1939, became a major in the Welsh Guards in 1943, and is a member of the Athenaeum, the Carlton, White's and Pratt's."

The old man beamed, looking proud of himself.

"You see, I've done my homework, my dear—?" he looked at Crawford with a smile, unabashed. "I do apologise, but your name obstinately escapes me."

"Crawford."

"Ah, yes. Our present Master. Master, I'd better call you. I've done my homework, you see—Master. *Who's Who,* that's a fine book. That's a book and a half. My only criticism is that perhaps it could be more selective. Then some of us would feel at liberty to include slightly fuller particulars of ourselves."

He turned in the direction of Dawson-Hill. "I apologise for not welcoming you before."

Dawson-Hill, who, unlike Crawford was quite at ease, went up and shook hands.

"I attended a lecture of yours once, Professor Gay," he said.

"I congratulate you," said Gay.

"It was a bit above my head," said Dawson-Hill, with a mixture of deference and cheek.

Gay was disposed to track down which specific lecture it had been, but Winslow, who had managed to support himself by leaning on a chair, enquired: "I confess I'm not quite clear about the purpose of this conference—"

"You're not quite clear, my dear chap? But I am. Indeed I am. But thank you for reminding me of my office. Yes, indeed. I must think about my responsibilities and the task in front of you all. Ah, we must look to the immediate future. That's the place to look."

"Do you wish us to sit round the table?" Brown asked.

"No, I think not. I shall very shortly be addressing you about your mission. I shall be giving you your marching orders. That is a solemn occasion, and I shall make every effort to stand up for my work. Yes, I want to impress on you the gravity of the task you are engaged in." He moved his head slowly from left to right, surveying us with satisfaction. "I remember absolutely the nature of my office and its responsibilities. I remember absolutely the circumstances that have brought you to me this evening. Meanwhile, I've been refreshing myself by the aid of some notes." From the side of his chair he pulled out a handful of sheets of paper, held them at arm's length, catching some light from the window, and studied them through a large magnifying glass. This took some time.

He announced: "To what I have to say in the preliminary

stages, I must request Eliot and Dawson-Hill to pay special attention. I should like to call them our Assessors. Assessors. That's a term and a half. But I find no warrant for the term. However. The Court of Seniors, as I hope you have been informed—it would be gross remissness on someone's part if you have not been so informed—has recently decided upon the deprivation of a Fellow. That decision hasn't been received with confidence by a number of Fellows. Whether they would have had more confidence if the Court of Seniors, as by right it should, had had an older head among them—it's not for me to say a wiser one—whether in those altered circumstances the Fellows would have had more confidence, why, again, it's not for me to say. This isn't the time to cry over spilt milk." Viewing his papers through the magnifying glass, he gave us a history of what had happened. It was a surprisingly competent history for a man his age, but again it took some time.

At last he said to Dawson-Hill and me: "That's as much counsel as I'm able to give you. The details of this regrettable incident—why, that's the task you've got to put your minds to. It's a task and a half, I can tell you. Now I propose to give you all my parting words."

He gripped the arms of his chair and tried to struggle to his feet.

"No, come, you needn't stand," said Brown.

"Certainly I shall stand. I am capable of carrying out my office as I decide it should be carried out. Indeed I am. Will you give me an arm, Eliot? Will you give me an arm, Dawson-Hill?"

With some effort we got him to his feet.

"That's better," cried Gay. "That's much better. Pray listen to me. This is the last chance I shall have of addressing you before your decision. As Moderator in this case of a deprived Fellow, being re-examined before the Court of Seniors, I give you my last words. To the Court of Seniors I have to say: This is a grave decision. Go now and do justice. If you can temper justice with mercy, do so. But go and do justice."

He stopped for a breath, and went on turning to Dawson-Hill and me: "To these gentlemen, members of the College, experienced in the law, I have to say this. See that justice is done. Be bold. Let no man's feelings stand in your way. Justice is more important than any man's feelings. Speak your minds, and see that justice is done."

Then he called to us, and we helped him back into his chair.

"Now I wish you all success in your tasks. And I wish you good-bye."

He whispered to us, as the others began to leave the study: "Was that well done?"

"Very well done," I said.

Dawson-Hill and I had followed the others and were almost out of the room, when the old man called us all back.

"Ah! I had forgotten something essential. Indeed I had. I must insist on your all hearing it. This is positively my last instruction." He looked at one of his pages of notes. "You intend to reach a decision on or before Wednesday next, am I right?"

"That's what we hope. But, speaking as Master, I can't guarantee it," said Crawford.

"Well spoken," said Gay. "That's a very proper caution. That's what I like to hear. In any case, the time's of no consequence. There will come a time when, I hope and pray, you'll be able to reach your decision. Stick to it, all of you, and you'll get there in the end. This is where my instruction comes in. I wish to be informed, before there is any question of your decision taking effect. As Moderator, I must be the first person to receive your decision. I do not feel inclined to insist on the whole Court of Seniors making this journey to my house again. It will meet my requirements if these gentlemen, Eliot and Dawson-Hill, are sent to me with the findings of the Court. Is that agreed?"

"Is that all right with you two?" Brown said under his breath.

"Agreed," said Dawson-Hill. I said yes.

"Our two colleagues have undertaken to do that," said Crawford.

"I shall be waiting for them day or night." Gay cried with triumph. "That is my last instruction."

As we went out, he was repeating himself, and we could hear him until we were out on the step. All this time the taxis had been waiting. When Brown got into ours, he peered at the meter and whistled through his teeth.

That was the only comment Brown allowed himself. Otherwise, while the taxi jingled back over the bridge, he did not refer to the next day, or the reason why the three of us were bundled incongruously together, driving through the Cambridge streets. He just domesticated this situation as he had done others before it. He enquired roundly, affably, prosily, about my family as though there was nothing between us. With banal thoroughness he asked if I or Dawson-Hill would find the time to see any of the university match: he speculated about the merits of the teams. It was all as flat and cosy as a man could reasonably manage. I wondered if Dawson-Hill saw through, or beneath, the cushioned prosiness of Brown.

There was nothing flat or cosy about dinner in the Combination Room that night. There were eight Fellows dining besides Dawson-Hill and me. Those eight were split symmetrically, four for Howard, and four against. The sight of Dawson-Hill and me seemed to catalyse the clash of tempers. A harmless question by Tom Orbell—how many nights would they be dining in the Combination Room before they went "back into Hall"—brought a snub from Winslow. G. S. Clark was asking Skeffington, politely but with contempt—"How can you possibly believe that? If you do, I suppose you're right to say so." This was not over anything to do with the Affair, but upon a matter of church government.

Someone made a reference to our visit. Winslow, who was presiding, said:

"Yes, I must say that this is a very remarkable occasion. But I suppose we oughtn't to ventilate our opinions while this business is what I believe, in the singular language of our guests' profession, is called *sub judice*."

"It's all one to me," said Dawson-Hill nonchalantly, "and I'm sure I can speak for Lewis."

"No, I suggest we'd better restrain ourselves for the time being," said Winslow. "Which, since I am credibly informed that some of our number are not now on speaking terms, may not be so difficult as might appear."

The air was crackling. Dawson-Hill set himself to make the party go, but instead of getting less, the tension grew. At the end of the meal, I told Winslow that he would have to excuse the two of us, since we wanted to discuss the procedure. He seemed glad to see us go. As we left the Combination Room, I noticed that Winslow was lighting his pipe, and Skeffington reading a newspaper. No one was willing to sit round to talk and drink wine.

TWENTY-SIX

DEFINITIONS BY A WINDOW

In the court, as we walked to my rooms, the sky was lighter than it had been that afternoon. On the breeze came a smell of acacia, faint because the blossom was nearly over, faint because the evening was so cold and dry. Immediately we went into my sitting-room, Dawson-Hill said: "I must say, they've given you the Number 1 dressing-room."

It was true, they had given me the college's best spare set. Dawson-Hill, so he said, observing mine, had to put up with one much inferior. He observed it with a dash of surprise and no discernible rancour. In fact, he seemed to draw an obscure pleasure from changes of fortune, from the sheer worldliness of the world.

When we had first met, he had been the young man with the future, the brightest catch among young barristers. I had been a young provincial, said to be clever, but not in his swim. He had been polite, because that was his nature: he had laid himself out to amuse, because he had rather people round him were happy than unhappy: but he hadn't expected to see much of me again. Our acquaintanceship had gone on like that for years. Then I left the bar, and he went on. He thought he had done pretty well. But he was a little surprised to find that, somehow, by processes which to him were pleasurably mysterious, I had become better known. He was surprised, but not in the least hipped. This was the world. Clever chaps bobbed up when you didn't expect them. It just showed that one often judged wrong. He was not an envious man, and nothing like so much a snob as he looked. He was ready to accept that I deserved what had happened to me. It made him like me more.

But, though he liked me more, he was as tough as he had ever been. He wasn't the opponent I should have chosen. Partly because he was in practice, and I had not done any real legal work for years. But much more because, though he sounded a playboy, he was hard-willed, the least suggestible of men.

As we sat in the window-seat, gazing into the garden on the cloud-grey summer evening, chatting casually before we started business, I had only one advantage. It was not just that I knew the background of the case better: that didn't count for much against a lawyer of his class. But I also knew the people better. That might cut both ways: it wasn't all gain: but it was all I had to play with.

"Perhaps we'd better settle one or two things," I said. We faced each other on the seat. It all looked slack, informal: it wasn't as informal as all that, and it went very quickly. "We can't expect them to keep to the rules of evidence, can we?" said Dawson-Hill.

"That won't happen," I said.

"We'd better tell them, when something wouldn't be evidence in court. Agreed?"

I nodded.

"Apart from that, it'll have to be catch as catch can. Agreed?"

Again I nodded.

"It's taken for granted we talk to members of the Court as and when they want us to? For instance, I am invited to dine with the Master on Monday night. I won't pretend the case isn't likely to crop up. Any objections?"

"None." He needn't have asked. There wasn't any analogy in law that I could think of. He had been asked down to advise the Seniors, who were also the judges: what was to stop him talking to them?

"Well, then, Lewis, I think it's for you to start to-morrow."

"What about your starting the case against Howard first?"

"No, no. You're arguing against a decision." Dawson-Hill gave his superior, mouth-pulled-down smile. "The Master made that clear at tea-time. And if he hadn't, it stands out a mile from the papers. No, no. You start to-morrow."

I should have to give way in the end; I might as well give way quickly. But it was a point to him. In this case, I would much rather he had to make the running.

"So who are you going to bring in to-morrow?" he asked, after I had acquiesced. This wasn't mild curiosity. He wanted to know the schedule of my case, and he was within his rights.

"Howard."

"You're starting with him, are you?" He was smiling. It was another point to him. He knew what it meant, the instant I said it—I was not confident of my chief witness.

"I fancy," he went on, with a touch of neutral professional malice, "that if I spend a bit of time on him, that might keep us most of to-morrow."

"I fancy it might," I replied. On Sunday, I reported, I should bring in Skeffington, Martin, Francis Getliffe. I didn't see why we shouldn't get them all into the morning session. Who was he going to call?

"Only one. The man Clark."

"What's he going to say?"

Again this was a professional question, and this time it was I who was within my rights.

"Character-evidence. Character-evidence of a negative kind, I'm afraid. Reports of your chap Howard discussing his work."

"Can you possibly think that that's admissible?"

"My dear Lewis, we've agreed, you can tell them what wouldn't be allowed in law."

"It's going pretty far."

"It's not going as far," said Dawson-Hill, "as Mr. Howard and his supporters seem to have gone. Or am I wrong?"

Sitting there in the subdued light, his face even more unnaturally youthful because one could not see the etching beneath his eyes, he might have been asking me to have a drink. And yet, I suddenly realised that he was committed. He was not just acting like an eminent lawyer doing a good turn for his old college. That was true, but it wasn't all.

Up to that moment, I had been taking it for granted that, as a natural Conservative, his feelings would be on the side of authority. I had also taken it for granted that, as a good professional, he would want the side that brought him down to win. Both these things were true—but they were nothing like all. Reasonable and dégagée as he sounded, he was as much engaged as I was. He was dead set against Howard, and perhaps even more against "his supporters." Another phrase which he used, in the same high, light, apparently careless tone, was "the Howard faction."

It was a warning. Now I had had it, I stopped that line of conversation.

Instead I said that it was time we defined what was "common ground." If we didn't, there was no chance of old Winslow keeping up with us, or even Crawford, and there would be no end to it.

"I can't for the life of me," said Dawson-Hill, once more off-hand, professional, "see how they're going to spin it out beyond Tuesday morning. And *that's* giving them all Monday to natter, bless them."

"Tuesday morning?" I told him he had never lived in a college.

The spirit of personal feeling had passed. We were down to business again.

"All right," said Dawson-Hill. "Common ground?"

"Do we agree that the photograph in Howard's thesis, reproduced in his paper, was faked? That is, a deliberate fake by *someone*?"

"Agreed." This was the photograph, with the expanded drawing-pin hole, which had set the affair going.

"Your line, of course, is that it was faked by Howard. Mine is that it was faked by old Palairet. Agreed?"

"Not within the area of common ground," said Dawson-Hill, sharp on the draw. It was the way we were going to argue, he conceded, but he wouldn't agree to more. I hadn't expected him to.

"But I think this," I said, "must be common ground. The missing photograph in Palairet's note-book. The caption under that photograph refers, in the opinions of the scientists I'm calling, to a photograph similar to the one in Howard's thesis and by definition faked. I don't expect you to admit that the caption does necessarily bear that meaning. But assume that the photograph were not missing and that it was faked—then is it common ground that it must have been faked by Palairet?"

"I don't see any need to accept that."

"I see great need."

"I'm sorry, Lewis, I'm not playing."

"If you don't, I shouldn't be able to leave it there. You see, the Court have listened to the college scientists often enough. I should have to insist on getting scientists from outside to examine Palairet's note-books—"

"You can't do that."

"Can't I?"

He stared at me.

"You can't wash this dirty linen in public, simply to prove a platitude. If there really had been a faked photograph stuck in the old man's note-book, then it wouldn't need outside scientists to tell us that in all reasonable probability, he must have produced the photograph himself—"

"That's all I'm asking you to agree on."

"It's extremely hypothetical and extremely academic."

"Well, if necessary, I should want responsible scientists to confirm it."

"The Seniors wouldn't be pleased if you brought them in."

I was sure—and I was counting on it—that he had been warned by the Master and Brown that, whatever he did, none of the proceedings must leak outside.

"I shall have to bring them in," I said, "unless you and I agree on this as common ground."

"Do you think the Court would dream for a moment of letting you?"

"In that case, I shall have to make myself more unpleasant than I want to."

"You wouldn't do your case any good," he said. "You wouldn't do yourself any good, as far as that goes. And it's remarkably academic anyway. I'm sorry, but I don't believe you mean it."

I replied: "Yes, I mean it."

Dawson-Hill was studying me, his eyes large, not as gay as the rest of the young-seeming face. He had met me as an acquaintance for nearly thirty years. Now he was trying to decide what I was like.

"Right," he said lightly, without a change of expression. "It's too trivial to argue over. Common ground."

Each of us said he had no other point to raise. We smoked cigarettes, looking out into the garden. Soon afterwards, with a cheerful, social good-night, he left.

Through the window I caught the scent of syringa mixed with the late night smell of grass. For an instant it pulled a trigger of memory, flooding me with feelings whose history that night I could not recall. Then my mind started working again in the here and now. I had not told Dawson-Hill that, over the missing photograph, I held a card whose value I was not certain of, and which I was still undecided whether or how to play. But I might have to.

One night a few weeks before, sitting with Martin, working up what I should say before the Seniors, both of us comfortable because we were on the same side, I had asked—what I was sure he had asked himself too—just why that photograph happened to be missing. I had said that of course it could have been an accident. I had gone on to ask whether it could have been deliberate. Neither of us replied: but I believed the same answer was going through our heads.

It had been a half-suspicion of mine for months, ever since, perhaps before, Martin and I had listened to Howard's outburst, and Martin had threatened him that if anyone else heard him it would ruin his case. It was the kind of suspicion that others must have had, so fantastic, so paranoid, that one did not bring it to the surface. With me, it had flared up as I listened to G. S. Clark at Brown's dinner-party.

Last Christmas, before Palairet's note-books reached Skeffington, there had only been one person with the chance to handle them. That was Nightingale. Was it credible that Nightingale had seen the photograph first, realised that it was a fake which proved Howard's story true, and pulled it out?

It didn't matter what I believed, but only what I could make others believe. If I were going to do the slightest good in front of the Court, I could not myself let out even the hint of a suspicion. That was simple tactics. To Crawford, Brown and Winslow, such a suspicion coming from me, as I acted as Howard's lawyer, doing my best with his case, would kill that case squalid dead.

And yet, that suspicion might have to be set to work within them. Staring sightlessly at the dark garden, I wasn't hopeful, I didn't see the way through. I couldn't do it. Who could, or would?

TWENTY-SEVEN

COMBINATION ROOM IN THE MORNING

Next morning I had breakfast late, as I used to when I lived in college. The kidneys and bacon, the hard toast, the coffee: the sunlight through the low windows: the smell of flowers and stone: it gave me a sense of *déja vu* and in the same instant sharpened the strangeness of the day. Under the speckled sunshine, I read my newspaper. I had asked Martin and the others to leave me alone this first morning before the Court. All I had to do was ring up the head porter and tell him to see that Howard was available in college from half-past ten. Then I went back to my newspaper, until the college bell began to toll.

The single note clanged out. It was five to ten, and we were due in the Combination Room on the hour. I walked through the fresh, empty, sunny court, the bell jangling and jarring through my skull. Through the door which led to the Combination Room, Arthur Brown, gown flowing behind him, was just going in. Following after him, from the lobby inside the door I borrowed a gown myself.

The bell tolled away, but in the room the four Seniors and Dawson-Hill had all arrived and were standing between the table and the windows. At night, the table dominated the room: but not so in the morning sunlight. The high polish on the rosewood flashed the light back, while outside the lawn shone in the sun. Seven chairs were set at the table, four on the side near the windows, the others on the fireplace side. Before each chair, as at a college meeting, were grouped a blotter, a pile of quarto paper, a steel-nibbed pen, a set of pencils. In addition to the college statutes, laid in front of the Master's place, loomed a leather-bound Victorian ledger with gold lettering on the back, a collection of Palairet's note-books, a slimmer green book also with gold lettering, and at least three large folders stuffed out with papers.

Good-mornings sounded all round as I joined them. If these had been my business acquaintances, it crossed my mind, they would have shaken hands: but in the college one shook hands at the most once a year, on one's first appearance each Michaelmas term. Arthur Brown observed that it was a better day. Nightingale said that we *deserved* some good weather.

Suddenly, with an emptiness of silence, the bell stopped. Then, a few seconds later, the college clock began to chime ten, and in the distance, like echoes, chimed out other clocks of Cambridge.

"Well, gentlemen," said Crawford, "I think we must begin."

Upright, soft-footed, he moved to the chair. On his right sat Winslow, on his left Brown; Nightingale was on the far right, beyond Winslow. They took up the places on the window side. Crawford pointed to the chair opposite Brown, across the table—"Will you station yourself there, Eliot?" Dawson-Hill's place was opposite Nightingale and Winslow. The seventh chair, which was between Dawson-Hill's and mine, and which faced the Master's, was to be kept—so Crawford announced—"for anyone you wish to bring before us."

Crawford sat, solid, image-like, his eyes unblinking as though they had no lids. He said:

"I will ask the Bursar, as the Secretary of the Court of Seniors, to read the last Order."

The leather-bound ledger was passed via Winslow to Nightingale, who received it with a smile. It was a pleased smile, the smile of someone who thoroughly enjoyed what he was doing, who liked being part of the ritual. Nightingale was wearing a bow-tie, a starched white shirt, and a new dark suit under his gown: he might have been dressed for a college wedding. He read: "A meeting of the Court of Seniors was held on April 22nd, 1954. Present the Master, Mr. Winslow, Mr. Brown, Dr. Nightingale. The following Order was passed: *'That, notwithstanding the decision reached in the Order of April 15th 1954, the Court of Seniors was prepared to hold a further enquiry into the deprivation of Dr. D. J. Howard, in the presence of legal advisers.'* The Order was signed by all members of the Court.

"That is all, Master," said Nightingale.

"Thank you, Bursar," said Crawford. "I think it is self-explanatory. I also think that we are all seized of the circumstances. Speaking as Master, I have nothing to add at this stage. Our legal advisers are now sitting with us. I have explained to them, and I believe the point is taken, that it is for Eliot to show us grounds why we should consider over-ruling a decision already given to the College. Eliot, we are ready to hear from you now."

I had expected more of a preamble, and I was starting cold. I hadn't got the feel of them at all. I glanced at Brown. He gave me a smile of recognition, but his eyes were wary and piercing behind his spectacles. There was no give there. He was sitting back, his jowls swelling over his collar, as in a portrait of an Eighteenth Century bishop on the linenfold, the bones of his chin hard among the flesh.

I began, carefully conciliatory. I said that, in this case, no one could hope to prove anything; the more one looked into it, the more puzzling it seemed. The only thing that was indisputable was that there had been a piece of scientific fraud; deliberate fraud, so far as one could give names to these things. No one would want to argue about that—I mentioned that it had been agreed on, the night before, by Dawson-Hill and me, as common ground.

"I confirm that, Master," came a nonchalant murmur from Dawson-Hill along the table.

Of course, I said, this kind of fraud was a most unlikely event. Faced with this unlikely event, responsible members of the College, not only the Court, had been mystified. I had myself, and to an extent still was. The only genuine division between the Court and some of the others was the way in which one chose to make the unlikely seem explicable. Howard's own version, the first time I heard it, had sounded nonsense to me; but reluctantly, like others, I had found myself step by step forced to admit that it made some sort of sense, more sense than the alternative.

I was watching Brown, whose eyes had not left me. I hadn't made them more hostile, I thought: it was time to plunge. So suddenly I announced the second piece of common ground. If the photograph now missing from Palairet's note-book V—I pointed to the pile in front of the Master—had been present there, and if that photograph had been a fraud, then that, for there would be no escape from it, would have to be a fraud by Palairet.

"No objection, Master," said Dawson-Hill. "But I'm slightly surprised that Eliot has used this curious hypothesis in the present context."

"But you agree to what I've said? I haven't misrepresented you?" I asked him.

Dawson-Hill acquiesced, as I knew he would. Having given an undertaking, he would not be less than correct.

While he made his gibe about the "curious hypothesis," I had glanced at Nightingale, who was writing notes for the minutes. Apart from the sarcastic twitch, his expression did not change; the waves of his hair, thick and lustrously fair for a man of sixty, seemed to generate light, down at the dark end of the table. Like a faithful functionary, he wrote away.

I went on: Who had done the fraud? Howard? or—we had all turned the suggestion down out of hand, but some of us couldn't go on doing so—Palairet? As I'd started by saying, I couldn't hope to prove, and possibly no one alive was in a position to, that Palairet had done it. The most I could hope to persuade them was that there existed a possibility they couldn't dismiss, at any rate not safely enough to justify them breaking another man's career. I should be able to prove nothing, I said. All I could reasonably set out to do before the Court was to ask a few questions and sharpen two or three doubts.

"Is that all for the present, Eliot?"

"I think it's enough to be going on with, Master," I said. I had spoken for a bare ten minutes.

Crawford asked Dawson-Hill if he wished to address the Court next. "No," said Dawson-Hill. He would reserve his remarks, if any, until the Court had heard testimony from the Fellows that Eliot was bringing before them.

Crawford looked satisfied and bland. "Well," he said, "at this rate it won't take too long before we put our business behind us." Then he added: "By the way, Eliot, there is one point I should like your opinion on. You repeated the suggestion which has of course been made to the Court before, and also to me in private—you repeated the suggestion, unless I misunderstood you, that it was Palairet who might have falsified his experiments. And you suggested it, again if I understood you correctly, not simply as a hypothesis or a *ballon d'essai,* but as something you thought probable. Or have I got you wrong?"

"No, Master," I replied, "I'm afraid that's so."

"Then that's what I should like your opinion on," he said. "Speaking as a man of science, I find it difficult to give any credence to the idea. I oughtn't to conceal that from you. Let me remind you, Palairet was moderately well-known to some of the senior members of the college. I should be over-stating things if I said that he was the most distinguished man of science that the college has produced in our time—"

Just for an instant, I could not help reflecting that Crawford reserved that place for himself, and to one's irritation was dead right.

"—but I have talked to men more familiar with his subject than I am, and I should not regard it as far wrong if we put him in the first six. He had been in the Royal Society for many years. He had been awarded the Rumford Medal of the Royal Society. Several of his researches, so I am informed on good authority, are classical beyond dispute. That is, they have been proved by time. The suggestion is now that at the age of seventy-two, he went in for cooking his results."

(Suddenly Crawford's Scottish accent, over-lain by fifty years in Cambridge, broke through and we heard a long, emphatic 'cōōking.')

"You think he could possibly, or even probably, have produced fraudulent data? Where I should like you to give us your opinion, is this—what reason could such a man have for going in for a kind of fraud that made nonsense of the rest of his life?"

I hesitated. "I didn't know him," I said.

"I did know him," Winslow put in.

He looked at me from under his lids. He had been staring at the table, his neck corded like an old bird's. But his hands, folded on his blotting-paper, stood out heavy-knuckled, the skin reddish, and neither freckled nor veined by age. "I did know him. He came up the year after the college had the ill-judgment to elect me to a Fellowship on the results of my Tripos."

"What was he like?" I said.

"Oh, I should have said that he was a very modest young man. I confess that I thought also that he had a good deal to be modest about." Winslow was in early-morning form.

"What was he like afterwards?" I went on.

"I didn't find it necessary to see him often. With due respect to the Master, the men of science of my period were not specially apt for the purposes of conversation. I should have said that he remained a very modest man. Which appeared to inhibit his expressing an interesting view on almost anything. Yes, he was a modest and remarkably ordinary man. He was one of those men who achieve distinction, much to one's surprise, and carry ordinariness to the point of genius."

I gazed at him. He had been a very clever person: in flashes he still was. Despite his disgruntlement, and the revenges he took for his failure, he was at the core more decent than most of us. Yet he had never had any judgment of people at all. It was astonishing that anyone who had met so many, who had such mental bite, who had lived with such appetite, who had strong responses to almost anyone he met, should be so often wrong.

Nightingale raised his head from his notes.

"Eliot hasn't answered the Master's question, I think."

"No—" I was beginning, but Nightingale went on:

"You've suggested, though of course we know the suggestion isn't your own invention, and we're none of us holding you to blame—"

He smiled quite openly, smoothing the lines from his face —"But you've suggested that a distinguished old man has gone in for a bit of scientific forgery, so to speak. And mind you, and I want to stress this once again to everyone here, a very petty bit of scientific forgery at that. I mean, this work of Howard's, or the work that's referred to in Notebook V, is trivial compared with the old man's real contribution. Nothing of this kind could possibly have added one per cent to his reputation. You're asking us to believe that a man absolutely established, right at the top of his particular tree, is going to commit forgery for the sake of that? Putting it in its lowest terms. I'm sorry, but it just doesn't wash. I think it's up to you to answer the Master's question."

Brown turned his head towards Nightingale. Crawford nodded.

Until then, I had not known how the Court worked among themselves. I had had no sense of the balance of power. It was clear, the instant one noticed the others listening to Nightingale, that we outside had underestimated him. He carried more weight than I liked. Not that he had been offensive to me; he was brisk, efficient, impersonal, speaking to me as though we were acquaintances doing a piece of business. That impersonal tone was a strength. And it was another strength, of course, that he was immersed in the detail. More than anyone there, he knew what he was talking about.

"I can't say anything very useful, as I didn't know Palairet," I replied to Crawford. "But do you want me to say why I don't think it's impossible?—"

"We should be interested," said Crawford.

I caught sight of Dawson-Hill along the table. His eyelids were pulled down in a half-smile of ridicule, or perhaps of professional sympathy. It seemed incredible to him, not used to academic meetings, that they should have rushed off in chase of this red herring. No rules, no relevance, in Dawson-Hill's terms, but instead they had obstinately got their heads down to the psychology of scientific fraud.

I did my best. I reproduced the names and anecdotes Francis Getliffe had told me, when we first talked about the affair, before the Audit Feast. Those frauds had happened. We knew nothing, or almost nothing, about the motives. In no case did money come in—in one, conceivably, the crude desire to get a job. The rest were quite mysterious. If one had known any of the men intimately, would one have understood?

Anyone's guess was as good as mine. But it didn't seem impossible to imagine what might have led some of them on, especially the more distinguished, those in positions comparable with Palairet's. Wasn't one of the motives a curious kind of vanity? 'I have been right so often. I know I'm right this time. This is the way the world was designed. If the evidence isn't forthcoming, then just for the present I'll produce the evidence. It will show everyone that I am right. Then no doubt in the future, others will do experiments and prove how right I was.'

The little I had picked up about Palairet—it didn't seem right out of his nature. I knew, I said to Winslow, that he gave one the impression of being a modest man. I should be prepared to believe that was true. But there was a kind of modesty and a kind of vanity which were hard to tell apart—and mightn't they, in fact, be one and the same thing? Reading the rubrics in his note-book, couldn't one at least think it possible that the aura of his personality had that particular tinge? Couldn't one at least imagine him getting old and impatient, knowing he hadn't much time, working on his last problem, not an important one, if you like, but one he was certain he knew the answer to? Certain that he knew how the world was designed? Almost as though it was the world designed by *him*. And mixed with that, perhaps, a spirit of mischief, such as one sometimes finds in the vain-and-modest—'this is what I can get away with.'

Catching Brown's gaze, I knew that I had made a mistake. It was not just that his mind was made up against Howard. It was also that he didn't like or trust what I was saying. He was a man of genuine insight, the only one on the Court. He knew the people around him with accuracy, compassion and great realism. But, although he had that insight, he had no use for psychological imaginings. As a rule, even when we were on opposite sides, he thought me sensible about people. This time, he was dismissing me as too clever by half.

It had been an awkward situation, and I had mishandled it. Under the pressure from Crawford and Nightingale, I had had no option except to take a risk, but I had shown bad judgment. Looking round the Court, I had to recognise that I had done more harm than good.

TWENTY-EIGHT

THE SOUND OF FALSITY

After the aside on Palairet, Crawford pushed the combination room bell, and the butler carried in a tray, on which a coffee-pot and jug struck sparks from the sunlight. He was followed by a servant, carrying cups upon another of the massive college trays. The Court settled down to drink their coffee. Dawson-Hill was interested in the silverware. What was the date of the trays? he asked, and Brown, behaving as though this were a comfortable party after Hall, replied with care. Dawson-Hill began asking about eighteenth century silversmiths. Each appeared to regard it as the most reasonable of conversations.

It was the kind of phlegm, oblivious of time, that I had met, chafed against and envied, learned to imitate without truly possessing, all my official life. Men of affairs weren't sprinters: they weren't tied to the clock: if you hurried them when they didn't propose to be hurried, you were not one of them.

The College clock was chiming a quarter past eleven before the trays were taken away. Crawford, settled in his chair, addressed me:

"Well, Eliot, I understand this is the stage in our proceedings when you would like to bring Howard in?"

I said yes. Crawford rang. After a wait of minutes, the door opened. First the butler, with a figure behind him. At the first sight, entering at the dark end of the room, Howard looked pale, ill-tempered, glowering. With one hand he was pulling his gown across his chest.

"Good-morning," said Crawford, "do sit down."

Howard stood still, undecided where he should go, although there was only the one chair vacant in front of him.

"Won't you sit down?" said Crawford, as though standing up might be a curious preference.

Polite, active, Dawson-Hill jumped up and guided Howard into the chair. Once again, Crawford seemed disinclined to take part himself. He merely asked Howard if he would mind answering questions put to him by "our colleagues," and then called on me to begin.

Turning half-left in my seat, trying to make Howard look at me—he was a yard away along the table—I could not get his eye. He was staring, and when I spoke to him he continued to stare, not at Brown but past him, into the corner of the room, where motes were jigging in parallel beams of sun. He was staring with mechanical concentration, as though he were watching a spider build its web.

All I could do with him, I had decided in cold blood weeks before, was to make everything sound as matter-of-fact as I could manage. So I started off on his career: he had come up to the College in 1939, hadn't he? And then he had joined the Army in '41? He could have stayed and gone on with his Physics—how had he managed to avoid being kept as a scientist?

His reply, like his previous one, was slow.

"I knew someone who got me put down for his regiment."

"Who was it?"

"As a matter of fact, one of my uncles."

"Did he find it easy?"

"I expect he knew the ropes."

Even then, he was ready to sneer at the influence which had always been within his reach. In a hurry I passed on. He had returned to the college in '45, taken Part II of the Tripos in '46? Then he had gone off to Scotland to do research under Palairet? Why?

"I was interested in the subject."

"Did you know him?"

"No."

"You knew his name and reputation?"

"But of course I did."

It would be fair to say that he had been impressed by Palairet's reputation and work, I pressed him? Just as young men are when they are looking for someone to do their research under? Was that fair? I had to press it. Reluctantly and sullenly, he said yes.

"When you arrived in his laboratory, who suggested your actual field of work?"

"I don't remember."

"Can't you?"

Already I was feeling the sweat trickle on my temples. He was more remote and suspicious even than when I talked to him in private. "Did you suggest it yourself?"

"I suppose not."

"Well, then, did Palairet?"

"I suppose so."

I persuaded him to agree that Palairet had, in fact, laid down his line of research in detail, and had supervised it day by day. More than a professor normally would? Maybe. Had he, Howard, found research easy?

"I shouldn't think anyone ever does," he said.

Some of the results he, or they, had obtained were still perfectly valid, weren't they? A longer pause than usual—No one's criticised them yet, he said. But there was one photograph which was, beyond any doubt, a fraud? He did not reply, but nodded. Could he remember how that photograph got into the experimental data? Palairet must have brought it in, he said. But could he remember how, or when? No, he couldn't. Would he try to remember? No, he couldn't place it. There were a lot of photographs, he was trying to write his thesis and explain them.

"This was a more striking bit of experimental evidence than the rest, though, wasn't it?"

"But of course it was."

"You can't remember Palairet first showing it to you?"

"No, I can't."

It was no good. To the Court, he must have seemed deliberately to be refusing an answer. To me, trying to pull it out, he seemed not to want to remember—or else his whole memory was thinner-textured than most of ours, did not give him back any kind of picture. Didn't he preserve, I thought to myself, any sense of those days in the laboratory, the old man coming in, the time when they looked through the photographs together? This was only five years behind him. To most of us, intimations like that would have flickered in and out, often blurred, concertinaed, but nevertheless concrete, for a lifetime.

I tried to gloss it over. I asked him if he found the fraud hadn't come to him as a major shock? Yes. He gave me no help, but just said yes. I went through his actions after the first letters of criticism had come in from the American laboratories, doing my best to rationalize them. When he was first accused, I was leading him into saying, he had just denied it. Why should he do any more? Fraud had never crossed his mind: why should he invent explanations for something he had never imagined? The same was true the first two occasions he had appeared before the Court. He had simply said that he had faked nothing. It did not occur to him to think, much less to say, that Palairet had done the faking. It was only later, when he was compelled to recognise that there had been a fraud, that he began to think that only one person could have done it. That was why, belatedly, so belatedly that it seemed an invention to save his skin, he had brought in the name of Palairet.

How much of this synoptic version I was managing to suggest—how much the Court took in, not as the truth, but as a possible story—I could not begin to tell. I had to do it almost all through my questions. His answers were always slow and strained, and sometimes equivocal. Once or twice he sounded plain paranoid, as in the public house with Martin, and I had to head him off.

All the time, I was thinking, another five minutes, a question which sets him going, and it might sound more credible. But that kind of hope was dangerous. This was tiring them; it was boring them. I was accomplishing nothing. If I went on, it could be less than nothing. I felt frustrated at having to surrender, but I gave it up.

Crawford looked at the grandfather clock in the corner of the room. It was nearly twenty-five to one.

"I am inclined to think," he said, "that is as far as we can go this morning. We shall have to trouble you—" he was speaking to Howard—"to join us again this afternoon. I hope that doesn't upset any other arrangements?"

Howard shook his head. This automatic courtesy, such as he received from the Master or Brown, was too much for him.

When the door had closed behind him, Crawford invited us to lunch with him in the Lodge. I wanted to say no, but I daren't leave them. As usual, one couldn't afford to be absent. So I listened to Dawson-Hill entertaining the others at the Lodge dining-table. Someone mentioned that a couple of heads of houses would be retiring this next year. "Which reminds me," said Crawford, "that I suppose my own successor will have to be elected at the end of the Michaelmas term. I take it there won't be any hitch about that, Brown?"

"I think it'll be looked after properly, Master," said Brown. He gave no sign that he was himself involved. He spoke as though he were making arrangements for the appointment of the third gardener.

As we walked in the Master's garden after lunch, Crawford discussed his plans for moving out of the Lodge. All clear by Christmas: his old house would be waiting for him. "Speaking as a husband," he said, "I shan't be sorry to get back. This—" he waved a short-fingered hand across the lawn over which tortoise-shell butterflies were performing arabesques towards the Lodge—"is *not* a convenient house. Between ourselves, no one knew how to build a house until the nineteenth century, and moderately late in the nineteenth century at that."

A butterfly traced out a re-entrant angle in front of us. On my face I felt the sun, hot and calming. We walked beside the long Georgian pond, the water-lilies squatting placidly on the water, and Crawford was saying,

"No, I don't know why anyone consents to come into the Lodge. As for any of you with a wife, I should advise very strongly against it."

Back in the combination room at a quarter-past two, the sun was beginning to stream into my eyes. Nightingale drew a blind, which up to then I had never noticed, so that the room took on the special mixture of radiance, dark and hush such as one meets in Mediterranean salons.

As soon as Howard was back in his chair, Dawson-Hill started in. The tone in his questions wasn't unfriendly; it had a good deal of edge just below the flah-flah, but so it had when he spoke to his friends. He kept at it for over two hours. His attack was sharp enough to hold them all, even Winslow, awake, alert, through the slumbrous afternoon. Dawson-Hill was having a smoother job than mine, I thought once or twice, as though I had been a young barrister again, with professional envy, professional judgment, resurrected. He was doing it well.

He limited himself to four groups of questions, and his line—any lawyer could have told—had been plotted out in advance. He sounded insouciant, but that was part of his stock-in-trade. There was nothing of the dilettante about his work that afternoon. He began by asking Nightingale to give him "the thesis."

This was a copy of Howard's Fellowship thesis, which

according to custom had been deposited in the college library. It was about a hundred and fifty pages long, typed—neatly typed, by a professional—on quarto paper. It was bound in stiff green covers, with the title and Howard's name in gold letters on the outside front cover and also on the spine.

"This does seem to be your thesis, doesn't it, Dr. Howard?" said Dawson-Hill, handing it to him.

"But of course."

Dawson-Hill asked how many copies there were in existence.

The answer was, three more. In the Fellowship competition, the college asked for two copies. He had used the remaining two for other applications.

"This is the show copy, though?"

"You can call it that."

"Then this—" There was a slip of paper protruding from the thesis and Dawson-Hill opened it at that page—"might be your star print?"

It was the positive which everyone in that room knew. It was pasted in, with a figure 2 below it and no other rubric at all. It stood out, concentric rings of black and grey, like a target for a small-scale archery competition.

"It's a print, all right."

"And this print is a fraud?"

I wished Howard would answer a straight question fast. Instead he hesitated, and only at last said, "Yes."

"That doesn't need proving, does it?" said Dawson-Hill. "All the scientific opinion agrees that the drawing-pin hole is expanded? Isn't that true?"

"I suppose so."

"That is, this print had been expanded, to make it look like something it wasn't?"

"I suppose so."

"What about your other prints?"

"Which other prints?"

"You can't misunderstand me, Dr. Howard. The prints in the other copies of your thesis?"

"I think I re-photographed them from this one."

"You *think*."

"I must have done."

"And this one, this fake one, came from a negative which you've never produced? Where is it, do you know?"

"Of course I don't know."

For once articulate, Howard explained that the whole point of what he had said before lunch was that he *couldn't* know. He had not seen the negative; Palairet must have made the print and the measurements and put them in with a set of other positives.

At that, Nightingale broke in.

"I've asked you this before, but I still can't get it straight. You mean to say that you used this print as experimental evidence without having the negative in your hands?"

"I've told you so, often enough."

"It still seems to me a very curious story. I'm sorry, but I can't imagine anyone doing research like that."

"I thought the print and the measurements were good enough."

"That is," I broke in, "you took them on Palairet's authority."

Howard nodded.

Nightingale, with a fresh, open look of incomprehension, was shaking his head.

"Let's leave this for a moment, if you don't mind," said Dawson-Hill. "I'm an ignoramus, of course, but I believe this particular print was regarded—before it was exposed as a fraud—as the most interesting feature of the thesis?"

"I shouldn't have said that," said Howard. (I was thinking, why didn't the fool see the truth and tell it?) "I should have said it was an interesting feature."

"Very well. Let me be crude. Without that print, and the

argument it was supposed to prove, do you believe, Mr. Howard, that the thesis would have won you a Fellowship?"

"I don't know about that."

"Do you agree it couldn't have stood the slightest chance?"

Howard paused. (Why doesn't he say Yes, I thought?) "I shouldn't say that."

Nightingale again intervened: "There's not a great deal of substance in the first half, is there?"

"There are those experiments—" Howard seized the thesis and began staring at some graphs.

"I shouldn't have thought that was very original work, by Fellowship standards," said Nightingale.

"It's useful," said Howard.

"At any rate, you'd be prepared to agree that without this somewhat providential photograph your chances could hardly have been called rosy?" said Dawson-Hill.

This time Howard would not reply.

Dawson-Hill looked surprised, amused, and broke away into his second attack.

"I wonder if you'd mind giving us some illumination on a slightly different matter," he said. "This incident has somewhat, shall I say, disarranged your career?"

"What do you think?" Howard replied.

"Not to put too fine a point upon it, it's meant that you have to say good-bye to being a research scientist, and start again? Or is that putting it too high?"

"That's about the size of it."

"And you must have realised that, as soon as this Court first deprived you of your Fellowship?"

"But of course I did."

"That was nearly eighteen months ago, seventeen months, to be precise?"

"You must have the date." Howard's tone was savage.

"So far as my information goes, during that time, that quite appreciable time. vou never took any legal action?"

It was the point Nightingale had challenged us to answer, at the Master's dinner-party after Christmas. I had no doubt that Nightingale had put Dawson-Hill up to it.

"No."

"You've never been to see your solicitor?"

"Not as far as I remember."

"You must remember? Have you been, or not?"

"No."

"You never contemplated bringing an action for wrongful dismissal?"

"No."

"I suggest you weren't willing to face a court of law?"

Howard sat, glowering at the table. I looked at Crawford: for an instant I was going to protest; then I believed it would make things worse.

"I always thought," Howard replied at long last, "that the college would give me a square deal."

"You thought they might give you much more of the benefit of the doubt?"

"I tell you," Howard said, his voice strained and screeching, "I didn't want to drag the college through the courts."

To me this came out of the blue. When Martin and I had pressed him, he had never said so much. Could it be true, or part of the truth? It did not ring true, even to me.

"Surely that would be more magnanimous than any of us could conceive of being," said Dawson-Hill, "in the circumstances as revealed by you?"

"I didn't want to drag the college through the courts."

"Forgive me, but have you really this extreme respect for institutions? I rather gathered that you had slightly less respect for existing institutions than most of us?"

For the first time that day, Howard answered with spirit.

"I've got less respect for existing society than most of you have, if that's what you mean. It's dying on its feet, and none of you realise how fast it's dying. But that doesn't mean I haven't got respect for some institutions inside it. I can see this university going on, and this college, as far as that goes, long after the system you're all trying to prop up is sunk without trace, except for a few jeers in the history books."

Nightingale whispered to Brown. Crawford, not put off by unplacatory statements, suddenly had his interest revived and was ready to argue, but Dawson-Hill got back to work. "Yes, and your interesting attitude towards what I think you called —existing society, wasn't it?—brings me to another question. What really were your relations with Professor Palairet?"

"All right."

"But you've given me the impression that they were slightly more intimate than one would naturally expect, between a very senior professor and, forgive me, a not yet remarkable research student. That is, the impression you've tried to give us is of someone coming in and out of your room, giving you pieces of experimental data and so on, very much as though he were a collaborator of your own standing. Does that sound likely?"

"It's what happened."

"But can you suggest any reason why we should think it likely? Didn't you give Professor Palairet sufficient grounds to be less intimate with you than with other research students, not more?"

"I don't know."

"But you must know. Isn't it common knowledge that Professor Palairet was in ordinary terms, a very conservative man?"

"He was a conservative, yes."

"Surely, actively so?"

"If you put it that way."

"Didn't he ask you to stop your open political activities while you were in his laboratory?"

"He said something of the sort."

"What did you say?"

"I said I couldn't."

"Didn't he object when you appeared as one of the backers of what I believe is called a 'Front' organisation? Scientists' World Peace Conference—wasn't that the eloquent name?"

"I suppose he did."

"You must know. Didn't he give you an ultimatum that, if you appeared in any such organisation again, you would have to leave his laboratory?"

"I shouldn't have called it an ultimatum."

"But that is substantially true?"

"There's something in it."

"Well, then, does all this correspond to the picture, a rather touching picture, I must say, of professor-student intimacy and bliss, on which your whole account of these incidents appears to depend?"

Howard stared. Dawson-Hill went on: "Further, I suggest to you that your whole account of these incidents doesn't make sense, whichever way one looks. If we assume, just for an instant, that Professor Palairet did perpetrate a ridiculous fraud, and we also assume the reality of this very touching picture of the professor-student intimacy, then we have to accept that he just gave you some experimental data and you quietly put them into your thesis and your papers as your own? Is that correct?"

It sounded like another point of Nightingale's. It was a valid one. From the start, Francis and Martin had been troubled by it.

"I made acknowledgments in everything I wrote."

"But it would mean you were living on his work?"

"All the interpretations that I made were mine."

"Does it sound likely behaviour on Professor Palairet's part—or on yours, as far as that goes?"

"I tell you, it's what happened."

Dawson-Hill smoothed back his hair, already smooth.

"I shan't keep you much longer, Dr. Howard. I know this

must be rather irksome for you. And the Court has had a tiring day." It was well past four. The sun, wheeling over the First Court, had begun to leak into the further window behind Nightingale's back, and during the last questions he slipped away from the table and drew another blind.

"Just one final question: when your work was criticised, did you take the advice of any of your scientific colleagues here? Did you take any advice at all?"

"No."

"You did nothing. You didn't produce the idea that Professor Palairet was in the habit of providing you with photographs. You didn't produce that idea for some weeks, if I'm not mistaken. My friend along the table—" Dawson-Hill smiled at me, superciliously, affably—"has done his best to make that seem plausible. Tell me now, does it really seem plausible to *you*?"

"It's what happened."

"Thank you, Master. I've nothing more to ask Dr. Howard."

Dawson-Hill leaned back in his chair, elegant, dégagé, as though he hadn't a thought or a care in the world.

"Well," said Crawford, "as has just been said, we've had a tiring day. Speaking as an elderly man, I think we should all do well to adjourn until tomorrow. The members of the Court of Seniors have all had opportunity to question Howard on previous occasions." (Crawford had been punctilious throughout in calling Howard by his surname alone, as though he were still a colleague). "I don't know whether any Senior wishes to ask him anything further now?"

Winslow, eyes reddened, but surprisingly unjaded, said: "I regard that as a question, Master, asked with the particle *num*."

"What about you, Eliot?" Crawford said.

During Dawson-Hill's cross-examination, I had been framing a set of questions in reply. Suddenly, looking at Howard, I threw them out of mind.

"Just this, Master," I said. I turned to Howard. "Look here," I said. "There's been a fraud. You didn't do it?"

"No."

"It must have been done, in your view, by Palairet?"

Even then he could not answer straight out. "I suppose so," he said at length.

"Of anything connected with this fraud you are quite innocent?"

He said, in a high, strangulated tone: "But of course I am."

As I signalled to Crawford that I had finished, Howard fell back in his chair, like an automaton. I felt—as on and off I had felt all day—something so strange as to be sinister. I had heard him speak like that when I believed him guilty. Now, so far as I was convinced of anything about another person, I was convinced that he wasn't. Yet, listening to him at that moment, I felt not conviction, but mistrust. What he said, although with my mind I knew it to be true, sounded as false as when I first heard it.

TWENTY-NINE

DISSERVICE TO AN OLD FRIEND

Back in my rooms after the day's session, I lay on the sofa. On the carpet the angle of the sunbeams sharpened, while I made up my mind. At last I put through two telephone calls: one to the kitchens, to say that I should not dine that evening: the other to Martin, asking him to collect the leaders of the pro-Howard party after Hall.

"In my rooms?" said Martin, without other questions. For an instant I hesitated. In college, nothing went unobserved. The news would go round before we had finished talking. Then I thought, the more open the better. This wasn't a trial-at-law, where an advocate mustn't see his witnesses. The only tactics left to us were harsh. So, after eating alone, I went to Martin's rooms in the full, quiet evening light.

As I was going up the staircase, Francis Getliffe followed me, on his way across from the Combination Room. We entered Martin's sitting-room together. There Martin was waiting for us, with Skeffington and—to my surprise—Tom Orbell.

It was Tom who asked me first:

"How did it go?"

"Badly," I said.

"How badly?" put in Martin.

"Disastrously," I said.

As we brought chairs round by the windows, from which one looked westward over the roofs opposite to the bright, not-yet-sunset sky, I told them that Howard was the worst witness in the world. I added that I had been pretty inept myself.

"I find that hard to believe," said Francis Getliffe.

"No," I said. "I wasn't much good."

I went on:

"A lot of people would have done it better. But, and this is what I wanted to talk to you about, I'm not sure that anyone would have done the trick. I've got to tell you that, as things are and as they look like going, I don't believe that this man stands a chance."

In the golden light, Skeffington's face shone effulgent, radiant, furious.

"That simply can't be true," he cried.

"As far as I can judge, it is."

Skeffington was in a rage, which did not discriminate clearly between Howard, the Seniors and myself. "Are any of us going to bear this? Of course we're not."

As for Howard, Skeffington was ready to abuse him too. In fact, I had noticed in Skeffington the process one often sees in his kind of zealot. He was still, as he had been from the day of his conversion, more integrally committed to getting Howard clear than anyone in the college. His passion for giving "that chap" justice had got hotter, not more lukewarm. But as his passion for justice for Howard boiled up, his dislike for the man himself had only deepened. And there was something else, just as curious. For Howard's sake, or rather, for the sake of getting him fair play—Skeffington was prepared to quarrel with his natural associates in the college, the religious, the orthodox, the conservative. All this on behalf of a man whom Skeffington, not now able to bear him and not given to subtle political distinctions, had come to think of as the reddest of the red. The result of this was to make Skeffington, in everything outside the Affair itself, more conservative than he had ever been before. He had taken on a rabid, an almost unbalanced, strain of anti-Communism. It was said, I did not know how reliable the rumour was, that he was even having doubts about voting for Francis Getliffe at the magisterial election—after all, Francis had been known to have a weakness for the Left.

So he was lashing out at the Court, at Howard, and, somehow projecting all his irritation, at me.

"I can't credit that you haven't got it wrong," he cried.

"I wish I had," I said.

"They can't help giving him his rights. Anything else it's dead out."

"Listen," I said, "this is the time that you must believe me."

Francis said:

"We do."

Martin nodded his head, so did Tom. I was sitting at the end of the semicircle, watching them as they faced the glowing cyclorama of the sky—Francis fine-featured and deep-orbited, Tom like a harvest moon, Martin composed, his eyes screwed up and hard. I looked at Skeffington, his head rearing handsomely above the others.

"You must believe me—" I said.

He said: "Well, you've been in there all day." It was an acquiescence, it occurred to me, about as graceful as one of Howard's.

Martin intervened:

"Right, then. Where do we go next?"

He knew that I had come with something to propose. What it was, he had not guessed.

Then I started. I wanted to shock them. It was no use going in for finesse. I said that the only question which might make the Court think twice was a question we had all thought about and kept to ourselves. That is, how had the photograph got removed from the old man's note-book? Could it have been removed deliberately? If so, by whom?

"The answer to that is simple," I said. "If it was removed deliberately, then it was by Nightingale."

I looked at Martin and reminded him that we had asked

ourselves those questions. I believed that, even to stand a chance of getting Howard off, it had to be asked in Court. I could not guarantee that that would work. It was risky, distasteful, and at the best would leave rancour behind for a long time. Nevertheless, for the short-term purpose of justice for Howard, I had to tell them that there was no alternative move at all.

The point was, were we justified in making it? It might do Nightingale harm—no, it was bound to do him harm, innocent or guilty. How certain were we of our own ground in suspecting him? Were we going to take the responsibility of harming a man who might be innocent?

The room was hushed. Martin looked at me, brilliant-eyed, without expression. Francis's face was dark.

It was Julian Skeffington who broke the silence.

"I've never been able to see how that photograph came unstuck," he said, without his loftiness or confidence. "I don't know what could make a chap do a thing like that. It's not a thing I expected to think of a chap doing. Especially when he's your senior and you're used to seeing him at dinner."

"Well?" I asked him.

"I don't pretend to like it. I wish there was another way."

"There's no other way of giving Howard a chance. Well?"

"If you put it to me like that," said Skeffington, reluctant but straightforward, "then I say we've got to go ahead."

"So do I," said Tom Orbell. "The trouble is, we've been too scrupulous all along!"

Francis cleared his throat. He disregarded Tom, and spoke straight to me.

"You were asking if we were justified, Lewis? I should like to say we weren't. But I can't do that."

This startled me.

"You really think we're right to do it?" I said.

"I'm afraid I've had a suspicion, from very early days."

"Since when?"

"I'm afraid—since the three of you came to see me in the lab last Christmas."

That was a shock. Then, an instant later, I had another, when Martin remarked:

"I'm sorry, but I disagree with you all."

"Have you altered your mind?" I broke out.

"No. I thought about it when we last talked, but I came down on the other side."

Mixed with my irritation, I was moved by sarcasm at my own expense. I had felt telepathically certain that we had agreed. It hadn't been necessary to say the words. It seemed bizarre to have been so wrong, about someone one knew so well. In the whole course of the Affair, this was the first occasion when Martin and I had not been at one.

"What are you holding back for?" said Tom.

"I don't believe we're entitled to do it."

"Don't you think it's possible that Nightingale pulled that photograph out—?" Skeffington's voice was raised. "Don't you remember that it was Nightingale who had it in most for Howard?" Tom joined in.

"Yes, I think it's possible," Martin replied to Skeffington. "But I'm not convinced it happened."

"I'm afraid I think it's ninety per cent probable," said Francis.

"I don't," said Martin. "You've always distrusted Nightingale, I know. So have you, even more so," he turned to me. "From what you've told me, it would have been remarkable if you hadn't. But you don't really believe in people trying to make a better job of their lives, do you? I know Nightingale isn't everyone's cup of tea, let alone yours. He's close, he's narrow, he's not very fond of anyone except himself and his wife. Still, I should have thought he'd tried to become a decent member of society. I'm not prepared to kick him downstairs again unless I'm absolutely sure."

Of these four, I was thinking, Martin was by a long way

the most realistic. Yet it was the men of high principle, Skeffington and Francis, whom no one could imagine doing a shady act, who could themselves imagine Nightingale doing this. While Martin, who had rubbed about the world and been no better than his brother men, could not believe it. Was it that realistic men sometimes get lost when they met the sensational—as though they had seen a giraffe and found that they couldn't believe it? Or was it more personal? In being willing to defend Nightingale's change of heart, in showing a heat of feeling which came oddly from him, and which had surprised us all, was Martin really being tender to himself? For he, too, of course, had tried to make something different out of his life.

"I think there's substance in what Martin says," said Francis, "but still—"

"Look here," cried Tom, eyes flat, face thrust forward, with the touch of cheerful hypomania which sometimes changed trigger-quick into temper, "from what old Lewis tells us, you've got this choice. Either you raise a doubt about Nightingale—which I must say seems to me a perfectly legitimate one, and it ought to have been brought out long ago—or else you leave Howard to be done down. What do you say, Martin? Is that all right?"

"It's a hard choice," said Martin.

"Well, you've got to make it."

"As far as I'm concerned," Martin replied, without any cover at all, "Howard's case will have to take its chance."

"I can't and won't sit down under that," said Skeffington.

"So that's what you'd let happen, is it?" said Tom.

"No," said Francis, "I'm afraid I've got to choose the other way. What about you, Lewis?"

"I'm with you," I said.

So we settled it. Then I came to the harder part. Who was going to "raise the doubt?" I told them that it would be useless for me to do it. I gave them the reasons I had thought over to myself the night before. And also, Nightingale and I had once been enemies: though it was years ago: men like Brown would not have forgotten. Did they agree?

There were frowns and heavy faces as they nodded. They had all seen where this must lead. "So it's got to be one of us," Tom said.

"Yes," I replied. The doubt would have to come out in Court next day, while I examined one of them.

Tom Orbell said the one word:

"Who?"

There was a long pause. The sky in the west was a luminous apple-green shading into cerulean blue above the college.

"I'm damned if I like it," said Skeffington, "but I'd better do it."

"I don't know enough about it, do I?" asked Tom. He was glad to be out of it, and yet half-disappointed.

Of them all, Skeffington was the last I should have selected. He did not carry weight. He had been so much the head and front of the Howard party that men did not listen to him any more. They would just dismiss this as another outburst, and the last.

I gazed at Martin. He would have been far more effective. He shook his head. "No, I can't go back on what I said. I'll do anything else I can: but not that."

Just as I was turning to Skeffington, resigned to making do with him, Francis said, in a tone strained, embittered and forced:

"No. I'm the best person to do it."

Martin looked at him in consternation. They had never been specially fond of each other, but Martin said with a touch of affection, almost protectively:

"But it's not much in your line, you know."

"Do you think I shall enjoy it?" Francis said. "But they'll listen to me, and I'm the best person to do it."

No man would more detest doing it. He was a man so

thin-skinned that he didn't like the ordinary wear and tear of a college argument, much less this. He was less cushioned than the rest of us. Although he had played a part in scientific affairs, he had done so by force of will, not because he fitted in. He had never toughened his hide, as most men do for self-protection, when they live in affairs. He had never acquired the sort of realistic acceptance which I, for example, could switch on. He continued to be upset when men behaved badly.

Yet despite all that, or really because of it, he was, as he said himself, the man the Court would have to listen to. Not only for his name, his seniority, but also because he was a little purer than most men.

Martin asked him to think again, but Francis was impatient.

His decision was made. He didn't want any more talk. He wanted to do it and get it over. He knew, just as well as the politically-minded, Martin and Tom Orbell, what in practical terms he was losing. All of us knew that up to that night he had a clear lead in the magisterial election. By this time next day, he would have lost one vote for sure, possibly more.

In Martin's room, no one mentioned the election. But I did, later that night. As soon as Francis had said that he was "the best person to do it," he got to his feet. All of us were constrained. There was some relief, certainly some expectancy in the air, but even a fluent man like Tom couldn't find any easy words. While they were saying good-night, Francis asked me if I would care to drive out with him and see his wife.

On our way out to their house, the same house I used to visit when we were young men, we scarcely spoke. I looked from the dashboard to the beautiful grape-dark dusk. Francis, silently driving, was both resentful at the prospect of next day, and also diffident. He had been in authority for so long, sometimes people disliked him for being overbearing, and yet he still curled up inside.

In the drawing-room, as soon as I went in, his wife Katherine cried out with pleasure. When I had first known her, nearly thirty years before, she had been a sturdy pony of a girl; now she was a matriarch. The clear, patrician Jewish features were still there, the sharp, intelligent grey eyes: but she sat statuesque in her chair, a big, heavy woman, her children grown up, massive, slow-moving, indolent, like those aunts of hers, other matriarchs, whom I had met at her father's dinner-parties when she and I were young. And yet, though the physical transformation was dramatic, though time had done its trick, and she sat there, a middle-aged woman filling her chair—I did not quite, at least, not with photographic acceptance, see her so. I did not see her as I should have seen her if I had that night come into her house for the first time, and been confronted with her—as I had been confronted with those great matriarchs of aunts, having no pictures of their past. Somehow anyone whom one has known from youth one never sees quite straight: the picture has been doubly exposed; something of themselves when young, the physical presence of themselves when young, lingers till they die.

We talked about our children. It seemed to her funny that her two eldest should be married while mine was six years old. We talked of her brother, to whom she was, after a break of years, at last reconciled. We talked of her father, who had died the year before. Then I said, in the warmth of associations flowing back:

"Katherine, my dear, I've just done Francis a bad turn."

"That's pretty gross, isn't it?" She glanced at her husband with her penetrating eyes. "What have you been up to, Lewis?"

"No," said Francis, "we've all got trapped. It's not his fault."

"In effect, I've done him a bad turn."

I explained what had happened. She knew all about the Affair: she was vehemently pro-Howard. Morally, she had not altered. She still kept the passion for justice, argumentative, repetitive, but quite incorruptible, that I remembered in her and her brother when they were young. At that time, that sharp-edged passion had seemed to me to be specifically Jewish: had I ever met non-Jews who felt for justice just like that? But now I had lived with Margaret for years. She had the same passion, just as contemptuous of compromise as any of my Jewish friends. If Margaret had been present that night, she would have judged the case precisely as Katherine did.

"You hadn't any option," she said to Francis. "Of course you hadn't. Don't you admit it?"

"No doubt that will comfort me a bit, when it comes to tomorrow afternoon." Francis, who still loved her, made that gallows-joke as though with her he had managed to relax.

"But it's an intolerable nuisance. No, it's worse than that —" I began.

"It's monstrous to have to make yourself unpleasant in just that way, of course it is," said Katherine to her husband.

"I meant something less refined," I put in. The way I spoke recalled to her, as it was meant to recall, a private joke. When I had first entered the great houses in which she was brought up, I had been a poor young man determined to get on. I had had to play down my sensibilities, while she and her friends had been free to indulge and proliferate theirs. So they had made a legend of me, as a sort of Bazarov, unrecognisably monolithic, utterly different from what I really was, and what they knew me to be. Somehow this legend had lasted half a lifetime: so that Katherine, whose fibres were tougher than mine, sometimes pretended at odd moments that she was a delicate, *fainéante* relic of a dying class being attacked by someone implacable and raw.

"Much less refined," I said. "Look, Katherine, if Francis doesn't become Master next autumn, it will be because of what he's going to do to-morrow. Perhaps he'll still get it.

But if he doesn't, it'll be on account of this business. I want you to realise that I am partly responsible."

"Why, I suppose he is," she said to Francis, in a tone I did not understand—angry? sarcastic?

"It's neither here nor there," he replied.

"If I'd not spoken as I did to-night—"

"It would have added up to the same thing in the end."

"Anyway," I said to Katherine, "I'm sorry it had to be through me."

She had been gazing at me. Her eyes were keen, appraising. Suddenly she laughed. It was a maternal laugh, a fat woman's laugh.

"You don't think I mind all that much, do you? I know the old thing wants it—" She grinned affectionately at Francis—"and of course, anything the old thing wants he ought to get. But between ourselves I've never really understood why he wants it. He hasn't done so badly anyway. And it would be an absolutely awful nuisance, don't you admit it? I don't mind telling you, I'm not panting to live in any beastly Lodge. Think of the people we should have to entertain. I'm not much good at entertaining. I'm getting too old to put up with being bored. Why should we put up with being bored? Answer me that."

She chuckled. "To tell you the truth," she said, "I've only got one ambition for the old thing now. That is, for him to retire. That's the only one."

Francis smiled at her. It had been a good marriage. But just at that instant, as she said 'that's the only one,' he couldn't lie to himself or even pretend to us that it was the only one for him.

THIRTY

THE WORD 'MISTAKE'

The next morning, Sunday, the Court of Seniors were sitting at the Combination Room table, waiting. They were waiting for Skeffington. He had been asked to be ready at half-past ten. There was no sign of him.

Impatiently, on edge because he was my witness, I went to the window and gazed into the sunny court. Turning back to the table, I asked Crawford if he would like me to ring up Skeffington's house. Just as he was replying, the butler came in. He told the Master that Dr. Skeffington was in the college; the head porter had seen him enter the chapel nearly half an hour before; he had still not reappeared.

"Thank you, Newby," said Crawford. "Bring him in as soon as he's available, if you don't mind."

When we were alone again, Brown told us that there was no service in chapel between eight and eleven that day. "He must be praying," said Brown. "That's what I get round to. He must be praying."

He added:

"Well, God forbid that I should cause any of His little ones to stumble, but I wish the man weren't such an infernal time about it."

"I'm very ignorant of these necromantic proceedings," said Winslow, "but I take it that Skeffington isn't attempting to bring supernatural influences to bear on our actions in this room? Or am I wrong?"

The old man was happy. He felt as though back in the

Cambridge of the Nineties, when unbelief, rude, positive unbelief, was fun. As he proceeded to inform the Court with relish, he still had exactly as much interest in "religious exercises" as he had in the magic of savage tribes.

"I suppose Skeffington would like us to see a difference between his activities and rain-making. But I confess I think it's a major intellectual error to endow his activities with a sophistication that they don't inherently possess. I must say, praying before giving evidence does seem a singular example of sympathetic magic. I find it a very remarkable thing for a supposedly intelligent man to do."

So, in private, did Crawford. Did Brown, who punctiliously attended college chapel, but, I often thought, out of social, not religious, piety, out of attachment to established things? It was neither they nor Nightingale who protested—but, from the opposite side of the table, Dawson-Hill, who said:

"I don't find it remarkable in the least, you know."

"Really?"

"I should have thought it was entirely natural."

Dawson-Hill smiled, self-possessed, unabashed. I should have remembered that he was a devout Catholic. I was ready for him to remind us that he had been to Mass that morning, but at that moment, the butler loudly called out Skeffington's name.

I cut my own examination short. Skeffington had nothing new to say, the Court had heard his opinion, fervent and lofty, times enough before. Everything fitted into place, once one saw Palairet had done it: the thing clicked, as it had clicked for him when he went through the notebooks: the missing photograph "told its own story": Palairet had done it, and nothing else was "on the cards."

I passed him on to Dawson-Hill, expecting them to be easy with each other. From the first question and answer, they couldn't get on. It wasn't that Skeffington gave anything away; it wasn't that Dawson-Hill had thought of anything subtle.

No, they just twitched a nerve of resentment in each other. Their eyes met only perfunctorily. Their handsome profiles were half-averted. Each of them was aware of his looks, I thought—to an extent which apparently irritated, not only more homely men, but also each other. Dawson-Hill took considerable care of his; his hair, that morning showing not a sliver of grey, was as burnished as an elegant undergraduate's. Was it the other's vanity each didn't like? They were both looking-glass vain.

There was more to it than that. Dawson-Hill saw someone "out of the same stable" as himself, belonging to just the same pocket of the upper middle-class, where smartness was making its last stand. That made the nerve of resentment quiver, when he found him hostile, in the enemy camp, in a case like this. Despite his tolerance, his free-and-easy fairness—Dawson-Hill was not devoid of either—he could not help feeling that this man should be on his side.

Then I thought again what I had thought the night before. What made Skeffington resentful was that, in everything but his sense of honour, he felt it too. Speaking before the Court that morning, he would have liked not to have quarrelled with their ruling. He wanted to become one of them—or rather, he did not so much want it as think that was his proper place. One could hear that "wish-to-accept" in his voice; it made him angrier with Dawson-Hill, with the Court, with all who disagreed with him. It made his rebellion more peremptory.

Round the table the Seniors were listening to him with formal politeness, not attention. He hadn't made much effect that day, but such as it was, it had been negative.

I was relieved to see him go.

Martin, who came in next, said precisely what he had contracted to say. He did not speak about the missing photograph. On all other points, he was careful, considerate, and unbudging. For himself, he said, he was convinced an injustice had been done. He could understand why others might not be convinced: wasn't it enough for them to see that an injustice might have been done? He was too practised a committee man to overstate his case: but he was also too practised to seem compromising where he didn't intend to be.

Dawson-Hill tried a few sighting-shots of questions, but then left him alone, with the final word:

"What it boils down to, if I understand you, is that, in a matter which is full of room for different opinions, you are giving the Court yours?"

"I think," said Martin, "it is rather more than that."

Crawford asked him the questions he had asked me, about Palairet and scientific fraud. Martin, more cautious than I had been, and a better judge of the Court, would not be drawn, except to say that he was forced to think Palairet had done it.

"Well, Martin," said Crawford, with a cordiality not so impersonal as usual, "that may be the point where we have to agree to differ."

When Martin had gone, and the rest of us went into the Lodge for lunch, I was sure that Dawson-Hill believed it was all over. He showed me the teasing and slightly guilty kindness that one shows to a rival who has done his best, when the best isn't good enough. I was also sure that not one of the Court was ready to change his mind. It was true, Brown as well as Crawford had not been quite unaffected by Martin. The most Martin had done was to make Brown reflect that they hadn't "handled the responsible chaps on the other side" too well. After they had "dug in their heels about this case,"—Brown felt immoveably that that was his duty—then they would have to spend some time and care "building bridges."

Brown sipped a glass of hock with sober content, Dawson-Hill reminisced about travels down the Rhine, old Winslow put away three glasses. Then Brown noticed that I was not touching mine. "You're not drinking, Lewis?" "It's very fine,"

Dawson-Hill said. "You oughtn't to miss it, you really oughtn't to." I said, not in the middle of the day. Brown was peering at me. He had noticed that I had been sitting silent. Did he suspect that I had not yet given up?

The Court regrouped itself in the Combination Room; the blind was pulled down; there was a smell of beeswax, furniture polish, Crawford's tobacco, honeysuckle from the terrace.

The butler cried out, as though rejoicing in the title:

"Sir Francis Getliffe!"

As Francis sat down, Crawford said:

"We are very sorry to drag you here on a Sunday afternoon."

"I should be distressed if anyone worried about that, Master."

"We know it's an infliction, but we hope you realise that we're grateful for your assistance."

"It couldn't possibly be an infliction, Master, if I can be of the slightest help—"

It was some time since I had seen Francis at a meeting. I had forgotten that, especially when uneasy, he took on a curious, stylised courtesy like a Spaniard in a play by Calderon.

Looking at him, my eyes made fresh by the tension so that I might have been looking at him for the first time, I thought that his face, also, might have been a seventeenth century Spaniard's. In shape, that is: long, thin, without much of a dome to the head. Not in colouring: the skin under the sunburn was pale and the eyes in the arched orbits were a kind of tawny yellow that I had seen only in Anglo-Saxons. They were splendid eyes, I suddenly realised, idealist's eyes, conceptualiser's eyes. Under them the skin was stained sepia and furrowed: those were the stains of anxious wear, the demands he had made upon himself, and they would not leave him now. The whole face was that of a man who had ridden himself hard, driven by purpose, ambition, and conscience.

Examining him, I began slowly. I wanted to get the courtesy peeled away. It didn't matter whether the Court thought I was spinning out the routine, making the best of a bad job. As I went over the old history, asking when he had first heard of the scandal, whether he had looked at Howard's published papers, formal questions of no interest, I could see Dawson-Hill, lounging in his chair as though this was dull stuff.

"For some time you took it for granted that Howard had faked the photograph in his paper?"

"Certainly."

"Accordingly, you accepted the verdict of the Court of Seniors, when they first deprived him?"

"In any circumstances I should want very strong reasons not to accept the verdict of the Court of Seniors of this college," said Francis, inclining his head to the Master and Brown, "and in these circumstances I thought their verdict was inevitable."

"When did you begin to think otherwise?"

"Later than I should have done."

That was better. His voice, light-toned and clear, had suddenly hardened.

"You began to think a mistake might have been made?"

"I should like to be clear about the word 'mistake.' "

"Let me ask you this instead. You began to think the Court had made a wrong decision?"

"I tried to explain that to them. Obviously I didn't go far enough."

Francis was now speaking with full authority. This was it, I thought. I was just going in for the *coup* when, maddened, I had to stop. There was one person who was not listening, either to full authority or anything else. Old Winslow, sedated by the heat and the glasses of hock, had nodded off, his nutcracker chin sunk low on his chest.

I stopped the question after the first word. Crawford enquired: "Eliot?"

I pointed at Winslow.

"Ah," said Crawford, without expression. "None of us is as young as he used to be." Gently he tugged at Winslow's gown.

The old man reluctantly, with saurian slowness, pulled up his head. Then he gave a smile rueful, red-lidded, curiously boyish.

"I apologise, Master," he said.

Crawford asked with medical consideration if he was all right.

"Perfectly all right, I thank you," said Winslow snappily, reaching out for the carafe of water in front of the Master's place. "Please resume your remarkable proceedings," he said to me.

With an eye on him, intent on keeping him awake, I asked Francis:

"You were saying that you hadn't gone far enough?"

"Certainly not."

"What do you now think you should have done?"

Francis answered, clear and hard:

"You asked me just now about a 'mistake.' I didn't accept the word. I ought to have drawn the Seniors' attention to what may—I do not say it was, but I do say most seriously that it may have been worse than a mistake."

There was no noise. Along the table I saw Nightingale, pen over the foolscap, in the middle of a note. He did not look up at Francis.

"I'm afraid I've not quite caught the drift of this," said Crawford. "Could you elucidate?"

"I'll try," said Francis. "I've never concealed my view that throughout this business Howard has behaved like an innocent and not very intelligent man. I've told you before that I believe his account of what happened is substantially accurate. I believe that most scientists who studied the facts would come to the same conclusion. They would, of course, as a consequence, have to accept that Palairet did this fraud."

"As the Master was saying to Martin Eliot before luncheon," said Brown, "that is just where we fundamentally disagree with him."

"How can you?" Francis spoke in a quiet tone, brittle but inflexible. "You've only been able to go on persuading yourselves because of one single fact. If that one photograph were present in Palairet's notebook, not one of you could even pretend to think that he wasn't responsible."

"The photograph, however, is not present," Crawford replied.

"That is what I meant by something possibly being worse than a mistake."

"If I understand your innuendo correctly," said Brown, "you—"

"I am not making an innuendo. I am stating a possiblity as clearly as I can. I believe the Court would be culpable if it did not take this possibility into account. It is: that the photograph now missing from Palairet's notebook was removed not by accident, but in order either to preserve Palairet's reputation or to continue justifying the dismissal of Howard."

"That is a very grave thing to say," said Arthur Brown. He was frowning, but not showing anger. I had no doubt that all the implications of what Francis had said were running through that cunning, politic mind—and at the same time outraging his feelings, because, tough and obstinate as he was, he was not willing that people should think he had done wrong or that he should think so himself.

"I know it," said Francis.

Beyond Winslow, Nightingale was no longer writing and

was gazing, together with the entire Court, at Francis. The lines on Nightingale's skin were visible, but no more than usual on a tiring day. The furrows ran across his forehead.

"I know it's a grave thing to say," Francis repeated. "I must ask the Court to remember that I've said it."

THIRTY-ONE

STATELINESS OF A MAN PRESIDING

Without another question, I told the Master that I had finished. Crawford turned to Dawson-Hill.

"Will you kindly proceed, then?"

Crawford's speech was as deliberate as usual, his moonface took on its formal, meaningless smile: but behind his spectacles his eyes had a smeared, indecisive look.

Dawson-Hill was in a dilemma. He was too shrewd a man not to have seen the crisis coming. It was not, however, the kind of crisis with which he had been trained to deal. Behind closed doors: the shut-in, senatorial faces: not an open word from any of the Court: not a name mentioned. And yet the feeling in the room had tightened like a field of force. Without any guide he had to judge that feeling.

It seemed to me that he had two choices. Either take the risk, come right out with it, ask who could have touched the photograph: or else damp the whole thing down, be respectful and polite to Francis, but get him out of the way and play for time.

The instant Crawford called on him, he began speaking, quick on the uptake, sounding quite casual. "This is extremely interesting, Sir Francis," he said, allowing himself a few seconds to make up his mind. Then he went on as though he had decided to take the risk. The notebook—Dawson-Hill kept referring to it, eyebrows stretched, as "this *famous* notebook." How much could Sir Francis help the Court about its history?

"I know no more than the Court does," said Francis.

Did Francis know anything of Palairet's habits or about how he'd kept his notebooks?

"I never even visited his laboratory."

Sensibly, Dawson-Hill was skipping the questions about legal proof. When the old man died, all his papers had been sorted out by his executor?

"So far as I know," said Francis.

Dawson-Hill glanced at Nightingale, who nodded.

The executor was himself an old man, a clergyman? And he had sent them, with long intervals between, in batches to Palairet's solicitors? The famous notebook being in the last batch? And the solicitors had passed each batch in turn on to the college?

As he asked these questions, Dawson-Hill was leaving gaps for the Seniors to break in. He was feeling his way, sensing how far he could safely go. If he gave them the lead, and one of them asked Francis just where and how he believed the photograph had been tampered with, then everything was on the table.

"And so the notebook arrived at the college?"

Francis said, "Of course."

Dawson-Hill looked across the table at the Court—Winslow was listening, hand propping up his jaw. Crawford sucked at his pipe. Brown sat back in his chair, firm and patient. Nightingale met Dawson-Hill's gaze. None of them volunteered a word.

Dawson-Hill had to make his decision. He could force the confrontation now—who had seen the notebook in the college? First Nightingale, then Skeffington, wasn't it? And so, what was Sir Francis Getliffe intending to say?

For any fighting lawyer, it was a temptation. But Dawson-Hill, trying to get the sense of the Court, felt that he mustn't fall into it. He drew back and went off on to an innocuous question. If I had been in his place I should have done just the same.

But, as he asked questions about Francis's opinion of Howard, he made what seemed to me a mistake in judgment, the first he had made since the hearing began. Francis had said that Howard's actions had been those of an "innocent and not very intelligent man." Dawson-Hill went in for some picador work. Was that really Francis's opinion? How long had it been so? Presumably he had not always thought Howard innocent? Not, in fact, until quite recently? Presumably, also, he had not always thought him 'not very intelligent?' When he supported him for his Fellowship, he could scarcely have considered him not very intelligent? Francis's estimates, both on character and ability, appeared to vary rather rapidly?

It would not have mattered that these questions were irrelevant. It did matter, or at least I thought it might, that Dawson-Hill let his temper show. Some of that temper came, of course, from pique. Until Francis spoke out that afternoon, Dawson-Hill had been certain that he had won. Now, looking round the uneloquent faces, he couldn't guess the end, but at least it was all to play for.

Yet there was something deeper than pique that made him more supercilious, sharpened the edge of his voice, drew him into addressing Francis with irritation as *Sir* Francis, with the accent on the title, as though Dawson-Hill had suddenly changed from an upper-class Englishman into a Maltese. It was deeper than pique, it was sheer dislike of Francis. For Dawson-Hill, despite his snobbisms and although he accepted the world, had a curious streak of emotional egalitarianism. He didn't like seeing people too miserable, and on the other hand he became irritated when he saw others in his view too well-endowed. He got on better with sinners than with the high-minded. He liked men best who were battered by life, had some trouble on their minds, were still high-spirited and preferably short of money. To him, Francis was a living provocation. He was too scrupulous, too virtuous: he was too conscientious, too far from common clay; he had done altogether too well; he had had success in everything he touched; he had even married a rich wife and had abnormally gifted children. Dawson-Hill could not bear the sight of him.

So Dawson-Hill, for once in his suave career, lost his temper. There was also a perceptible surge of temper on Francis's side. Francis, much nearer common clay than Dawson-Hill supposed, had a good robust healthy appetite for disliking those who disliked him. Further, he had no use for men as elegant as Dawson-Hill, as beautifully dressed, as youthful-looking, men whom he dismissed as *flaneurs*.

Their exchanges became more caustically smooth from Dawson-Hill, more contemptuous and impatient from Francis. I saw Brown peering at them both. He began to write on the paper in front of him.

"Sir Francis," Dawson-Hill was asking, "don't you agree that Dr. Howard, whose character you have praised so generously, showed a really rather surprising alacrity in accepting his professor's data?"

"I see nothing surprising in it."

"Should you say it was specially admirable?"

"It was uncritical."

"Shouldn't you say it was really so uncritical as perhaps to throw some doubt on his moral character?"

"Certainly not. A good many stupid research students would have done it."

"Do you really think it specially creditable?"

"I didn't say it was creditable. I said it was uncritical."

Just then Brown had finished writing his note. He placed it carefully on top of Crawford's pad. Crawford looked down, scrutinised the note, and, as Dawson-Hill was beginning another question, cleared his throat:

"I think there may be a measure of feeling among my

colleagues," he said, "that this might be as far as we can usefully go this afternoon. Speaking as Master, I'm inclined to suggest that we adjourn."

Winslow inclined his head. Crawford then asked Brown if he agreed, as though Brown's note had had no more effect on his, Crawford's action than if it had been a love-poem in Portuguese.

"I am also inclined to suggest," Crawford said, once more as though the idea had occurred to him out of the blue, "that this is a point where the Seniors might spend a little time gathering the threads together. I think it might be convenient if you let me provide you with tea in the Lodge—" he looked along his side of the table, from Winslow to Nightingale. "So shall we let Eliot and Dawson-Hill off for the rest of the afternoon?"

There was a murmur. There were ritual thanks from the Master to Francis Getliffe. Then the Seniors, led by Crawford, filed through the inner door of the Combination Room into the Lodge.

That left Dawson-Hill, Francis and me alone together. Not one of us could find a word to say. For an instant, Dawson-Hill's social emollience had left him quiet. As for me, it was a long time since I had felt so awkward. Heavy-footedly, I asked if he would be dining in hall. "Alas, no," he said, getting back into his social stride, telling me the house where he was going.

Francis said to me that he would see me before I returned to London. Nodding to Dawson-Hill, he left the room. I went out after him, but I did not want to catch him up. I did not want to speak to anyone connected with the Affair. I walked quickly through the Court, beating it to the shelter of my rooms.

I knew well enough what I was doing. It did not look like it, but I was touching wood. People thought that I was cautious and wary, easily darkened by the shadows of danger ahead. So I was. But also, all my life, I had been capable of being touched by too much hope, and in middle age I was so still. In fact, as I grew older, some of my inner weather reminded me more and more of my mother's. She too had been anxious and had over-insured: over-insured literally, in her case, so that years after her death I kept coming across pathetic benefits she had taken out in my name, with the Hearts of Oak and the other insurance companies, into which she, like the poor of her time, paid her pennies a week.

While at the same time, more superstitious each year she lived, (and I believed that in my fibres the same was true of me) she invented formulae for good-luck every week, as she filled in her forms for the competitions in *John Bull, Titbits* and *Answers*. She had hours and days astrologically chosen, in which to write her great bold clumsy words: and another lucky hour in which to post the envelopes. She used to take me to the pillar-box when I was a child. I would hear the envelope flap-thud into the dark: and then she would look at me, and I knew that in her heart she had already won the prize. "When our ship comes home," she would say, and at once sternly warn me about "counting our chickens before they were hatched." With an air of harsh realism, she told me that we mustn't expect the first prize every week. Yet she not only expected it; as she warned and reproved me for too much hope, she was simultaneously working out the ways to spend it.

I was very like her. It sometimes seemed to me that it was the anxious, the far-sighted, the realistic, who were most susceptible to hope. Certainly I could still be drunk with it. And the word "still" really had no meaning. In middle-age I was invaded by hopes exactly as I had been as a young man. No one had learned more about the risks, the probabilities, the realistic expectations of careers: and yet, in secret moments. I had learned nothing. For a long time, as I came to know more about myself, I had developed strategies to protect me and others from these surgent moments which—in their own existence, in their own euphoria—I could not suppress.

By myself that evening, therefore, I would not allow a thought to stray towards the case. If I did so, I should just feel that it was in the bag. Much more I wished to avoid meeting Martin or Skeffington, above all the Howards. If I did so, I should warn them how, in situations like this, anything could still happen. In the words I used, in the reasons I gave for staying in suspense, few people would be more guarded. And yet beneath the words there would be a feeling which completely contradicted them, and anyone who heard me would know it. It didn't take a perceptive person, as I had learned to my own and others' cost, to catch and believe the tone of irrepressible hope.

So I kept to myself, had a bath, took a book out into the garden and read till dinner time. When I arrived in the Combination Room I found, and was glad to find, that none of the principals was dining. Winslow, still in the Lodge, so the butler told me, had just sent word for them to strike his name off the list. Tom Orbell was the only partisan whose name was there. As soon as he entered he said, seeing me alone, "How is it going now?"

"Oh, it's still early days," I said in a judicious, reproving tone, the model of a middle-aged, responsible, experienced man, a man with a public face.

I did not let him say any more about the Affair, and no one else wished to. It was a small party, and a very young one. When Tom picked up the list, and noticed that Lester Ince was presiding, he said:

"Now that isn't exactly my idea of the *douceur de la vie*."

Two or three of the young Fellows came in, among them Ince, who, turning upon me a bland, benevolent and ceremonious gaze, said: "I'm very pleased that you're able to be with us to-night. We're all very pleased."

It might have been the Master or Brown speaking. For an

instant, Tom Orbell and I were taken by surprise. It even occurred to me that Ince was mimicking. But he was just feeling his position as Senior of those present. He addressed me in full: he did not feel it right to call me "Lew." He knew that he was in the chair, and he had set himself to make a proper job of it.

Dinner proceeded with decorum. After the meal was over he announced: "I think I should like to present a bottle to mark the first time that I have presided in this room."

Nothing could be more stately. On hot summer nights like this, it was a college custom to go on to the terrace outside the Combination Room, sit on a balustrade abutting the Master's garden, and drink white wine. In less reverential moods, I had heard Lester Ince object to this practice, on the simple but severe grounds that sitting on stone gave him piles, and that white wine was better described as cat's piss. Not so that night. He led the way on to the terrace, planted a firm, masculine, Trollopian backside on the balustrade, proposed his first toast in Barsac and inclined his head gravely, with ceremonial pleasure, when Tom Orbell toasted him as donor of the wine.

Looking up, one saw, over the roof of the hall, the sky so densely blue that it seemed tangible. The air was quiet. As five of us sat there on the terrace it was—especially to me, basking in it—the most placid of evenings.

Two of the young men got up to go.

"Must you leave us?" said Ince.

They said they had work to do.

"We shall miss you," said Ince, as a kind of presidential blessing. With disappointment he looked at Tom Orbell, the only Fellow left. "I was going to ask them, I thought to-night was a good night for it, isn't it time we really began to think about this election?"

He meant, of course, the magisterial election. To Tom,

who had been thinking of it for a couple of years past, the question seemed astonishingly cool.

"I suppose we ought to pay some attention to these things. It's our own fault if we're too lazy and then find that other people have been ganging up. It's a bore, but we probably ought to get hold of things and put some weight behind them. We'd better see that we get something sensible done."

It appeared as though he had been preparing for this speech as soon as he found that he was senior for the night. I was thinking how, like most apolitical men, he thought politics were very easy. He didn't see any complexities about them. For him, it was just the righteous but inert against the unrighteous but active. If only he and other men of good will applied themselves, all would come right.

It was an approach that could scarcely have been less endearing to Tom Orbell, who wrote about politics, whose dream-life was a politician's, and who, except in his persecuted moments, knew by instinct what the texture of politics was like.

Tom looked flushed and cross. In the warm evening, beads of sweat were standing out above his temples, where the hairline was going back.

"I think," he said, at his most mellifluous, "that there is something obviously sensible to be done. But then, I've always declared my interest."

Sitting dignified between us, Ince did not pretend, as in his more intransigeant turns, not to comprehend the phrase.

"Who are you thinking of, then?" he said.

"I've made it quite clear, I should have thought," replied Tom Orbell. "I'm voting for Arthur Brown."

"No," Ince reflected, "I don't think I want him."

"But why ever not? He's—"

"He's been here a bit too long," said Ince. "No, we've got to take some action before things go too far."

"Don't you realize," Tom asked, with an expression of

'God give me patience,' "that things have gone pretty far already? Don't you realise it's a moral certainty that it's going to be either Brown or Getliffe—"

"No, I won't have Getliffe," remarked Ince, as though that settled it.

"Why not?" I put in.

"I won't have a scientist," said Lester Ince. "I've got quite a different idea—"

"Who is it?" cried Tom.

Ince gave us a long, slow, subtle, satisfied smile. "G. S. Clark." He sat back, with the confidence of M. de Norpois mentioning the name of Giolitti, with the modest expression of an elder statesman who has produced the solution, obvious but so far concealed from others of less wisdom, out of his hat.

"God love my blasted soul!" Tom broke out. "Hasn't it occurred to you that the man's a monster? Hasn't it occurred to you that he's a ridiculous monster? Look here, I'm a Tory and I suppose you'd say you weren't. I love my religion and so far as I know, you haven't got any. But do you want, any more than I do, a man who sees a Communist under every bloody bed?"

"Everyone's got some bee in his bonnet," said Ince, temperately.

"Well, please enlighten me as to what you *do* see in him," Tom went on, beginning to show his silken, unstable courtesy and talking down his nose.

"He's independent."

"With great respect, I doubt it."

"I'm afraid," said Ince, in his new, stately manner, "I have to take people as I find them. I find him original. I find that he's not one of anyone's gang. And I'd like to tell you what a lot of people are thinking nowadays. It's time we got outside the gangs. We've got to keep our eyes open for men who stand on their own. And we shan't get a man in this college who stands on his own more than G. S. Clark does."

"So that's what you think, is it?" said Tom.

"I should like to hear your opinion of him," Ince turned to me.

I shook my head. "If I'd been asked to imagine an improbable nomination," I said, "I couldn't have imagined one as improbable as that."

"Look here," Tom broke out furiously, "I suppose you haven't given the faintest thought to the consequences, if you go ahead with this spectacular idea? I can tell you, and it's useless to deny it, things look pretty even just now between Brown and Getliffe. It looks like nine votes certain for Getliffe and seven for Brown, and the others not yet committed. If you go ahead with this spectacular idea, all you'll achieve is perhaps subtract a vote or two from Brown, including making Clark withhold his own vote. So with classical ingenuity, you will give Getliffe a long lead and probably let him in by default. Which is exactly the result you say you want the least. I suppose you hadn't thought of those consequences? Or I suppose that isn't the idea behind your spectacular idea?"

Tom was ready, as usual too ready, to smell out a conspiracy. Ince's face, up to that point rubbery, benevolent and composed, had taken on a frown.

"I've been listening to that kind of talk until I'm sick and tired," he said. "I'm just not prepared to play. All I'm prepared to do is to pick out the man I think best and say so and stick to it."

"Thus cleverly producing the consequences that you say you don't want."

"Damn the consequences. As for what you're telling me, there's only one answer to that." Suddenly Ince's stateliness had dropped away. His presidential manners had got lost. He said: "There's only one answer. Stuff it."

As they were glaring at each other, the butler came out on to the terrace.

"Mr. President," he said to Ince, "may I have permission to deliver a telephone message?"

"By all means," replied Ince, shining with sedateness once again.

The butler came to my side, and in his clear confidential whisper said: "Mr. Nightingale's compliments, and he would much appreciate it if you could do him the favour of calling in his rooms as soon as you conveniently can to-night."

THIRTY-TWO

ONE ENEMY TO ANOTHER

Walking through the third court to Nightingale's rooms, I was getting ready for a scene I did not like. In the golden pacific air my nerves were sharpened. I felt the mixture of combativeness, irritation and fear. My thoughts were all over the place: I even found myself thinking, with a childish sense of being ill-used, 'It's too nice a night to go and have a quarrel.'

After the warm, flower-scented court, the staircase, not yet lighted, struck dank as a well. As I climbed to the third floor, the landing was bright, flooded by the sunset. My eyes were dazzled, coming up from the dark floors beneath, and I could scarcely read Nightingale's name above the door. When I knocked and went in, he had the curtains drawn and both the reading lamp and an old-fashioned central chandelier switched on. He stood up, and in silence gave me an eager and charming smile.

He asked me to sit down, pointing to the one good arm-chair in the bare room. There was a church hush.

I was the first to make conversation. I said that I had glanced up at the Bursary, expecting to find him there.

"No," said Nightingale, "I don't believe in living over the shop." He went on to say that he had occupied these present rooms ever since he was first elected and added: "And that's longer ago than I'd care to think. If it comes to that," he spoke to me civilly, as though we shared a rueful pleasure, "it must be a long time since you were up here last. *That* must be longer ago than either of us cares to think."

It had, in fact, been before the war. I had only been inside that room twice during the time we were both Fellows. Our relations had made it unlikely that I should visit him. And yet, Nightingale seemed to remember that period, when he was bitterly miserable, when he and I were barely on speaking terms, not sentimentally, not with affection, but with something like respect.

Perhaps he was one of those men, so self-absorbed that everything that has happened to them is precious, who don't want to dismiss an enemy from their minds, provided they have known him long enough. The bare fact of knowing him long enough gives him some claim upon them. Just then, he was speaking to me—whom he had always regarded as an enemy, that night with specific cause, and who in turn disliked him more than most men—as though we had something in common.

I looked round the room. It was as I dimly recalled it, bleak, both less cosy and less personal than most Fellows' rooms. An oar, relic of undergraduate rowing, was hung along one wall. On his desk stood a large photograph of his wife, pudgy, amiable, full-eyed, which couldn't have been there in my time. I noticed on the walls photographs which must also have been recent, groups of officers in the desert. In one Nightingale sat in the middle, wearing shorts and a beret. In another he was placed two from the left of a famous soldier, whom I happened to have met. I asked about him.

"Oh, they'd kicked me upstairs by then," said Nightingale. "They'd decided I was an old man, and no good for fighting any more."

It occurred to me, he was oddly modest about his war. He had been a field officer in his mid-forties; I couldn't think of many amateurs who had done as much. I said that I knew his commander, Lord Gilbey. During the war, stories had collected in Whitehall among officials not given to hero-worship, about his personal bravery. I asked Nightingale about this.

"Oh, he didn't much mind being shot at," he said. He added: "After all, he's been paid to be shot at all his life, hasn't he?"

"But still," I said, "he must have quite abnormal physical courage."

"I suppose he has," said Nightingale.

"I must say I envy it."

"I don't think you need," said Nightingale.

Suddenly I realised, what had been at the back of my mind all along, that I was talking of one very brave man to another. Like it or not, one had to admit that Nightingale's courage in both wars was absolute.

"I've seen too much of it to be impressed," he remarked. "I don't think you need envy it." He said it with something like a sneer, but quite kindly. He was not a man with any interest in understanding others: he was too knotted in himself for that. Certainly he had no interest in me, except as one who filled him with resentment. Yet, just for an instant, he seemed to understand me better than if he had been fond of me. He spoke—it was bizarre, in the tension of that evening—as though he were reassuring me.

There was another, and a longer, church-like hush. We had finished all the conversation we could make. We had not, we had never had, a thought in common. We were both controlling ourselves, ready to wait.

At last Nightingale said:

"I wanted to talk to you about this afternoon."

"Do you?" I replied.

"I should like to know why Getliffe said what he did."

"He must have felt it was his duty," I said.

"I take it *you* were responsible for this?" His voice was still controlled, but there was a strained, creaking note within it.

"I think that, for anything that concerns his actions, you'll have to ask Getliffe himself. Isn't that right?"

"Do you imagine for an instant that I can't see the power behind the scenes?"

"Do you imagine that I or anybody else could persuade Getliffe to say a word he didn't believe?"

"I want to know why he said this."

"Now look," I said, speaking as violently as he had done but more quietly, "this will get you nowhere. The point is, Getliffe has said it. And what he says it's quite impossible for the Seniors to ignore. That's the brute fact—"

"Do you think we're trying to ignore it? What do you think we've been doing since we adjourned?"

He emphasized the "we" as though, through being on the Court, he still drew not only strength but pride. I looked straight at him. The bones of his forehead, under the thick, wavy fair hair, were strong. He had crows' feet beneath his eyes, fine lines on his eyelids. The delicate etching of his skin seemed not to match the heavy, almost acromegalic, bones. His eyes stared full into mine—they were lustrous, innocent eyes, they held feeling but no insight. As we gazed at each other, the corners of his mouth stretched, as if he were using his muscles, his whole physical force, to master himself. He spoke in a voice which, though monotonous, was low, and said:

"I hope you'll listen to me, Eliot."

I said yes.

"I know we haven't always seen eye to eye. I don't know how much I was to blame. I don't mind telling you this—if I had my time over again, I should try not to say some of the things I've said."

It wasn't an intense statement. It didn't contain remorse. Yet it sounded sincere, and curiously business-like.

Before I could reply, he asked me:

"I suppose there are some things you've said you'd like wiped off the record, aren't there?"

"Of course."

That seemed to satisfy him.

"We haven't always seen eye to eye," he repeated. "That's agreed on both sides, but it oughtn't to affect the issue."

"What do you mean?"

"You're no man's fool, Eliot," he replied, still in the same level, businesslike fashion. "You know as well as I do, and better, I shouldn't be surprised, that this afternoon got us into deep water."

In contrast to his tone, his stare was illuminated.

"Now I'm asking you to help us out of it," he said. "I'm asking you to put the past into cold storage and help us out of it."

I was having to keep myself matter-of-fact. All his energy, his strained obsessive energy, was pouring out of him. His words were flat; yet one wasn't listening to them, but to the force behind them. It made the air in the room seem denser, the light more dim.

"So far as I can see," I said, "there's only one conceivable way out."

He took no notice of me.

"We've got into deep water," he went off again. "You know as well as I do, and a good deal better, that a suspicion was raised this afternoon. We're intended to suspect that someone may have falsified the books to do this man Howard down. We're intended to suspect someone. Someone? It might be me."

I looked at him without speaking.

There was a pause.

He said:

"I don't expect you to worry about that. Why should you? But I tell you that it isn't the issue. It isn't what we think of one another. We've seen a lot of things happen to one another. I'm not talking about what might happen to either of us now. I don't expect you to worry about that. But I do expect you to worry about something else."

He went on: "If this goes on, what's the end of it going to be? If people begin suspecting as you want them to, then I can tell you the result, and I hope it's one you haven't thought of. They suspect someone. All right. I tell you, it might be me. Someone in this college. An officer of this college. What is going to be the effect on the place?"

He was speaking very fast, half-inarticulately, but with passion.

"I'd give a lot to keep the college out of danger, Eliot. I hope you would. I don't mind saying, it's done everything for me. I don't mean when I was a young man. A bright young man ought to be able to look after himself. No, it's done everything for me when I was afraid I was going to peter out. They trusted me. They gave me an office. It's the only thing anyone's ever elected me to. I've done my best not to let them down. I tell you, that office is the best thing that ever happened to me. Do you wonder that I'm not prepared to see anything bad happen to this place? That's why I'm talking to you. I'd give all I've got to keep it safe."

I believed him. I believed him without the flicker of a doubt. It wasn't the easy-natured who were most seized by that kind of loyalty. It wasn't the successful: old Gay had as little as a man could reasonably have. It wasn't the self-sufficient. No, most of all it was those like Nightingale who were self-absorbed without being self-sufficient. For an instant, I wondered, was that also true of Howard? When I heard his mumbling statement that he was thinking of the college, I had thought he was confused, I had dismissed it. Was I being too sceptical, were these two alike in that one spot? Was it possible that when Howard gave his reason for not suing the college, a reason that he only half-admitted to himself, that it was there?

With Nightingale, the force of his feeling beat down on me. It was so strong that, not only recognising it but overcome, I lost all certainty of what he was like, much less what he had, or had not, done. I could not be sure at that moment whether I believed he had ripped out the photograph in cold blood. All I was sure of was this ferocious, self-bound loyalty. Whether I suspected him or not, had become remote or indeed, meaningless. And yet I could simultaneously and quite easily imagine that if the photograph had come his way, and if it seemed to threaten his idea of the college's honour, then he would have had it out—without his conscience being troubled, even though it meant victimising Howard, because this was an act of conscience too.

I had to struggle to keep detached, that is, detached enough not to give a point away.

I replied:

"No one wants to do the college the slightest harm."

"I'm glad to hear you say it."

"No one," I said, picking out the words, "would want to press the suspicion you mentioned further than he had to. But—"

"Yes?"

"As I said before, there's only one conceivable way out. If the Seniors can change their decision against Howard, then no one's going to cause any unnecessary trouble. But if the Seniors can't change their decision, then I'm afraid it would be very difficult to stop."

He was waiting for me to continue, but I had finished. The telephone rang. I could hear him replying to the porter's lodge, saying that he wouldn't be long. He looked at me, his eyes shining:

"Is that all?"

"I can't say any more to-night."

"Do you want to speak to your—friends?"

I said:

"That would make no difference."

He acted as though exhilarated, and not disappointed. He seemed only to have heard the half of my reply, the anodyne half. He seemed not to have grasped what the reply meant. Or perhaps he was still borne up by the excitement of having spoken without constraint. Cheerfully, in a tone hearty and almost friendly, he said that he would have to go, his wife was waiting for him in the car outside the college. Together we walked down the stairs and through the courts. Nightingale looked up at the sky, where the first stars were coming out.

"Now I call this something like weather."

We were walking as though I might never have left the college, as though we were a pair, not of friends exactly, but of friendly acquaintances, who had been colleagues for twenty years, and were, without noticing it, getting old together.

Outside the main gate, the car was drawn up by the kerb, the door open, Mrs. Nightingale looking out.

"Hullo," she said, "what have you boys been up to?"

"Oh, just talking a bit of shop," said Nightingale.

She got out on to the pavement, so that Nightingale could climb in to drive. As he did so, she patted him affectionately and then stood chatting to me. She was as unselfconscious as anyone I had known. She was so easy that, though at sight she was not specially attractive, she took on an attraction of her own. And yet, the instant I heard her ask what we had been doing, and saw her great eyes glance at him, I was positive about two things. First, that she had known exactly what we had been talking about, and second, that, in the midst of the suspicion about him, she did not suspect but know. I was positive about something more. She was easy, she was good-natured, she would far rather the people round her were happy than unhappy. If he had not done what he was suspected of, she would be glad. But if he had done it, then she would not only know, she would talk about it with him, she would enjoy the complicity, and she would—for though she had good feelings, she had no kind of conscience—amiably approve.

V

THE CURVES OF JUSTICE

THIRTY-THREE

THE SIGHT OF A BLANK SPACE

The bell tolled, sunlight spotted the carpet, as I came into the Combination Room on the Monday morning. The Seniors were all there standing by the fireplace. Even as we exchanged good-mornings, one could feel the strain in the air. It was not the specific kind of strain that one meets going into a group of acquaintances, when they are hiding bad news from one. I had no guide as to what had been said among themselves, either the night before or that morning; but I knew almost at once that they were split.

Dawson-Hill came in, not from the college door as I had done, but from the inner one which led to the Master's Lodge. I was wondering, how early did this conference begin? Dawson-Hill's hair was burnished, he smelled of shaving lotion. "Good-morning, my dear Lewis," he said, with his bright, indifferent smile.

We took our places at the table. Slowly, with neat fingers, Crawford packed and lit a pipe. He sat back in his chair, his face as unlined as ever, his body as still: and yet, as soon as he spoke, I was sure that for once his complacency was precarious.

"I'm inclined to think," he said, "that certain statements made by one of our colleagues involve us in a certain amount of difficulty. I'm going to ask you to address your minds to the wisest way of removing the difficulty, remembering, of course, the responsibility before the Court."

He sucked at his pipe.

"Eliot, these statements concern your side of the case. Are you able to give us a lead?"

Although I was looking at Crawford, I could feel Nightingale's gaze upon me. This had been pre-arranged, I thought. They were leaving the move with me. As for an instant I hesitated, a voice came from Crawford's right:

"With your permission, Master."

Crawford turned, face and shoulders, to look at old Winslow.

"Do you wish to speak now?" Crawford asked him.

"If you please. *If* you please."

Crawford held up his hand in my direction, as though I needed shutting up. Winslow bent his head down over the table, like a great battered bird investigating the ground for food; then, twitching his gown away from his collar, he stared up at us from that bent posture. His eyes were bold, unconcerned, almost mischievous.

"As you all know, Master," he said, "I speak as a complete ignoramus. When I hear the interesting subjects discussed so intelligently by everyone else on this Court, I marvel slightly at how remarkably little I know of these matters. However, there are limits even to my incapacity. Yesterday afternoon, of course I may delude myself, I thought I captured the general drift of what Francis Getliffe was trying to tell us. Unless I am considerably mistaken, he was trying to tell us something which is perhaps a shade out of the ordinary run. He appeared to be giving us, as his considered opinion, that the unfortunate Howard might conceivably have been what I believe is nowadays known as 'framed.' And that if this possibility should happen to be true, then it appears that one of the Fellows, one of our singular and reputedly learned society, must have been guilty of *suppressio veri*. To put it with the maximum of charity, which is probably, as is usually the case, totally uncalled-for.

"I have been considering these rather unusual possibilities, but I see no reason to invent complexities where no complexities can reasonably exist. It seems to me impossible, much as one perhaps might wish it, to pretend that Getliffe did not mean what he said. It seems to me *a fortiori* impossible for this Court not to act accordingly. No, I have to correct myself. No doubt nothing is impossible for this Court, or for any other committee of our college. Shall I simply say that it is impossible for me? Of course, I know nothing of Getliffe's subject. But I have always understood that he is a man of great distinction. I have never heard anyone suggest that his character is not beyond reproach. For what little my opinion is worth, I have always thought very highly of him. Indeed, Master, may I bring it to a point?"

"Naturally."

"Thank you, thank you. I need only remind you of what I think is common knowledge. Shortly, my dear Master, your remarkable reign is coming to a close and you will subside into obscurity with the rest of us. In the ensuing election, I have never so much as contemplated another candidate than Getliffe. If you will forgive the turn of phrase, I soon both expect and hope to see him in your place."

Winslow gave a grim, nutcracker smile at Crawford, reminding him of supersession and mortality. He gave another past Crawford at Brown, reminding him of Winslow's opinion of his chances.

"I confess," Winslow went on, "I should find a certain inconsistency in supporting Getliffe as our next Master and not paying attention to his statement of yesterday afternoon. I do not propose to exhibit that inconsistency. I should therefore like to give notice, Master, that on this Court I intend to vote for the re-instatement of Howard, or if you prefer it, the quashing of his deprivation, whatever peculiar form of procedure we find it appropriate to use. I suggest that this is done forthwith. Of course," said Winslow, "it will make the Court of Seniors look slightly ridiculous. But then, the Court of Seniors *is* slightly ridiculous."

Quiet. Whatever else had been talked about and decided, this hadn't, I was certain. No one there had expected Winslow's *démarche*. Further, I was certain, after watching the others respond to Winslow, that among themselves much had been left unspoken. Was that because Nightingale had not left them? Hadn't Crawford and Brown talked by themselves?

"Is that all?" enquired Crawford, flatly but politely.

"Thank you, Master. That is all."

It had sounded like an outburst, like a free, capricious act. Yet in fact, Winslow was running along an old groove: it wasn't often or for long that men of eighty could get out of the grooves their lives had worn, and despite his spirit, gusto and relish, Winslow had not done so that morning. He had always had a standard of suitable behaviour. His tongue made that standard sound odder than it was. Actually, it was as orthodox as Brown's, and in depth not so independent: for Winslow believed what responsible people told him, as now with Francis Getliffe, while Brown, however comfortably he spoke, in the long run believed no one but himself.

No, Winslow's standard of behaviour had nothing special about it. Nor, as far as that went, had the history of his life. It was not in those terms, but below them, that he was interesting.

His life had, of course, been by his own criteria a failure. He was fond of saying so. He explained how, of three inadequate bursars in succession, he had been the worst. He was prepared to expand on his "lifetime of singular lack of achievement." He believed he was telling the truth. In reality, except when he spoke of his son, living God knows how in Canada, nearly forty and without a job, taking his allowance and never sending a letter, he liked talking about his failure. "I always felt I was slightly less crass than most of my colleagues. And indeed that was not making a superlative claim.

Nevertheless, even compared with their modest efforts, I've done quite remarkably worse." Speaking like that, he got the feeling of being unsparing and honest. Yet he wasn't. As he talked he believed he was a failure: but his fibres told him otherwise.

He had never been easy with men. He had never made close friends. He was both too arrogant and too diffident. And yet, at eighty, he still kept a kind of assurance that many disciplined, matey and, by his criteria, successful men, never attain at all. It was the kind of elemental assurance of someone who had after all lived according to his nature. It was the kind of assurance that one meets sometimes in rakes and down-and-outs—very likely, now I came to think of it, in his own son. It was the kind of assurance that both gave, and at the same time derived from, the strongest animal grip on life.

Crawford looked at Brown and said:

"I think we must take note that our Senior colleague has declared his intentions."

"If you please, Master," said Winslow. "*If* you please."

I too had been looking at Brown. He knew, both of us knew, that Winslow would from now on never budge.

"I suppose it is slightly premature for the Court to try to formulate its decision," said Crawford. He said it with the faintest inflection of a question. From his left hand Brown, for once, did not help him out. Brown sat back, receptive, vigilant, without a word.

Without a word, we all sat there. For an instant I felt triumph. The case had cracked. Then, in a tone slightly harsh but businesslike, Nightingale said: "I should regard it as premature, of course. I totally disagree with almost everything we've heard from Mr. Winslow. I can't begin to accept that that is a basis for a decision. I move that proceedings continue."

At last Brown spoke, steadily and with weight:

"I have to agree with the Bursar."

"In that case," said Crawford, in resignation, "I'm afraid we come back to you, Eliot."

Again, before I started speaking, I was interrupted: this time by Dawson-Hill.

"Master, with apologies to my colleague, may I—?"

Crawford, who was getting fretful, shut his eyes and nodded his head, like one of the mandarin toys of my childhood.

"I would like to make just one plea," said Dawson-Hill. "I haven't the slightest intention of depriving my colleague of an argument on his side of the case. I am sure he knows that I haven't the slightest intention." He gave me his groomed, party smile. "But I would like to ask if he can see his way to leaving Sir Francis Getliffe's statement as it stands. Naturally this statement can't be ignored by the Court. But with great respect and humility, I do suggest that if my colleague takes it further we face a prospect of getting into situations of some delicacy, without any gain either to his arguments or mine. I'm fully aware that anything said to this Court is privileged. Nevertheless, I do urge on my colleague that we avoid delicate situations where we can. I know he will agree with me, it is quite obviously incontrovertible, that none of Sir Francis Getliffe's speculations are provable in law. With great respect, I do suggest that we leave them now."

Again, Nightingale was watching me. He was wearing a new butterfly bow, red with white spots, jaunty under the stern masculine jaw. In his eyes the pupils were large. This was the second version of his appeal to me.

I had made my choice long since. I said:

"I'm sorry, Master. I can't present a fair case for Howard with one hand tied behind my back."

"All right!" It was Nightingale who said it, his voice gravelly. This was the first time violence, open violence, had broken into the room. He was furious, but furious not so much from a sense of danger as because he had been turned down. "Put your cards on the table. That'd be a change for us all."

"If you don't mind," I said—I was playing to provoke him —"I'd rather put Palairet's notebook on the table."

"I should like a simple answer to a simple question," Nightingale cried. "How much of all this is intended for me?"

"I don't think," I said, "that the Bursar should conduct my case for me."

"I'm afraid that's reasonable," said Dawson-Hill, sounding both embarrassed and not used to being embarrassed, across the table to Nightingale.

But Nightingale was a daring man. Passions, long banked-down, were breaking out of him. They were not, or only in part, the passions of the night before. Then he had spoken to me, an old enemy, with the intimacy that sometimes irradiates enmity. Now he wasn't speaking to me personally at all. He hated me, but only as one of many. He was speaking as though surrounded by enemies, with himself all set to hack his way out. He had lost his temper: but as with some active men, having lost his temper made him more fit for action, more capable of looking after himself.

"I want to know," he said, "whether what Getliffe said yesterday was intended for me? Or what this man is telling us this morning?"

Deliberately I did not answer. I asked Crawford if he minded my having Palairet's notebook open on the table. "Perhaps," I said, "the Bursar can help me find the place." I got up from my seat, went round the table behind Crawford, took the note-book and stood with it at Nightingale's side.

"It's somewhere near half-way through," I said. "We ought to have had it tagged."

Nightingale was watching the leaves as I furled them through. "Later than that," he said, not pretending that he was lost.

"There it is, isn't it?" I said.

"Yes," said Nightingale, gazing carefully at the page but without expression.

Everyone was watching him as he studied the page.

I brought back the open notebook into the centre of the room, and placed it on the table in front of Crawford's place. The right-hand page was numbered in ink, a hundred and twenty-one. The date, also in ink, stood on the left of the top line. Two-thirds of the page was empty, except for the trace of gum marking out the sides of a rectangle, where the photograph had been. At the bottom of the rectangle, nearer the middle than the left-hand corner, was a scrap of the print, perhaps a quarter of an inch square. Getliffe and the rest had agreed that this scrap told nothing. Beneath the rectangle, in the bottom third of the page, the caption took up three lines of holograph, in a neat Edwardian script. It was written in pencil, and looked fainter than when I had seen it before. It also looked insignificant, something domesticable that couldn't cause trouble.

"There, gentlemen," I said.

I had judged my line by now. I began:

"You heard Getliffe give you his opinion yesterday. No one gives that kind of opinion lightly: and you all know Getliffe as well as I do. He said it was possible that the photograph which used to be on this page—" I had put a finger on the notebook—"had been torn out. Not by chance."

"I want to know whether that was intended for me." Nightingale's voice swept across the room.

"Of course," I said, not replying to him directly, "Getliffe felt justified in saying that the photograph might have been torn out. Not by chance. But he didn't feel justified in speculating about—by whom? We can't know. I should think it quite likely that we shall never know. From the point of view of this case, or for those who have been convinced for so long of Howard's innocence, it doesn't matter. All that I need remind you of is that this note-book passed through several hands before it looked like *this.* It's not my function to attribute motives. I assume, as Getliffe does, as other physical scientists in the college do, but not the Bursar, that there was a faked photograph on that page. That faked photograph could have been seen by several people. As Getliffe said, someone who was pro-Palairet, or anti-Howard, might have desired that photograph out of the way. That is as much as anyone has any right to say. But I think I might remind you of the history of the note-book."

Carefully, for I had a double purpose, since I had at once to keep the suspicion on Nightingale and leave both him and the Court a tolerable way out, I went through the history step by step. The last entry was on April 20, 1952. Palairet had died after a long but not disabling illness, on January 5, 1953. He might—I said it casually, but I could feel a jolt—have ripped the photograph out himself. Why not? He might have got tired of being silly. If it were still there when he died, the note-book stayed in his laboratory for months: a laboratory assistant could have access: would he have known or cared? Palairet was a solitary worker, but there were two or three research students about. No one had thought of talking to them.

"Red herrings," said Nightingale.

Some time in the autumn of '53, a time probably impossible to define now, I said, the executor had moved the note-book, part of the last batch of scientific remains. The executor was a clergyman of eighty, quite unscientific. On December 13, 1953, the note-book and other papers had reached Palairet's solicitors. On December 15, 1953, it had arrived at the Bursary.

"And now," I said to Crawford, "may I ask the Bursar one or two questions?"

"Are you prepared for that, Nightingale?" Crawford asked.

"Of course I am."

I spoke diagonally across the table. "You were the first person in the college to see the note-book?"

"Of course I was."

"Do you remember when?"

"Probably the day it arrived."

"Do you remember—this page?"

"You'll be surprised to know I do."

"What did it look like?"

"I might as well say, I hadn't much time to get down to Palairet's papers. I happened to be busy at the Bursary. Some of my predecessors managed to do the job in two hours a morning, but I've never been clever enough."

His eyes rolled, so that I could only see crescents of dark against the whites. It was the kind of spite that one used to hear from him when he was a younger man, when everything had gone wrong. It was spite against Winslow, who had been a mediocre Bursar while Nightingale was an exceptional one. It was revenge against Winslow for his speech that morning.

But Nightingale, though at his tensest, sounded matter-of-fact as he went on. "I didn't have much time to get down to the papers. But I think I remember skimming through the note-book. I think I remember one or two things on the right-hand pages."

He was speaking like a visualiser. I asked: "You remember this page?"

"I think so. Yes."

"What did it look like?"

"Not like that."

Everyone there was taken right aback. Though I went straight on, I was as astonished as the rest.

"What then?"

"There was a photograph there, top half of the page."

"What sort of photograph?"

"Nothing like the one in Howard's thesis. Nothing wrong at the corners."

"What did you do?"

"I just glanced at it. It wasn't very interesting."

"You say there was nothing faked in the photograph. What about the caption?"

"I was too busy to worry about that."

"Too busy?"

"Yes, too busy." His voice rose.

"You just looked at this photograph? The rest of the page was like this, was it?" I pushed the note-book towards him.

"Yes."

"You looked at the photograph? Then, *what did you do?*"

He stared at me. In an instant he said:

"Just put the book back with the rest of the Palairet dossier, of course."

The night before, in the violence of his feeling, I hadn't known what I believed. So now, gazing at the empty page, I lost my sense of fact. I could see him, on a December morning, also gazing at the page: either at the photograph securely there, or at the gap after he had torn it out. Everything seemed equally probable or improbable. It was a sort of vertigo that I had felt as a young man, when I did some criminal law: and since, in the middle of official security: or dazzled by the brilliance of suspicion. Somehow, immersed in facts, in the simple, natural facts of a crime, one found them diminish, even take the meaning out of, the lives in which they played a part.

In the midst of the facts of the crime, there were times when one could believe anything. Facts were hypnotic, facts were neutral, facts were innocent. Just as they were for those who had done a crime. If Nightingale had ripped out this photograph, it could seem such a simple, such an innocent act. It might seem unfair that there was all this fuss about it. It was more than possible, it was easy—I had known many who had managed it, I had myself, when I had performed an act which damaged others—to forget, because the act itself was so innocuous, that one had done it at all.

"You put it back with the photograph still there, you mean?"

"Of course I mean that," Nightingale cried violently.

"But the photograph had disappeared when the note-book was next opened?"

"That's what we've heard."

Up to that point, Nightingale had given me nothing. Suddenly I saw him enraged, his eyes rolling with hostility again.

"I'm sorry," I said, "have I misunderstood? The next person to look at the note-book was Skeffington, wasn't it?"

"I've been told so."

"Well, then, when he looked at the note-book the photograph was missing?"

"We've heard a lot," said Nightingale, "of no one making allegations against any particular person. Two can play at that game. I'm not going to make an allegation against any particular person. But why shouldn't one of Howard's friends have taken out the photograph? The perfectly genuine photograph? Just to get this started again? Not to make any bones about it, just to point their fingers at me?"

"But that could only be Skeffington?"

"You're saying that, I'm not."

"Could anyone call him one of Howard's friends?"

"You can answer for them. I'm not going to."

"Can you imagine Skeffington doing any such thing for any man or any purpose in the world?"

"Some of them have imagined things against me, haven't they?"

It was past one o'clock. There I left it. As soon as the afternoon sitting began, I knew that, though I hadn't broken through, I had done something. The last five minutes of the morning, Nightingale's accusation against Skeffington—those were what Dawson-Hill was trying to wipe out. The accusation was fantastic, Dawson-Hill was as good as telling Nightingale as he questioned him: wouldn't he reconsider and retract it?

For a long time Nightingale was obdurate. He had made no allegations against anyone, obstinately he repeated. Dawson-Hill handled him with gentleness and respect. Gradually one could see the lineaments of Nightingale's face changing in response. But Dawson-Hill did not get the retraction, the total return to the plane of efficiency and reason, that he was working for. Later, he was working for another answer which he did not get. He was anxious because Nightingale had admitted to seeing the photograph. How much could Nightingale really trust his memory? Couldn't this particular recollection be wrong? Wasn't it possible, or even likely, that the photograph was already torn out when the note-book first came under Nightingale's eyes? Dawson-Hill wanted an open, easy yes. It took him ingenuity to make Nightingale tolerate the bare possibility.

The open, easy answers came at last, in reply to the last two questions.

"You see nothing to make you believe that Palairet faked any photograph at any time?"

"Of course I don't."

"You still believe that Howard was guilty?"

"I believe that," said Nightingale, in a fierce, daring and tireless tone, "as much as I believe anything."

Letting down the tightness in the room, Dawson-Hill then asked Crawford about the time-table for the next day, Tuesday. G. S. Clark had already been told to be ready first thing in the morning. After that, Dawson-Hill presumed, he and I would make our final remarks.

"That sounds reasonable to me," said Crawford.

That afternoon he had wilted, much more so than Winslow, who spoke next:

"My dear Master, I confess the word 'reasonable' doesn't seem to me to be specially appropriate. I seem to remember remarking this morning that, without further mummery, we should reinstate this man. With your permission, may I repeat that?"

"I'm afraid the consensus of opinion this morning was that the hearing should go on," said Crawford.

"We hadn't the benefit, I might point out," Winslow snapped, "of to-day's interesting proceedings. I should like to hear others' views."

Crawford was going through the motions of presiding. Nightingale broke in:

"You know mine."

"It is?" Crawford asked.

"It doesn't need saying. I stick to the Court's decision."

"So the Bursar and you," Crawford said to Winslow, "appear to cancel each other out."

"Very remarkable," Winslow replied.

"Brown?"

Crawford turned to his left. All day long Brown had been quiet, quieter than I had ever seen him at a meeting. He had passed no notes to Crawford. Now he said, still sitting back, his expression heavy but his voice practised and level:

"I'm inclined to think that we've gone too far to try to short-circuit things now. This may be a time when it would be a mistake to spoil the ship for a ha'p'orth of tar. As for my opinion, Master, I should like to reserve it until Wednesday."

"Well then," said Crawford, "we meet to-morrow." He had suddenly begun to look like an old man. In a tone sharp and petulant, he went on: "I wish I could see more agreement among us. As far as my own opinion goes, I shall attempt to give some indication of it to-morrow afternoon."

THIRTY-FOUR

CRIPPLE WALKING ON THE LAWN

"He's all man," said Irene with glee. She was not talking of a lover, but of her son, away at his preparatory school. She and Martin and I were sitting on their lawn before dinner on the Monday evening. I had not long arrived. Martin, whose face had caught the sun, was lying back in his deck chair, his hand to his eyes, squinnying towards the bottom of the garden.

Martin also was talking about the boy. He was out of comparison more protective than she was. In the weekly letter home, Martin read undertones of trouble, concealed from parents, which she laughed off.

"He's all man," she cried. "He'll be as wild as a hawk, one day. That will be something."

Martin smiled. Even he, the most cautious of men, did not find the idea unpleasant. As for her, she adored it. I was thinking, Martin's love for the boy was tenacious, deep, more spontaneous than any other affection he had ever had. She loved the boy too, perhaps as much as Martin did, but in a way that was not in the ordinary sense maternal. She was a good mother; she was conscientious, to an extent that people who had known her in her raffish days could scarcely believe. And yet really she loved the boy looking upwards, not downwards, looking towards the time when he was a man, and would take her out and tell her what to do.

Once, when she was young and chasing a man twice her age, I had heard her squeal with delight and say that she was good at daughtering, not at mothering. It was truer than she thought. Somehow, in her own family, where she looked from the outside a bulky, ageing woman, she would feel younger than any of the men.

That was already so in her marriage. In calendar years she was older than Martin: she looked older. But, now they had been married fifteen years, she had come to behave like a daughter to a father, who was wilful, capricious, but who was her one support: to whom under the teasing and the disrespect, she felt nothing but passionate respect.

It seemed to suit them both. Against all the prophecies, against the forecasts of wiseacres like myself, the marriage had worked. As she walked back into the house to put dinner on, stoop-shouldered, thickening, still active and light on her feet, from his chair Martin's eyes followed her. It was not till then that he asked me about Nightingale. He had kept from her, I felt sure, how he had been more scrupulous, more gentle, than the rest of us. Perhaps he knew that that was an aspect of him, surprising to his friends, surprising even to himself, that she would not wish to see.

"How did Nightingale take it?" As he asked the question, he was puzzled to see me grin. It just happened that his tone had not been at all gentle. Somehow it brought back to mind one of old Gay's saga men enquiring how some unfortunate hero had faced an ordeal, such as having his house burned over his head.

"Well, how did he take it?" Martin repeated.

I described the day. Martin listened with concentration. He was careful not to say whether he thought Nightingale's behaviour pointed to guilt or innocence. He was too experienced to worry me with doubts just then. I was in the middle of it; he was not going, even by a fraction, to weaken my will. As usual, he was leaving nothing to chance. It rested with Crawford and Brown now: what were they going to say?

"It ought to be all right," I said.

Dawson-Hill was dining with Crawford that evening, wasn't he? Martin asked.

"I don't know that I like that," he reflected. He insisted that I ought to see Brown alone on the following, Tuesday, night. After all, Brown was a friend and a good man. Despite all this faction, I could still talk to him as a friend. It might be worth doing. Martin was sure that it was worth doing. I was not eager, but Martin pressed me. Would I mind if he fixed it up straight away? I said that anxiety was running away with him. "Never mind," said Martin, and went away to telephone.

He returned across the grass with a furtive smile.

"Uncle Arthur wasn't any keener on it than you are. But he'll see you in his rooms tomorrow night at nine o'clock."

After dinner, the four of us were sitting near the window looking out over the wide lawn. On the further side, G. S. Clark had come down his own steps and was walking near the edge—so that he kept in the full evening sun, out of the shadow of the elms. He was walking slowly, dragging his useless leg. It took him minutes to reach the bottom of the garden, turn, go on with his exercise. Yet his locomotion, though it was painful and laborious, did not look so. There seemed a jaunty, almost wilful air, in the way he pulled up the bad leg and then set off for his next step, as though this wasn't a very good way to walk, but one that, out of eccentricity, he happened to prefer.

There was a murmur of voices from inside the house, and Irene left us. I heard her saying from the passage between her kitchen and the Clarks', "Yes, he's here."

"I know it," came Hanna's voice, clear, the intonation off-English.

The two women came into the drawing-room and walked towards us, Hanna neat and catlike by Irene's side. The previous month, Hanna had been letting herself go: but now her hair, which had strayed grey and wispy, was glossy black again, trim on the shapely Hamitic head. Despite her age, she had re-attained something of the look of a student—an intelligent, well-groomed student, eager, argumentative, ratty.

"I can't stay long," she said, refusing to sit down.

I pointed to her husband, doing another limp across the lawn.

"I know. He will tire himself." For an instant she spoke like a nurse.

Then she said:

"He appears before the Court tomorrow? You know that?"

I replied that of course I did.

"This is all beastly!" cried Hanna. "This is rotten!" She was angry with me because she was having to be disloyal. Whatever feelings she had had for Clark had been corroded: but she was a woman who wanted to be loyal, who thought she would have been happy being loyal, and somehow luck and history had always tripped her up. She wanted to be loyal to a cause, to be loyal to a man. She did not like to lead a shabby life. Her politics were pure and impersonal; she was not predatory in her human relations. And yet, for reasons which with all her intelligence she did not understand, she was constantly finding herself in traps like this.

"I thought you must be warned. *He* will say—" she glanced with black eyes on to the lawn—"that Howard does not know what truth is. He will give examples about Howard talking of his scientific work."

She went on:

"*He* believes that no one with Howard's opinions has any conception of truth at all. Or any other of the private virtues. He believes that. He means what he says. That is the strength."

She cried:

"Are you ready for that, Lewis?"

"I think so."

"Don't underestimate him."

I said that I didn't, which was true. But Hanna would have liked a more fiery response. With an ill-tempered toss of her head she said:

"I never know where I am with you Anglo-Saxons. I never know when you're going to be soft and when you're going to be tough. Living your life, Lewis, I suppose you must have had to be tough in your time."

Martin told her gently:

"He'll have it in hand."

"Will he?" she asked.

Once more she refused to sit down. She could not stay long, she said, watching for Clark to begin his climb into the house. But she did stay just long enough to give a display of subtlety. How many of the younger Fellows had I seen, said Hanna, mondaine, brimming with the sophistication of Central Europe, travelled, experienced, twice-married, since I arrived in the College? She didn't mean Howard, of course—for whom, being vixenish as well as subtle that night, she expressed contempt. "The dullest sort of left-wing camp-follower." She didn't mean Howard—but which of the others, she said with an inconsequence so airy that it knocked one down, had I managed to see?

It showed the subtlety of a schoolgirl of sixteen. I saw Irene's eyes, narrow and sly, glinting towards Martin. They were both amused, but they were amused with a touch of concern. For Martin and I were fond of Hanna, and so, more oddly, was Irene. And here Hanna was trying, by guile, to get us to talk of Tom Orbell.

When he had first begun to lavish worship on her, she hadn't paid much attention. Then she had come to like him. With her usual lack of instinct, she had let her imagination dwell on Tom. She was at a stage—perhaps for the first time in her life—when being loved could compel love. Maybe already, the first crystal of feeling had become sharp within her. I hoped not. She was hard, she could be viperish, but she was also generous. She had never begrudged those she knew the good things that had come their way—not successes, which she didn't mind about, but the serenity and the children she had never had. I was afraid, I was sure Irene was afraid, that this was another of her boss-shots. Tom was a gifted man, and a man of force: but I believed it suited his nature to give his love without return. Once she responded, with a vulnerable, impatient, mature love, he might be frightened off. That would mean humiliation for him—but for her, it could be worse than that.

THIRTY-FIVE

THE INNER CONSISTENCIES

From the beginning of the Tuesday morning session, G. S. Clark was sitting opposite the Master, his face fresh, his eyes sky-blue, looking frail, like one of Dickens's saintly, crippled children in the midst of able-bodied men. As I listened to him, he did not seem either saintly or crippled. He was the best witness who had come before the Court. He knew exactly what he had come to say, and without fuss, qualification or misgiving, said it. He did not believe in Howard's honesty, he told Dawson-Hill; he made no bones about it; he did not believe he was straight either as a man or a scholar. That was true in general and in particular. Clark said he couldn't trust a scientist who said there might be "something in" Lysenko, who went in for complicated apologetics when faced with attacks on the truth. To Clark that chimed with all he knew of Howard, and with one piece of evidence in particular.

This piece of evidence he wanted to give the Court. Clark did not claim much for it; but it did show, he said, what Howard thought about his science. The incident had happened three years before, while Howard was in the middle of his work with Palairet. Clark could date it precisely, because it took place on the first day of the Yorkshire match at Fenner's.

"I was walking across Parker's Piece," said Clark. Listening, I remembered hearing that he never missed a match. He took a passionate, vicarious joy in the athletic life. "And

Howard caught me up. That's not very difficult, at the pace I have to go." He gave his fresh smile, with the absence of self-pity so complete that it was embarrassing. "I was surprised to see him, because I knew he was working up in Scotland. But he told me he was staying in college for the week-end. I asked him how his research was going. He said that he was fed up. I tried to encourage him a bit—I said that not even a scientist could expect a new discovery every day of the week. I don't want to put words into his mouth, but I think I remember how he replied. He said something very close to this: "I'm not interested in any damn' discoveries. All I'm interested in is cooking up a thesis. Then I can publish a paper or two by hook or by crook. That's the way everyone's playing this game. And I'm going to play the same game too."

It sounded the literal truth. As Clark spoke, he had the expression, open-eyed, credulous and observant, that I had seen in professional security officers. He was not the man to invent: and indeed, if anyone had wanted to invent evidence, they would have invented something more damaging than that. It did not seem very damaging. It was an anti-climax after all the preparation. Yet I felt that everyone there was trusting his word, and at the same time liking him.

Soon it was my turn. I asked at once:

"I accept the conversation you've reported, completely. But is it really significant?"

"Recalling it in the light of what's happened," said Clark, "I think it may be."

"I should have thought," I said, "that those remarks are just what you might expect, from a young man disappointed, in a bad patch, with his work not coming out? I should have thought a lot of us at that age might have said very much the same?"

"With respect, and admitting that my own standards of

behaviour haven't been what I should like—I don't think I should."

"Have you forgotten," I said, "what it's like to be chafing because things aren't going right? Did you never make a cynical remark when you were in that state?"

"Not that kind of remark," said Clark. He gave me a sweet smile. I had to keep my voice from getting rougher. He provoked me more than most men did. Yet his manner towards me stayed benign and friendly.

"What's more," he said, "I've never heard a scientist talk like that about his scientific work."

"You can't seriously believe that Howard announced to you—you've never been a special friend of his, have you?—that he was going in for fraud?"

"All I'm entitled to believe, on the strength of what he said that morning, is that he's not a man of good character."

"What do you mean by good character?"

"Yes," G. S. Clark replied, "I was afraid that you and I might not see alike on that."

"I'm sure we don't." I spoke harshly and I made sure that the court recognised the harshness. I had decided that my only tactics were to change my tone. With the same edge, I asked: "Why did you want to appear here at all this morning?"

"I'm sorry," he said, still equable, "but I understood any Fellow had a right to do so. Perhaps the Master will correct—"

"Of course you had a right to," I said. "But most Fellows didn't exercise it. Why did you?"

"I can't answer for others' sense of their responsibility, can I?"

"I'm talking about your sense of your responsibility. Why did you want to come?"

"Under the correction," said Clark, "I thought I had something to tell the Court."

"Why did you think it was worth telling?"

My tone had hardened further. The Master was stirring, clearing his throat, ready to stop me. Clark stayed unbullied, obdurate.

"That is what," he said, "I've been trying to explain."

"You didn't appear just through personal animus?"

"I'm sorry, Eliot," Crawford was beginning, but Clark said:

"I'm quite prepared to answer, Master. I can honestly say that I have no personal animus whatsoever against this man."

His confidence was unshaken. Brown was frowning; the Court was against me. But he was going where I wanted to lead him.

"I accept that. It might be less dangerous if you had," I said. "But you have political animus?"

"I don't approve of his political convictions."

Still the Court was against me.

Still they felt—one could sense it in the room—that what he stood for, not always what he said, was right.

"I meant rather more than that," I said. "Don't you really think that a man of his convictions is a bad man?"

G. S. Clark was so set that he didn't budge. He said:

"I'm never quite happy at judging character outside the Christian framework."

"You've got to. Don't you really believe that a man of Howard's convictions isn't to be trusted in any circumstances?"

"In many circumstances, I believe his convictions would be an obstacle to my giving him trust as I understand it."

"Don't you really believe that he's not a man of the same kind as yourself?"

Clark gave a smile sweet and obstinate. "I believe there are certain differences."

"Don't you really believe that such men ought to be got rid of?"

"Really, Master," Dawson-Hill protested, "you can't permit that question—"

Clark was still smiling. I let it go at that.

In my last speech, which was a short one, but which was interrupted by lunch, I tried to make much of Clark's special kind of prejudice. Could the Court really give the faintest encouragement to the view that character and opinion went hand in hand? Wasn't this nonsense, and dangerous nonsense? Didn't we all know scientists—and I named one—whose opinions were indistinguishable from Howard's, and whose integrity was absolute? Wasn't it the chronic danger of our time, not only practical but intellectual, to let the world get divided into two halves? Hadn't this fog of prejudice, so thick that people on the two sides were ceasing to think of each other as belonging to the same species—obscured this case from the beginning? Hadn't it done harm to the college, to Howard himself, and to the chance of a just decision?

I said this without emollient words. G. S. Clark had given me the opening, and I was talking straight at Crawford, some of whose beliefs I thought I might still touch. But it was not only tactics that made me speak out so. Just as tenaciously as Clark believed what he had said that morning, I believed this.

Then I said, and this time I was talking straight at Brown: "As a matter of fact, I've come to know Howard moderately well on account of this business. I don't say that he would be my favourite holiday companion, but I think he's an honest man."

It was then that we stopped for lunch, which was a sombre, creaking meal. Nightingale, alone of the four Seniors, did not look tired; he seemed buoyed up by the energy of strain, just as, in an unhappy love-affair, one is as springy as though one had been taking benzedrine. Outside the Master's dining-room the sunlight was brilliant. Crawford and Brown, not altering their habits by a single tick, drank their ritual glasses of wine, but I noticed that old Winslow, as though determined to keep his lids propped up, drank only water.

When we were back in the combination room I did not go on long. I said that, in the whole hearing, there had been just one critical piece of testimony—Francis Getliffe's. He hadn't produced a new fact: but he had produced a new and dangerous possibility. What he had said couldn't be unsaid. He had deliberately told the Seniors it mustn't be. No one wanted to bring up new suspicions, which would only fester because they couldn't be proved. No one wanted to institute new proceedings. Surely the best, and as far as that went the only course, was to declare a moratorium. Howard's innocence had to be officially recognised. Those I represented could not be content with less. But they were quite prepared to regard anything else that had been said or done as though it had not been. I finished, looking across the table:

"I don't believe there's any other course for the Court which is either prudent or just. If the Court doesn't do it, I can't see how the college will be worth living in for a decade. Just for policy's sake, even if there were only a shade of doubt about Howard, I should try to persuade you to avoid that. But in my view there is no shade of doubt—so it isn't only policy or ordinary human sense that I'm asking you to act on. Those would be good reasons for altering your decision about Howard. But the best reason is that the decision—although most of us would have made it in your place—happened to be unjust."

Dawson-Hill was quite unjaded. He had the stamina of a lawyer trained for trials. He showed less wear and tear than anyone present. Yet, like me, he chose to cut his speech short. Partly, I thought, he felt the elder men were exhausted. Partly, like me, he couldn't get any response in that strained but deadened room. His tone throughout, under the casual mannerisms, was sharper than at any previous time, sometimes troubled, and often edged.

"Can Sir Francis Getliffe be wrong, I ask myself?" he demanded, at his most supercilious. "I can only conclude that, just occasionally, in the world of mortal circumstances, the answer might conceivably be yes. Of course, I recognise that Sir Francis is most high-minded. Even those of us who disagree with him on public issues recognise that he is more high-minded than is given to most of us. But I ask myself, Can a man so high-minded, so eminent as a scientist, conceivably be wrong? Is it possible to be high-minded and at the same time rather curiously irresponsible?"

Dawson-Hill was sitting upright, with his head thrown back. "I have to conclude that the answer may be yes. For after all, his speculations before this court—and with all my veneration, my heartfelt veneration for Sir Francis, I am not able to call them more than speculations—might involve the good name of others. They might, by a fantastic stretch of improbability, involve the good name of a most respected member of this Court. Dr. Nightingale faced this issue plainly yesterday morning, and it would, I know, be going against his wishes, it would be less than fair to the respect that we all ought to bear him, if I didn't state it just as categorically now." He inclined his head to Nightingale, whose eyes lit up. "I put to you this possibility. It might be considered by some that, if this Court reverses its decision, if it reinstates Howard, then it is giving some weight to Sir Francis's speculations. It might even be considered by some that it indicated a lack of confidence in Dr. Nightingale. Could one blame Dr. Nightingale if he took that line himself? I am not authorised to say that he or others will take that view. I mention it only as a possibility. But I suggest that it exists."

That was bold. Bolder than I counted on, or wanted. Afterwards, the rest of Dawson-Hill's speech went according to plan. Dismissing Getliffe's speculation, he said, he came back to the much more natural alternative, which sensible men had taken for granted all along, that the photograph had disappeared by accident, that probably it had disappeared before the Bursar saw the note-book, and that he had, to his own inconvenience, suffered a trick of memory, that it had been a genuine photograph, and that the caption was just an old man's ill-judged comment, "perhaps a shade too optimistic, for his own private eye." Surely that was the rational explanation, for rational men who weren't looking for plots and conspiracies and marvels?

"Which brings me to the very simple alternative with which the Court had to cope in the beginning," he said. "Regrettably, there has been a piece of scientific chicanery. We all know that, and it is a misfortune which the college didn't deserve. The Court previously had to choose and still has to choose, between attributing this chicanery to one of two men. One was a man rightly honoured, an eminent scholar, devout and pious. The other is a man whom we can form our own opinions of. Master, I am a rather simple man. I don't possess the resources of my distinguished colleague. I don't find it easy to despise good old men, or to find virtues in those who have renounced all that most of us stand for. If I had been a member of the Court, I should have made the same choice as the Court has made before. I now suggest to the Court that in spite of the painful circumstances, all it can do is repeat that same choice and re-iterate that same decision."

As he stopped, the grandfather clock in the corner racketted, coughed, whirred, and then gave a stroke just audible, like the creak of a door. It was a quarter past three. Crawford blinked, and said: "Thank you, Dawson-Hill. Thank you both." Staring straight in front of him he said: "Well, that brings us to the last stage in our labours."

"Master," said Brown, quick off the mark, "I wonder if I might make a suggestion."

"Senior Tutor?"

"I don't know whether you or our other colleagues feel as I do," said Brown, "but as far as I'm concerned, listening to what to all of us have been difficult and distressing arguments, I think I've almost shot my bolt. I wonder whether you would consider breaking off for to-day, and then the Seniors could meet in private to-morrow morning when we're a little fresher?"

"In private?" Crawford looked a little bemused, listening, as he had done for so many years, to Brown's guidance.

"I don't think we need call on our legal friends. We've got to reach a settlement on the basis of what they've said in front of us. Then we can perhaps discuss the terms of the settlement with them tomorrow, later in the day."

For an instant Crawford sat without responding. Then he said: "No, Senior Tutor. I gave notice yesterday that I should have something to say this afternoon. Speaking as Master, I wish to say it before we finish to-day's hearing."

He said it with a mixture of dignity and querulousness. In exhaustion, he was letting something out. Right through his Mastership, for fifteen years Brown had held his hand, told him which letters to write, advised him whose feelings wanted soothing. He had used Brown as a confidential secretary: had he noticed how much he depended upon him? Until the Affair, it had been a good Mastership. Did he know that he had Brown to thank for that? Now, when for once he asserted himself and upset Brown's protocol, one saw that he did know; but he didn't thank Brown for it. It was the kind of service which no one ever thanks a grey eminence for.

"As I've just told the Senior Tutor," Crawford announced to the room at large, "I wish to make a statement myself. But first of all, am I right in assuming—" he turned to Winslow—

"that you are of the same way of thinking as you were yesterday?"

Nightingale's voice came from beyond Winslow.

"I certainly am. I should like the Court to know that I agree with every word of Mr. Dawson-Hill's."

"You're continuing to vote against re-instatement?" said Crawford.

"Of course."

Winslow leaned forward, hands clasped on the table, looking under his eyebrows with a subfusc pleasure:

"For myself, Master, I can only acknowledge the Bursar's most interesting observation. Like him, however, I find it remarkably difficult to change my mind. I think that answers your question, Master?"

Crawford sat back in his chair. His physical poise stayed with him, the poise of a man who had always been confident of his muscles. But his voice had lost its assurance altogether.

"Then we cannot avoid a disagreement. I think, as I thought yesterday, that it is time for me to speak." He was looking straight in front of him, past the chair, now empty, where the witnesses had sat. "And speaking not as Master but as a man of science, I have to say that there are things in this hearing which have given me cause for much regret. Not only having to deal with this distasteful business of scientific cheating, which is, by its nature, a denial of all that a man of science lives for or ought to live for. But apart from that, there have been other things, straws in the wind, maybe, which give reason to think that contemporary standards among a new scientific generation are in a process of decline. We have had a report this morning, of this man Howard, whom we elected a Fellow in a scientific subject in all good faith, expressing lack of interest in his research, as though that were a permissible attitude. It would not have been a permissible attitude in the laboratories here fifty years ago. When I was beginning my own research, I used to *run* to my laboratory. And before that, I used to *run* to my lectures. That was how *we* felt about our work."

I had never heard Crawford reminisce, or show the slightest trace of sentimentality. For an instant, he was maundering. He jerked himself together: "But we must give our minds to that decline in standards on another occasion. We now have to conclude the deplorable business for which we've been sitting here. I find it almost intolerable to have had to devote thought and attention to this deplorable business. There have been times, I confess, when it has seemed like asking bloodstock to draw a cart. But it has not been possible to escape. I cannot assess how much nearer we have been brought to wisdom. For myself, speaking as a member of the Court, all I know is that I can see my own course of action."

Someone stirred. Crawford's face and body were quite still.

"I find it distressing not to have more factual certainty. I do not take the view, held apparently by some, that in matters of this kind one can usefully see into other people's minds. Speaking as a man of science, I do not apprehend the suggestions made why such and such a person may have done such and such. For myself, I have to fall back on first principles. My first principle is to discount what may have been happening in peoples' minds and to give weight to the man who knows most about the concrete phenomenon."

He went on. "That brings me straight away to our colleague, Getliffe. Here I might add something, from my own position, to what has been said by the Senior Fellow present. As he rightly told us, Getliffe is a distinguished man of science. He has served twice on the Council of the Royal Society, overlapping on one of those occasions with myself. He has not yet been awarded the Copley Medal—" said Crawford with satisfaction, who had—"but in 1950 he won the only slightly less distinguished Royal Medal. I must say, I cannot find it within me to disregard a man of such credentials. We have known for some time, of course, that he was uneasy about the Court's original decision. I was never comfortable, as my colleagues will remember, that he was not altogether with us. But I was under the impression, which I believe was not completely false, that he was prepared to concede that there was a genuine margin for disagreement. Speaking both as Master and as man of science, I feel that on Sunday, before the Court, he removed that impression. I have hoped all along that this wretched business could be settled without too much disturbance. But though nothing we can do now will please everybody, I think there is only one thing I for myself can say or do. I do not know that Getliffe convinced me that Howard was, beyond the possibility of doubt, innocent. He did convince me, however, that no body of sensible men, certainly no body of men of science, could say that he was guilty. Therefore I find myself obliged to believe that he has received less than fairness, and that he should be reinstated by this Court. I have to say so now."

I lit a cigarette, looking across at Brown. Was it all right? I was thinking, Crawford, who for so long had been permanently middle-aged, had suddenly seemed old. I had seen the same change and the same symptoms in predecessors of his: men quite different from him except that they had just come to the critical point. He was thinking now only of the mainstay of his life: and for him, the mainstay had been his science, his position among scientists. Not that he was a man, one would have thought, who needed to buoy up his self-esteem: yet that had been the purpose, the meaning, the lustre of his life, and in his seventies, when he thought about it, as he did increasingly, it gave him happiness.

He had enjoyed being Master, just as he enjoyed any honour that came his way: but to him it had really been an honour, not a job: his only ambition in the Lodge had been a quiet reign and no fuss. He had no involvement in other people, and very little feeling for them. Like many men whose human interests burn low, he was often, for that very reason, comfortable to be with, just because he made no demands. It was from the same source that he derived his dignity, his kind of impersonal tact. And yet, in the end, it had let him down. Throughout the Affair, he hadn't been able to draw on enough reserves of feeling to give the college the leadership it needed. This was painful to him, it had aged him: not so much because he felt inadequate as because, step by step, he had found himself dragged into scenes of personal emotion. For, again like many men themselves not involved, he had a dread, superstitious or pathological, of feeling in others. The undertow of violence, of suspicion, of passion, had dragged at everyone in the Court: but he was the only one who had felt it like an old man's illness.

Without any hurry, as though he were discussing giving a grant of ten pounds to a choral exhibitioner, Brown said:

"Master, I'm afraid this puts me in a rather awkward position."

He meant that the decision now rested with him. He said it without anxiety, for though he was far-sighted he was not anxious. He said it without drama, for no one was less histrionic. Yet his expression was full of care and feeling.

"I admit," said Brown, still in a round, conciliatory tone which contradicted his expression, "that I am a little sorry that everyone has committed himself rather further than I should be prepared to do this afternoon. I am right in thinking, Master, that we shall have an opportunity to exchange views tomorrow? That is, when the Seniors meet in private?"

"If you wish it, Senior Tutor."

"Thank you, Master. I don't feel able to come down finally one way or the other, until I've slept on it."

Crawford was gathering his gown round him, ready to rise, when Brown went on:

"If you will allow me one last thought to-day. I have a feeling that it is only fair to Eliot, who has given us so much of his time and trouble." He faced me with a slight smile. "I have listened most carefully, as we all have, to his representations. We are all seized, as I am sure he knows, of the complexities of this case and its repercussions. Some of those repercussions, I am certain that he will recognise, are no fault of this Court. We have been given very pointed warnings by our other friend, Dawson-Hill. Of course Eliot will realise the responsibility those warnings put upon us. In most circumstances, as everyone in this room knows, I think, I should be the first person to look for a compromise. But I'm afraid I should have to stick in my heels against a compromise, if and when it might imply casting even the insinuation of approval upon blame thrown against valued colleagues and innocent men."

THIRTY-SIX

SPECIAL KIND OF IRRITATION

At six o'clock, in the Howards' flat, I was listening to them talking to an Indian but preoccupied by the news which I had had no chance to break. If it had been good news, I would somehow have slipped in a word. Did they know that? They were both, Howard especially, more anxious than when they waited in Martin's room in April. Howard had taken two stiff drinks in a quarter of an hour.

The Indian, whose name was Pande, had been in the room when I arrived. He had a small, delicate, handsome head, fine-nerved by the side of the Howards. He was drinking orange-juice while the rest of us drank whisky. Laura was trying to persuade him to sign some protest. He was too polite to say that he did not want to, too polite even to change the conversation. As Laura got up to fill a glass, I noticed that she was pregnant. With her strong, comely figure, she carried the child lightly; it might be already six months gone. She saw my glance, and gave, to herself, not to me, a smile that was a mixture of triumph and *pudeur*.

"You must see—" she said to the Indian, standing over him.

Very politely, Dr. Pande did not quite see. I was thinking, he would have called himself a progressive, as they did: but he was nothing like at home with them. They were too positive. With his nerves, at least, he would have been more at home with a quiet reactionary, like G. S. Clark. Once more the useless rat-race of anxiety went on in my mind: what words exactly had Brown used? Could they mean anything but their obvious meaning, that he had decided against us and that we had lost? Was he warning me that it was no use trying to move him that night?

The Howards, though they had kept unswervingly to persuading the Indian, kept slipping glances in my direction, making attempts to read my face. But they were so tough and disciplined that they stopped themselves trying to hurry Dr. Pande out.

Howard was replying to one of his expressions of doubt.

"That's all very well. But objectively, it's holding up things. We haven't got time for that."

Howard was a shade less pertinacious than his wife. Soon he was telling Pande that he needn't add his signature until next day. Pande gave a sigh, and with a jubilation of relief, looked round him.

"You'll sign tomorrow?" said Laura.

"I will talk to you. Perhaps on the telephone," said Dr. Pande, as, very light, very ectomorphic, he went out of the room.

We could hear his footsteps down the stairs. They looked at me.

"Is it all right?" asked Laura.

"No," I said. "I've no comfort to give you."

Laura flushed with shock. For the first time I saw tears in her eyes. While Howard stood there, his mouth open, not putting a face on it, not aggressive, for once undefiant. But I did not feel protective to either of them. For him I felt nothing at all, except a special kind of bitter irritation. It was the kind of irritation one feels only for someone for whom one has tried to do a good turn and failed: or for someone for whom one has tried to get a job, and who has been turned down.

Laura recovered herself. What had happened? I told them there had been a division on the Court. That was as far as I felt like going or could safely go. Howard pressed me for names, but I said that I couldn't give them. "Damn it," he said, "are you an M.I.5 man?" It seemed to me that he was capable of believing that literally.

The Court would issue its finding the next day, I explained. Laura was back in action. So it wasn't all settled? So there were still things that might be done?

"Are you *doing* them?" she cried.

I said that I was doing all I could think of. I did not tell them that I was seeing Brown that night. Their hopes were reviving, despite anything I said. I repeated, I didn't believe anything I could do was relevant now: I had no comfort to give them.

As soon as I left their flat and got down into the street, I felt an anger which couldn't find an outlet, a weight of anger and depression such as made the brilliant summer evening dark upon the eyes. I was not angry for Howard's sake: he remained more an object of anger than its cause. I didn't give a thought about injustice. No, the thought of Howard, the thought of Laura, the thought of seeing Brown, they were just tenebrous, as though they had added to my rage, but were looked at through smoked glass. There was nothing unselfish, nothing either abstract or idealistic about my anger, nothing in the slightest removed from the frets of self. I was just enraged because I hadn't got my way.

Slowly I walked by St. Edward's Church and out into the Market Place. I bought a newspaper, as automatically as one of Pavlov's dogs, at the corner. I went into the Lion, drank a glass of beer, and was staring at the paper.

A thick, throaty voice came from over my shoulder.

"Why, it's the man himself!"

I looked up and saw Paul Jago, heavy, shabby, smiling.

He asked me to have another drink and, as he sat down beside me, explained that his wife had gone off to a sick relative. It was a long time, he said, since he had walked about the town alone in the evening, or been into a pub. He was studying me with eyes which, through the thick lenses, were still penetrating, in the lined, self-indulgent face.

"Forgive me, old chap," he said, "am I wrong, or are you a bit under the weather?"

The quick sympathy shot out. Even when he was at his most selfish, one felt it latent in him. Now it was so sharp that I found myself admitting I was miserable. About the Howard case, I said.

"Oh, *that*," Jago replied. Just for an instant his tone contained pride, malice, an edge of amusement. Then it softened again. "I'm rather out of touch about that. Tell me about it, won't you?"

I did not mind being indiscreet, not with him. I did not even rationalise it by thinking that, as a Fellow entitled to a place on the Court, he had a right to know. I let it all spill out. It seemed natural to be confiding in this ageing, seedy man, with the wings of white hair untrimmed over his ears, with the dandruff on the shoulders of his jacket. Yet we had never been intimates. Perhaps it seemed more natural just because he was seedy, because he had allowed himself to go to waste, had made a cult of failure and extracted out of it both a bizarre happiness and a way of life. It was not only his sympathy that led me on.

He soon grasped what had happened in the Court. His mind was as quick as his sympathy, and, although he had perversely misused it for so long, or not used it at all, it was still acute. About Getliffe's statement and Nightingale's answers the day after, he asked me to tell him again.

"I want to be sure," he said. He gave a curious smile.

It was after half-past seven, and I had already told him that I was calling on Brown at nine. He invited me to have dinner at an hotel. When I said that I didn't want much of a meal, he humoured me. He went back with me to the college, where we called at the buttery and, like undergraduates, came away with loaves of bread, a packet of butter and a large slab of cheese. In my room, Jago greedily buttered great hunks of crusty loaf. At the same time, his eyes lit up, he listened to me repeat in detail what Nightingale had said the day before and what Brown had said that day.

THIRTY-SEVEN

APPEAL

Eating a crust, butter sliding on to his fingers, Jago listened to me. Although the sun shone outside, in the room it was cool twilight, and the diffused light gave delicacy and sharpness to his face. He did not criticise or doubt. Once or twice he asked for an explication. He nodded. Suddenly he broke out:

"Say no if I'm imposing myself—"

"What do you mean?"

"Do you mind if I come with you to see Brown?"

It was a surprise and not a surprise. He was immersed in the drama. I had known that he was wanting to take a part. Was it just good-nature? He was a man of charm: maybe he still, just for an evening out, so to speak, liked proving that the charm wasn't lost. Or was it remorse, having turned me down before? Remorse, and the self-satisfaction that things would have gone better if the college had been in his hands?

"I've got a feeling," said Jago, "that Arthur Brown might pay some attention to me. We were close, once."

On the stroke of nine, we walked together over the cobbles at the foot of Brown's staircase. After the week's heat, the smell from the wallflowers beneath the ground floor windows was dusty and dry. When we had climbed the stairs, I went first into the room. Brown's greeting was friendly, but not open. When he saw Jago behind me, he grimaced with astonishment.

"My dear Paul!" he cried. He crossed the room and shook hands with Jago. "How ever long is it since you've been in here?"

"Longer than I like to think," said Jago lightly. "And I mustn't come in now on false pretences, must I?"

"What's this?" But Brown had known as soon as he saw Jago.

"I'm afraid I've come to add my representations to Eliot's, you know."

"Is that fair?" asked Brown.

"Don't you think it is?" said Jago, without self-consciousness.

"Anyway," said Brown, "it's very good to have you here, whatever you've come for."

Brown's affection and pleasure were genuine. Tactically, he was on his guard. He did not need teaching that Jago would try to work on him; nor that, without a purpose, Jago would not have come. It was he who warmed to the reconciliation, if that was what it was, not Jago. And yet Brown had watched Jago let himself slip; he had watched him contract out of all human obligations, except one. To Brown, whatever his luck, any indulgence like that was outside his nature. He was a stoic to the bones; whatever tragedy came his way, the King's government, the college, his relations with his friends, had to be carried on. He disapproved of Jago's abandonments; he scarcely understood them and in a sense he despised them. (Perhaps he also envied someone who could so totally let his emotions rip?) Further, he knew, no one better, that Jago had turned against him. But none of this, though it might have changed Brown's affection for him, had uprooted it. Brown's affections, in spite of—or more truly, because of—their being so realistic, were more tenacious than any of ours. He could not change them as he did a suit of clothes or a set of tactics. It was a handicap to him, I used to think, as a politician: perhaps the only handicap he had.

Brown went through the ritual of drink-offering without hastening his pace.

"I've got a little white Burgundy waiting for you," he said

to me. "I had an idea it might be rather restful after the work you've had to put in. Paul, unless my memory escapes me, you never cared much for it, did you?"

Brown's memory did not escape him. Jago asked for a sip of whisky.

"I don't think that's very difficult," Brown replied, going out to his gyp-room and bringing back whisky bottle, siphon and jug of water to put by Jago's side.

"There we all are!" said Brown, settling into his chair. He told Jago that he was looking well. He asked after his garden. He was ready, just as though he were an American business-man, for an indefinite exchange of cordialities before getting to the point. Whoever first came to the point, it would not be he. But it was not really a battle of patience. Jago would have lost it anyway, but he was not playing. Very soon he gave a smile and said:

"I've been hearing a good deal about this case to-night."

"Have you, Paul?"

"And about what's happened in the Court—of course, I don't question what Eliot's told me—"

"I'm sure," said Brown, "that you're right not to."

All of a sudden, Jago's tone sharpened.

"Am I right, Arthur," he leaned forward, "that you've seen this case all along in terms of people? In terms of your judgment of the people concerned?"

Brown's stonewall response did not come quite so pat. He said:

"That may be fair comment."

"You have always seen everything that way."

Jago spoke affectionately, but with weight of knowledge, as though drawing on their associations of the past and on history each could remember, as though he still possessed the moral initiative he had had when they were both young men. If I had used the same words to Brown, they would not have meant the same.

"I shouldn't regard that," said Brown, "as entirely unjust."

"But for once, in this case, it may have made *you* entirely unjust."

"You can't expect me to accept that, Paul."

"I put it to you," all Jago's reserves of force were coming out of him, together with a sadic spirit, "that you've never been vain about much except your judgment of people?"

"I shouldn't have thought that I claim much for myself in that respect."

"Don't you?"

"I hope not," said Brown.

"More than you think, Arthur, more than you think."

"Only a fool," said Brown, "claims that he knows much about people."

"Only a fool," Jago darted in, "claims it in the open. But I've known wise men, including you, who claim it for themselves."

"I can only say again, I hope that isn't true."

"Haven't you assumed all along that young Howard couldn't be innocent?"

"That's not quite fair," said Brown steadily, "but I don't want to shilly-shally. Put it another way: everything I know about the man makes me think that he could possibly be guilty."

Jago had an intent, sharp smile.

"As for Nightingale. Haven't you assumed all along that Nightingale was above reproach? Haven't you closed your mind to what Getliffe said? Haven't you refused to believe it?"

"I should find it very hard to believe."

"Why do you find it hard?"

Brown's high colour went higher still. He started in a burst of anger, his first that night.

"I regard it as abominably far-fetched."

"Were you always so convinced that Nightingale was above

reproach?" Jago spoke quietly, but again with weight and knowledge. When Brown had been his closest friend and had run him for the Mastership, it had been Nightingale, so they thought then, who had done them down.

After a pause Brown replied: "You have good reason not to like him, Paul." He paused again. "But we should never, even then, have thought him capable of this—"

"I should have thought him capable of anything," said Jago. "And I still do."

"No." Brown had recovered his confidence and obstinacy. "I can't see him like that."

"You're being blinder than you used to be—"

"You mustn't think that I'm specially fond of him. I don't mind telling you, we haven't got much in common. But it sticks in my gullet not to do one's best for the chap with a record like his."

A military record, Brown meant. Was this one of the reasons, I suddenly thought, for what had baffled me all along—Brown's loyalty to Nightingale and the origin of it? Brown, who on medical grounds missed the first war, had the veneration for physical courage of those who doubted their own. But, more than that, he had a kind of veneration for the military life. Tory, intensely patriotic, he believed, almost as simply as he might have done as a child, that, while he was sitting in his college rooms during two wars, men like Nightingale had kept him safe. He was one of those rare men who liked recognising his debts. Most of us were disposed to deny our gratitude. Arthur Brown was one of the few who actually liked not denying his.

"I feel," Brown said, "a man like that deserves a bit of looking after."

"You mean, that you won't let yourself see him as straight as you let yourself see anyone else?"

"I mean," Brown replied, unmoved, "that when I sit next to him in hall I am prepared to make a few allowances."

"Arthur," said Jago, "do you realise how much you're evading me?"

"He's not an easy man. And I like an easy man," said Brown, with impenetrable obstinacy. "But I feel he's entitled to a bit of protection."

"You mean, you won't let yourself entertain any suspicion of him, however reasonable?"

"I do not admit for a second that this is reasonable."

"You won't even admit the possibility, not even the possibility, that he did this?" Jago said with violence.

"As I think I've told you, I should find it very hard to admit that."

It was then I thought Jago had come to the end, and so had we all.

Jago switched again.

"I should like to tell you something about myself, Arthur."

He had spoken intimately. Brown, still on guard, said yes.

"I should like to tell you something about my wife. I've never said it to anyone, and I never thought I should."

"How is she, Paul?" asked Brown. He said it with warmth.

"You never liked her much, did you? No—" Jago was smiling brilliantly—"none of my friends did. It's too late to pretend now. Oh, I can understand how you feel about her. And I hope you understand that I've loved her all my life and that she is the only woman I have ever loved."

"I think I knew that," Brown said.

"Then perhaps you'll know why I detest speaking of her to people who don't like her," Jago flashed out, not only with love for his wife, but with intense pride. "Perhaps you'll know why I detest speaking of her in the way I've got to this very moment."

"Yes, I think I do." Now Brown was speaking intimately.

"I've never spoken to you or anyone else about the last election. I suppose I've got to now."

"It's better to let it lie," said Brown.

"No. I suppose everyone still remembers that this man Nightingale sent round a note with a reference to my wife?"

"I hope that's all long forgotten," said Brown, as though to him it really was a distant memory, one pushed for good sense's sake deep down.

"I can't believe that!" cried Jago.

"People don't remember these things as you think they do," said Brown.

"Do you imagine I don't remember it? Do you think that many days have passed when I haven't had to remember every intolerable thing that happened to me at that time?"

"It's no use saying so, but I've always wished you wouldn't dwell on it."

"It's no use saying so. Don't you think my wife remembers everything that happened? Most of all, the note that this man Nightingale sent round?"

Brown nodded.

"If it hadn't been for what Nightingale did then, she believed then and she still believes things might have gone the other way. So she thinks she ruined me."

"Looking back," said Brown, "for any comfort it may be worth, I don't believe it made a decisive difference—"

"That's neither here nor there," said Jago, brilliant, set free. "My wife does. She did so at the time. That is what I have to tell you. Do you know what she did, three months after that election was over?"

"I'm afraid I can guess," said Brown.

"Yes, she tried to take her life. I found her one night with her bottle of sleeping-pills empty beside her. And a note. You can imagine what the note said."

"I can."

After an instant's pause, Jago glanced straight at Brown and said: "And so I feel entitled to ask you not to rule out the possibility, the bare possibility, that this man Nightingale may have done something else. I admit there's no connection.

So far as I know, he may have been spotless ever since. But still I feel entitled to ask you not to rule the possibility out."

Brown said: "You're not making this easy for either of us, are you?"

"Do you think," cried Jago, "that it's been easy for me to tell you this?"

Brown did not reply at once. I heard the hiss and tinkle as Jago refilled his glass.

Then suddenly Jago, as though in a flash he had seen Brown's trouble, made another switch.

"You won't admit the possibility, not even the possibility, that in any circumstances Howard might be innocent?"

For an instant Brown's face lightened, as though he welcomed Jago's question, put that way round.

He said:

"Will you repeat what you've just asked me?"

When Jago had done so, Brown sat without expression. Then he said, slowly and deliberately:

"No, I can't be as positive as that."

"Then you do admit the possibility that the man's innocent?" Jago threw back his head in triumph.

"The bare possibility. I think I shouldn't be comfortable with myself unless I do."

I lit a cigarette. I felt the illogic, the anti-climax of relief.

"Well, what action are you going to take?" Jago pressed him.

"Oh, that's going much too far. I shan't even have my own mind clear until tomorrow."

With friendly roughness Jago went on:

"Never mind the formalities. There's some action you must take."

"I've still not decided what it is."

"Then it's pretty near time you did."

Jago drank some whisky, laughing, exhilarated because he had got home.

"An old dog can't change his tricks. I'm not as quick as some of you," said Brown, domesticating the situation. "You mustn't expect too much. Remember, both of you, I've only admitted the bare possibility. I'm not prepared to see other people blackguarded for the sake of that. And that's as far as I'm able to go to-night. Even that means eating more of my words than I like doing. I don't mind it with you, Paul, but it isn't so congenial elsewhere. Still, I've got this far. I think I shouldn't be entirely easy if we didn't make some accommodation for Howard."

Brown did not like saying he had been wrong. He liked it less than vainer men: for, genuinely humble as he was, believing without flummery that many men were more gifted, he nevertheless had two sources of pride. One was, as Jago had told him, in his summing-up of people: the other was in what he himself would have called his judgment. He believed that half his colleagues were cleverer than he was, but he didn't doubt he had more sense. Now, for once, that modest conceit was deflated. And yet he seemed, not only resentful, but relieved. For days, I suspected, maybe for weeks, his stubbornness—which, as he grew older, was becoming something more than tenacity, something more like an obsession—had been fighting both with his realism and his conscience. Brown had had his doubts about the Howard case. Perhaps, as with many characters of exceptional firmness, he had them and did not have them. He didn't mind, in secret he half-welcomed, the call Jago had made on his affections. For Brown had been able to use it as an excuse. Just as Jago was not above working his charm, his intensity, for his own purposes (was this half-revenge, I had been thinking? Had he exaggerated the story he had just told?), so Brown was not above working the strength of his own affections. He was really looking for an excuse inside himself for changing. The habit of stubbornness was becoming too strong for him. He was getting hypnotised by the technique of his nature. He was glad of an excuse to break out. His affection for Jago gave him precisely that. It allowed him, as a visit from me alone almost certainly would not have done, to set his conscience free.

There was another reason, though, not so lofty, why Brown welcomed an excuse to change. His own stubbornness, his own loyalties, had been getting in the way of his political sense. He knew as well as anyone that during the Affair, he had mismanaged the college. If he stuck in his heels, he would go on mismanaging it. In the end, since much of Brown's power depended on a special kind of trust, it would take his power away.

It had been astonishing to me, throughout the Affair, how far stubbornness could take him. He was a supreme political manager. Nevertheless, his instincts had ridden him; they had ridden him right away from political wisdom; for the only time in his career as a college boss, he had not been sensible.

But now at last, triggered by that night, his conscience and his sense of management, which pulled in the same direction, were too strong.

In euphoria, Jago was talking about the college, rather as though he were visiting it, from the loftiest position in the great world outside, after a lapse of years. He mentioned Tom Orbell, who had been his last bright pupil. Brown was unbuttoned enough to say:

"Between ourselves, Paul, I hope that young man gets a very good job *elsewhere*." None of us needed an explanation of that sinister old college phrase. It meant that a man, even though a permanency, as Tom was, would be under hard pressure to apply for other posts. It was getting late, and Jago and I stood up to say good-bye.

"Don't let it be so long before you come in again," said Brown to Jago.

"It shan't be long!" Jago cried.

I wondered how long it would be.

"It shan't be long!" Jago hallooed back up the stairs.

When we got into the court, I realised that he was unsteady on his feet, on feet abnormally small and light for such a heavy man. I had not paid attention, but he had been drinking hard since we arrived. I should have liked to know how much he drank with his wife at home. Cheerfully he weaved his way at my side to the street door.

The fine spell had broken. The sky was overcast, a bleak wind blew into our faces, but Jago did not notice.

"Beautiful night!" he cried. "Beautiful night!"

He fumbled his key in the lock, until I took it from him and let him out.

"Shall you be all right?" I asked.

"Of course I shall be all right," he said. "It's a nice walk home. It's a beautiful walk home." He put a hand on my shoulder. "Go and sleep well," he said.

THIRTY-EIGHT

AN ORDER IN THE BOOK

Out of the window, as I sat at breakfast next day, the garden was dark; the room struck cold. All the morning the room struck cold, while I waited for a message from the Combination Room, where the Seniors were having their last meeting. To myself, I had given them an hour or so to find a formula. By twelve o'clock there was still no news. I couldn't judge whether the delay was good or bad. I rang up Dawson-Hill, who also was waiting in his room: no, he had heard nothing.

There were no books in the guest-room. I had read the morning papers twice over. I ate the relics of the bread and cheese which Jago and I had brought in the night before. Between one and half-past I telephoned the porter's lodge. The head porter told me that the Combination Room lights, which had been on most of the morning, were now turned off. The Seniors must have gone to lunch.

As soon as I heard that, I went quickly through the courts to the college library, took out a couple of books, returned to my rooms. I was anxious enough to telephone the porter's lodge again: had there been a message during the minutes I had been away? When they said no, I settled down to read, trying to stop myself speculating: but I was ready to hear the college clock, each time it struck.

It had just struck half-past three, when there was a knock at my door. I looked for the college butler. It was Dawson-Hill.

"I must say, Lewis," he said, "the old boys are taking their time."

He was not cross, not in the least worried, except that he had to catch the last train back to London.

"I suggest," he said, "that we both need a breath of fresh air."

Leaving the window open on the garden side, he said, we should be within earshot of the telephone. So we walked on the grass between the great chestnut and the palladian building. The wind was rough, the bushes seethed, but Dawson-Hill's glossy hair stayed untroubled. He set himself to entertain me with stories which he himself found perenially fascinating: of how the commanding officer of his regiment had mistaken X for Y, of how Lord Boscastle had remarked, of a family who were the height of fashion, 'What ever made them think *they* were aristocrats?' He was setting himself to entertain me. His laugh, which sounded affected and wasn't, cachinnated cheerfully into the windswept March-like garden. By this time I was worrying like a machine that won't run down. I could have brained him.

At half-past four his stories were still going on, but he had decided that we both needed a cup of tea. Back in my rooms, he rang up the kitchens: no one there yet, in the depth of vacation. He took me out to a café close by, leaving a message with the porter. No one had asked for us when we returned. It was after five when, sitting in my room, Dawson-Hill cachinnating, I heard another knock on the door. This time it was the butler.

"The Master's compliments, gentlemen, and he would be grateful if you would join him in the Combination Room."

As he walked in front of us through the court, it occurred to me that this was how the news of my Fellowship had come. I had been waiting in Francis Getliffe's rooms (without suspense, because it had been settled beforehand), the butler had knocked on the door, given me the Master's compliments, and led me in.

Again, this dark summer afternoon, the butler led us in. On the panels, the wall-sconces were shining rosily. The Seniors sat, Winslow with his head sunk over the table, Brown bolt upright, Nightingale with his arms crossed over his chest. Crawford gazed at us, face moonlike, back to his normal composure. When he spoke his voice was tired, but nothing like as jaded or spiky as on the day before.

"Pray be seated, gentlemen," he said. "We apologise for keeping you all this time. We have had a little difficulty in expressing our intention."

In front of him and Brown were sheets of foolscap, written on, passages crossed out, pages of holograph with lines across them, attempts at drafting, discarded resolutions.

The butler was leaving the room, when Brown plucked at Crawford's gown and whispered in his ear.

"Before you go, Newby!" called Crawford.

"Thank you very much for reminding me, Senior Tutor. We are under pledge, as I think the Court will remember, to communicate our decision to Professor Gay, who was appointed by the College Moderator in this case. I believe it was agreed that our legal colleagues here would report our decision to the Moderator, as soon as it was signed and sealed. Is that correct?"

"Certainly, Master," said Dawson-Hill.

"In that case," Crawford said to the butler, "I should be obliged if you would give a message to Professor Gay's house asking him to expect these two gentlemen this evening."

No one was smiling. No one, except me, seemed to resent this final interruption.

The door closed.

"So that's all in train," said Crawford, and Brown steadily nodded.

"Well, gentlemen," said Crawford, "perhaps now we can dispatch our business. I should like to make a preliminary observation. Speaking not as Master but as a member of the college, and as one who has spent half a century in academic life, I have often felt that our internal disagreements sometimes generate more heat than light. I seem to recall making a similar comment on other occasions. But, with deference to my colleagues, I doubt if that has ever been more true than in this present one, which, I am thankful to say, we are now concluding. Speaking as an academic man, I am sometimes inclined to believe in the existence of a special *furor academicum.* However, speaking now as Master about this special and unfortunate occasion, I have to say that it is one of our responsibilities to diminish the heat which it has generated. In the course of our very protracted and careful discussions in this Court, especially to-day, I need hardly remark that no one has ever entertained a thought that any Fellow of the college—with the solitary exception of the man whom the Court originally deprived—could possibly have acted except with good intentions and according to the code of men devoted to science or other branches of learning."

This wasn't hyprocrisy. It was the kind of formal language that Crawford had been brought up in. It was not very different from the formal language of officials. It meant something like the opposite of what it said. It meant that such thoughts were in everyone's mind: and that for reasons of prudence, face-saving and perhaps a sort of corporate kindness, the thoughts had to be pushed away. Crawford went on. Maddened for him to come to the point, I heard phrases of Brown's put in for Nightingale's benefit. I heard the damping-down of crises, the explaining away of "misunderstandings," the respectful domestication of Francis Getliffe.

At last Crawford said:

"I hope that conceivably these few superficial remarks may give our legal colleagues some idea of the difficulties we have found ourselves in, and of the way in which our minds have been working. I think it remains for me now, as Master of the College and President of the Court of Seniors, to let them know our finding. This finding has already been composed in the form of an order. When we have heard any observations our legal colleagues may have to make, the order will be inscribed in the Seniors' Order Book."

He scrabbled among the papers in front of him. He picked up one sheet.

"No, Master, fortunately not," said old Winslow. "This is one of the resolutions, one of the perceptible number of resolutions, if I may say so, that you and I didn't find altogether congenial."

"This is it, Master," said Arthur Brown, as unmoved as a good secretary.

"Thank you, Senior Tutor." Crawford took off his glasses, replaced them with another pair, settled back in his chair, quite relaxed, and read.

"June 30th, 1954. At a Meeting of the Court of Seniors, held this day, present the Master, Mr. Winslow, Mr. Brown, Dr. Nightingale, it was resolved with one dissentient; that, after the hearings on June 26th, 27th, 28th, 29th, held in the presence of legal advisers, the testimony is not sufficient to support the Order for the Deprivation of D. J. Howard, dated October 19th, 1952, and that the Order for such Deprivation is hereby quashed. It was further resolved that Dr. Howard's Fellowship should be presumed to have continued without interruption during the period of deprivation and that he should be paid dividends and commons allowance in full: and that his Fellowship shall continue until it lapses by the effluxion of time."

"Is that all right, Dawson-Hill?" Crawford asked, as he put down the paper.

Just for an instant, Dawson-Hill flushed. Then, nonchalantly, with his kind of patrician cheek, he said:

"I don't pretend to be entirely happy about it, Master."

"If you have anything further to say—?"

"Would that be the slightest use?"

"We are very grateful to you both," Brown put in, "but I

really think we've got as far as discussion can reasonably take us."

"Are you satisfied, Eliot?" Crawford asked.

As I listened, I had felt nothing but elation, savage elation, the elation of victory. But it was a long time since I had heard the singular eloquence of college Orders. It took me a moment to realise that it was not all victory. Like the other Research Fellows since the war, Howard had been elected for four years. We had assumed that, if he were reinstated, the period of deprivation wouldn't count against his term. They were counting it, by the simple method of paying him, so that he would slide out as early as the Statutes allowed: this device had occurred to no one before.

"When does his Fellowship run out?" I enquired.

Brown, who saw that I had taken the point, replied:

"December 13th this year."

"Well," I said, "you're giving him half a loaf."

"No, Lewis," said Brown, "we're giving him a reasonable deal according to our lights. We think we should be ill-advised to give him more."

"He will, of course," said Crawford, "still be eligible for an official Fellowship if and when a vacancy crops up. Though I doubt whether it would be in his own best interests to hold out much hope of that."

Brown spoke to me; "No, Lewis, he's getting more than half a loaf. He's getting the substance of what he wants. He won't have a black mark against him, his Fellowship will have run its course. As for the way we've done it, we're entitled to consider ourselves."

They all waited, the clock ticked in the silence, as I made up my mind.

"For myself," I said, "I think I can accept that. But I'm not certain that all the Fellows I am representing will do."

"They'll be seriously irresponsible if they don't," Brown said. He added in a tone unusually simple and direct: "This isn't altogether plain sailing, you know. You'll do your best to persuade them, won't you?"

Crawford, still relaxed in his chair, inclined his head, not his body, first to the right, then to the left. With a satisfied smile he said:

"Well then. That is agreed."

He went on:

"I will now ask the Bursar to enter the Order in the book."

The draft was passed along to Nightingale, who had the order-book already opened. He said, as though he were excited, but excited in a not unpleasurable way:

"I take it that I enter my own dissent. I don't know whether anyone's ever had the chance to do that before!"

Fair hair bent over the book, he dutifully wrote. Winslow, turning away from him, was making remarks sharp with mischief about the resolutions that Nightingale wouldn't have the "trouble of inscribing." I got the impression that much of the day Brown had been drawing up forms of words by which the Seniors ruled out most of the evidence, and by inference protected Nightingale: but that when they became specific, Winslow had said that he would enter his dissent and when they were woolly, Winslow, with some aid from Crawford, had jeered them away. All his life he had loved drafting: This had been his day.

Nevertheless, fighting Brown on those clauses, Winslow and Crawford had given way about Howard's tenure. That was a compromise, and the more one thought of it the more indefensible it seemed. It wasn't like Brown, even, though it was his work. He was both too shrewd and also too magnanimous not to know that when one admitted being wrong, one ought to go the whole hog and be generous. I didn't believe that they were aiming at keeping Howard from voting at the election, though incidentally they would do just that. No, I believed that, in some fashion which in the future Brown himself would be hard put to it to disentangle, much less justify, this was an attempt to make a gesture in favour of Nightingale, against the man who, even if he were innocent, had caused the trouble.

Meanwhile, Winslow was expecting Nightingale to resign. Winslow had been brought up in a Cambridge stiff with punctilio, pique and private incomes, and where, when men were criticised, they had a knack of throwing resignations on to the table, as in fact Winslow had done himself. It seemed incredible to him that Nightingale should not resign. Each minute, with relish, the old man was expecting it. I was not. I didn't doubt that Nightingale, who had still four years to go as Bursar, would finish his term of office down to the last second of the last day. If there were coldness, or something like ostracism, from Winslow and others, he would take that, thickening his carapace, under which he would feel ill-used, perhaps at times persecuted, imagining attacks, becoming offensive in return.

Nightingale finished writing, and placed the book in front of Crawford. I got up, and when they had signed, stood behind them and studied the page. The order was as Crawford had read it, written in Nightingale's neat, schoolmistressish hand. Underneath were the three signatures, R. T. A. Crawford, M.C., G. H. Winslow, A. Brown. At the bottom of the page ran two lines inserted by Nightingale before the others signed:

"Dr. Nightingale, Bursar of the College and Secretary of the Court of Seniors, wished to have his dissent recorded. Alec Nightingale."

Everyone was standing up. Nightingale reverentially put a large piece of blotting-paper on top of the order and closed the book. Then he looked out of the window into the gloomy evening and said to no one in particular, with the meteorological interest that never seemed to leave him;

"Well, we've had the last of Spring."

The Court, despite the day-long sitting, did not seem

anxious to break up. It was the disinclination to part one sometimes sees in a group of men, gathered together for whatever purpose, never mind what the disagreements or inner wars have been. Crawford asked us all if we would like a glass of sherry. While the butler brought in decanter and glasses, Winslow was saying that, as soon as the Long Vacation term began, he must summon the first full pre-election meeting.

"You'll soon be vanishing into oblivion!" he said to Crawford, with an old man's triumph, prodding him with his retirement, "You'll soon be no one at all!"

We stayed and talked. They went on about the timetable of the election, though no one mentioned the candidates' names. It was nearly seven, and I said that Dawson-Hill and I must soon be off on our mission to old Gay. As I said that, Brown, whom I could not remember having ever seen gesticulate, covered his face with his hands. He had just thought, he said, that under the Statutes Gay, as Senior Fellow, still had the prescriptive right to convene the election and to preside at it. "After our experience with him over this business," said Brown, "how are we going to dare to try and keep him out? How are we going to keep him out at all? I wish someone would answer me that."

Dawson-Hill was shaking hands all round. As Brown saw us ready to leave, he had another thought. He spoke to Crawford: "If our friends are going out to Gay's, then I think we ought to send a copy of the Order to Howard himself. I have a feeling that it's only right and proper."

It was the correct thing to do; but it was also good-natured. Brown detested Howard, he had behaved to him with extreme prejudice, but he was not the man to see him kept in unnecessary suspense.

THIRTY-NINE

VIEW OF AN OLD MAN ASLEEP

In the taxi, along the Madingley Road, through the dense, grey, leafy evening, Dawson-Hill sat with an expression impatient and miffed. He did not like losing any more than most people; he was bored by having to visit Gay.

"Well, you've got away with it, Lewis," he observed.

"Wasn't it right that I did?"

But Dawson-Hill would give no view about Howard's innocence. He went on talking in an irritated, professional tone.

"I must say," he said, "you played it very skilfully on Monday morning. I don't see how you could have got away with it unless you'd used that double-play. You'd obviously got to raise the dust about Nightingale and give them an escape-route at one and the same damned time. Of course, if you'd gone all out against Nightingale, it would have been absolutely fatal for your chap. That stood to sense. But still, I must say, you did it very neatly."

He added: "You've always been rather lucky, haven't you?"

"What do you mean?"

"My dear Lewis, people say you always have the luck." He broke off: "By the way, I confess I think Nightingale's had a rough deal. The one thing that sticks out a mile to my eye is that he's as blameless as a babe unborn."

The trees, the garden hedges went by. I had been thinking, how odd it was if acquaintances thought one lucky. It was the last thing anyone ever thought about himself.

Then, sitting complacently back, tired and smug with winning, I heard what Dawson-Hill said of Nightingale. Could it be true? All my instincts told me the opposite. Sitting back, I let in only the vestige of the question, could it be true? If so, it was one of the sarcasms of justice. One started trying to get a wrong righted; one started, granted the human limits, with clean hands and good will; and one finished with the finite chance of having done a wrong to someone else. And yet, in the taxi, windows open to the chilly, summer-smelling wind, it was I who was smug, not Dawson-Hill.

He was enquiring what nonsense we should have to listen to from old Gay. How long would he keep us? Dawson-Hill could not miss his train, Gay or no Gay, senile old peacocks or no senile old peacocks. Dawson-Hill had to be in London for a late-night party. He told me the names of the guests: all very smart, all reported with that curious mixture, common to those who love the world, of debunking and being himself beglamoured. It was remarkably tiresome, he said, to have to endure old Gay.

The taxi went up the drive. As Dawson-Hill and I stood on the steps of the house, he said, like the German officers on the night the war began: *"Nun fängt es an."*

The housekeeper came to the door. Her first words were: "I am so sorry." She looked distressed, embarrassed, almost tearful. She said: "I am so sorry, but the Professor is fast asleep."

Dawson-Hill laughed out loud, and said, gently and politely: "Never mind."

She went on, in her energetic, Central European English, "But he had been looking forward to it so much. He has been getting ready for you since tea-time. He was so pleased you were coming. He had his supper early, to be prepared. And then he goes to sleep."

"Never mind," said Dawson-Hill.

"But he will mind terribly. He will be so disappointed. And I dare not wake him."

"Of course you mustn't," said Dawson-Hill.

She asked if we would like to see him, and took us into the study. The room was so dark it was hard to see anything: but there Gay lay, back in his chair, shawl over his shoulders, beard luminiscent in the vestigial light, luminous white against the baby-clear skin. His head was leaned against the side-wing of the chair. His mouth was open, a dark hole, but he was not snoring. With all of us dead silent, we could hear his breaths, peaceful and soothing.

We tiptoed out into the hall. "What is to be done?" said Dawson-Hill.

We could leave the copy of the order with a note signed by us both, I said.

"He will be so disappointed," said the housekeeper. Tears were in her eyes. "He will be heart-broken like a little child."

"How long before he wakes?" asks Dawson-Hill.

"Who can tell? When he has what he calls his 'naps' in the evening, it is sometimes one hour, sometimes two or three."

"Don't worry, Mrs. Nagelschmidt," said Dawson-Hill, "I will stay."

She flushed with happiness. He had remembered her name, he was so polite, and all was well. I said it was very hard on him: I would volunteer myself, but I was dining with my brother, and afterwards might have to do some persuasion with the Howard faction.

"That's important," said Dawson-Hill. "No, you can't possibly stay. It's all right, I will."

"And your party?"

"I suppose," said Dawson-Hill to the housekeeper, "I may telephone, mayn't I?"

"You shall have everything," she cried. "You shall sit in the drawing-room. I will make you a little dinner—"

I asked how he was going to get back to London. He said that he would have to hire a car.

It was pure good-nature. Half an hour before, we had seen

Brown's good-nature; that one took for granted, it fitted deep into his flesh and bone. But Dawson-Hill's came as a shock. I remembered the stories of his good turns to young men at the Bar, done secretively, and with his name kept out. Those stories, whenever I met him and heard his prattle, I only half-believed. Now I broke out:

"You're a very kind man, aren't you?"

Dawson-Hill coloured from hairline to collar. He was delighted to be praised, and yet for once uncomfortably shy. His face seemed to change its shape. The lines, which as a rule ran downwards, giving him his air of superciliousness and faint surprise, suddenly went horizontal, broadening him out, destroying his handsomeness. He looked like a hamster which has just filled its cheek-pouches, shifty, but shining with chuff content. In a manner as gauche as an adolescent, he said, in a hurry:

"Oh, I don't think we'd better talk about that."

FORTY

WALKING OUT OF THE LODGE

When I got to Martin's house, Margaret was there to welcome me. She had come up to take me home next day. She was bright-eyed because we had won; she wanted nothing except for us to be by ourselves. Irene was yelping with general disrespectful glee: the room was warm, swept by currents of slapdash content.

But Margaret was bright-eyed, not only with joy, but with a kind of comic rage. Within five minutes of her arriving at the house—so they told me—Laura had been on to her by telephone. The Seniors' decision was an outrage: of course Donald's tenure ought to be prolonged by the entire period during which he had been deprived. Would Margaret see that that was done? and would she also sign a letter which, when Margaret mentioned it, I recognised as the one they had been forcing upon Dr. Pande?

"It may be a perfectly reasonable letter," cried Margaret. "But I'm sick and tired of being pestered by that awful woman."

"I thought you got on rather well with her?" said Martin, with a glint of malice.

"That's what you think," Margaret said. "I've had more of her than I can stand. What's more, I don't believe, as some of you do, that she's under her husband's thumb. I believe she's the bloodiest awful specimen of a Party Biddy, and I never want to see her again as long as I live."

On the tenure of Howard's Fellowship also, Margaret's

conscience had worn thin. She would have struggled to the last to get him justice. But she did not see, she was saying happily, still pretending to be irascible, why he should get more. The way he had done his research, his lack of critical sense, his taking his professor's evidence—that wasn't even second-rate, it was tenth-rate. The man was no good. He ought to count himself lucky to get what the Seniors were giving him: he ought to count himself lucky and keep quiet.

Martin said that he hoped we could convince the others so. As he spoke, we were eating dinner.

"You haven't got to go out again to-night?" Margaret asked me. "You've had a horrible day, you know you have."

In fact, I was very tired. But I was not too tired to think, with the disrespect of love, that Margaret was not above a bit of rationalisation when she wanted something for herself. Was she really so sure that Howard had got his deserts? Was she really speaking so impartially as her academic relatives would have done? When she wanted to forget it all, stop them wearing me out, and be together?

Martin had already called a meeting. It would be dangerous, he said, not to "tie up" the offer at once. By a quarter to nine we were back in college, sitting in Martin's rooms, cold that night after the house we had just left.

Francis Getliffe arrived soon after. We had brought our chairs round the table, which stood between the chimneypiece and the windows, the curtains of which were not drawn, so that one could see the cloudy, darkening sky. A standard lamp stood by the table, leaving one end in shadow: Martin switched on a reading-light on a desk near-by. As Francis sat down he said: "Of course, we've got to accept it."

"I don't know whether there's going to be any trouble," said Martin. "But look—"

He was speaking to Francis—"you'd better let me run this. You've done enough already."

He said it in a considerate tone. I believed he was speaking out of fairness. Though he had not told me, I fancied that, when the election came, he intended to vote for Brown: but he knew, no one better, that in saving Howard, Francis had done himself harm. Martin had, of course, foreseen it on the evening when Francis volunteered to speak out. Martin, with the fairness into which he was disciplining himself as he grew older, was not prepared to let him do more. Certainly Francis seemed to take it so, for he said: "Good work." It was the most friendly interchange between the two that I had seen.

Skeffington and Tom Orbell came in together, Tom with that air of being attached to balloons by invisible strings which emanated from him when he had been drinking. He gave us a euphoric good-evening. Then Howard followed with a nod, but without a word, and sat in the remaining chair, head bent on his chest, eyes glancing to the corner of the room.

"I couldn't collect any of the others who signed the memorandum," said Martin. "They're nearly all away, but this is a quorum. I suppose you all know the terms of the Seniors' decision?"

"I should think we do," said Tom ebulliently.

"It seems to me to give you—" Martin was addressing himself down the table to Howard—"everything essential. What do you think?"

"I think," said Howard, "that it's pretty mingy."

"It's a bad show," said Skeffington, paying no attention to Howard, almost as though he were invisible. Loftily he bore down on me: "It's a bad show. I can't understand how a man like you could let them give us a slap in the face like that."

"Do you think it's quite as easy?" I said in temper. It occurred to me that I had not received a word of thanks, certainly not from the Howards. It occurred to me simultaneously that I did not remember seeing a group of people engaged in a case they all thought good, who did not end in this kind of repartee.

"It ought to be," said Skeffington.

"You're not being realistic, Julian," Martin said.

"If this is being realistic, then I'm all in favour of trying something else," said Skeffington. "What do you think?" he asked Francis Getliffe.

"I agree with the Eliots," said Francis.

"Really," replied Skeffington, with astonishment, with outrage.

It was Francis's remark, made quietly and without assertion, that sent Tom Orbell over the hairline—the hairline which, when he was drunk, separated the diffuse and woofy benevolence from a suspicion of all mankind. He was not very drunk that night: he had come in exuding amiability and good-will. Of all the young men in the college, he was the most interesting, if one had the patience. He had by a long way the most power of nature; he was built on a more abundant scale. Yet it was hard to see whether that power of nature would bring him through or wreck him. Suddenly, as he heard Francis's remark, he once more saw the lie in life.

"So that's what you think, is it?" he said, talking down his nose.

"We've got no option," said Francis.

"That's all right. If you think so." Tom thrust his great head forward. "But some of us don't think so. We've got the old men on the run, and this is the time to make them behave decently for once. I don't know what Lewis was doing not to behave decently, except—" his suspicions fixed themselves on me—"that's the way you've got on, isn't it, playing safe with the old men?"

"That's enough, Tom." Martin spoke sharply.

"Who says it's enough? Haven't you done exactly the same? Isn't that the whole *raison d'être* behind this precious bargain? I don't like the Establishment. But I'm beginning to think the real menace is the Establishment behind the Establishment. That's what some of you—" he looked with hot eyes at Martin, at Francis, at me—"are specialists in, isn't it?"

"Can it," said Skeffington. He was the only man who could control Tom that night. "What I want to know is, how are we going to set about it?"

"Set about what?" asked Martin.

"Getting this decision altered, of course."

Gradually, as Tom sobered himself, the two of them began to shape a proposition. The time ticked by as we sat round the shadowed table. Only Howard, at the end removed from the rest of us, did not speak at all. The argument was bitter. Martin was speaking on the plane of reason, but even his composure Tom frayed. Francis was getting imperative. I heard my own voice sounding harsher. While Skeffington would not budge from his incorruptibility. Somehow absolute and full recompense had to be given, pressed down and running over.

"We're going to have our pound of flesh," cried Tom. "We insist on complete reinstatement. Payment in full for the period of deprivation. *And* the Fellowship to run from this day with the period of deprivation added on. We won't be fobbed off with less."

"That's stretching it," said Skeffington. "We can't ask for payment for the deprivation if we get the period tagged on. *That's* the decent thing."

"So that's what you think," said Tom, turning on his ally.

"It's not on, to ask for money too."

"Very well, then." Tom lowered at us across the table. "Julian Skeffington's willing to let you off lightly. I'd disown you first, but I'll come in. You'll have to go back to your friends and make them give what he's pleased to call the decent thing."

"You're seriously suggesting that we go back to the Master straight away?" said Martin.

"What else do you think we're suggesting?" Tom burst out.

"Look here," I intervened, "I've sat through the whole of these proceedings. I know, and you don't know, what the feeling is. I tell you that we shouldn't stand a chance."

"You want to make it easy for everyone, don't you?" Tom attacked me again.

"He's dead right," said Francis.

"Now we listen to the voice of Science, disinterested and pure, the voice of Intellect at its highest, the voice that we shall always associate with Sir Francis Getliffe," Tom declaimed.

"Hold it," said Skeffington. "You say," he turned to me, angry with Tom as well as with us, stiff-necked, "that if we go back to them we shan't get any change?"

"Not the slightest," I said.

Tom was beginning another burst of eloquence, but Skeffington stopped him.

"I'll take that," he said to me. "We've got to take that. You know what's what. But that doesn't write us off—"

"What else can you do?" said Martin.

"It's pretty clear," said Skeffington. "We start all over again. We beat up a majority of the Fellows, and we send the Court another memorandum. We accept their withdrawal, but we tell them we're not satisfied. We tell them they've got to do the decent thing. We'll put in the proper terms of reinstatement, just to leave no room for argy-bargy."

"That's what I like to hear!" cried Tom.

There was a pause. Martin glanced at me, then at Francis and began to speak:

"No. I'm sorry. You can't do it."

"What do you mean, we can't do it?"

"How do you think you're going to get your majority?"

"We'll beat them up just as we did before."

"You won't," said Martin. "Not to put too fine a point on it, you won't get me." They were interrupting him, but he said sternly: "Now listen for once. We've been in this too, every inch of the way. I haven't done much. But if it hadn't been for Lewis, I doubt if we'd have got any sort of satisfaction. If it hadn't been for Francis Getliffe, I'm quite sure we shouldn't. Well, we've done our piece. And that's enough."

Both Skeffington and Tom were speaking, the voices were jangling round the table, when there came an interruption. Howard, who after his first remark had not said a word, who had been sitting with jaw sunk into chest, noisily slammed his hand on the table and pushed back his chair.

He said, in a grating tone:

"I'm fed up."

"What?" cried Tom.

"I'm fed up with being talked about. I'm not going to be talked about any more by any of you," he said. He went on:

"They seem to have decided that I'm not a liar. I suppose that's something. I'm not having any more of it. You can go and tell them that it's all right with me."

On heavy feet, he clumped out of the room.

He was innocent in this case, I had no doubt. And he had another kind of innocence. From it came his courage, his hope, and his callousness. It would not have occurred to him to think what Skeffington and Tom had risked; and yet anyone used to small societies would have wondered whether Skeffington stood much chance of getting his Fellowship renewed, or Tom, for years to come, any sort of office. Howard did not care. He still had his major hopes. They were indestructible. Men would become better, once people like him had set the scene. He stamped out of the room, puzzled by what had happened, angry but not cast down, still looking for, not finding, but hoping to find, justice in this world.

Martin, with face impassive, eyes sparkling, said:

"Well, that appears to settle it."

Haughtily Skeffington announced:

"I shall write to the Master on my own."

"I advise you not to, Julian," said Martin.

"I shall have to," Skeffington replied, obdurate and sea-green.

"But still," said Martin, "as far as we're concerned, that's settled it?"

Skeffington nodded. He said:

"It's all you can expect of a chap like that. He's got no guts."

It was the first recognition of Howard's existence he had made all the evening. He did it seriously, his head uptilted, without a glint of humour, whereas Tom, his great frame shaking, his cheeks moist and roseate in the cool room, was billowing with laughter. He tried to speak, and emitted little squeals. All he could say was:

"Give me your hand, Martin. Give me your hand, Lewis."

When we went down into the Court, there was a light shining in the Master's study. "We'd better get it over," said Francis, and he, Martin and I walked across to the Lodge. The front door was unlocked, and we went in and climbed the stairs. As soon as I opened the study door, I saw Crawford on one side of the fireplace, Brown on the other.

"Good-evening to you, gentlemen," Crawford said. He offered us a night-cap of whisky, but I said that we had not come to stay.

"Perhaps I can act as spokesman," I said. "It's straightforward, Master. We've been talking to some of the signatories of the last memorandum. We've been talking about to-day's decision of the Court. All I need say is that it's been accepted."

"Splendid," said Brown. He got up, stood beside me, and took my arm. He had noticed what I had not said. Quietly, as Crawford was talking to the others, Brown said in my ear, "You've done us all a service, you know."

Crawford was saying at large:

"Well, I'm glad this business is settled without breaking too many bones." He called to me as though he had never had a doubt in his life: "I think I remember saying to you in this room last week, Eliot, perhaps we worry too much about forms of procedure. I think I remember saying that in my experience sensible men usually reach sensible conclusions."

He said it with invincible content, with the reverence of one producing a new truth. Martin, who was in high spirits, glanced at me.

We went down the study stairs. Crawford pulled back the great oak door. Out in the court the chilly wind was blowing, so strong that the staircase lanterns sprayed and shook in the midsummer dark. Crawford walked out of the Lodge with Brown on his right hand, Getliffe on his left. Following after them, Martin once more glanced at me, eyes sharp, half-sarcastic, half-affectionate. Did he mean what I thought he meant? That, within six months, Crawford would be walking out of the Lodge for good, and one of those two would be walking in?